Also By Leigh Michaels

The Mistress' House

Just One Season in London

The Wedding Affair

Leigh Michaels

sourcebooks
casablanca

Published by Sourcebooks Casablanca, an imprint of Sourcebooks, Inc.
P.O. Box 4410, Naperville, Illinois 60567-4410
(630) 961-3900
FAX: (630) 961-2168
www.sourcebooks.com

Printed and bound in the United States of America
QW 10 9 8 7 6 5 4 3 2 1

One

WHEN THE HEAVY BRASS KNOCKER FELL AGAINST THE front door, the crash echoed through the cottage. Olivia ignored it. She wasn't expecting callers; she wasn't prepared for callers; and she didn't want to greet callers.

But barely half a minute later, the knocker dropped once more. She abandoned the bread dough she'd been kneading and wiped her hands on her apron. The baking was late already, and this interruption wasn't going to help.

As she crossed the narrow hall, she noticed a dusting of flour on her blue muslin skirt and brushed feebly at it, but she managed only to make the smear look worse.

The man waiting on the doorstep was short, stout, and past middle-aged. His face was red, as if the warmth of the day was too much for him, or perhaps his neck-cloth was just too tight. He looked astounded to see her there. "Lady Reyne, where are your servants today?"

All two of them? Olivia wanted to answer. But she didn't think Sir Jasper Folsom really wished to know that this was the housemaid's weekly afternoon out or that Nurse was upstairs putting Charlotte down for her nap. And since he hadn't asked about Kate Blakely, who was Olivia's guest, she felt no need to explain that Kate had gone to call at the vicarage.

At any rate, Sir Jasper was Olivia's landlord, not her keeper, so she didn't feel obliged to tell him why she was the only one available to answer her door in the middle of a sunny Wednesday afternoon.

She smiled vaguely. "I find it terribly boring to sit and be waited on, Sir Jasper."

"You are a most unusual lady, ma'am. I have come to collect the next quarter's rent."

"Of course." Olivia hesitated and then stepped back. Better, she thought, not to have this conversation on the doorstep. "Would you care to come inside?"

He looked startled at the invitation, though an instant later he had masked the expression. He bowed and followed her into the tiny parlor, where the single window stood open and a fire had been freshly laid, ready to light in case the evening should turn cool.

Sir Jasper took off his hat and looked around the room. "Quite delightful."

Threadbare was the word Olivia would have used for the furnishings Sir Jasper had supplied along with the cottage, but she supposed there was a certain cozy charm about the mismatched chairs and the way personal items—a smock she was hemming for Charlotte, a shawl Kate had started knitting last night—were sprinkled around.

Don't be so snobbish, she told herself. The cottage wasn't grand, but it was home in a way that her previous residence had never been, and she was grateful to Sir Jasper for offering it at a rent she could afford.

At least, she had been able to afford the rent until now. She braced herself to tell him that at this moment she could not pay the entire amount she owed, but she found she couldn't come straight out with it.

"I don't keep ale in the house," Olivia said, "since we do not as a rule have gentleman callers. But I can offer you tea."

Sir Jasper smiled, displaying yellowing teeth. "That would be most welcome, my lady."

Olivia escaped to the kitchen and made the tea, rehearsing her speech under her breath as she waited for the tea to steep.

When she returned to the parlor with the tray, Sir Jasper turned from his inspection of a perfectly hideous sampler that was hanging on the wall. His gaze flicked over her a little more closely than was proper, and he smiled widely.

Olivia felt a flicker of alarm. Surely he hadn't interpreted her comment as evidence that she regarded *him* as a gentleman caller, rather than simply as the landlord...?

"I see you appreciate my mother's needlework," he said.

Olivia had found the sampler wadded in a cupboard when she moved in, and she had hung it only because it was large enough to cover a badly stained spot on the wall. But she lied without a qualm. "I was delighted to add it to the everyday view from my favorite chair. If you could clear a corner of the table, Sir Jasper—I do beg your pardon for having to ask."

"Not at all, my lady. With your servants away, I am happy to assist." He moved a book, a half-written `letter, and Kate's as-yet-unrecognizable shawl out of Olivia's way so she could set down the tray.

Olivia poured the tea and drew a breath to begin explaining.

Sir Jasper sipped. "I'm sure you're excited by the news. The entire countryside is agog."

"What news?" She was almost relieved to be interrupted, though also surprised. Rarely did anything worthy of comment happen in Steadham; Olivia found the quiet to be one of the village's greatest attractions.

"The wedding, of course. Lady Daphne's wedding." He looked startled when she didn't react. "You did not receive an invitation? I would have thought... The festivities are to be held here. At Halstead, to be precise."

Halstead—one of the few country houses in England that had only one name, as if the single word made it clear to any audience what was being discussed. The country seat of the Duke of Somervale, the manor house at Halstead lay less than a mile from the village if one walked across the fields and the park. But the estate was so large and self-contained that when the family was not in residence, it was easy for the villagers to forget the manor lay so close by.

In the months since she had arrived in Steadham village, Olivia had seen Halstead only from a distance. Apparently that wasn't going to change in the foreseeable future. But then, she would have expected nothing else.

Sir Jasper went on, "The wedding itself is to be in the village church, I understand."

He *understood*? Then Sir Jasper must not have

received an invitation, either. That surprised Olivia much more than the fact she had not been included on the guest list—for though Sir Jasper was a mere baronet, he must have been a neighbor of the Somervale family for years.

"I felt sure you would be invited," he mused. "As the widow of an earl… but the duchess is even higher in the instep than I believed."

"It's hardly a snub for me not to be included, Sir Jasper. So far as I am aware, I have never met any of the family, and I doubt the duchess even knows I've taken up residence in the neighborhood." *Or would care in the slightest, if she knew.*

Sir Jasper's face had tightened as if the mere mention of a snub had made his own exclusion sting more.

So Olivia hurried on. "Perhaps it's a very small wedding—just the family."

"A *small* wedding? For one of the Somervales? That family doesn't know the meaning of the word."

The firm click of the empty cup as he set it down made Olivia fear for her mother's china; she had managed to save fewer than a dozen good pieces as it was.

"But perhaps you are correct," Sir Jasper went on. "Now I must continue my rounds. The rent, Lady Reyne?"

Olivia's fingers trembled as she took her reticule from under the smock in her sewing basket and opened it. "I can give you half of the rent today, Sir Jasper, but I'm not able to pay for the entire three months right now. I had hoped to make an agreement in regard to the remainder."

He was silent for so long that the rattle of a carriage wheel in the road outside the parlor window seemed to echo through the room. "What sort of agreement did you have in mind?" His tone was low and suggestive.

Dread trickled down her spine, but Olivia kept her voice level. "I shall be able to give you the remainder at the beginning of next month."

He sniffed. "And I'm to simply take your promise for that, I suppose."

"I am not accustomed to having my word questioned, Sir Jasper. In any case, I would still be paying in advance—just not quite as far ahead as before."

"And then I suppose you plan to continue this practice month after month? I'm not accustomed to waiting for what is owed to me, my lady. What's the difficulty, anyway?"

That's my affair and none of yours. But thumbing her nose at a man when she was asking him to do her a favor wasn't wise. "I'm sure you know that after the death of her father, Miss Blakely has become my guest, and—"

"Adding another mouth to feed in your household was no decision of mine," Sir Jasper said sharply. "I see no reason for me to be inconvenienced by your folly."

"I am not asking you to sacrifice the rent payment or even reduce it, only to postpone collecting the full sum."

"And I'm telling you I'm not inclined to do so. I've been offered twice the rent," Sir Jasper said slyly. "I'd agreed to the bargain with you, so as an honorable man I couldn't go back on it. But if you're not paying on time, then I'm free to change the terms or let the place to another tenant."

Olivia tamped down the desire to snap at him that if he actually had a tenant who would pay more, he should seize the opportunity. She couldn't take the risk that he would throw her out.

This was her own fault. If she'd had the full sum and handed it over promptly, he wouldn't have been able to hold her to ransom.

"But perhaps we could come to an... arrangement," he went on.

Her skin crawled at the oily note in his voice. But perhaps her imagination was running away with her, and he only meant that his price for waiting would be an outrageous amount of interest. He surely couldn't mean that he wished to pay court to her, could he? His wife had died long since, and Sir Jasper had to be close to twice Olivia's age, for his sons were grown.

How she wished she had not invited him inside or offered tea! If he got the idea that she would welcome his suit, she would have to disillusion him, of course—and gently. She hoped he would not nurse resentment.

"The widow of an earl," he said softly, "living in an out-of-the-way village in a cottage where she cannot afford the rent. Your options are limited, Lady Reyne. You can't take in lodgers, for the place isn't large enough to house them even if you didn't already have enough hangers-on to feed."

Hangers-on? Olivia wondered if he thought her daughter a millstone. With an effort, she kept her expression neutral.

"You can't take a job as a governess or a companion, for no fine lady would hire an employee who was encumbered with a child. But I can think of one thing the widow of an earl could do nicely."

He didn't sound much like a man who was trying to fix his interest with a lady, but surely he couldn't be suggesting something short of marriage. Was he?

He chuckled. "Oh, *that's* a fine lady's expression, all right. There's no doubt your blood is blue, the way you've gone all arrogant and scornful as you pretend you don't know what I'm talking about. It's nothing you're unfamiliar with, either. You have a daughter."

Olivia tried to control her breathing, knowing that he was watching the effect of her short, shallow breaths. He licked his lips, his gaze focused on her breasts.

"I might waive the rent altogether if you were satisfactory in bed," he said. "I'd want a whole lot more than a taste, of course—*my lady*. But we'll start with a kiss today as interest on the debt."

Olivia felt as paralyzed as a rabbit caught in the open with a hawk diving for the kill. Then she heard the click of footsteps on the stairs as Nurse came down, and she pulled herself together with an effort.

Sir Jasper had heard, too. "I thought you said your servants were out."

And so you assumed I invited you in on purpose. Perhaps thought I intended to seduce you. Olivia stood up and said coolly, "What a pity you must be leaving now, Sir Jasper."

She thought for an instant that he would refuse to leave after all. But as he put on his hat, he said darkly, "You think about it, my fine lady. As of today, the rent increases to twice the figure we agreed on when you moved in."

She couldn't stop herself from squeaking in protest.

He grinned. "You're the one who broke the terms of the agreement. So if you don't pay up, one way or the other, you'll be moving out come the end of the month."

Olivia only wished she could leave the cottage—and Sir Jasper—behind. She showed him to the front door to be certain he left and because if she called for Nurse to see him out, there would be questions about why she was pale and shaken.

Sir Jasper stepped outside and turned to face her as if to add some new condition to his demands. The gate separating the cottage's garden from the road banged shut. Olivia looked up, expecting to see Kate returning from her calls. She was half-embarrassed to be caught in this predicament and half-grateful for reinforcement from her friend.

Instead she saw a carriage standing in the road just beyond the wall. A footman wearing the white wig and deep blue and silver livery of the Somervales started steadily up the path, his tread measured. He looked as if he'd marched a good distance already today. He reached the steps, bowed, and held out a folded parchment.

"For Lady Reyne," he intoned. "From the Duchess of Somervale."

Sir Jasper's jaw dropped.

Olivia knew she should have enjoyed the moment. Instead, she took the parchment reluctantly. The folded sheet was surprisingly heavy, adorned with silver ribbon and a large blue wax seal carrying the imprint of the Somervale crest, which she recognized from the ironwork on the estate gates.

"So the duchess didn't leave you out after all," Sir Jasper said. "You fine folk all stick together, don't you, my lady?"

The footman's eyes widened in shock as his gaze ran over Olivia.

She thought that no matter how many copies of the invitation he had delivered in the neighborhood—and if *she* was included amongst the wedding guests, then every other person who had even a hint of noble blood must have been invited as well—this was surely the first he had handed to the guest herself while she stood at her front door decorated with flour and bits of bread dough. But he was too well-trained to actually say so.

"You look very tired," she told the footman. "If you would like refreshment—"

He bowed politely. "Thank you, ma'am. But the invitations were sent down from London—a great box full—and we must see them all into the proper hands today." He retreated to the gate and climbed onto the perch at the back of the carriage, which slowly pulled away.

Olivia broke the seal and looked down at the parchment.

Her Grace, the Duchess of Somervale, requests that Lady Reyne honor the company with her presence at the marriage of Her Grace's daughter, Lady Daphne Elliot, to the Marquess of Harcourt, on Friday, 30 August 1816, at Halstead.

One could scarcely turn down a duchess's invitation, no matter how uncomfortable it was to accept. So Olivia would be going to a wedding.

Sir Jasper peered greedily at the invitation, and Olivia could sense his hot breath against her skin.

"I wonder if your fine friends will loan you money," he mused. "If they don't, my offer is still open." He tipped his hat and walked away.

Olivia stood on the step for a long time, trying to draw enough warm air into her lungs to thaw the chill that his proposition had left deep inside her. But the effort didn't seem to be working.

❧

Kate Blakely had never exactly enjoyed visiting the sick and needy members of the parish, because the people she was calling upon were in distress. As the vicar's daughter, compassionate calls had been expected of her. However, now that the visits were no longer a part of her duties, she found herself missing the people, as well as the distraction from her own troubles that her regular rounds had provided. Sitting at the bedside of an ailing parishioner helped her to remember that even though her own choices seemed limited at the moment, she still had options.

So after her household duties were finished at the cottage, she had left Olivia mixing bread and stopped by the vicarage with her basket to ask if the housekeeper could spare some produce or preserves to take to the sick.

"I wouldn't ask, Mrs. Meecham," Kate told the housekeeper, "except that I'm a guest in Lady Reyne's house and can hardly take things from her larder to give to others."

"Besides which, Lady Reyne has little enough to

keep her own household fed and nothing to spare."
The housekeeper filled Kate's basket to brimming.
"You're to take what's left home to her ladyship."

"You're very generous, but Lady Reyne does not
care to accept charity."

"It is not charity when her ladyship is housing and
feeding you, despite the fact that you should still be
living right here in your own home."

"Mrs. Meecham, this is not my home any longer.
The new vicar will take up his post at any moment,
and I could hardly be in residence when he appears. I
feel fortunate Lady Reyne offered me shelter."

"Your father served this parish for thirty years, God
rest his soul, and ever since your mother died, you've
been right there alongside him. It's a crime for you to
lose your home and your security because that good
man died too young."

Kate didn't argue, because they'd covered this
ground so many times that the discussion had lost all
of its intensity.

One of the housemaids popped her head into the
kitchen. "There's a carriage drawing up in front,
ma'am."

Mrs. Meecham whipped off her apron and smoothed
her dress. "That'll be the new vicar. You'll stay and
meet him of course, Miss Blakely?"

"Oh, no," Kate said hastily. "Not today. He'll be
tired after his long journey."

The maid was shaking her head. "It's not that kind
of a carriage. It's marked with the duke's crest, and a
footman's coming up the walk."

Kate's heart gave a little flutter. After so long, she'd

almost given up, but perhaps her letter to the duchess hadn't been ignored after all.

"Then go open the door and see what he wants, foolish girl," Mrs. Meecham ordered. As the maid left, the housekeeper's eye fell on Kate once more. "As for the new vicar, you'll have to meet him sometime."

"Whenever he arrives to take up his post, he can find me at Lady Reyne's cottage." Kate knew she sounded stubborn, so she added more softly, "I would not wish him to believe I was trying to push myself into his household or instruct him as to how to go on."

"Who better to guide him than you, with all your experience in this parish? Since he's your own cousin, I expect he'll want your opinion about how best to begin with his new flock."

Kate didn't argue the point, for she was far more interested in why the Somervale footman was at the door. Perhaps the duchess had been away and had only now received Kate's letter...

The housekeeper added a new loaf of crusty bread to the basket, already weighed down with preserves and bottled fruit, just as the maid returned to the kitchen. She held a folded parchment in her hand. "It's for you, miss. From the duchess."

Kate broke the seal on the parchment, while trying to keep her hand from trembling. If the duchess had agreed to help her find employment...

Her Grace, the Duchess of Somervale, requests that Miss Katherine Blakely honor the company with her presence at the marriage of Her Grace's daughter, Lady Daphne Elliot...

Kate stared at the parchment. It was not the letter she had hoped for. Not an offer of help or advice. It wasn't even *personal*. The lump in her throat threatened to choke her.

Mrs. Meecham was shamelessly looking over Kate's shoulder. "So Lady Daphne's getting married in less than a month's time. Halstead must be all aflutter."

The big house would be *en fête*, Kate thought. Full of people from the upper classes of society.

Kate had written to the duchess because she was the only person able to help. But with an entire houseful of the rich, famous, and idle… Surely one of them could provide the help Kate needed to leave Steadham. And the invitation to Lady Daphne's wedding made it possible for her to meet them.

With a sudden—and rare—burst of warm feeling toward Lady Daphne, Kate forgot all about her calls and the loaded basket, and she walked back to Lady Reyne's cottage, thinking hard.

                         ❧

Once again, Penelope Townsend had lain awake late into the night, listening for noises from the bedroom next to her own. But even with the windows thrown wide to catch the few cool night breezes that London afforded, the house on Berkeley Square was too well built for sound to travel. So she had tossed between her fine linen sheets, wondering when or if her husband had come home, until sometime in the wee hours when she had finally dropped off to sleep.

In the morning, out of sorts at having slept badly and not long enough, she was roused by the clatter of her lady's maid bringing in her chocolate. As Etta opened the curtains, Penelope sat up wearily and ran her hands through her hair. As usual, it had popped out of her overnight braid and was straggling around her face, her curls as thick and springy as wires and completely unmanageable. Etta draped a satin bed jacket around Penelope's shoulders and set the tray on her knees. The maid's eyes fell on Penelope's hair, and she sighed.

Penelope didn't blame her. Etta's skills were wasted on a mistress with few natural recommendations; if not for the enormous wage Penelope's father paid her, Etta would never have taken what she seemed to think was a thankless job.

Lying next to the fat little china chocolate pot was a folded sheet of paper, and Penelope's heart jolted. Could this be a note from her husband?

The page crackled as she unfolded it, and she noticed that the seal had been broken already. It was only a letter that must have arrived for her with the morning's post. A letter that someone else had already opened...

Before she could work up the energy to be offended that someone had read her mail, she realized it was an invitation inscribed in perfect calligraphy on rich, yellowish parchment.

Her Grace, the Duchess of Somervale, requests that The Earl and Countess of Townsend honor the company with their presence at the marriage of...

Penelope turned the sheet over to check the address. It was indeed directed to both of them—and no servant would have dared to break the seal of a letter that was addressed to the earl. Which meant her husband must have opened it himself.

"Is his lordship at home?" She was proud that her voice didn't quiver.

"Yes, my lady. The footman was fetching his hat and stick when I came upstairs."

That meant the earl was on his way out of the house for the day. *Again*.

Penelope bit her lip. "Bring me a dressing gown. I'm going downstairs right now."

Etta looked startled. And well she might, Penelope thought—for every other time her mistress had asked whether the earl was at home, it had been so she could avoid him, not seek him out. "But… my lady, you're not…"

"Will you get my dressing gown, or shall I?"

Etta's gaze fell, and she retrieved the satin and lace robe that matched Penelope's nightgown—part of her trousseau. Not that it mattered any more, Penelope thought as she tossed her hair back over her shoulders. Before Etta could fuss any more about her going out into the public areas of the house in her nightclothes, Penelope was descending the stairs. The broad marble treads felt deliciously cool against her bare toes.

The Earl of Townsend was in the hall accepting his hat, gloves, and walking stick from the hands of the senior footman. The earl didn't seem to hear the whisper of Penelope's satin hem against the stairs, for he didn't look up.

Penelope cleared her throat. "May I have a moment, my lord?"

The footman's hand slipped and he dropped the walking stick, which clattered against the marble floor.

The earl turned slowly turned toward the staircase.

"Ma'am?" His voice was coolly polite—the same tone in which he addressed a servant who had made a very messy error.

Her toes twisted nervously against the marble as she regarded him. He was every inch the gentleman this morning. His coats always fitted perfectly; his gloves were always spotless, and his face always handsome and unlined, no matter what hour of the night he had returned home.

Too late, she realized what she must look like this morning—hair tumbled, gown creased and awry. No wonder Etta hadn't wanted her to come downstairs. Penelope was not surprised when the earl's gaze grew even chillier than usual.

"I saw the invitation," she managed finally. "Is it your intention to attend the wedding?"

"Of course I will attend. Lady Daphne Elliot is a member of my family. I believe she's some sort of cousin, but no doubt your father could enlighten me on the precise relationship, since he has studied my pedigree with far more concern than I have."

His voice was beautiful, she thought. Even the sarcastic edge that sometimes turned it into a weapon failed to make his deep tones seem any less musical.

He adjusted his hat. "Good day, ma'am."

Though he'd answered the question she had asked, Penelope was left feeling just as uncertain. "Wait." She flinched at the way he set his jaw; she hadn't meant to issue a command. "Is it your wish that I attend the wedding as well?"

"You will attend," he said coolly, "because the duchess has ordered it." He bowed, and without hurry, went out. The sound of the footman closing the door behind him was oddly final.

And that, Penelope thought grimly as she climbed the stairs once more, had been all the answer she needed. She was going to the wedding only because the Duchess of Somervale had left the earl no option but to bring her.

◈

The Duke of Somervale had arrived at Halstead barely two hours earlier, but already he was daydreaming of being somewhere else. *Anywhere* else. Even London.

The fact that he would consider leaving the country seat he loved to go haring off to London—hot, dusty, and smelly as the city would be in the last half of August—brought him up short.

Simon focused his gaze once more on his butler, who was standing straight and square directly in the center of the library, and tried to take in what Greeley had just told him.

The eventual outcome was plain, Simon thought. *Daphne's wedding is going to kill me.*

The butler raised an enquiring eyebrow. "Your Grace?"

"Did I say that out loud, Greeley?"

"I didn't quite catch…"

"Good." Simon leaned back in his chair. "You must be mistaken. My mother cannot possibly have invited enough people to Daphne's wedding that every bedroom in the whole of Halstead is committed."

Greeley cleared his throat and looked unhappy, but he didn't back down.

"My mother doesn't *know* enough people to fill every bedroom at…" Simon's protest wasn't literally true, for the dowager duchess of Somervale knew everyone. Worse yet, everyone knew *her*. Still, she didn't generally go round inviting every person whose name she recognized to parties, much less to a once-in-a-lifetime event like her daughter's wedding.

Suspicion darkened Simon's voice. "Greeley, you're not trying to tell me she's tossed me out of *my* bedroom, are you?"

"No, sir. The duchess would never assign a guest to your suite, for she has a far deeper appreciation of the consequence required by the position of His Grace of Somervale than…" The butler coughed. "That is…"

"Than I do, you started to say." Simon pushed himself up from his chair and crossed the library to the terrace door that stood open to the perfect summer sunshine. From out on the lawn, somewhere around the corner of the house and out of sight, came the sound of girlish giggles. A positive chorus of girlish giggles.

Simon felt the color drain from his face. "They're already invading? But the wedding is still almost a week away!"

"The bridesmaids have all arrived, sir. Her Grace left plenty of time for final fittings of all the gowns, since there are precisely a dozen young ladies."

"Twelve? It takes *twelve* bridesmaids to get Daphne down the aisle?"

"Also, a few members of the family have already made their appearance. Colonel Sir Tristan Huffington explained that since he did not wish to chance missing the festivities, he set out early in case travel conditions became difficult."

"Nonsense. The summer's been fine, and the roads are in excellent condition. He set out early so he could enjoy Halstead's amenities for an extra week."

"And Lady Daphne's godmother is in residence as well, to offer her support to the bride."

"Now there's a misnomer," Simon muttered. "*Godmother*, I mean. If that woman has ever been on nodding acquaintance with the Almighty, I'll swallow my best hat. All right, Greeley, you've made your point. How many will be sitting down to dinner tonight?"

"Twenty-two, sir."

"And if that's only the vanguard…" Simon sighed. "Thanks for the warning, old chap."

But Greeley stood as still as if his toes had melted into the plush rug in front of the desk. "Just one more thing, sir. Mrs. Greeley observed to me as she was making the bedroom assignments that an unusually high proportion of the guests Her Grace has invited to stay here at Halstead are young, unmarried ladies."

"What's strange about that? Most of my sister's friends must be young, unmarried ladies." But there had been a note in Greeley's voice that sounded almost as though he was sounding an alarm.

The butler bowed. "As you say, sir. The mixture of guests is quite coincidental—and that's what I informed Mrs. Greeley."

Coincidental. The word seemed to hang in the quiet air of the library until another, closer ripple of feminine laughter pushed it aside.

A shadow fell across the polished floor from the

terrace outside, and Lady Daphne gave a shriek and burst into the library. "Simon—you're home at last! Now the celebration can really begin. Come and make your curtsies to my brother, everyone. Simon, these are my bridesmaids."

As his sister threw her arms around him, Simon looked past her to a dozen young women in pastel muslin gowns, all of whom seemed to be curtseying at once. Tall, short, plump, thin. Light hair, dark hair, red hair, golden hair...

As they milled around on the terrace, smiling and bobbing up and down, the group looked remarkably like decorative goldfish in a pond. Fish, Simon thought wryly, who had scented food. Fish who were churning the water to a froth as they battled to reach the center of the action, where they'd have the best chance of capturing the promised treat.

Him.

A dozen bridesmaids. Every last one of them, he'd wager, was absolutely eligible—from a good family and with an acceptable dowry. And this wasn't even the full guest list.

Greeley's warning had been right on target. No wonder Simon had been feeling itchy; he'd been set up like a target on a pistol range.

He didn't blame Daphne, of course. The young women in question might be her friends, but he knew where to place the blame for this scheme. He looked over his sister's upswept black hair to catch the butler's eye. "Greeley, where will I find my mother? And send a message to the stables. I'll need a groom to deliver some letters for me this afternoon."

Since he could hardly walk out on his sister's wedding, he had no choice but to spend the next week playing the role of Prince Charming to a horde of potential Cinderellas. But he'd be damned if he'd do it alone. A wise man knew when to call for reinforcements.

Daphne's wedding, he thought grimly, *is going to kill me*.

Two

THE SILENCE IN THE SMALL GARDEN BESIDE THE COTTAGE was disturbed only by the occasional cluck and scratch of one of the neighbor's chickens, the sharp cries of children as they chased an escaped pig through a nearby courtyard, and the scrape of Olivia's hoe as she loosened dirt around a hill of runner beans. She almost didn't hear the squeak of leather as a rider shifted in his saddle in the road just outside her garden wall.

Kate looked up from the patch nearby where she was thinning a row of carrots. "There's Sir Jasper riding past again."

Every muscle in Olivia's body tightened.

Sir Jasper's nasal voice rang out. "My lady, and Miss Blakely. I see you are both well occupied today in raising vegetables. What an interesting hobby you have."

"We manage to amuse ourselves." Olivia kept her voice light.

He bowed, tipping his hat with an ironic flourish, and rode on.

Kate pushed herself back from the carrots. "I don't understand that man. I'm really starting to think he cherishes a *tendre* for you, since he can't seem to go half a day without passing by the cottage. Yet when he sees you outside, he never makes a push to do anything more than pause for a moment's conversation."

I should have told her right away, Olivia thought. But on the day that Sir Jasper had made his proposition, Kate had been absorbed by the invitation to Lady Daphne's wedding and had not noticed that Olivia was quieter than usual. At any rate, Sir Jasper's offer had been so insulting that Olivia herself had scarcely believed what she was hearing. She'd been afraid that Kate—not having heard the conversation firsthand— might think Olivia had imagined the whole thing or misunderstood Sir Jasper's intentions.

But whether it had been wise to keep her own counsel or not, Olivia had stayed silent then. To tell Kate now, more than three weeks after the incident, would be even more difficult.

Three weeks in which she had made little headway toward solving her problem.

She had managed to eke out the rent payment that was truly due, though only by squeezing the household budget till it squealed in pain. But if Sir Jasper insisted on doubling the rent as he'd threatened, Olivia would come up short once again. She had quietly looked around the village for another house, but there was none to be found in Steadham. She had no resources to go some-where else, and even if she could afford the fare to travel, there was no one whom she could ask to take her in.

In any case, she couldn't simply pick up her daughter and leave. She felt responsible for Nurse as well, and Maggie the housemaid, and now even Kate.

"I'm not sure we'll ever make you a gardener, Olivia," Kate said gently.

Olivia looked down at the hill of runner beans, chopped off at ground level and already wilting under the warm sun. "I let my mind wander, and my hoe must have slipped."

A childish soprano chimed in, "I will dig, Miss Kate!"

Olivia looked across to where Charlotte was standing on a bench in the grape arbor that nestled against the garden wall, plucking the lowest-hanging fruit from the vines. The little girl looked a bit like a grape herself with her hands and her round cheeks smeared with sticky bluish-purple juice. After eating her fill, she had gathered up the hem of her pinafore in one small hand, forming a makeshift basket to hold the extra fruit. Juice from the grapes she'd smashed dripped through the fabric, down her skirt, and onto her tiny shoes.

Olivia winced at the idea of trying to get juice stains out of Charlotte's yellow muslin dress and decided it might be easier to fix a pail of juice and dye the entire thing purple. Or whatever color grape juice would end up becoming if mixed with yellow muslin. Kate would know.

Or perhaps Olivia wouldn't bother, for the dress—though still wide enough to fit Charlotte's slender body—was already too short. Her baby was rapidly growing up; Charlotte would be three within a few weeks.

Olivia sighed. She could find enough fabric to make dresses for her daughter. A few of her old gowns remained in the cottage's attic—once fashionable things she had no use for in Steadham—and she could salvage the material and trimmings for the child. But where she would find money for new shoes...

Sir Jasper had been right on a number of fronts. Olivia could not take in lodgers, for there was no space. Because she had a child, she could not seek out any sort of job that required living in the employer's house, which largely wiped out the possibility of earning a wage.

She looked down at the wilting runner beans. She couldn't even grow vegetables to sell or barter, for if she couldn't manage to keep from killing the ones she had hoped to use to feed her small family, there would never be any left over.

And she couldn't continue to live on the narrow edge like this. One unexpected expense, one illness, one unforeseen need, and the precarious life she had built in Steadham would come crashing down—as it almost had three weeks earlier when Sir Jasper had made his not-quite-veiled demand.

I can think of one thing the widow of an earl could do nicely, Sir Jasper had said. *I might waive the rent altogether if you were satisfactory in bed*.

Such an arrangement was out of the question, of course; she felt ill even thinking about it. And yet... every day, women chose men to marry based not on respect or fondness, but solely because they could provide food and shelter.

This is different, she told herself firmly, for there would be no end to Sir Jasper's demands. A wife might not have many rights, but an unwilling mistress had fewer yet.

A barouche rattled by—glossy black and gleaming, with a pair of footmen riding up behind, clad in the blue and silver Somervale livery. Olivia barely had a glimpse of the hats of the two ladies inside, for the coach was moving quickly. *Too quickly for safety*, she thought. *What if the pig—or worse yet, the children who were chasing the pig—ducked out from between two cottages and into the path of the carriage?*

"That was the duchess," Kate said. "I couldn't see who the other woman was, but surely Lady Daphne wouldn't wear that very strange hat."

"With the wedding less than a week off, I'm surprised Her Grace is only now arriving."

Kate shrugged. "Perhaps she just hasn't come into the village before. The cottage isn't the center of gossip, and the duchess has never kept me informed of her movements."

Her voice was firmly controlled, but Olivia knew Kate well enough to hear the note of strain underneath. At least, Olivia thought, the duchess should have been polite enough to answer Kate's letter—even if she couldn't actually help.

"Perhaps they're going to inspect the church," Olivia said. "Or to discuss the ceremony with the new vicar. Has he arrived yet?"

"I don't think so. Mrs. Meecham would have sent me word. The duchess should remember what the church looks like. She was married there, and the family used to spend most of the year at Halstead until the duchess took Daphne off to London to be presented."

"That's the first time I've heard you refer to Lady Daphne without her title."

Kate blinked. "Did I? It's how I always thought of her, though heads would have rolled if I'd said as much to her face."

"So the duchess *is* a stickler, I see."

"Not the duchess. When Daphne was Charlotte's age, she would stamp her foot and scream whenever one of the children forgot to use her title."

"At *Charlotte's* age? Odd that you remember it so precisely, for she must be only a few years younger than you are."

"Four, I think. She must be twenty now." Kate finished the row of carrots and stood up to stretch. "Simon, on the other hand... the duke, I mean... is delightful. He's funny and charming and handsome, and he doesn't stand on ceremony."

Olivia moved on to the next hill of runner beans, determined that this time the plants would survive her tending. "*Simon*, is it? How well do you know him, Kate?"

A tinge of pink flared in Kate's cheeks. "He used to come to the vicarage for extra tutoring sometimes when he was down from Oxford."

"And to see you?"

"Of course not. He used to talk to me about all the women he fell in love with—though that's taking the term lightly, for even Simon knew he was never serious about any of them. And before you go on about me using his name, he wasn't the duke then."

"Only the marquess of something-or-other," Olivia teased. "A different thing entirely, I'm sure. But why, if you knew the duke so well, didn't you write to him for assistance?"

"Are you mad? If he recommended me for employment, everyone would think he was passing along a cast-off mistress."

"I suppose you're right," Olivia admitted. "But if he's less high in the instep than his mother and sister are…"

"In any case, after the duchess didn't answer me at all, I could hardly turn to the duke. But there has to be someone at this wedding who's a possibility."

Olivia dug her hoe deep into the soil. "Now you almost sound as if you're planning to set your cap for one of the guests, Kate."

Kate's laugh sounded brittle. "Hardly. Even if I wasn't old enough to be on the shelf, I'm a vicar's daughter with no dowry. I can't think of any woman who's less likely to inspire a marriage proposal, especially from the sort of gentlemen who will gather at Halstead next week."

"You can't? What about a widow who has a three-year-old daughter and not a penny to her name?"

"That's true. We are neither of us prizes on the marriage market, are we, Olivia? I had hoped that the duchess would recommend me to someone who needs a companion or a secretary or a governess. But surely someone in that crowd will hire me. I simply must find that person."

Kate's voice held a note of determined optimism, but Olivia suspected she had to work at it. No matter what Kate said, it would be no simple task to ferret out guests who might be in search of an employee from among a crowd of merrymakers.

"You've been very quiet since that day as well,

you know," Kate said. "Tell me, what has kept *you* thinking so hard since you were invited to Lady Daphne's wedding?"

Not the wedding, Olivia thought.

From out in the street, a man's shout cut through the village noises, so loud and close at hand that Olivia jumped. The sharp blade of the hoe grazed her toes and sliced off another entire hill of runner beans. She whirled around, ready to lambaste the thoughtless fool who was making such a noise, and her heart leaped into her throat.

The scene burned itself into her vision as if everyone and everything had frozen in place. She saw her daughter perched on tiptoe on the narrow back of the bench. How had Charlotte managed to climb up there? And how was she keeping her balance?

Except—she wasn't.

One of Charlotte's small hands still clutched her pinafore-basket full of grapes, while the other was stretched out to a particularly juicy and tempting bunch that dangled just beyond her fingertips. But she wasn't looking at the grapes; she had turned her head toward the street as if the shout had startled her.

And as Olivia watched in horror, unable to reach her baby, Charlotte toppled off the back of the bench, over the wall, and out into the street, landing almost under the feet of a glossy black gelding.

The horse reared. Olivia tried to choke back her scream. From the corner of her eye, she saw Kate starting across the garden toward the gate. But that was too circuitous a route for Olivia, who flung herself straight toward the arbor instead. She stepped up onto the bench, sat on the back rail where Charlotte had perched, and swung her feet around and over the wall. Below her, Charlotte lay fearfully still in the dust, flat on her back.

The horseman had drawn the gelding away and dismounted, flinging the reins to a boy who came running from the cottage next door. Just as Olivia jumped from the wall into the street, the horseman knelt in the dust beside the child and reached out as if to gather her up.

"Don't," Olivia cried. She thrust out a hand to hold him away as she dropped to her knees beside the child. "Haven't you done enough damage by frightening her into falling and then trampling her?"

He looked up then, and midnight-blue eyes blazed at her. "I? My good woman, how dare you accuse *me*?"

"Because you caused this accident! Calling out—"

"Why do you think I shouted? I saw her start to fall, but I was too far away to reach her and hoped to alert someone else to her peril."

Olivia was barely listening. Charlotte's eyes were open wide, and she was staring as if in disbelief. Olivia brushed at the front of Charlotte's dress, trying to determine if she was breathing.

"It's not blood she's drenched in," the horseman said. "Only grape juice."

"I know that much, thank you," Olivia snapped.

Charlotte gasped, wheezed, and gave a thin, reedy wail.

"Oh, thank God," Olivia said. "She only got the breath knocked out of her."

The horseman's eyes narrowed. "Thank God indeed,

for the person who was supposed to be supervising her was of no use whatsoever! I assume you are that person?"

His gaze slid across her with arrogant ease, and suddenly Olivia saw herself as he must see her— wearing her oldest and most faded dress with a floppy-brimmed hat to hold off the sun, and every inch of her coated with dust. She must look like a nursery servant who had been pressed into service in the garden.

"What in the devil do you mean by allowing a child to climb into such a precarious position?"

Charlotte's wail grew steadily louder. Olivia helped her sit up, and the child huddled against her mother. "There, darling. Don't let him frighten you any more. Perhaps he'll stop yelling now and go away."

"Gladly," the horseman said coldly, and stood up.

Olivia hadn't expected him to comply, and remorse swept over her as her normally good manners finally began to reassert themselves. Now that she was no longer terrified for her daughter's life, she was stunned by the recollection of what she had said. Perhaps he *had* only been trying to help. And she *was* at fault for not watching Charlotte more closely.

"Sir," she began. "I—" Still kneeling in the dirt, she had to look a long way up to his face, but her gaze caught at the level of his knees instead. The soft pale leather of his buckskins was stained with dirt and… "You have grape juice all over you."

He didn't even bother to look. "It's of no importance."

"The stain will never come out of the leather."

In good conscience, she had to offer to compensate him for the damage. The accident was her fault; he would not have knelt in Charlotte's puddle of juice if Olivia had been doing her duty. She had no idea where she would find the money to replace such a costly item—but this was, in a sense, a debt of honor, and so she must pay it.

She patted her daughter's back and tried to make herself utter the words.

Kate pulled up beside them, out of breath. "Your Grace," she gasped.

Olivia's hand froze in midpat.

"Miss Blakely." The gentleman shot a glare at Olivia. "Ma'am."

Olivia's mind felt like congealed mud. Bad enough that in the momentary madness of terror for her daughter she had insulted *any* gentleman. But to have insulted the Duke of Somervale, the premier gentleman of the entire district...

Without taking his gaze off Olivia, the duke snapped his fingers. The boy who had been holding the reins of the black gelding led the animal across the street. The duke tossed him a coin, and the boy grinned and backed away.

"Your Grace," Olivia said. Her voice didn't sound quite as shaky as she felt. She gathered Charlotte into her arms and stood up. "I most humbly beg your pardon." She attempted a curtsey, but with Charlotte snuggled against her shoulder, it was a sadly ungraceful obeisance.

The duke's gaze was as chilly as the village water trough had been all the past winter. "You will understand, I am certain, that the timing of your apology makes me find your change of heart less than convincing."

"Truly, sir, I..." Olivia bit back the rest. What was

the point of abasing herself, after all? He would never understand the panic a parent felt and how the sight of a child in danger could sweep away good judgment. What had Kate said about him? He fell in love lightly, fell out just as quickly, and was incapable of faithfulness. What would such a man know about the deep love one person could feel for another, much less a mother for a beloved child?

Kate also had said he was delightful and funny and charming and handsome, Olivia reminded herself. Well, she would have to agree with *handsome*. His hair was so dark it looked almost blue where the sunlight kissed it; his form was tall and lean and muscular; and his features were regular and classical, apart from a tiny scar next to his left eye. His face might even be pleasing, she thought, if he didn't appear to have been hewed out of a chunk of granite.

"Your Grace," Kate said again. She sounded breathless.

Olivia was still keeping a wary eye on the duke. "Oh, don't for heaven's sake *beg*, Kate. I'm the one he's annoyed at. I'm quite certain he won't rescind *your* invitation to his sister's—"

"Olivia, *don't*," Kate whispered. "That's not…"

A woman's voice interrupted. "Miss Blakely, Mrs. Meecham at the vicarage told me I would find you here. I wished to call on you and extend my condolences in person for the loss of your father."

Olivia turned slowly. She knew what she would see, even though she had been so absorbed in staring at the duke that she hadn't heard the creak of wheels or the jingle of harness as the duchess's barouche had returned and pulled up in the road.

The two ladies inside leaned forward in their seats as if intrigued by the standoff. The one who had spoken was middle-aged and wearing a dashingly stylish hat. Her hair, once just as dark as the duke's, was now threaded liberally with silver. Her companion was older, with a mass of multicolored feathers on her head, a nose that would have done a hawk proud, and sharp, beady black eyes.

"Your Grace," Olivia said feebly, trying to curtsey to the duchess. Charlotte shifted restlessly in her arms, throwing her off balance.

The duke swore and cupped his hand under Olivia's elbow as if he thought she was about to fall down. His grip was not gentle, and his voice was grim. "No doubt this time you'd manage to drop her on her head."

Kate moved toward the barouche, curtseying so elegantly that Olivia felt like a clumsy ox.

Charlotte reached out to pat the pristine white folds of the duke's neckcloth, and Olivia watched in horror as a tiny purple handprint took perfect shape on the linen, right under his chin.

The duchess was talking animatedly to Kate, but her companion sat up even straighter, peering at the duke through a quizzing glass. "Oh, Somervale," she chirped. "You're always *so* original. Tell me, are you planning to make purple-spotted clothes the new fashion now?"

❧

Penelope hovered anxiously as her maid packed for the trip to Halstead, watching every fold of tissue paper as Etta briskly laid gowns and shoes and shawls and wraps and headdresses into the series of trunks and hatboxes that had been brought down from the attics and lined up across the bedroom.

"Must I really take my entire wardrobe?" Penelope ventured finally. "We're to be there for less than a week."

Etta didn't pause. "You'll need to change clothes at least four times a day for walking, riding, picnics, carriage outings, dinners, dancing—and at a moment's notice. You'll not embarrass me by looking less than your best." She looked quite fierce.

The butler tapped on the bedroom door. "My lady, Mr. Weiss has asked if you are at home."

The last person Penelope wanted to talk to today was her father. "I must help with the packing. Goodman, please tell Mr. Weiss that I—"

Etta said, "My lady, to speak plain, you're in my way. I'll accomplish a great deal more if you aren't standing over me."

When even her maid didn't need or want her, things were in a sad state indeed. "If you're quite sure you can manage, Etta, I'll go down." Penelope paused only to make sure her hair wasn't falling out of its pins before she descended to the drawing room.

Ivan Weiss was standing before the bow window overlooking Berkeley Square. His hands were clasped behind his back, and he was rocking on his heels as if he was impatient to mark this visit off his calendar and get on with more important matters.

And that was probably true, Penelope thought. Once he'd settled his daughter by marrying her off to the Earl of Townsend, her father had dusted his hands of her and returned to his first love, the brewery that had produced his fortune.

The fortune which in turn had made Penelope such a notable heiress that she was of interest to an earl despite the lack of anything resembling blue blood in her lineage.

And you agreed to the match, Penelope reminded herself. *So it's hardly fair to blame your father for how it's turning out.*

"Good afternoon, Papa," she said as he turned from the window. She dropped a deep, elegant curtsey.

Ivan Weiss beamed. The one way Penelope could always command his attention was by demonstrating the ladylike talents she'd learned at the expensive boarding school he'd sprung for. He made no pretense of appreciating art or music, but his opinion of his Penny's talents was far higher than her own—or that of her teachers. Every time she curtseyed to him, he would laugh with delight.

So she always curtseyed to him as deeply as she would have done to the queen, had she ever been properly presented at court, before she offered her cheek for his kiss. "What brings you to Berkeley Square today, Papa?"

"I hear you're packing up for a stay at Halstead." Delighted pride filled his voice. "My girl to be a guest at Halstead!"

Of course he would have heard, Penelope thought. Ivan Weiss provided ale to every fine residence in the West End of London, along with most of the inns and coaching houses within range of his headquarters, and with each delivery his men made, they seemed to return gossip to their employer.

"The wedding of a duke's sister is about as close

as you can get to royal," he went on. "I called in just to see whether you need anything extra. Dresses or female fripperies?"

"No, Papa. There's no time, anyway, but I already have everything I need."

He laughed. "Never thought I'd live to hear a woman say that! But here—you might like something new anyway." He pulled his hand from behind his back and held out a velvet box. "Women always like jewelry, and having a new bauble to flaunt will help make you feel at home with those fine society tabbies."

Penelope took the box with reluctance. Ivan Weiss's taste in jewelry was no better than his eye for art, and his choice was guaranteed to be the most startling one in view. Penelope had long since given up trying to modify his ideas of what was fashionable.

Today's offering was a gold brooch bearing a central stone that was dark yellow and as big as her knuckle. It looked like an unwinking cat's-eye, and it was so heavy that it would drag down any dress she pinned it on. But the good manners her father had paid so much to instill in her made her say, "This is very thoughtful of you, Papa."

He looked her up and down. "You seem a little peaked. Are you increasing, Penny?"

She shook her head.

"I think maybe you are," he offered hopefully. "Your mother looked the same way—a little pinched in the face—when she was first carrying you."

Far better to be honest, Penelope thought, than to face deeper disappointment later. "I am not with child, Papa."

Ivan Weiss's face fell. "Well, what's keeping you then? I'm getting to be an old man, and I want little ones to dandle on my knee. A whole raft of them, starting with a grandson who'll be an earl one day himself."

Yes, Penelope thought. *Now we reach the crux of it.*

He looked at her darkly. "Are you telling me there's something wrong with that fancy earl of yours? I'd think, seeing as how producing an heir is the only thing that will increase the allowance I pay him, he'd be working hard to get you in the family way." He eyed her shrewdly. "Or maybe he's doing his best, and it's *you* that's the problem, Penny?"

She wanted to tell him it wasn't her fault that her husband refused to do his duty. And yet... perhaps it *was* her fault. If a wife was so displeasing to her husband's eye that he could not bring himself to share the marriage bed, then who else could possibly be to blame but the wife?

Penelope had heard tales whispered under the blankets at her boarding school of how men behaved with women, but masculine hesitation to leap into a bed had not figured in any of those stories.

Nor had the duenna Penelope's father hired to chaperone her through her brief betrothal given so much as a hint of why a man might not avail himself of any woman who was accessible to him. Quite the contrary, in fact. Though her discussion of wedding-night mechanics had been brief and—in Penelope's view—singularly unhelpful, the one thing Miss Rose had been clear about was that by the morning after her wedding, a bride would have no doubts left regarding what a husband and wife did together.

So if the man was not the problem, the woman must be.

If I had tried harder to lure him to my bed...

Perhaps Lady Daphne's wedding was not something to be dreaded after all, but an opportunity to be seized. They would be away from their normal routine, away from the London house that held such mixed memories, away from the bad habits they had fallen into.

And perhaps in a different place and surrounded by happiness and liveliness and the joy of another bride and groom, they might yet find their way to some kind of real marriage.

Even if she had to seduce him... if she could only figure out how *that* was done.

Penelope decided she'd think about a plan later. In the meantime, she squared her shoulders and faced her father. "Yes, Papa. I'm the one who's to blame."

He let out an exasperated whoof. "Damn it, Penny—"

She hadn't heard the drawing-room door open, but suddenly she felt a whisper of air stirring against her neck and turned to see her husband standing on the threshold.

The earl displayed his usual air of languid grace. He was dressed in fawn-colored pantaloons and a bottle-green coat today, and the tassels on his Hessian boots were still swinging. Somehow the dark green of the coat threw reddish highlights into his curly, dark brown hair.

What was he doing at home in the middle of the day? Since the morning more than three weeks ago when she'd confronted him over the invitation, Penelope had barely seen him. In fact, she'd scarcely caught a glimpse of him during daylight in the entire three months they'd been married.

But then she hadn't seen much of him at any other time of day, either. Occasionally he dined at home and they silently occupied opposite ends of the long table. Once in a while he stepped aside politely as she passed in a hall. But since the very first night after their wedding, when he had come to her bedroom only long enough to tell her that he would not be returning…

She hoped he hadn't heard what her father had said. A man like the Earl of Townsend, with all his culture, couldn't understand one like Ivan Weiss who had rough edges aplenty.

"Mr. Weiss," the earl said gently, "pray allow the *fancy earl* to pay his compliments."

Penelope winced, though she had to admire the way the earl had delivered the sarcastic comment as delicately as he would flick his whip to brush a fly off the ear of one of his horses without injuring the animal. She had seen him do it once, when he had taken her for a drive through the park in his curricle, right before their wedding…

Her father turned brick red from embarrassment—or rage. But he said, calmly enough, "You're going to a wedding at Halstead, I understand."

"Yes, I am a distant relative of the Somervales. I'm sure you can tell me, sir, whether Lady Daphne is my third cousin or my fourth. I do find genealogy such a tiring pursuit."

"It appears you have no stamina at getting descendants, either," Ivan Weiss said dryly.

The earl's gaze turned steely.

Ivan Weiss did not seem to notice. He reached into his pocket and drew out a letter. With slow, deliberate movements he unfolded the paper and held it up as if to peruse the words.

The earl hadn't moved, and a bystander would probably not have noticed a change in his expression, but Penelope had become so closely attuned to his every attitude that he might as well have shouted that he recognized the sheet of paper. Whatever was written there, he knew about it—and seeing it made him uneasy.

"Regarding this remarkable communication," Ivan Weiss said, "the answer is no."

"I had assumed as much, sir, since you did not deign to answer."

Weiss plowed on as if he hadn't heard. "I will not fund such a misguided venture at this time. My terms have not changed, and since you know quite well what they are, there's no sense wasting breath in further discussion until you've taken the necessary steps to meet my requirements. You understand?"

The earl bowed. "Of course, sir. I pray you will excuse me. I must depart for Halstead sooner than planned, at the request of the duke, so I must make arrangements."

"Sooner?" Penelope was startled. "Then I must get back to my packing, too."

Ivan Weiss scoffed. "Why do you think I hired that harridan of a maid for you, Penny? Let her do the work." He eyed her closely. "I'm getting to be an old man, you know. Time's a-wasting." He kissed her cheek, bowed stiffly to the earl, and departed.

Silence descended on the drawing room. But despite what her husband had said about being pressed for time, the earl made no move except to pour himself a glass of port. He sipped and studied Penelope over the rim of the glass.

Penelope felt shivery inside. He hadn't looked at her like that since... since their wedding night, she thought. And then everything had gone wrong.

"What was that all about?" she asked. "The letter, I mean."

"Nothing of significance."

She didn't believe him, for there was a note of heaviness underlying his voice that said her father's refusal had mattered very much indeed. In any case, the earl would not have asked for a favor from the father-in-law he detested unless the matter was vital.

Surely Ivan Weiss wouldn't have rejected a reasonable request... would he? "My father is a good man at heart."

"Indeed." The earl's tone was clipped. "I see you have a new trinket. Have I missed an occasion? Your birthday, perhaps?"

Penelope had forgotten the box she held. "No. It's a sort of celebration gift... because of the invitation to Halstead."

"May I see it?"

Reluctantly, she opened the box to display the brooch.

His gaze flickered. "A remarkable piece. Shall I see you wearing it at the wedding?"

Though she had thought she was learning to recognize his moods, this one defeated her. Was there a tinge of humor in his voice? No, it must have been entirely her imagination. She looked down at the brooch. "I think not, for the gown I plan to wear is pink. You said we're to go early to Halstead, my lord?"

"The duke has requested me to come as soon as I can, but you need not make haste."

Penelope wondered why he had been summoned ahead of time. If she was really a wife, she could ask what was going on. "When do you go?"

"I will leave tomorrow morning, so I must warn my valet of the change in plans."

"Tell me what hour, and I'll be ready."

"You must not disturb yourself, ma'am. I'll drive down tomorrow in my curricle, and you can come in a few days in the carriage."

Along with the rest of the baggage, Penelope thought. "A drive in your curricle would be quite nice," she said with determination.

"This is hardly the same as a brief jaunt through the park. The trip to Halstead takes hours, and you would be exhausted and wind-burned long before we arrived."

"I will manage. In any case, if my father should hear I was staying in town while you have gone ahead without me…"

His eyes went dark. "Do not attempt to blackmail me. I no longer have any reason to fear losing your father's good will."

She wondered again what request he had made in his letter. "But *I* do," she confessed.

For a long moment they stood in silence, gazes dueling. Then he said, "Very well. I leave at nine. If you wish to come, be ready then—and leave any notion of complaining behind." He set his glass down hard on a nearby table and went out.

Absently, Penelope took out her handkerchief and wiped up the port that had sloshed over the fine finish.

That's a beginning, at least, she thought. The trouble was that she had no idea how to go on.

Three

THE SITUATION, SIMON TOLD HIMSELF FIRMLY, COULD only improve.

As matters stood, the Duke of Somervale was on display in the middle of the village street, being gawked at by every cottager within shouting distance. He was standing next to a termagant who had a tongue so sharp that she could flay a squirrel without using a knife. He had half a gallon of grape juice soaking his buckskins and staining his neckcloth. Even his horse seemed embarrassed to be seen with him, for the gelding tugged at the reins, anxious to be off.

And perhaps most annoying of all, Lucinda Stone had had the brass to laugh at him.

Simon tipped his head back so he could level a cold stare at her. Lady Stone might be his sister's godmother and his mother's friend, but she stood in no special place with him, and the sooner she realized it, the better.

"I see you've finally learned to appreciate your own consequence, Somervale," Lady Stone went on blithely. "Your mother will be pleased about *that.*

You have quite a nice sneer—though it would be far more effective if you were still sitting on the back of your horse so you could literally look down your nose at me."

She was right, and her tone was so sly that Simon couldn't help but burst out laughing.

The woman standing next to him, so close his hand still hovered under her elbow, took a step back as if she was startled by the sound.

"Even dukes laugh now and then," he muttered, turning to inspect her. At first he had thought this sharp-voiced female must be the child's nurse, but now that he took a second look, he could see that this woman was no servant, regardless of how she was dressed. Her features were fine and delicate, and her hands were small—though because of her rough gloves, he couldn't see whether they were as dainty or soft as a lady's were expected to be. And her accent was an educated one. Perhaps she, like Miss Blakely, fell somewhere in between the nobility and the lower classes.

The finely turned ankle and the slender calf she'd displayed as she jumped down from the wall had caught his eye even in the midst of his concern for the child. And now that the child was no longer in danger, he found himself thinking again of the flash of bare skin, the peek at forbidden territory…

Simon had seen his share of women's legs, and a good many of them had belonged to well-born ladies. But no ankle had ever seized his attention like this one, making him want to explore. He'd never been much of an ankle man anyway; he was more likely to notice a generous bosom, something this woman did not have. While her shape was pleasantly rounded—so far as he could tell under the almost shapeless gown—no one could call her proportions voluptuous.

He realized he was staring when sparks of gold flared in the hazel depths of her eyes, and he was annoyed. Why was she offended by him taking a second look? She'd gone all soft and mushy as soon as she'd found out who he was, but now she was spitting fire merely because he'd taken her up on her unspoken invitation to pay closer attention to her attributes!

And what was Kate Blakely thinking anyway, being friends with a woman like this one? The soft-hearted vicar's daughter must have taken up with a wayward acquaintance. But why? For the well-being of the child, perhaps.

He turned his attention to the little girl. She seemed to be all right now, though she was huddled close against the woman's shoulder. She was, however, peeking at him through long, dark lashes. He had no notion of how old she might be, but she was fine-boned and small, except for what seemed to be very long legs. Her eyebrows had a haughty arch that looked odd against the babyish roundness of her face, but a closer look told him that her brows matched those of the woman who held her. Definitely mother and daughter.

The duchess had not stopped talking—but then, Simon thought, she seldom did. He'd just have to be patient and let her run down. She was rattling on about some sort of letter. He let his gaze drift past the child and back to the woman who held her. She might not be as well endowed as some, but she was well proportioned. A neat little armful, in fact...

"My dear Miss Blakely, how very right you were to move out of the vicarage, regardless of what Mrs. Meecham believes to be your due. What an uncomfortable situation you have been in, since your father's death."

The gelding nudged Simon's shoulder and whinnied, and the little girl's eyes went wide as she stared at the horse.

"Your letter did not catch up with me until I reached Halstead, but I understand from Mrs. Meecham that you are well settled here at the cottage for the moment."

Simon's mystery woman set the child down and stepped forward. "I am happy to have Miss Blakely as my guest, Your Grace."

"Your Grace," Miss Blakely said, "may I present my hostess and friend—Olivia, Lady Reyne."

Lady Reyne? Simon felt the impact of the title like a blow to his abdomen, for it meant there must be a Lord Reyne somewhere. But of course she would have a husband, for she had a child. Why was that fact something to bother him?

And hadn't he heard something about a Lord Reyne? From one of the gossips, perhaps?

"Oh, yes," the duchess said. "My housekeeper mentioned you had moved into the village, Lady Reyne. I hope you will enjoy—"

Lady Stone snorted. "Do get on with it, Iris. My delicate skin has had about all the sun I can stand for one afternoon."

Delicate skin, my arse, Simon thought. Lady Stone's face generally looked as if she was the end product of a tannery.

"Very well, Lucinda," the duchess snapped. "I must tell you, Miss Blakely, that your letter came to my attention at a most convenient time, for indeed I do know of someone who is in great need of your assistance—me! Daphne has invited a dozen of her friends to be her bridesmaids, and they have already arrived at Halstead. I confess I underestimated how exhausting a houseful of young ladies can be. I would like you to come and help me until the wedding."

"You must have run mad to even consider it, Iris," Lady Stone put in.

"Having them all in one place seemed a good idea. Fittings and all." The duchess gave an airy wave of her hand. "But the dressmakers have been very efficient, and the young ladies are at loose ends. Miss Blakely, I beg you will assist me in keeping them entertained."

And prevent them from making fools of themselves around the gentlemen, Simon thought wryly. *Including me, I hope.* He heartily endorsed the idea, though he didn't have a great deal of confidence in its success. Even Miss Blakely, efficient though she undoubtedly was, would have her hands full with the assignment.

"The gel's in mourning, Iris," Lady Stone put in. "She can't go to parties."

Simon was still looking at Lady Reyne. *She* didn't seem to be in mourning. That dress was nothing short of a crime—faded, baggy, and roughly the shape of a sack—but it wasn't black. In fact, he thought, it might once have been a fetching shade of blue. So

Lord Reyne wasn't recently dead—or perhaps he was not dead at all. How aggravating that he couldn't remember the casual mention.

The duchess had barely paused. "That doesn't signify in the least, Lucinda. Being a chaperone is hardly like *enjoying* parties, after all. I shall expect you to take up your duties tomorrow, Miss Blakely, at the earliest time that is convenient for you. I'll send a carriage for you and your baggage. Of course you'll remain at Halstead for the duration."

Simon blinked in surprise. Was his mother going to house her new companion in the attics? Or had Greeley been mistaken when he said she'd filled every single bedroom?

Lady Stone spoke up. "Perhaps, Miss Blakely, your friend will be able to assist you in your duties. I am persuaded that the young ladies would benefit from having Lady Reyne's undivided attention as well."

Simon felt his jaw drop. He had always known that Lucinda Stone had a lopsided view of the world, but to ask a woman who couldn't keep both eyes on her child to help chaperone a dozen lively young ladies and prevent them from getting into trouble…

The duchess's teeth seemed to snap shut, but she said politely enough, "Of course, Lady Reyne. I am persuaded you would be an excellent influence."

Simon tried to stifle a snort.

Lady Reyne heard him despite his efforts, for the look she shot at him was so pointed that it should have punctured his throat.

The little girl's bonnet had been knocked off by her fall and was still lying in the road at his feet. He stooped to retrieve it, dusted it off against his buckskins, and held it out. The child hesitated and looked past him at the horse with wariness in her gaze.

Simon made a funny face at her and was rewarded with a giggle as she edged just close enough to reach for the hat. She was truly unhurt then, he thought with relief.

"The invitation is very flattering, Your Grace," Lady Reyne said. "But I am afraid I must decline because of my duties at home."

"Your daughter, you mean?" Lady Stone asked blandly. "Do bring her along, Lady Reyne. Perhaps the young ladies would enjoy having a live doll to play with… or even if they don't, Somervale apparently will."

❧

Kate could barely restrain herself. The moment the carriage had gone out of sight, with the duke riding beside it, she hugged herself and spun around in the middle of the road, sending up a little whirl of dust around her feet. "Everything is all right after all! The duchess wasn't ignoring me. She just hadn't received my letter."

Olivia took Charlotte firmly by the hand. "Or else she simply didn't bother to answer until she realized what a predicament she's put herself in. *Twelve* young women, Kate!"

"I'm sure Lady Daphne's bridesmaids are all perfectly well-bred. High-spirited, of course, as young women often are. But it's not as if the duchess has adopted a group of foundlings."

Olivia shook her head. "The foundlings might be

easier to control. I'm glad that you're to have Her Grace's help with the search for an employer, but Kate, it seems an overwhelming job."

"Then come and help me. With two of us—"

"Oh, no. Her Grace only issued the invitation to me because she didn't wish to appear rude by contradicting her friend. I'd seem a rare sort of climber if I didn't take the hint and refuse." Olivia let the garden gate drop shut behind them. "Kate, you do realize the duchess made no promises whatsoever?"

"I'm sure she'll treat me well. You said yourself she doesn't wish to be rude."

"No, I said she doesn't wish to *appear* rude."

"Anyway, I'll be at Halstead all week. I can look around for myself, get to know all the guests, and consider who I'd like to work for. Think of it, Olivia—I might even have a choice of positions. That's even better than if the duchess had recommended me to one of her friends."

Olivia smiled. "Indeed it is, my dear. And I know you'll make the most of the opportunity."

The garden gate creaked behind them and Kate looked up.

A man stood just inside the wall, dressed entirely in black from head to foot. He was an inch or two taller than Kate, stocky and square, with thick shoulders and a jaw that was already running to jowl despite the fact that he was probably no more than thirty-five. "Have I the honor of addressing Miss Kate Blakely?" His voice was deep and sonorous.

Kate stepped forward.

He bowed. "The Reverend George Blakely, at

your service. I am your distant cousin, of course, as well as the new vicar of the parish, here to take up your father's yoke."

And about time, too, Kate thought.

As if he had read her mind, he bowed. "I was regrettably detained by the demands of my previous parish. But I look forward to quickly making my place here. I hope you will be of assistance in that endeavor, Miss Blakely."

Kate's answer was automatic, born of years of expectations of the vicar's daughter. "Of course I would be happy to do whatever lies within my power, but…"

The crease between Mr. Blakely's brows eased, and he smiled widely. "I am honored. Since you have seen fit to agree, then all is decided."

"*What's* decided?"

"What your father wished for us, I believe, Miss Blakely. I look forward to the privilege of making you my wife."

❧

Penelope was out of bed at dawn, and well before nine o'clock she descended the stairs. She was wearing the best of her walking dresses, and her hat was pinned firmly in place, anticipating the breeze that would be created by a swift ride in a high, open carriage. A light cloak was draped over her arm, and she carried her reticule and her jewel case.

She had left Etta still frantically repacking the smallest of the portmanteaus—trying to fit in everything she insisted Penelope would need until the baggage wagon arrived—all the while muttering about mistresses who took odd notions. When Penelope left the room, Etta had been saying something about behavior unfitting a countess.

But Penelope had made up her mind. Whether or not she had a spare chemise or even a hairbrush to her name, she was going to be in the earl's curricle when it pulled away from Berkeley Square at nine o'clock.

If, indeed, the earl was ready to leave at the appointed hour. Penelope doubted that would be the case, for she had heard him moving around the house in the small hours of the morning. If he'd been drinking at his club—and she assumed he must have been, for he generally didn't make so much noise when he came in that she could hear him in the hall outside her bedroom—he would not even be awake yet at nine.

At any rate, she suspected he had named the hour only to shock her out of the idea of accompanying him and not because he truly planned to leave then. Still, if she was sitting by the front door when his horses were brought around, he could hardly go off without her.

The senior footman was closing the front door as she came down, and a wave of suspicion washed over Penelope. Had all the stumbling around last night been a ruse? Perhaps the earl had left even earlier than he had told her he would.

The servant sent a sideways look at her. "His lordship's in the breakfast room, my lady."

"Thank you, Martin." Penelope started toward the back of the house, pretending to ignore his wide-eyed surprise that she hadn't turned in the opposite direction. Perhaps, she thought, after this week at Halstead the servants would have to readjust their thinking completely.

The earl was at the breakfast table. Instead of eating, however, he was nursing an ale—and he didn't appear to be enjoying it.

So her first guess had been correct. "It appears you have a head this morning, my lord."

"Clever of you to notice," he growled.

Penelope set her reticule and jewel case down on the table and went to the sideboard. She poured half a cup of coffee from the pot and regarded the dark fluid thoughtfully. "This is strong enough, I think. Goodman," she told the butler. "Please ask Cook to send in the juice of a lemon, along with a small pot of honey."

She set the cup aside and selected eggs, ham, and toast from the sideboard. "If you would pass me the teapot, my lord," she said as she sat down.

"I thought you were getting coffee. I could smell it from across the room—nasty stuff."

"The coffee is for you, as soon as the lemon juice arrives."

He eyed her blearily. "You're quite the managing wife this morning. What has caused you to make such a shift?"

Penelope buttered her toast and opted for partial truth. "I have been fixed in Berkeley Square for three months now, and I don't intend to miss the opportunity for an outing."

"Even if it means spending half the day in my curricle?"

She heard the challenge that lay under his perfectly polite words, but she chose to ignore it. "I am looking forward to some country air. At any rate, you're said to be an excellent whip, my lord—at least when you're not in your cups, so by sobering you, I'm assuring I'll be safe." She dug her fork into her scrambled eggs.

The earl snorted. "You'd be perfectly safe with me whether I'm in my cups or not."

The butler returned with a cruet. Penelope stirred lemon juice into a full cup of coffee and set it in front of her husband.

He looked at it as if it were a worm crawling on his neckcloth. "What is this?"

"I know you have no fondness for my father, my lord, but you must own he knows ale and its aftereffects."

"I was drinking brandy last night."

"The result cannot be far different, no matter which variety of spirits you were imbibing. Drink it, and you'll feel better." Penelope applied herself to her breakfast and pretended not to notice whether he complied.

He sipped and made a face. "You forgot to add the honey."

"That's for later—after you've downed the coffee." She polished off her toast and eggs, considered having a second serving of ham, and decided against it. The fresh air would no doubt give her an appetite, but a fast drive on a full stomach couldn't be the best of ideas. After curing her husband's morning-after woes, it would be too ironic if she were to become carriage-sick.

The earl was looking doubtfully into the coffee cup. "You're quite sure this is a treatment, not a punishment?"

"I do not know from my own experience, you understand."

"I should think not." He took one more swallow and pushed the cup away. "I'd prefer to have the head."

Penelope was determined to let nothing interfere with her equilibrium this morning. "As you wish, my lord."

The butler came in. "The curricle is at the door, my lord. And Mr. Carlisle has arrived."

Penelope gathered up her reticule and jewel case. "Mr. Carlisle?"

The earl paused to hold the door for her. "Andrew Carlisle. He is also a friend of the duke's, and we have both been summoned to Halstead. We made plans to go down together."

Penelope said faintly, "You mean… in your curricle?"

There was a glimmer in the earl's eyes. "He has none of his own, you see."

She could picture the scene. The high, narrow seat of a curricle—intended for just two passengers—with a gentleman on each side and Penelope squashed in the middle for hours…

"Are you *certain*," the earl asked politely, "that you still feel strongly about leaving Berkeley Square for an outing today?"

❧

The occupants of the cottage were up early, for though the duchess had said Kate was to come whenever it was convenient, Olivia knew that whenever the Somervale carriage arrived, Kate would need to step in immediately.

At the moment, Kate looked anything but ready. She was pale and silent. Olivia wondered whether it was the task she had taken on which was upsetting Kate, or the ridiculous offer from the new vicar.

"Did you sleep at all last night?" Olivia asked finally.

Kate shook her head. "I lay awake and thought about how to answer. I never expected…"

"If the next words out of your mouth are 'It's quite a good offer, you know,' I shall throw the water jug at you, Kate. I wouldn't be at all surprised if you're thinking that you should accept. You've been offered a home, a place in the world, a familiar routine. You could go straight on with your life—running the vicarage, visiting the sick and needy, and arranging flowers for the altar each week."

Kate nodded eagerly. "Just as I did while my father was alive."

"*Almost* as you did when your father was alive. But the one change is a very large one."

"Being a wife, you mean." Kate crumbled her toast. "You've never talked about what it was like to be married, Olivia."

Olivia suppressed the shiver that ran through her. "And I don't wish to speak of it now. Just take it from me, Kate. This offer feels easy, I grant, but just because something seems obvious doesn't make it the right choice."

"Well, I must own that I'd prefer Mr. Blakely had waited until he knew me for more than four minutes before concluding we should suit, but—"

"*Four* minutes? Do you think it was so long?" Olivia asked earnestly, and was rewarded with Kate's first smile of the day. "At least don't answer him right now. Wait to see who's at Halstead and consider your other options first."

"I would have my own home, you know."

"Marriage is forever, Kate. When you take a job, you can leave if your employer isn't compatible or pleasant or kind. But when you marry…" *You'd be better off as a mistress*, she wanted to say. *At least then you'd have some bargaining power.*

She didn't realize until she saw the sudden glow of warm sympathy in Kate's gaze how much she'd admitted about her own marriage. But just then, through the cottage's open window, she heard the jingle of harness and the thud of hooves as a carriage drew up in front. "Promise me you won't rush into this. At least make him court you. Find out what sort of man he is."

Kate swallowed the last of her tea and jumped up. "I won't answer Mr. Blakely until the wedding is past. Will that do?"

Olivia was so relieved she felt silly. "I only hope you can keep him dangling so long," she said, "for I'm quite sure *he* thinks you've already agreed!"

❦

The earl's curricle, like everything else he owned, was stylish without being showy. Unlike the rig that Penelope's father drove—a conveyance almost as garish as the jewelry Ivan Weiss chose for his daughter—the Earl of Townsend's curricle was very plain and shiny black. His horses had been curried to such a polish that their coats matched the paint as well as each other. Though Penelope was no judge of horseflesh, she had no doubt of their quality. She wondered how the stable boys told the animals apart. The shape of a hoof, perhaps, or the precise color of the eyes? She could see no other difference.

She looked at the horses longer than she otherwise might have done, trying to distract herself from the ride to come. But when she heard the earl greet his friend, she could no longer pretend Andrew Carlisle wasn't there. She smothered a small sigh and turned to the young man who waited on the top step.

He was not the tulip of fashion that she had expected any friend of the Duke of Somervale to be. Instead, he was neatly but soberly dressed in well-worn riding garb, and at the railing by the base of the stairs a roan horse waited—saddled, bridled, and fresh from the stable. He was not as elegant or highbred as the earl's carriage team; this was an animal intended to cover long distances efficiently.

Andrew Carlisle had come prepared to ride. Despite what the earl had said, Penelope was not going to be the pressed-ham filling in one of those ridiculous sandwiches the gentlemen called for when they were too absorbed in gambling to rise from the table.

She chewed her lip and looked warily at the young man. "I'm so sorry, Mr. Carlisle. I didn't realize how disobliging I would be to take your place in the curricle. Surely you can't intend to ride all the way."

"Take my place?" the young man said blankly. Then he started to grin. "You mean Charles let you believe I would allow him to drive me to Halstead? The truth is, Lady Townsend, I detest riding in a carriage of any sort. It's a milk-toast sort of man who needs a curricle and a team and an entire system of roads to get himself across country."

"Milk toast? Keep talking that way, Andrew, and I'll have to plant you a facer."

"Have no fear your husband will come to fisticuffs on your front step, my lady," Andrew Carlisle said, "for he knows quite well he couldn't carry out his threat. Give me a horse any day. I'll cross the fields, jump the gates, and be there long before the curricle arrives."

For the first time in the three months of her marriage, she heard the earl laugh as if he was genuinely entertained. "Don't believe him, ma'am. Andrew's real reason for riding everywhere is that if the company is dull, he can saddle up his horse and escape before anyone is the wiser."

Penelope was so startled at the idea that the earl might have *teased* her—misled her on purpose simply because it amused him—that she whirled to face her husband, tripped over her ruffled hem, and nearly slipped off the step.

Each man shot out a hand to steady her, but the earl moved more quickly, catching her arm as she flailed madly in an attempt to keep her balance. She felt as clumsy as a cow, having to be pulled back onto the stair.

Andrew Carlisle looked thoughtful. "Now, Charles, don't manhandle the lady. Even though she did look for a moment as though she would take a swing at you, I'm quite certain you deserve it." His smile was endearingly crooked and his green eyes were alight as he swept a bow. "May I help you into your chariot, my lady, and show you how a gentleman comports himself? It's dead sure Charles will never be able to demonstrate the finer points of—"

The earl's right hand was still firm on Penelope's elbow; his left feinted toward Andrew Carlisle's jaw, and the young man stepped nimbly back out of reach with a grin.

Penelope's cloak had slipped aside, and through the thin muslin of her sleeve she could feel the suppleness of the earl's driving glove, the kid as warm as his own skin would be, barely an inch from her breast. Her nipple seemed to reach out for him, and she felt herself flush and tense. If he turned his hand in the slightest...

"Yes, Andrew," the earl mocked. "Do demonstrate. Seeing *you* giving lessons in etiquette will be something new."

Penelope's breast felt chilly as her husband's fingers relaxed and dropped away. She forced a laugh as she allowed Andrew Carlisle to take her hand and help her up into the curricle.

But she wished the earl had been the one who stood there while she climbed up, with her skirt brushing his coat sleeve and him supporting her with the iron strength of his arm.

❧

Shopping was not a major pastime for the females of Steadham village, for the shops were small and mainly devoted to necessities. But in a dusty little corner of the dry-goods store, high above the bolts of plain coarse cloth, Olivia discovered a box piled with lace and trimmings.

"Left over when the dressmaker died," the proprietor

said. "Back in the old duchess's day, Halstead kept her busy. Now the ladies shop mostly in London."

"Fashions were different then." Olivia sorted through the box. The lace was good, though it was mostly scraps too small to make anything but a pincushion, but the braid might be useful. "A dressmaker would have been occupied just keeping all the embroidery and ruffled lace in good shape in those days."

"Nobody knew what to do with these things, so they ended up here." The shopkeeper poked at a bit of lace with a stubby finger. "Not much call for delicate things here in Steadham. Not that the womenfolk around here wouldn't like them, but they've a need to be practical. What use is a piece of lace with no more strength than a cobweb?"

He was no doubt right about the durability, Olivia thought, considering the contents of the box must be twenty years old. Still, if her fingers were nimble enough, she could retrim her best dress in such a way that she wouldn't stand out as a three-years-out-of-style dowd at Lady Daphne's wedding. The new decoration would only have to last one wearing, for no matter how long Olivia lived in Steadham, there would never be such a social occasion again.

She fingered a length of braid. "How much for this?"

The proprietor eyed her steadily. "You'd be doing me a kindness to take the whole box off my hands," he said, and named a price.

He was asking little enough, but she had no coins to spare. Olivia kept her smile in place. "Just the braid," she said steadily, and the proprietor grumbled as he untangled the braid and wound it up neatly for her.

As Olivia left the dim shop, blinking against the strong afternoon sunlight, a group of young women came down the street. They strolled along in pairs, their brilliant array of gowns and stylish parade of hats and parasols a sharp contrast to the duller colors of the fabric bolts she had just surveyed.

Toward the back of the group, Olivia spotted Kate. As the parade paused outside the dry-goods shop to debate the question of going in, Kate stepped aside to join her friend.

Olivia said quietly, "Are you walking them to the village to keep them out of trouble?"

"*Out* of trouble? The duke commented that he would be absorbed in business this afternoon—in the village—so suddenly Daphne's bridesmaids felt in need of taking the air. They all started out, though some turned back. Too far to walk on a warm day, they said."

"Even to admire a duke? Though surely they would find it easier to brush up against him at Halstead."

"I'm sure you don't need me to explain that he's escaped to the village rather than summoning the tradesmen to come to him. There he is now, coming out of the inn."

From the corner of her eye, Olivia had already noted the duke. His sheer size and the breadth of his shoulders in a finely cut, dark blue riding coat would have commanded the attention of anyone passing on the street. But beyond good looks, there was something about the way he carried himself...

A sense of entitlement well wrapped in arrogance. She turned her back to him.

"Truly," Kate said, "I've never seen such a pack of females outside of a kennel."

"They're not as well-bred as you'd hoped, then? I'm sorry, Kate."

"They're too naive to realize how notorious he is."

"Perhaps they don't care, so long as there's a chance to end up as a duchess. It would be quite a coup if one of them nipped in under the very noses of all her friends to snatch him up."

"They're guileless, that's certain. They were all excited last night when Daphne said she'd ask the duke to put up a diamond bracelet as a prize in an archery contest she's planning for later in the week."

"Surely the Duke of Somervale has more sense than to go around giving diamond bracelets to girls who've barely come out."

"Of course he does. But when Daphne whispered that Simon's valet keeps a selection always at hand—an entire chest full of diamond bracelets, she said, so the duke is never without a gift to woo a mistress—the girls were drawn like moths to a flame."

The only surprise there, Olivia mused, was that the duke's sister knew of his exploits. "A chest full of diamond bracelets to woo a mistress?" She gave a gurgle of laughter. "To get rid of her afterwards, more likely. If that is the sort of tale being shared at Halstead, how I wish I could be around when Lady Daphne starts telling ghost stories to her friends!"

A deep voice interrupted. "Lady Reyne, I hardly thought it possible to insult me, my sister, and every one of her friends in less than a minute. But I should have realized *you* would find a way."

Olivia had expected he would already be surrounded by the half-dozen eager young women, so she had felt it safe—as well as advisable—not to watch him. What a foolish idea that had been. She faced him and raised her chin. She should be getting used to him looming over her... but surely yesterday he hadn't seemed quite so tall. "I intended no insult, Your Grace."

"Really? You expect me to believe it was an accident for you to call me a cad, my sister an embroiderer of tales, and her friends gullible—all in the same breath?"

Olivia smiled. "You'll have to choose one or the other, Your Grace. Either I believe you *do* have a chest full of diamond bracelets and your sister told the simple truth, or I believe you *don't* and she was having fun with her friends. I'm afraid it's impossible for me to have insulted you both." She congratulated herself for avoiding the question of Lady Daphne's bridesmaids altogether. If they believed that faradiddle, then *gullible* was hardly a strong enough word.

Kate bobbed a curtsey. "Your Grace, I..."

"I don't blame *you*, Miss Blakely, though your taste in friends seems questionable."

"Sir!" Kate's fair skin flushed. "I must protest." Then she seemed to think better of it.

The bridesmaids, having found the dry-goods store wanting, had flocked back onto the street, surrounding the duke. Kate began shooing them away toward the potter's shop.

Olivia didn't move. *Diamond bracelets*, she thought.

If only Sir Jasper had thought to offer her a diamond bracelet—something worthwhile, instead of merely forgiving her rent—she might have been tempted...

No, not even the most expensive diamond bracelet in the world could make Sir Jasper tempting.

But the Duke of Somervale was a different proposition altogether. Diamond bracelets, and the security such jewels represented, must be merely the icing on the cake for his mistresses.

What Olivia herself couldn't do with the proceeds of a diamond bracelet!

"*Do* you keep a chest of diamond bracelets to woo your mistresses, Your Grace?" she asked sweetly.

"Certainly not, Lady Reyne."

Olivia told herself it was just as well, if only because she wouldn't know the first thing about converting a diamond bracelet into ready money. "What a relief it is to know that, sir."

His expression didn't change, but his eyebrows went up. They were, despite what Olivia had thought yesterday in the midst of their confrontation over Charlotte's too-still body, nice eyebrows—aristocratic, with a strong arch.

Walk away, she told herself. But the sparkle in his midnight-blue eyes said that if she did, he would consider he had routed her.

"A relief, I mean, to be assured you're so sensible," she went on. "Surely you keep rubies and sapphires and emeralds on hand as well, set in necklaces and brooches. After all, not *every* woman appreciates diamonds—or bracelets, for that matter."

For an instant he stared at her, and Olivia's insides quaked. However great the temptation to bait him, what in heaven's name had made her succumb to it?

Then he threw back his head and laughed.

He really was gorgeous, she thought. Kate was right. He could be charming and funny and delightful…

Stop right there, Olivia told herself, *and think before you dig yourself into a hole you can't climb out of.*

But she opened her mouth again anyway. "However," she said softly, "I happen to be one of the ones who does. Appreciate diamond bracelets, I mean. So if you're thinking of wooing another mistress anytime soon, Your Grace, do keep me in mind."

Four

AND THEN THE INFURIATING FEMALE SMILED AT HIM AND walked away.

So Lady Reyne was the kind of woman who appreciated diamond bracelets! She didn't look it, Simon thought. There wasn't a drop of ornamentation anywhere around her today, and while her gown was more attractive than the bag she'd been wearing yesterday in her garden, that was saying very little. Her dress was no indication that the woman had expensive tastes. Its style was at least three years out of date, as was the bonnet that perched saucily on her glossy dark curls.

The gown was also the style of a younger woman. Not that Lady Reyne was exactly in her dotage, but pale pink muslin was more appropriate for a debutante. However, no mere debutante would be capable of flinging forth a lure like the one she had just dangled before him.

So Lady Reyne was in the mood for dalliance, eh? And what made her think all she had to do was snap her fingers to snag the Duke of Somervale? He wanted to laugh at the idea that she believed she could attract him. He'd seldom met a woman who was less to his natural taste.

His gaze followed her down the street, just as a gentle breeze flitted by and pasted the thin muslin to her figure. Perhaps she might have a few more charms than he'd suspected. Though she was hardly voluptuous, she also wasn't the straight, hard-edged stick he'd imagined. And just as the glimpse of her ankle yesterday had made him want to look further and longer and higher, the curve of her leg and the gentle sway of her hips under the lightweight fabric, so fleetingly revealed by the helpful breeze, fed his curiosity. Her derriere appeared to be exactly the right size for a man's hand— *his* hand—to cup. He wondered how she would feel under him...

He shook his head. Perhaps the heat, or the oppressive atmosphere produced by being pursued by so many nubile females, was turning his brain. His gaze had only lighted on Lady Reyne because she'd flung out a challenge, not because he was attracted to her.

Daphne was whimpering something about the long walk and how one of her bridesmaids had worn a blister on her toe. "You will drive us all home, Simon, won't you? We can squeeze together in your curricle."

The Duke of Somervale's hackney service, he thought absently. Did Daphne seriously believe he couldn't see through the excuse? He wondered if they'd draw straws to see which ones would end up pressed most closely against him.

Like a rowboat drifting down a gently flowing stream, his attention slid away from his sister and back to Lady Reyne. *If you're thinking of wooing another mistress…* Clever of her to turn the subject, to distract his attention from his accusation that she'd insulted him. It would serve her right if he took up her invitation and made her think he was seriously considering her offer. He would enjoy watching her stammer and stumble around.

Unless she'd really meant it. And in that case, maybe he'd just enjoy *her*—for if she was as saucy in bed as she was in the street…

"Philippa's ankle hurts," Daphne went on. "And it's too warm to walk all the way."

Yes, the afternoon was definitely warm. Simon sympathized with the stray dog that lay panting in the shade of the dry-goods shop, his tongue hanging almost to the dirt. He understood exactly how the animal felt. Odd, though, for Simon hadn't felt hot until Lady Reyne had started talking about diamond bracelets…

For the last time, he tugged his attention away from the figure swaying seductively down the street—Lady Reyne was going out of sight anyway—and back to Daphne.

"There are seven of you," he said calmly. "I would have to make several trips."

Daphne nodded. "It wouldn't take long. It's only a mile." A blush rose in her cheeks. "I mean…"

"It's a little over a mile by road. The shortcut path is barely half that—just a short walk, after all. I think you're caught in your own trap there, Daphne, since you could all walk home in less time than I could ferry you. Nevertheless, as a gentleman I shall provide transport for the ladies who wish to ride."

She smiled. "You are the best of brothers, Simon!"

"The innkeeper owns a big, old carriage that should suffice to hold you all at once—if he can clear out the vermin in a timely fashion."

And once I have the young ladies settled, he thought, *I may have some additional business to transact for myself—with a slightly older lady.*

&co&

When faced with the threat of sharing a carriage with mice, the bridesmaids decided to walk after all. Kate noted that Philippa's problematic ankle seemed to miraculously heal, as did Emily's blistered toe. And no one complained about the heat anymore. They did, however, walk so slowly and listlessly that Kate thought they would never get out of the village, much less all the way back to Halstead.

"Perhaps you don't wish to sit down to dinner with the duke?" she asked finally. "Because at this rate, you'll be lucky to arrive in time for breakfast tomorrow."

"You're very dull, Kate," Lady Daphne complained. "I can't think why Mama hired you. We do not need a chaperone, for we are perfectly able to look after each other. Perhaps she felt pity for your situation. With no home and not a suitor in sight…"

A suitor. For a few minutes, Kate had forgotten about Mr. Blakely and his offer. All she had to do was say the word, and she would have a home, a husband, a place in the world. Even Lady Daphne couldn't turn up her nose once Kate was betrothed. And she would no longer have to listen to the condescending chatter of a group of ill-mannered and arrogant girls.

They're not entirely bad, Kate told herself. Daphne was the worst, but then she always had been; the rest must be particularly daring because they were off the rein for the first time.

Kate strolled along, lost in reflection. If she accepted Mr. Blakely's offer, she would be a person to be respected. Of course, as the vicar's wife she would still have to treat people like the Duke of Somervale with the utmost tact and diplomacy. But she could have pointed out—with utmost tact and diplomacy, of course—that the duke was being completely irrational to accuse Olivia of insulting him. In fact, as a moral leader she would have been responsible for doing so.

And then there were purely practical matters. She would not have to rely on the duchess for a recommendation or scramble to obtain introductions to people who might hire her. She would not depend for her living on pleasing an employer day after day. She would not risk losing her place or her home by speaking up. She would no longer be a drain on Olivia; instead, she could help her friend in small but significant ways.

And she would be able to look ahead with confidence at the future—right here in this familiar village, among these familiar people, and in the same familiar house. There was something to be said for knowing exactly where one's destiny lay. Steadham village might feel stifling at times, but it was comforting as well.

She walked on, musing about the things she'd like to do when she was truly the mistress of the vicarage. She'd always disliked the pictures in the dining room; now she could change them. For her bedroom, she could choose new bed hangings and draperies…

Then she realized the sunny room at the back of the vicarage, overlooking the garden, wouldn't be her bedroom anymore. As the wife of the vicar, she would move into the principal bedroom—and share it with her husband. She would sleep with Mr. Blakely in the same bed where she herself had been born, and someday she would give birth there to her own children...

Her thoughts skittered away from the idea. She told herself it was because that room still seemed to belong to her parents.

Just as they were about to leave the road outside the village for the shortcut path across the fields, Kate heard hoofbeats and carriage wheels behind them. The young ladies suddenly perked up and looked around.

The curricle that approached would have been glossy black except for the dust of the road. Perched high on the seat was not the duke, as the bridesmaids had obviously expected, but two people—a handsome man wearing a curly-brimmed hat and a lady wrapped, despite the heat, in a lightweight blue cloak that billowed in the gently stirring air. As the carriage slowed, something about the lady's profile drew Kate's attention.

In utter astonishment, Kate said, "*Penny?*"

The lady's face glowed. "Kate! I had no idea you would be in the neighborhood! Is your home near Halstead? Oh, my dear—I'm so sorry. I didn't know you were in mourning. What a pity we've lost touch. Perhaps we'll have an opportunity to catch up now."

Kate couldn't remember exactly how much time had passed since she'd heard from Penny Weiss, but

Penny's life must have changed considerably since their last exchange of letters. A lady might ride in an open carriage for a short distance with any gentleman. But this was obviously no casual drive, and since Penny had no brothers or cousins whom she could accompany without risking her reputation, the man driving the curricle had to be her husband.

Big changes indeed, Kate thought. She hoped that whoever Penny had married deserved her.

She had barely registered the fact that a horseman rode to one side of the curricle until he spoke. "Miss Blakely, we meet again."

Kate's heart began to thud. That voice—low and rich and beautiful… Years had passed since she had heard Andrew Carlisle speak, but it took only five words to carry her back to the summer when she'd been seventeen. "Mr. Carlisle," she said crisply.

Lady Daphne was aglow. "Andrew, you sly fox! I thought you weren't coming to my wedding!"

Andrew Carlisle bowed and swept off his hat. "Lady Daphne. I did not immediately see you among the lovely flowers that surround you."

But he saw me instantly, Kate thought. *Because I stand out so obtrusively in my black… and because I am not a lovely flower!*

Daphne stretched up her hand to him. "You wrote that you were obligated to Lord Winchester and couldn't leave."

Obligated to Lord Winchester? Kate wondered what that meant. Was he a private secretary of some sort? What a comedown that must seem for the young man who had wanted to seek adventure, to see the world…

"I expected to be there for some weeks yet, instructing his two sons," Andrew said easily. "But the young men progressed more quickly than expected, and Lord Winchester rewarded them with a period of liberty before they go to Oxford in the autumn."

Leaving Andrew at loose ends, Kate deduced—unemployed before he had planned.

One of the bridesmaids wrinkled her nose. "Instructing? Do you mean you're a *tutor*? Were you teaching them Latin and such?"

Kate thought if Andrew had said he was a hangman, the bridesmaid would have used much the same tone.

"Mostly *and such*," Andrew said, "because I never was good enough at Latin myself to teach it."

How richly ironic it would be for Andrew to make his living as a tutor now, Kate thought. They had only met because he had required extra tutoring himself from Kate's father to get through Oxford...

"Come down from there," Daphne demanded, "and be presented to my bridesmaids. Then we won't hold up his lordship's horses any longer." She made a little curtsey to the gentleman in the curricle.

Kate almost let out a whistle before she regained control of herself. Penny's husband was *his lordship*?

The gentleman threaded his horses between the bridesmaids, and as the curricle passed, Penny leaned down toward Kate. "Shall I see you at Halstead?"

Kate nodded. "We have much to talk of, it seems."

The earl flicked his whip, and the curricle rattled away.

"So that's Penny Wise," Daphne said. "How perfectly common of her to hang out of the curricle."

The nickname grated on Kate, though she'd heard it many times. Some of the girls at school had thought it a clever play on words.

Andrew Carlisle dismounted, draped the reins of his gelding over his arm, and made his bow to each of the bridesmaids as Daphne presented them. "I am honored, ladies." He offered his arm to Daphne. "*Penny Wise*? Is that what you called her?"

Kate said, a bit sharply, "To be accurate, she's Penelope Weiss."

Andrew's green eyes gleamed in the sunlight as he surveyed Kate. "And now she's Lady Townsend."

Daphne sniffed. "What a sad comedown *that* is for Charles. An earl having to marry a brewer's daughter just because she has pots of money and he has none. You know, I always fancied him myself, but a match simply wasn't possible."

Kate said, "But surely, Lady Daphne, with your lineage as the daughter of a duke, you are every bit as great an heiress as Penny Weiss."

A shocked silence descended over the group. Daphne's look was so sharply venomous that Kate thought herself lucky not to drop on the spot. She suspected Andrew had to bite back a grin—not that she cared what he thought, of course.

Perhaps I should reconsider the idea of being a governess, Kate thought. And if the other jobs open to a lady of quality required the same standard of deference to the employer's opinions that she had so miserably failed to demonstrate just now, she might have to cross those off her list as well.

Kate told herself, *There's always Mr. Blakely*.

The gates of Halstead had come into view before the earl spoke. "A friend from your days at school, I perceive?" he asked politely.

Penelope stopped looking back over her shoulder. She would see Kate again soon; how gauche to crane her neck. What a blessing, though, to know she would have a friend at Halstead to help her through this difficult week.

"Indeed. Miss Blakely was the best of friends. When I arrived at school, she was the only one of the older girls who…" She stopped suddenly and felt her face begin to burn.

She knew he glanced at her, and she caught a glimpse of curiosity in his expression. Or perhaps it was surprise. *As though he believed someone like me would have no feelings.*

The curricle rattled up a long drive and made a sweeping turn in a crushed-stone courtyard before drawing up before a wide front door. Penelope had been too absorbed in her own thoughts to pay much attention to the house, and now she was too close to get the full effect—four stories of stone and brick stretched upward only a few feet from her, making her feel no larger than a toy. "It's as big as a palace," she whispered.

A groom came running to take the horses. The earl climbed down and stretched up a hand to help Penelope down. Stiff from the long last stage of their drive, she fumbled a little as she started to descend. Her toe slid on the iron footrest, and the earl caught her around the waist and lifted her down.

She felt breathless… weightless… as though he'd shifted her body from one spot to another but left her heart somewhere behind. She'd thought Andrew Carlisle strong when he'd helped her up into the curricle that morning, but now the difference was clear.

Her husband offered his arm, and Penelope laid her hand carefully on his sleeve, took a deep breath, and marched up the stairs and into the enormous entry hall.

The footman who had opened the doors for them looked stunned. "His Grace said the *gentlemen* would be coming."

The earl frowned. "Please inform the duchess that the Earl and Countess of Townsend have arrived."

Penelope could not remember him voicing her title before, at least in her hearing. A little flicker of warmth lit deep inside her at the tone of his voice; he seemed to be demanding respect for her. And the way he'd lifted her down had made her feel warm all over. Even the way he'd looked at her—perhaps that look of his hadn't been condescending after all but compassionate toward a girl who had been seriously out of place at the boarding school where Ivan Weiss had sent her.

Perhaps her instincts had been right, and things were going to be different between them here at Halstead. Once more, hope began to flutter deep inside her.

After the brilliant sunshine outside, Penelope was half-afraid she would stumble. She paused and looked around, waiting for her eyes to grow accustomed to the dimmer light in the entrance. A group of young ladies who were crossing the hall tossed curious glances at her, but they didn't stop giggling. An old lady with beady dark eyes and the nose of a predatory bird paused at the foot of the stairs as if to study her.

The footman had disappeared, but Penelope hadn't noticed where he'd gone until a small lady with dark hair laced with silver spilled out into the hallway. "Charles, my dear!" She stretched out both hands to the earl. "Welcome, Countess. Your husband has been like an extra son to me since the days when the boys played together. I thought Simon said he'd asked you to bring Mr. Carlisle as well, Charles. No? Well, it's a blessing, in a way, if he can't come."

The earl said smoothly, "We encountered Lady Daphne and her party on the road, and Andrew is walking the rest of the way with them."

The duchess's eyes narrowed. "Indeed. Then we have a problem. Mrs. Greeley reserved the two blue bedrooms—the suite near the top of the main stairs— for you and the countess. But since I wasn't expecting your wife to arrive until later in the week, I had thought to put Mr. Carlisle in the adjoining bedroom for a few days. We'll have to sort out where to put everyone instead. Suites are at a premium, I'm afraid."

"As fond as Andrew is of his horse," the earl said, "I'm sure he'd be happy in the stables, Your Grace. Or surely you could put all the gentlemen in the east wing, like old times."

Was that a hopeful note in his voice? Penelope had no idea where the east wing was, but it sounded very far away from the blue suite at the top of the main stairs. So much for her still vague plan to seduce her husband during their visit. If the bedroom arrangements made it even easier for the earl to avoid her here at Halstead than in London, then nothing would change.

"I've already filled the east wing," the duchess said crisply. "The bridesmaids are there. Come and have tea in the drawing room while Mrs. Greeley arranges something."

The old lady who had been standing quietly at the foot of the stairs raised one hand to rub her beak of a nose. "Don't be silly, Iris. Townsend and his bride don't need two bedrooms. After all, they're *newlyweds*."

The word seemed to bounce off the marble lining the entrance hall, smacking Penelope in the face. The duchess's eyes widened in shock. Even the giggling girls fell abruptly silent.

Under her hand, Penelope felt her husband's arm tense till it felt like iron, and her cheeks began to burn. No matter what the earl said next—no matter how he went about excusing himself from her bedroom—one thing was certain. Penelope knew this was going to be the most humiliating moment of her life.

"I… Please, Your Grace." Penelope gulped, suddenly afraid to continue.

The duchess made a sharp gesture. "Don't be foolish, Lucinda. Maids *and* valets coming and going in a single bedroom? It would be more crowded than Bond Street on a busy shopping day. No, the earl and countess must have the blue suite. Mr. Carlisle will content himself with whatever Mrs. Greeley finds. If it's a room in the village, he can count himself lucky."

The earl's muscles relaxed under Penelope's hand, and he moved with languorous grace to escort her to the drawing room.

But Penelope was still taut as a wire. If the duchess hadn't interrupted, what would she herself have said? Had she been about to plead with her hostess to spare her embarrassment? Or would she have begged the duchess to force the earl to share her bed?

⚜

As Olivia walked down the village street, she was perfectly aware of being watched, and she exerted all of her self-control not to burst into a run to get out of the duke's sight. Still aghast at her own behavior and feeling weak in the knees, she reached the cottage with relief.

The housemaid fluttered out of the tiny parlor, so excited the feather duster was trembling in her hand. "My lady—"

"Maggie, dusting does very little good if you then shake the duster *inside* the house."

Maggie looked down as if startled to see what she was holding. "Sorry, ma'am. I just can't hold still. I was doing the marketing when one of the girls from Halstead told me about the toffs coming to stay for the wedding. Think, my lady, of all the hot water they'll need carried!"

Lugging brass cans full of hot water up several flights of stairs wasn't a pastime Olivia wanted to put her mind to, but the direction of Maggie's conversation was clear. "You're wondering if I'd mind you leaving me to work at Halstead."

"Yes, ma'am. I don't want to go away—this is a good place, truly. But Mrs. Greeley needs all the extra help she can get just now. The pay is good because of all the extra people, and there might even be gifts when the guests leave. So if you can do without me…"

Olivia couldn't refuse the girl such an opportunity when she herself was barely able to afford Maggie's wages. "Of course. Nurse and I can manage for a while. And you'll be welcome back whenever you wish to come."

Maggie beamed. "Thank you, my lady. I'll make your tea first, while you sit down and rest. It must be hot outside, for you look so warm. You're all pink in the face."

If snow had been falling, Olivia thought, she'd still have been pink after her squabble with the duke. "Thank you, Maggie, but you should speak with Mrs. Greeley right away. You wouldn't want to find out the jobs have already been filled."

Anxious at the possibility, Maggie took the duster along in her haste to change her apron and be on her way.

Olivia went to the kitchen and put the kettle on the fire. She had plenty to do; with Kate and Maggie both gone, she'd be busier than ever. But first Olivia was going to reward herself with a few free minutes and a precious spoonful of tea leaves.

Though, under the circumstances, the idea of a reward was not exactly appropriate. *Penance* was more like it. What had gotten into her, anyway?

You'd be better off as a mistress, she had almost said to Kate this morning. *At least then you'd have some bargaining power*.

That thought must have still been lurking in the back of Olivia's mind, or she would never have said what she had to the duke. *If you're thinking of wooing another mistress anytime soon, Your Grace…*

She shook her head ruefully. If she was fortunate, she would not come face to face with him ever again. Surely on Lady Daphne's wedding day, he'd be too busy to notice her and so easy to pick out of the crowd that it would take no effort at all to stay out of his way.

Her tea was steeping when she heard the knocker fall. She couldn't think of anyone who would be calling—at least, no one she wanted to receive—so she ignored the summons. She cut two thin slices from the loaf she had baked that morning, added butter to the plate, and poured her tea into a china cup so thin and dainty that it was practically transparent. No heavy, serviceable pottery mug for her today. A solid reminder that she was a lady would not be amiss.

A moment later, she heard a footstep in the passage. No—*multiple* footsteps. One set must be Maggie, ready to leave for Halstead and her interview with Mrs. Greeley. But the other was definitely heavier, masculine…

Olivia sighed. She really could not support a conversation with Sir Jasper today.

She looked up as Maggie appeared, followed by a very tall gentleman who stopped in the doorway between the narrow, dark hall and the kitchen. The little maid, speechless for once, bobbed a curtsey and ducked out the kitchen door.

Olivia almost dropped the teapot. "You can't call on me here!"

The Duke of Somervale stepped into her kitchen, and suddenly the room felt small and airless. "Surely that's an odd reaction from a lady who suggested only a few minutes ago that she would like to be my mistress."

"I didn't." Olivia felt herself turning pink. "Well, not exactly. What I said was that I like diamond bracelets."

"Ah, yes. And you know this because you have so many already and would like to add another to your collection?" His gaze rested on her with an ironic twinkle. "I have called on you to continue the discussion."

"I was being nonsensical—challenging you like that—and you know it. In any case, I meant a duke can't call on a lady in her kitchen. It simply isn't done."

He dismissed the ridiculous line of argument with a gesture. "Shall we go into your garden, then?"

No, she thought. *Sir Jasper might see. Anyone might see…*

Before Olivia could protest, he plucked a second china cup from the high shelf she had strained to reach. He added the teapot, the plate of bread and butter, and her already cooling cup to the tray she had started to arrange and carried it all outside.

She directed him to a hidden corner where a low hedge of rosebushes sheltered a couple of crude seats some previous tenant had shaped from fallen logs. "What a very intimate spot in which to discuss… diamond bracelets." The duke set the tray down with a flourish, dusted off the makeshift chairs with a spotless handkerchief, and bowed her into one of them.

He won't be staying long, Olivia thought as she watched him take the other, almost—but not quite—concealing his wince. Not only would the caliber of the tea fall far short of what he must be used to at Halstead, but the ambiance was seriously lacking.

No, she wouldn't have to put up with him for more than a few minutes. He surely couldn't intend to press the subject.

"Only a few minutes ago, you offered me a bargain. Did you mean what you said?"

Olivia took a breath to deny it. *Of course not*, she would say. *I wouldn't be your mistress for any number of diamond bracelets…*

But she couldn't force herself to utter the words.

In less than a week, Sir Jasper would be back to demand the rest of the money he said she owed. If she couldn't pay it all in hard cash, he would renew—perhaps even increase—his demands. And though she would never give in to the blackmail he had threatened, a bargain with the Duke of Somervale would be different.

Different? Exactly how *is it different?* asked an inconvenient little voice in the back of her mind. *A mistress is a mistress!*

She took a deep breath. It *was* different, she told herself, in several ways. She might be on the edge of desperation, but this solution was her own idea, and therefore she would be the one in control. Instead of being held to Sir Jasper's demands, she would be the one to set the terms. Also, she was proposing to enter into an affair, not the sort of enslavement Sir Jasper seemed to have in mind. And this would not be a lengthy arrangement. Even Kate, who admired the duke, had said he was not the sort to be faithful to anyone, and taking a mistress was by definition a fleeting transaction.

By trading her virtue for valuables, she could gain

security not only for herself but for Charlotte. This temporary arrangement would make all the difference in paying for a decent life for both of them, buying their freedom from men like Sir Jasper and providing a few extras—a governess, perhaps, and a good school.

Perhaps most importantly, her daughter was still young enough that Charlotte would never have to know what her mother had done to secure her future.

"Yes," Olivia said steadily. "I meant it."

For an instant, the world seemed to hang in the balance.

"Good," the duke said. "Then we have some bargaining to do, my lady."

∾

She was pale, Simon thought, and though she was plainly determined, she didn't look excited at the prospect of making love with him. She looked more as if she was waiting to have a tooth extracted.

Even a fool could see the marriage bed had not been a place of pleasure for her, and Simon was anything but a fool. He felt his blood stir at the thought of being her first lover, at least in the real sense of the word. The one who would introduce her to all the pleasures of illicit lovemaking. He would slowly enjoy every inch of her and, at the same time, show her how to pleasure herself as well as him.

As a trysting place, the isolated corner of her garden held only a few advantages. There was an interesting patch of moss, dappled with sunlight under the over-hanging branches of an old oak tree, that might be soft enough for a makeshift bed.

But she had not yet committed herself beyond the point of retreat. The idea of tossing her down on the moss, inviting though it was, would have to wait. This filly was skittish. She would need to be coaxed, gentled to his touch.

And in any case, he reminded himself, that wasn't what he really wanted from Lady Reyne. At least, it wasn't *all* he wanted.

She was looking at him warily, as if she could read the turmoil inside him, and he could feel her begin to withdraw.

"Bargaining," he said again, and watched the hazel of her eyes grow darker. His voice felt rough, and he deliberately masked the passionate edge—for only a foolish man would spook the lady before she was entirely his. "I am prepared to be generous to get what I want. Would you like two bracelets, my lady? One for each wrist?"

She wet her lips.

She couldn't have meant the gesture to be seductive, for it simply wasn't in her. Not yet, at any rate. Still, the sight of the slick pink tip of her tongue sent desire jolting through him, and he heard himself say, "Shall we seal the bargain with a kiss?"

"We haven't made a bargain yet," she said warily. "Why are you willing to pay more than I asked for?"

"Because," Simon said, "I want more than you offered."

He watched the play of emotions on her lovely face and wondered what sort of depravity she was imagining. Nothing too perverted, he suspected, for she was still innocent. What fun it would be to discover and fulfill her fantasies...

But it was time for plain speaking.

"For the next week," he said firmly, "until my sister's wedding is safely past and the last guests leave Halstead, I want to court you."

Five

WITH ANDREW CARLISLE ADDED TO THE GROUP, THE bridesmaids no longer dawdled and drooped. Not that his presence made any real difference to Kate, for he behaved exactly as a gentleman could be expected to—strolling along between two of the well-born young women, flirting gently with all of them, and rarely deigning to notice the help.

Nevertheless, even the occasional glance or smile in her direction made him as annoying as a speck of granite in Kate's shoe—too small to make a fuss over, too large to ignore.

One of the bridesmaids asked Andrew about Lord Winchester. "My father said he's hanging out for a bride. Is it true?"

Another of the girls sniffed. "Not if he has sons, Horatia. Weren't you listening?"

Andrew seemed to bite back a smile. "He was widowed some time ago, but he married again last winter. That is why—" He broke off. "I am sorry to disappoint you, Miss Horatia."

Kate wondered what he had started to say instead.

That is why... How would Andrew have finished that sentence, if he hadn't thought better of it?

She was relieved when they reached Halstead and she could retreat, if only for a few moments, to the cool and peaceful bedchamber she'd been assigned. The duchess had insisted Kate have a room all to herself, located in the main part of the house and not the distant wing where companions and other not-quite-servants were usually housed. Mostly, Kate suspected, the duchess's order arose because she wanted Kate to be always available to her, not from a particular concern for Kate's comfort. Nevertheless, Kate was grateful for the quiet.

She splashed cool water over her face, sponged the dust off her black dress, tidied her hair, and within a few minutes was as ready as she'd ever be to return to her duties. Though the young ladies who had shared her walk would no doubt take much longer to refresh themselves, a half-dozen others had not gone all the way to the village, and by now the duchess would likely be impatient for Kate to take over.

At any rate, Kate told herself, she wouldn't have to concern herself with Andrew Carlisle for the moment, for he had excused himself at the door to take his horse around to the stables. "He's a dear old friend," he'd told the bridesmaids, "and I prefer to see to his care myself."

The bridesmaids had giggled all the way up the stairs about how odd Mr. Carlisle was to consider himself friends with his horse. Kate thought the comment had been a reasonably tactful way for Andrew to get away from the clingy females. No doubt when he finally did return to the house, he would vanish into one of the masculine bastions and not be seen again until dinner.

Which was just fine with her.

As Kate reached the foot of the stairs, Mrs. Greeley stepped out of the shadows. "Miss Blakely, I have no choice. I must move you out of the green room to accommodate another guest. I'll have one of the maids take your things over to the east wing instead."

So much for Kate's cool and peaceful bedroom, her sanctuary, her retreat. She hadn't even spent a single night there. "The east wing?"

"You'll be closer to the bridesmaids if they need you," Mrs. Greeley offered hopefully.

Kate laughed and went on to the drawing room, which seemed remarkably full of people.

Lady Stone, who occupied the most comfortable chair, and Colonel Sir Tristan Huffington, with his shoulder propped against the marble mantelpiece, were sniping at each other—but there was nothing new about that. A cluster of bridesmaids occupied a corner as they whispered together. They'd bear watching, Kate thought. And near the duchess was Penny, on a settee next to her husband. Her spine was absolutely upright as their boarding school instructors had taught, but she was making what sounded like random answers to the duchess's comments.

The duchess looked exasperated, and as her gaze fell on Kate, relief gleamed in her eyes. "Come here, my dear," she said smoothly. "I understand you know Miss... I mean, the countess... from your time together at school. You must have much to speak of." She stood up briskly and shook out her skirts. "And I—"

At the door, the butler cleared his throat. "Your Grace, Mr. Blakely requests a few moments with you and Lady Daphne."

"Mr. Blakely?" The duchess blinked as if expecting to see a ghost standing behind the butler.

"The new vicar is a cousin of my father's, ma'am. He arrived yesterday."

"Oh, yes. I'd forgotten there was a relationship. No doubt he wants to talk about the wedding, but what a horridly inconvenient time to call… Put him in the small morning room, Greeley. I'll be there in a moment. Goodness knows where Lady Daphne is."

"She went up to change her dress after our walk, I believe. Would you like me to ask her to come down?" Kate's offer was halfhearted; she could imagine how Daphne would react to being hurried along for the vicar's convenience.

"Yes, please," the duchess said briskly. "And perhaps on your way, you'll show Lady Townsend to the blue suite at the top of the stairs so she can rest and refresh herself. Mrs. Greeley seems to have gone missing."

Penny got to her feet with obvious relief, and Kate led her out. For a moment, she had forgotten the vicar entirely, but as they left the drawing room, Kate saw that though the butler was attempting to show Mr. Blakely into the morning room, the vicar was taking his time and admiring the grandeur of Halstead.

"What a remarkable staircase," he said. "The way it branches and hangs in midair without visible support! And the colors of the room."

I wonder if he's warming up his voice for the duchess, Kate thought. He sounded as if he thought his throat were a musical instrument and he was testing his range.

"Her Grace is to be complimented on her taste— *Miss Blakely?*"

Now Kate knew he'd practiced his slow, sonorous voice, for when he was startled, his tone skated upward into a nasal-sounding tenor.

"What are *you* doing here?" He sounded scandalized. "A young woman in mourning, visiting a house full of wedding festivities! I am *shocked*—"

Before Kate could defend herself, the duchess spoke from behind her. "Mr. Blakely!" Her voice held the crack of a whip. "Your cousin has graciously put aside her personal loss to assist me during this busy time, and I don't know what I would do without her. Surely her willingness to give service to others in their time of need is an expression not of frivolity but of true Christian charity!"

The vicar's Adam's apple pumped as he swallowed hard. Kate could see him reassessing his position with this potentially valuable patron.

"Of course, Your Grace. I spoke in haste, thinking only of what others—those of less pure mind—might think to see her here. But if *you* approve—well, no one could object."

Over his bowed head, the duchess winked at Kate, who gave a quick tug to Penny and started up the stairs.

The vicar went on, "I admire my cousin for her most virtuous of motives. I am happy to confide in you, Your Grace, that I plan to quickly make her my wife."

Penny's eyes went wide. Kate smothered a groan

as she looked back over her shoulder to see how the duchess might react to the pronouncement.

And saw Andrew Carlisle lounging in the shadow of the front door.

Well, what of it? she asked herself crossly. What Kate chose to do with her life was nothing at all to him. And Andrew Carlisle was nothing at all to her.

❧

Kate's groan pulled Penelope back to the moment. During the entire time that she'd sat in the drawing room—which could have been no more than a quarter hour, though it had felt like an age—Penelope had been in a sort of fog, afraid she might fling herself at the duchess's feet and beg for her help. Exactly what sort of help, Penelope wasn't certain.

But the vicar's pronouncement—*that* she could deal with. "You don't sound very happy about it, Kate. *Are* you going to marry him?"

Kate didn't answer directly. "I don't suppose you want to hire a companion, Penny? You and I have always gotten along well. I could wind skeins of needlepoint yarn for you or keep you company on long walks."

"Then you're not betrothed? I must own I'm glad, as he hardly seems a fit match for you." Penelope felt herself color, for surely the same could be said of her own husband.

Kate pushed open a door. "This is the blue suite. You have your choice of rooms, I suppose, though this is the more feminine of the two. I suspect…" She opened a cupboard. "Yes, your things have already been unpacked."

"Already? The duchess has very efficient housemaids."

"And you have very few possessions," Kate said. She sounded curious.

The bedroom was spacious, with a high ceiling and two huge windows overlooking the drive and park at the front of the house. A pair of upholstered chairs were drawn up near the fireplace, and Penelope tried to focus on them. But she could not ignore the enormous bed with its tall posts, puffy mattress, and deep blue silk hangings.

If things had gone just a tiny bit differently…

They're newlyweds, the elderly lady had said—and for just an instant the duchess had looked at Penelope as if seeking confirmation.

If at that moment Penelope had simply smiled happily, laid her head against her husband's shoulder, and looked up at him adoringly… then they would be sharing this room. And as of tonight, everything would change.

But she had done nothing of the sort. Though she had felt a tinge of regret for letting an opportunity slip away, she could not deny the wave of relief that had followed. She knew she hadn't imagined the way the earl's body had gone rigid at the very idea of sharing her bedroom—and she was glad not to have to face his wrath, as she surely would have done had she manipulated him into such a public display.

"Are you all right, Penny?" Kate walked across to the washstand. "Shall I ring for a maid to bring you hot water? This pitcher is barely warm."

"A cool rinse will be refreshing. We had a long drive, and I think I'll rest for a while." She took off her hat and set it atop a cabinet. "Besides, aren't you supposed to be fetching Lady Daphne?"

Kate made a face. "She's not going to want to be fetched—but yes, I must go and make the effort. Perhaps we can talk later? I want to hear all about your wedding."

Penelope did not settle down to rest, however. As soon as Kate was gone, she began to explore the room. Her meager wardrobe occupied less than a tenth of the cupboard Kate had opened, and two more cabinets stood entirely empty. But the cupboards and dressing table— even the huge, high bed—did not call to Penelope. She couldn't keep herself from looking at the door on the far side of the room, and she was drawn to look beyond.

Tentatively, she turned the handle and peeked into another blue bedroom, almost the twin of her own. If anything, the bed was even larger, draped with silk in a slightly darker shade of blue—or did the color seem different only because the drapes were closed here and the light was dimmer?

There was no evidence of occupation except for a pitcher on the washstand that felt warm against her hand. She tiptoed across the carpet and opened a cabinet. Several coats, a pile of shirts, a heap of neck-cloths... Somehow, she thought, the earl's valet had fit a great deal more into a small portmanteau than Etta had managed. Even though his manservant had been left behind to come with Etta and the baggage wagon, the earl would have no difficulty in turning himself out well. But then, he never did look anything other than cool and elegant.

Penelope could feel her hair, relieved of the weight

of her hat, springing into random curls that must stick out in all directions.

The door leading into the main hallway creaked open and Penelope tensed—too nervous to run. The earl came in very quietly, and she turned to face him, biting her lip and waiting.

He glanced around the room, perhaps making certain there was no servant to overhear.

"To what do I owe the honor of this visit, ma'am?"

Why *had* she come to his bedroom? And having been discovered there, why hadn't she simply apologized and retreated?

Because you want to change things, Penelope reminded herself. "I thought perhaps we could talk about… our situation."

"Now? And here?"

"Why not? In London, you're never at home. On the drive, Mr. Carlisle was riding alongside. Here, there are no maids or valets to interrupt unless we call for them."

Without a word he took off his coat, draping it over the back of a chair. His cravat was next; he tossed it atop the coat, but it slid off to pool on the floor. He unfastened the band at the neck of his shirt. His fingers were long and strong and supple, and though Penelope was a good five feet away, she could almost feel the warmth of his fingertips brushing against the smooth linen as though it had been her skin.

He glanced at her. "Don't let me stop you. You were saying?"

Penelope looked away. "I've been thinking about your letter, my lord. The one to my father. It seems to me that he did not absolutely reject your request."

And I wish you would tell me what that request was, she wanted to add.

He paused, fingers clasped on the next button. "His refusal seemed quite definite to me."

"But it wasn't. Not really. He said he wouldn't agree *at this time*. But surely he meant if you meet his terms…"

"I would call them *demands*."

"Perhaps." Penelope took a deep breath. "At any rate, we both know what he wants. It's been three months, my lord, since the wedding. It seems to me it is time to take the next step."

The earl didn't answer. Slowly, he stripped off his shirt.

Penelope's mouth went dry at the sight of so much bare skin. His chest was unexpectedly broad, and under the light furring of hair, she could see each muscle so clearly defined and distinct that she would be able to draw him from memory. Her heart was pounding.

He laid the shirt aside and came to stand directly in front of her. She had been even closer to him, of course, on their wedding day—but this was different. He seemed so much bigger than she'd realized, and that bare chest was so much warmer… What would it be like to be pressed against him? Under him?

She shivered a little.

He moved past her to the washstand, poured warm water from the pitcher into the basin, and bent to splash his face.

Penelope watched the muscles flex in his back and arms. Then, feeling as if she was only half-awake, she reached for a towel to hold out for him.

He looked at her over the edge of the linen square.

"I must beg your pardon. I did not realize how strongly your father has pressured you for an heir until yesterday when he visited in Berkeley Square, and even then I did not comprehend how concerned you are about providing one in order to satisfy him." He blotted his face and folded the towel.

The careful way he matched up the corners told Penelope exactly how tightly he was controlling himself, for she couldn't imagine him caring whether a towel was neat or not.

"You must not disturb yourself over the matter," he went on. "Mr. Weiss cannot cut off your allowance, for my solicitors saw to that in the marriage contracts."

She took a moment to find her voice. "That's not…"

"I understand it is not money but fear of disappointing your father that worries you most." He laid the damp towel aside. "But there is no need for these desperate maneuvers. I have no intention of claiming my husbandly rights."

Desperate? He thought she was desperate? And he was letting her down easily, as gently as was possible in these horrid circumstances.

She kept her back straight as she turned to walk out of the room.

"Penelope," he said softly. "I am sorry."

"So am I, my lord." She didn't look back. "So am I."

❧

"Court me?" Olivia's words came out as nothing more than a squeak, so she had to try again. "What do you mean, *court me*?"

The duke shrugged. "What everyone means, I

suppose, when they use the phrase in speaking of an unmarried man and a widow. You must have noticed the bridesmaids in the village today, circling around me like a troop of Dianas on the hunt."

"That would have been difficult to miss."

"With days to get through before the wedding, I do not intend to be harried into leaving my home simply because schoolgirls are taking aim at my title with every arrow at their disposal. Neither am I willing to run the risk that one of them might succeed in compromising herself into requiring an offer of marriage."

"I doubt that would be possible without assistance from you."

He snorted. "Then you know very little about the matter. I have been pursued by every debutante who has come on the marriage market—and her mama— for the past five years."

"Not because of your modesty, I warrant," Olivia said under her breath.

"Thus there are few tricks I am unfamiliar with. But twelve of these chits will be ever present in my home for a week to come. Add in the fact that my mother shows every sign of turning a blind eye to their antics, and one of them might slip under my guard in any of a hundred possible ways."

"And you, sir, would be dished. Married before you even had a chance to figure out what had happened. But if the problem is the bridesmaids, I don't see why you want to court me."

"I should have said, of course, I wish to *pretend* to court you."

"But of course. That goes without saying." Olivia

started to laugh. "You really are in a pickle, Your Grace, if you think courting *me* is going to discourage those girls. They'd never believe you were serious about someone like me. I've not even completed my mourning period."

"They don't have to admire you," he said. "Only find you a formidable enough challenge to make them turn to easier prey."

"That's comforting," Olivia muttered.

"I am well known to prefer women with more depth and experience than any schoolroom miss possesses. And I have already started to supply the easier prey as well by calling on all my friends to join me at Halstead for the wedding."

"I can't imagine they'll thank you for turning them into targets."

"I have warned the unmarried ones of the risks. But with an adequate number of males on the ground this week, the bridesmaids' attention will be split. With luck, we'll all come out the other side without being leg-shackled."

"There's a flaw in your logic, of course. After you spend a week courting me, what happens when the wedding is over and you don't need me as cover anymore?"

"Then you will jilt me. Coldly, heartlessly, and publicly."

"And quite stupidly as well," she pointed out, "for no woman with sense would even contemplate jilting a duke once she'd captured him. You'd do better to carry out the jilting yourself, you know. It makes no sense for *me* to be the one to back out of a betrothal."

The duke said coolly, "Because jilting me would

ruin your reputation, you mean? And being my mistress wouldn't?"

He had a point there, Olivia had to admit. "If I were your mistress, no one would know anything about it. But if you court me openly, and then I break off the connection—"

"Why should the reaction concern you? Are you worried about how you'll be received next Season in London?"

Olivia had no intention of appearing in London again until Charlotte's first Season, if then. But there was no reason to invite speculation by saying so.

"If you're suggesting I should give you provocation, ma'am…"

"Oh, that should present no problem," Olivia muttered. "Just watching you draw breath in your usual arrogant fashion would be provocation enough for me to cancel a wedding. But I see you are determined to think you're right, so I won't argue the matter any further."

"Then we are in accord?"

"Not just yet. For me to agree to carry off this charade—jilting and all—you'll have to make it worth my while."

"Of course you will keep the gifts I give you."

"How perfectly paltry of you, Your Grace. You know quite well an unmarried woman isn't allowed to accept anything of substance from her betrothed."

"She can accept a ring. You wouldn't be able to keep the Somervale ring, of course—"

"Yes, I imagine your mother would have something to say about *that*."

"But we could say you preferred a diamond instead."

Olivia shook her head. "No matter how nice the ring, it's nothing against the worth of a duchess's coronet. So if you're going to be able to trust me to do as you wish, instead of holding you to your supposed promise of marriage—"

"As if you could force me into it." He stood.

Not because he was insulted, Olivia thought, but because he couldn't abide the rough chair anymore. "You're afraid of a pack of schoolgirls, but not of me?"

"The schoolgirls have innocence on their side, and society protects them because of it."

"Or at least they have the appearance of innocence, which is nearly the same thing."

"While you, my lady—forgive me—have an aura of scandal. When a lady vanishes from her husband's house only days after his funeral is held…"

"…a thoughtful gentleman would conclude there is a reason. But perhaps I should not expect so much of *you*, Your Grace. How did you happen to hear of that?"

"One of the guests already at Halstead is something of a gossip. When I asked if anyone knew of a Lord Reyne, Colonel Sir Tristan Huffington was happy to enlighten me. Your late husband was much older than you, with pockets sadly to let. When he died, you promptly removed yourself from his ramshackle house, and no one knew where you had gone."

Olivia's lips felt stiff. "The colonel is well-informed."

"Since I am aware of your history, you must realize how foolish threats are."

"Still, you'd be wise to pay me so well that I'd prefer to have the money instead of being stuck with you—even considering the coronet."

"*Three* diamond bracelets?"

"Don't be silly. I only have two arms. I'd prefer money, anyway—or better yet, some kind of continuing payment."

"That sounds uncomfortably like blackmail."

"Not at all, for I would never trust you to continue the payments once the bargain was finished. I can't recall what it's called when a servant is pensioned off. No doubt you know."

"You mean an annuity?"

"Yes, exactly. That would do nicely. You may fund an annuity for me. Then I can be independent, and you can forget all about me once I've jilted you. And you needn't think I'm planning to rob you, Your Grace. I suspect my idea of a large sum is far different than yours. It will cost you less to buy me off than it would to support one of Daphne's friends for a year. That much is certain."

"I wonder if you're worth it." His gaze slid slowly over her. "Are you up to the job?"

"Do you want my honest assessment? Making twelve bridesmaids believe you're so besotted you can't possibly have eyes for one of them isn't my problem at all. It's yours. I need only stand still and look somewhat decorative. All the convincing will be on your side."

"Your disarming frankness makes me less inclined to pay your price."

"It's entirely up to you, of course." Olivia's breath felt shallow. What was she doing, anyway, arguing against the most rewarding bargain she'd ever been offered? Was she mad? "It was your idea to pretend to court me, instead of having the simple little affair I suggested."

He said very deliberately, "Oh, not *instead of*. I meant, *in addition to*."

Olivia's breath rasped in her throat. His voice sounded hot and dangerous. She forced herself to laugh. "Touché, sir."

"The truth is, Lady Reyne, I don't pay my mistresses. To keep my mother from matching me up with an empty-headed schoolgirl—*that's* worth a pension. But don't think for a moment I'm rejecting your initial offer. I'm only adding my own set of terms to what you proposed."

She felt the heat of his gaze washing over her, and her insides went liquid. How could he have such an effect when he wasn't even touching her?

"I'll have your answer now." His voice curved like warm velvet against her skin. "Shall we seal our bargain with a kiss?"

Olivia finally managed a full breath. "Only if you provide earnest money."

"You don't trust my word?" He shrugged. "I don't have a diamond bracelet—or an annuity—on my person, I'm afraid. The ladies who draw my eye tend not to lose interest in me so quickly that I must woo them with gifts in advance."

"How nice for you. But you're in for a rude shock where I'm concerned."

He smiled slowly. "So we do have a bargain."

Without taking his gaze off her face, he unfastened the gold and sapphire stickpin nestled in the folds of his neckcloth. He folded her fingers around the warm metal. Then he raised her hand to his lips.

His mouth was warm against her skin, moving

slowly over the back of her hand, his fingers cupping hers. Intimate as the gesture was, Olivia was relieved. She'd thought for a moment he meant to do more. But a mere kiss on the hand—even though it was her bare hand, and even though heat rippled up her arm—*that* she could stand.

He pulled her closer, lifting her hands to rest them on his shoulders and then wrapping one arm around her while his other hand came to rest under her chin. His fingertips splayed across her throat, each pad barely touching, yet sensation arced through her. She tipped her head back in an instinctive attempt to avoid the contact and looked directly into his eyes.

She saw satisfaction in his gaze and knew she'd acted exactly as he'd expected. "Such a cooperative little mistress you're going to be," he whispered, and his lips came down on hers.

His mouth was warm, mobile, and gentle—asking rather than taking, exploring rather than plundering. He kissed her so thoroughly that she forgot how to breathe. Her world narrowed until the only thing that still existed was sensation—the smooth wool of his coat under her hands, the tiny rasp of beard against her cheek, the scent of his soap, a tangy taste as the tip of his tongue teased her lips open, the coolness of air moving against her breasts, and then the gentle tug of his mouth against her nipple as he bent to sample and explore... How had he opened the bodice of her gown without her noticing?

"You said a kiss," she protested.

He raised his head and smiled. "That's a valuable sapphire you're holding. I intend to get my money's worth." His voice was husky, trailing across her ears as gently as his mouth had caressed her breast. He pulled her closer and kissed her again, more possessively this time. His thumb gently circled the peak of her nipple until she arched against him, pushing her breast against the warm smoothness of his palm.

"Tonight," he whispered against her lips. "I will come to you tonight."

❦

The vicar's call on the duchess had been a short one, and Her Grace had apparently opted not to include Lady Daphne after all—for as Kate came down the stairs, Mr. Blakely was being shown to the front door. Before she could even think of dodging into a side room to avoid him, his sonorous voice rang out across the breadth of Halstead's entrance hall. "Miss Blakely, a moment if you please."

Kate weighed the possibilities. If he was aiming to lecture her, it would be better to hold this conversation in private. But if he intended to renew his courtship, then the last thing she wanted just now was to be alone with him.

She compromised by taking him into the reception room nearest the entrance but pointedly leaving the door open. The chamber was tiny; the furniture was the uncomfortable sort chosen to discourage casual callers from lingering; and the air felt chilly even in the middle of August—though perhaps that was more a matter of disuse than of actual temperature.

Kate ignored the straight-backed wooden chairs and stopped in the center of the room, her hands folded demurely, waiting to see what was on the vicar's mind. Mr. Blakely looked at her even more closely than he had the previous afternoon in Olivia's garden, as if he was truly seeing her as a person for the first time.

Then he smiled broadly. "Miss Blakely, I had no idea you were so closely connected to the premier family in the district. To be on such terms with the duchess that she relies on you… I must say, however, perhaps there is such a thing as too much discretion in these matters. Your modesty is admirable, of course, not wishing to put yourself forward or seem to boast of who you know. But not to have even hinted to me of your connection, when you must have known how crucial such a bond can be to the pastor of a flock—"

From the corner of her eye, Kate caught a glimpse of movement in the doorway.

Andrew Carlisle stood there. "So sorry. Since the door was open, I thought the room was empty."

"The vicar was just leaving," Kate said.

"I thought perhaps he might be," Andrew agreed. "Let me walk you out, sir."

He was gone barely a minute. Kate had folded her hands on the back of a chair and was deciding how long she must wait before she could safely duck away when Andrew returned.

"Please accept my condolences on your loss," he said. "Your father was a brilliant man."

"Thank you. I appreciate your sympathy."

The silence drew out. "I've missed you, Kate."

"It's Miss Blakely to you, Mr. Carlisle."

"Only in public," he said softly. "What has happened to you? You can't mean to marry the vicar."

"Why on earth shouldn't I? It would be a perfectly good match. He's a godly man."

"And he's so aware of his state of grace, too. You have changed, Kate, if you truly find someone like Mr. Blakely a tempting prospect as a lifetime partner. Or is it not the man but his situation that attracts you? Is security so important to you now?"

"What business is it of yours?"

"None, I suppose—except that we were friends."

"Were we?" Kate wet her lips. "You liked to tell me stories. That is true. I recall you plotting to venture up the Amazon by canoe. Did your dreams come to nothing?"

Andrew smiled. "There are many kinds of adventure, Kate. That one was probably the most crack-brained of my many schemes, but I am flattered you remember them still. Do you recollect all the others as clearly? And have you wondered sometimes which of those dreams I might be pursuing?"

Kate was speechless. The sheer conceit of the man, to think she'd had nothing better to do on any given day than to contemplate where in the world he might be! "The only thing I wonder," she said tartly, "is why no cannibal ever boiled you in your own impertinence. Since none has, the obvious conclusion is that you have never come face to face with one!"

In the silence that followed, the Duke of Somervale looked around the half-open door of the reception room. "Andrew, I might have guessed it would be you here annoying Miss Blakely. You always were quite good at it."

Andrew laughed. "I was starting to wonder if you had done a bunk altogether, Simon."

"Couldn't figure out how to get by with it," the duke admitted. "Now stop bothering Miss Blakely and come do the pretty with me. We might find you an heiress among the bridesmaids, you know."

Of course, what the duke was really saying, Kate thought, was, *Stop wasting your time on Miss Blakely…*

And that was quite all right with her.

There are many kinds of adventure… She wondered precisely what Andrew Carlisle had meant. Not, of course, that she intended to ask.

❦

After her bath, Penelope pressed one of the housemaids into service to assist her into her simple dinner gown. Anyone could do up buttons, after all. But Maggie was utterly useless at arranging hair, so Penelope was putting the finishing touches on a very simple twist when the earl came into her bedroom. When he silently appeared over her shoulder in the dressing table mirror, her hand slipped and she stabbed her scalp with a hairpin.

He looked surprised to see her almost ready to go down. "Dinner will not be served for nigh on an hour, ma'am."

He had called her by her name earlier, Penelope thought wistfully. Now the coldness had returned. She steadied her fingers and pushed the hairpin into place. "With the house so busy, I thought it best not to wait till the last moment."

"One of the other ladies' maids would be happy to assist you. You need only make a request."

"I don't like to ask," Penelope admitted. "Each of them has duties aplenty already, and Maggie has been quite helpful."

His expression softened a little. "You dislike being a trouble to anyone, don't you?"

The little maid stopped fluttering about the room gathering up Penelope's discarded clothing and bobbed a curtsey. "No trouble at all, my lord. I'm that pleased to help."

Slowly, the earl's gaze slipped away from Penelope to rest on the maid and then on the hip bath that stood beside the fireplace. "Indeed? I wonder—Maggie, is it?—if you would go and order me a bath. The tub looks very inviting."

Maggie dropped the pile of intimate belongings squarely in the center of the carpet, obviously without giving a thought to the mess. "I'll order hot water this minute, my lord, and send a footman to move the tub into your bedroom."

The earl stretched. "No need. It's fine there." He stripped off his coat.

Penelope felt her insides shimmer as she remembered seeing his bare chest this afternoon, and she told herself she was very glad she'd decided to hurry through her toilette rather than watch his performance again.

All that warm, smooth skin… Even the memory left her feeling dazed. She wondered if the hairs on his chest were coarse or soft, and whether those well-defined muscles were as hard as they looked.

A wiry lock of her hair sprang loose and tumbled

down her neck. Penelope fiddled with another hairpin and tried not to watch in the mirror as the earl slowly unwound his neckcloth and laid it aside. She wondered if every woman within range was susceptible to losing her mind as the earl undressed; the maid had seemed no more immune than Penelope herself, the way she'd hared off to take care of his request.

Trying to keep her gaze off her husband, Penelope looked instead at the small heap of clothing on the floor. A silk stocking trailed out of the pile, and a lace-edged chemise spilled across the Aubusson carpet. They were intimate items that, under other circumstances, she would have been embarrassed to have on display. But he seemed to pay no notice. As if there was nothing new to him about seeing a woman's undergarments trailing across a bedroom floor...

No doubt he *was* used to the sight, and perhaps that helped to explain why he had chosen not to share her bed. If he had a mistress...

The idea had occurred to her before, of course, but for the first time she allowed herself to dwell on what that woman would be like. She would be tiny, beautiful, witty, and accomplished—all the things Penelope wasn't. And her hair would fall naturally into glossy ringlets, not the wiry, uncontrollable mass that Penelope had to deal with.

"You wear no jewels this evening?"

"It would be foolishly showy to add gems to the simple styles I can manage myself. Like adding sweet icing to a loaf of coarse black bread and pretending it is cake."

She knew she sounded cranky, but she couldn't stop herself from picturing the sort of woman he would take as a mistress. One who would look delicious draped in diamonds…

She stabbed viciously at the back of her head with the hairpin. "This thing will not stay in." She supposed pretending a snit was a great deal better than taking the chance he might guess something closer to the truth.

He came up behind her. He was still wearing his shirt, though the front gaped open to display a tantalizing wedge of warm, smooth chest. His fingertips skimmed her shoulder blade just where the edge of her bodice met skin and then trailed up the back of her neck, scooping up the wayward lock of hair along the way. Gently he tucked the ends into the twist and smoothed the palm of his hand from her nape to her crown. Then he took the pin from her suddenly numb hand and anchored his work in place.

Penelope's breath had stuck in her chest until she couldn't exhale, and her gaze seemed glued to his reflection in the mirror.

"As soon as we return to town," the earl said quietly, "I shall go to your father and tell him I am incapable of fathering a child. Then he must accept the facts and stop blaming you."

What he said wasn't true, of course. Penelope knew he wasn't incapable, simply unwilling. He had married her because he had little choice, but her noble husband was so reluctant to mix his blood with hers that he preferred to let the direct branch of his family die out rather than mate with her.

Behind him, the door opened to admit a line of maids carrying cans of hot water.

Penelope stood and gathered up her reticule and escaped.

Six

As THE GUESTS WERE SUMMONED TO THE DINING ROOM that evening, Simon was startled when his mother announced she had given up the notion of a formal seating chart in favor of dining *en famille.* With the numbers of men and women so wildly uneven, and so many of the bridesmaids of roughly equal rank, arranging the order of precedence as etiquette demanded would have been a nightmare.

But though he hadn't been looking forward to having Lady Stone—who was the senior female guest and therefore entitled to the seat at his right—as a dinner partner tonight, he *had* expected to get a reprieve from the bridesmaids for the duration of the meal.

He shot a dark look at his mother, who ignored him, and bowed politely to Lady Stone, offering his arm to escort her in to dinner. She surveyed the group of guests and then gave him a sly smile. "Are you a betting man, Somervale?" Her voice was low. "Five guineas says the tall brunette and the little blonde will trample their friends to claim the seats next to you."

He looked at the two—already quivering like

racehorses beside the drawing room door—and said firmly, "I would win the wager, my lady."

"Then it's a bet," she announced. "How do you plan to keep them from it? Make me sit beside you instead?"

"Nothing so crude, ma'am. Since my mother has suspended the rules, I will seat you in my chair at the head of the table between the young ladies, and I'll take a place elsewhere."

She gave a great rusty laugh. "I like you, Somervale—but you don't play fair."

"Backing out of your debt of honor, my lady? I think you owe me five guineas."

"We'll go double or nothing next time. Where will you sit instead?"

In the kitchen, he wanted to say. "I think anywhere beneath the salt should be safe."

In fact, however, he enjoyed the evening far more than he had expected. Andrew Carlisle flirted impartially with every bridesmaid within the reach of his voice, and Colonel Sir Tristan Huffington told Kate Blakely about his war service and how much he appreciated a woman who was old enough to understand what he was talking about.

When Lady Stone interrupted with a sniff, saying, "There *are* no women old enough to understand what you're talking about, you old goat. Miss Blakely is merely more polite than most," Simon surprised himself by laughing.

But most of all, he passed the time in looking forward to the end of the evening—when the company would have dispersed enough that he would no longer be missed and could leave Halstead for his visit to Lady Reyne. To *Olivia*. A beautiful name, as smooth and as sweetly rounded as she herself was...

Simon kept one eye on the clock as the port went round the table after dinner. As soon as he decently could, he broke into the colonel's monologue about everything that the War Office had done wrong in the most recent conflict and suggested the gentlemen move to the drawing room.

"Fine by me," Andrew Carlisle said. "But you amaze me, Simon. I thought you invited us because you *didn't* want to spend time with the ladies. If you tell us now that you're trying to fix your interest with one of them before the rest of your unmarried friends arrive tomorrow..."

Simon muttered something about wanting to get the evening over with. Andrew's knowing smile was no worse than Simon's mother's; when the gentlemen appeared in the drawing room, the duchess's self-satisfied expression set Simon's teeth on edge.

Eventually the ladies began to trail off upstairs. Charles suggested to Andrew that they play a game of billiards; Sir Tristan cornered Kate Blakely and Lady Townsend to finish his dissection of the war; and Simon was finally able to escape.

As he entered his bedroom, he was thinking only about how quickly he could change into riding clothes and leave the house, and it took him a moment to realize the room wasn't empty.

Damnation. He'd let his guard down—he'd been thinking about Olivia again instead of the danger now ever present in his house—and he had only seconds to act before whichever bridesmaid who had laid a trap for him made her move.

He started to back out of the room, but as a figure shifted in the shadows, Simon's gut relaxed. He knew that shape—and it wasn't a bridesmaid. "Hemmings, I thought I told you not to wait up for me tonight."

His valet bowed his head. "I felt it wise to remain until you were safely returned, sir."

"I'm not three years old, Hemmings," Simon said dryly. "I don't need a nursemaid." *Of course*, he thought, *thirty is no safer than three, in some circumstances*.

"Exactly, Your Grace. However, as I was gathering up your things earlier, one of the young women tried the door. She *said* she'd taken a wrong turn in the corridor while trying to find her bedroom." His sniff made clear exactly what Hemmings thought of the excuse.

"You're certain she wasn't headed right next door? My mother didn't assign one of the bridesmaids to that room, did she?" He'd almost forgotten the other bedroom in his suite, the one reserved for a duchess. His mother was capable of putting whichever girl she favored directly under his nose. And Greeley had warned that every room in the house was in use…

"No, sir. I have locked the room reserved for your duchess. As soon as I have helped you into bed, I shall make up a pallet on the sitting room floor for the night. Just in case."

Now there was a picture—his valet sleeping across his doorway like a faithful hound on guard. Simon scratched his jaw thoughtfully. "You see, Hemmings, I'm not planning to retire just yet. In fact, I'm going out for a ride. Excess energy, you know."

"I shall keep watch as I await your return," the valet said stolidly.

Well, there's a problem. What good was being a duke, anyway, if he was unable to come and go as he pleased? He could hardly have Hemmings waiting up for him when he might not be back till dawn...

"Also," the valet went on, "it appears someone may have been inside the room earlier, because the sapphire stickpin you were wearing today seems to have gone missing."

"I lost it," Simon admitted. "Er—if you've been protecting the sanctity of my bedroom all this time, have you had dinner?"

"No, sir, but it was a small sacrifice to make for your safety."

"Then you must go down and raid the kitchen, for I can't have you getting weak and sickly just now. The key to this room must be somewhere around here. I'll lock the doors when I go out so no one can possibly invade. You can go to bed and not fret."

The valet resisted. He insisted on helping Simon to change into riding garb, and he was still making his disapproval clear when Simon turned the great key and went down to the side door nearest the stables.

The sooner everyone knew he was courting Lady Reyne, Simon thought, the better.

But first, he intended to enjoy tonight.

❧

Kate found dinner to be the most pleasant part of her day. Though there was no controlling what the bridesmaids might say, once all of them were seated at the long table, there was a limit to what they could *do* to get themselves into trouble.

She didn't realize she'd loosed a long breath until the colonel said, "No wonder you're relieved. I thought myself that two of them were going to get into a hair-pulling contest right there in the drawing room. What did Lady Stone say to stop them cold? I couldn't quite hear."

"She congratulated them for finding a way to make themselves memorable to the duke."

"Humph. I would have thought Lucinda could come up with an *interesting* strategy."

"You know Lady Stone?"

"Since long before she became a Stone. Back when she was only the size of a pebble, you might say." He gave a rusty laugh. "Before I joined the army—a good many years ago."

Politely, Kate asked him about his career. As he droned on about life in the quartermaster corps, she listened with half an ear, keeping the other half tuned for the bridesmaids.

Beyond the colonel, a few places on down the table, where she couldn't quite avoid seeing him, Andrew Carlisle was surrounded by young women who hadn't been able to push closer to the duke. A couple of them had been on the walk this afternoon, and Kate noted they seemed much less interested in their dinner companion than the two who hadn't—and who seemed to be quizzing him. One of them said, "How are you related to the duke, Mr. Carlisle?"

"Not at all," Andrew said cheerfully. "Though I do have a relative who's a viscount."

The girl's face brightened, and Kate could see her mind working. A viscount wasn't high on the list of nobility, so marrying one was nothing like the coup of snaring an earl or a duke. Still, it *was* a title, higher on the scale than a baronet…

Kate wondered if the bridesmaid would work out a way to tactfully ask Andrew whether he was close enough in the line of succession to be worth cultivating.

Andrew let an instant pass while he contemplated the platter of roast beef that a footman was offering to him. "But he—the viscount—is on my mother's side of the family."

Kate had to hide a smile behind her napkin. Obviously Andrew was aware of the duke's reason for inviting him, so he was making clear to the girls that he was no catch at all in the marriage stakes. On the other hand, he seemed to be saying he could be a great deal of fun if they *didn't* have marriage on their minds.

But then, Andrew Carlisle had always been fun. Kate wondered if her own face had been as horribly transparent as the bridesmaid's was, during the summer when she'd been seventeen. Andrew had been staying at Halstead that year as Simon's guest, and both had come each day to the village for extra lessons with her father. Kate had been much more innocent back then than the bridesmaid was—and Andrew had been much less smooth than he was now. But she had been head over heels in love with him, nevertheless…

She turned quickly back to the colonel. "And then?" she prompted. "Where were you sent after your service in the American colonies?"

No sooner had the last course been removed than the duchess rose to sweep out of the room, pausing beside Simon's chair as he politely stood to see the ladies out. Kate was just close enough to hear her murmur, "Don't be too long before you join us, dear."

Simon gave his mother a suspicious look.

Lady Stone added blandly, "Iris only means too much port isn't good for the colonel's gout. She'd never be clumsy enough to admit she's anxious to give the girls another shot at you, Somervale."

Once in the drawing room, with no gentlemen to impress, the bridesmaids drooped until Lady Daphne gathered them up in a corner to plan the morrow's activities. "We'll ride in the morning." Two of the girls whined, but Daphne cut them off. "I realize some of you look a great deal better on horseback than others do, but everyone must have a chance to shine. Besides, if all of us go, then every gentleman will be required, in order to properly escort us. We can have a picnic in the abbey ruins down by the river."

Ruins, Kate thought, which would offer a magnificent opportunity for one or more of the girls to wander off and have to be rescued by a gentleman…

Kate made a note to send word to the stables and the kitchens—for it would not occur to Daphne that horses, saddles, and picnics did not appear simply because she wished for them.

"A morning on horseback," Lady Stone said. "Fresh air, fresh horseflesh, and fresh young women. What could possibly go wrong?"

Kate tried in vain to fight down a hysterical giggle. "What could go *wrong*? My lady…"

Lady Stone stared at her, one eyebrow raised.

Kate had already marked governessing off her list of possible careers, and now it had become apparent that she was missing the necessary skills to be a companion, if she couldn't stop herself from laughing at odd statements made by elderly ladies.

Perhaps it was time to remind herself of the advantages of marrying Mr. Blakely. *If I could only think of some.*

In the moments when her attention was diverted, one of the bridesmaids had begun to entertain the rest with a cruelly accurate imitation of Andrew's voice as he'd left them at the door of Halstead that afternoon. "Yes, indeed," she drawled, "my horse Dobbin is my very best friend, don't you know."

Suddenly all urge to laugh was gone; how dare this privileged young woman make fun of someone who was unable to strike back? Kate was about to intervene when she realized that for once, the duke had obeyed his mother—at least it seemed the gentlemen had sat over their port for only minutes before coming to join the ladies.

The bridesmaids weren't expecting them so soon—especially the one who, with her back to the door, was so caught up in her performance that she didn't notice the newcomers. "Don't you think I even look like my horse?" she asked earnestly. Her voice was slightly husky, with a wicked similarity to Andrew's accent. "He's the more handsome, of course."

The girl standing next to her gave her a hard poke. The bridesmaid turned round so fast she lost her balance and stumbled into Lady Daphne, who said something under her breath about clumsy oafs.

Andrew laughed. "You've quite a gift for mimicry, Miss... what was your name again?"

The erring bridesmaid flushed a most unbecoming shade of scarlet and dropped a ragged curtsey.

Kate was nonplussed. In one lightning-fast stroke, Andrew had disarmed the young woman's jest while making clear she wasn't important enough for him to remember her name.

"Well played," Lady Stone murmured. "How I wish I'd had a bet riding on the outcome of that little stunt!"

Andrew Carlisle was in no need of Kate's meager attempts to defend him. In fact, she thought, she could do worse than to learn from the master.

❧

Without Kate's cheerful chatter and Maggie the housemaid rattling around as she carried out her duties, the cottage seemed very quiet. Or perhaps, Olivia admitted, the silence was inside her head and came from the oppressive knowledge of what she had committed herself to do. She managed to behave normally through the evening, but only because she knew the duke would be too busy with his guests to arrive on her doorstep anytime soon.

She helped to give Charlotte her supper, tucked her in, and offered a story. Her little girl considered. "Tell me Cinderella, Mama."

Olivia wanted to howl at the irony of her choice. A heroine wearing rags, a hero who possessed even more arrogance than wealth... How could anyone over the age of three believe two such different people could ever achieve a truly happy ending? "How about the lady and the duke instead?" she muttered. "Only the names and the ending have changed."

Charlotte shook her head firmly and put her cheek down against her mother's breast to listen. By the time Cinderella dropped her slipper as she left the ball, Charlotte was sound asleep—and Olivia was delighted not to have to once more recite a happy ending that was so foolishly saccharine.

Olivia settled the little girl against her pillow and looked across the room to where Nurse was sewing by firelight, hemming a new pinafore for Charlotte to replace the one ruined by grape juice. Where she'd found the fabric, Olivia didn't know—and she wasn't about to ask.

After tonight... or, more accurately, after the next week... things would be much easier. She would focus on that.

She took her hair down to brush and braid it, and changed into the nicest nightgown she owned—which wasn't saying much, she realized as she gave the garment a good inspection. The once-fine lawn fabric had grown limp with age and multiple launderings. She put on a dark wrapper and went downstairs to check that the fire was banked and the house secured.

And to wait.

It seemed an age to Olivia before she heard the soft neigh of a horse. A little later, she caught the hushed sounds of footsteps in the garden and opened the door.

The Duke of Somervale loomed up out of the night. For a moment, as his shadow swayed in the light of her single candle, he seemed supernaturally large, and she quailed at the thought of giving herself to him. If he swooped on her…

He paused on the step. "I found a shed at the bottom of the garden for my horse. There was even hay there."

"Stale, I'm afraid, since I've had no horses here since I moved in."

"He'll manage well enough—and will appreciate the rations in his own stable. Do you ride?"

"I used to."

"My sister is arranging an outing tomorrow. You must join us." He stood very still, looking at her.

Checking out the bargain he'd made, she thought. The candlestick trembled in her hand.

He took it before the wax could spill over her wrapper and blew out the flame. "Come outside with me. The stars are beautiful. It's a very fine night."

She was too startled to object as he took her hand and led her back to the secluded nook where they had toyed with tea that afternoon. Despite the overhanging branch, the stars were indeed beautiful—like a scattering of gems on a field of black velvet. She was startled to see that on the ground, over the patch of moss, he had laid a thick blanket he must have brought with him.

"Come and sit with me," he said. "Not the most elegant of furnishings, but more comfortable than the chair you offered me this afternoon."

She laughed, and in the faint starlight she saw him smile.

The blanket was soft, though it smelled of horses. A moss-covered hump underneath formed a natural pillow, so she lay back to better study the night sky. "I never learned their names." She pointed at the brightest of the stars. "What is that one?"

"Some other night I'll teach you about stars." His voice was thick as he stripped off his coat and boots and stretched out beside her.

Olivia studied his face, suddenly all sharp angles in the dim light. Her breath caught in anxiety. Could she go through with this?

But there was no choice left now. Whatever she wanted no longer mattered, for a man who had come so far would not be denied.

Still, his kiss was unexpectedly gentle, as soft as a spring shower, and she relaxed a little. Lying here next to him, with the scent of roses and moss and grass and horses and hay, was pleasant.

He braced himself above her and kissed her with what seemed infinite patience. He tasted her as if she were a dessert too rich to gobble—nibbling at the corners of her mouth and teasing her lips with the tip of his tongue until she relaxed and allowed him to explore.

Only then did his hand move to her wrapper, untying the belt and spreading the garment wide to expose the almost sheer fabric of her nightgown. Slowly he unlaced the bodice. Her nipples peaked as a whisper of cool air passed over them, and he palmed her breast to warm her, watching all the while.

An arc of heat ran all the way from the nipple, where his thumb lazily traced the rosy aureole, down between her legs, and she felt herself flush with embarrassment. He gave a soft chuckle and let his hand slide down over her ribs, her hip, her leg, and then back up under her nightgown. His touch was firm and masterful—he was claiming every inch of her as his. He explored her calf, her knee, her thigh. She let him spread her legs, though she bucked despite herself when he rested his palm over her mound.

"You're so soft," he whispered, and kissed her deeply once more as his fingertip slid slowly inside her. He found a most sensitive spot, and she mewled in protest. "Has no one ever touched you there before, my dear?"

He sounded surprised, and Olivia felt a wash of uneasiness as he withdrew his hand. What if he found her inadequate? Surely these were things a fallen woman should be familiar with. "I'm not much of a mistress, I fear," she confessed.

He smiled. "I assure you I do not feel the lack." He laid her palm against the front of his breeches. His erection strained the fabric, and as she felt the size of him, Olivia trembled. But a mistress had duties… Uncertain of what to do, she rubbed a little, and he pulled her hand away.

She was instantly chagrined. "I'm truly sorry. You must tell me what you like—and what you don't."

"I like *that* far too much to let you continue just now." He released himself from her. Though the night was not chilly, Olivia shivered without his strong warmth beside her. He drew her wrapper up around her shoulders.

"I don't understand." She felt breathless. "I thought…"

He knelt between her legs, and she subsided. At least she knew now what to expect, and she braced herself for his invasion.

But instead of settling on top of her, he spread her knees wider, his hands warm against the sensitive flesh at the top of her thighs. He stroked the slit of her womanhood with his thumb, and Olivia arched at the unexpectedness of his touch.

"That's the way," he whispered. "I want you wet and hot and eager when I take you."

Olivia tried not to sigh. As if he could simply command such a thing… as if she could produce such a response from sheer determination. Since she had only a vague idea of what he was talking about, how could she meet his desires?

So at this, too, she was bound to be a failure. She wondered how long he would wait before he realized what he asked was impossible. And would he be angry then?

He bent his head, and at the first flick of his tongue, she arched up from the blanket. "You're exquisitely sensitive," he murmured, and the vibrations of his voice sent a rumble through her belly as though the earth was moving under her. She tried to pull away, but he held her, and ever so gently he licked.

The delicate little nub of flesh quivered under the pressure of his tongue. Gradually she relaxed as she came to believe that however odd the sensations he was creating—however odd that he wanted to touch her *there*, and in such a way!—she would be safe from harm with him. And yet, at the same time, pressure was building inside her, and there was nothing relaxing about it. The conflicting sensations puzzled her.

He stopped for a moment, and she jerked up off the blanket. He laughed and went back to caressing her.

She felt empty, hollow, and lonely, but she knew what would make her feel better. Even as she marveled at the idea that she wanted to be possessed—to have him inside her—the need grew beyond bearing. She fumbled again, trying to reach for him, and when she could only capture his shoulder, she tugged at the fine linen of his shirt, trying to pull him up to her.

He left her then, and she was bereft for a moment until she realized he hadn't abandoned her but was only unfastening his breeches. She tried to help, running her fingertips over him to find the lacings, and he gave a breathless murmur and pushed her hand away. A moment later he stretched out on the blanket beside her, and as she turned to him, he rolled onto his back and lifted her over him.

His penis—hot and thick and urgent—nudged between her legs and found her opening, and he clutched her hips. Olivia tried not to think about the size of him, and how he would thrust into her—but he didn't press. Instead he raised her slightly and said, "Take your time."

She wriggled a little, and he groaned. Slowly, she settled down over him, taking him inside her inch by inch, feeling his heat sliding deeper inside her and meeting her own, filling her slowly and easily.

So that was what he had meant when he had said she should be wet and hot. It seemed she could do as he asked after all. And as for eager—she felt herself tighten around him, urging him deeper, and met his gaze in wonder.

His hands moved upward to cup her breasts as the full length of him slid home inside her. Her wrapper nestled closely around them like a cocoon, a dark shadow against the blanketed moss.

Slowly, he thrust and retreated, thrust and retreated, and she caught the rhythm and rode it, shifting a little to increase the sensation. Her mouth was dry, her throat tight, her breathing harsh. Something very important, she knew dimly, lay just out of her reach…

"You learn quickly." His voice was hoarse. "Come for me, Olivia."

An instant later, she knew what he meant—knew what she had been striving for. He held her hips and ground himself up inside her and held steady while she came apart as her climax took her. She cried out and threw her head back, arching against him.

When she collapsed, limp and sated, he stayed still for another few seconds before he rolled her under him. She could feel both his hunger and the tautness of his control, and she urged him on until his restraint broke and she welcomed the violence of his thrusts. Before he was finished, she was calling out along with him as another climax rolled over her.

Minutes passed before she could breathe again without gasping, and she thought from the way he lay across her that he was having some trouble getting air himself. When he shifted his weight off her, she was reluctant to let him go. But he didn't go far. He snuggled her against his side and said, "Next time we'll do better."

"Better than that?" she asked doubtfully, and he laughed and kissed her, and suddenly her body was thrumming again to his touch.

Seven

COULD THERE REALLY BE SO MANY SHOOTING STARS on a single evening, Simon wondered, or were his eyes going bad? Probably just his eyes, he decided, for nothing else seemed to be working right, either, in the wake of the most powerful orgasm he could remember. His brain was fuzzy and his muscles were limp, too.

Not that he was feeling concern about any of it. Everything had worked just fine when it counted. A little loss of vision or muscle control afterwards was a small price to pay.

He followed another flash streaking across the sky and then turned his head to see if Olivia might have seen this one or if he really was imagining things.

Her eyes were closed. Her long dark lashes lay against the curve of her cheeks, shadowed in the soft moonlight. Her breathing was even—more than he could say for his, he admitted—but she looked every bit as bonelessly relaxed as he felt.

Any minute now she would open those glorious hazel eyes—and then no doubt she'd open her outrageously kissable mouth and start making demands.

An *annuity*, for the love of God.

He'd believed that only a woman who was very experienced—and very disillusioned with her previous lovers—would even have thought of such a thing. Perhaps she'd been fobbed off with a bracelet made of paste and had decided to take no such chances in the future.

The only surprise was that she had let him sample the merchandise so thoroughly before she had her reward—for though that had been a valuable sapphire stickpin, in the overall picture it was a mere trifle. But perhaps that meant she was a skilled negotiator—for having once tasted her, there was little he wouldn't give to be allowed into her bed and into her body.

On the other hand, he'd swear the woman lying next to him was almost as innocent as a virgin— nowhere near so experienced as to have planned that strategy. At least, she had been innocent before he'd made love to her, and he was fiercely glad that he was the one who had initiated her.

Lady Reyne was a puzzle he meant to investigate. He would get to the depths of her…

In more ways than one. Almost instantly, with no more stimulation than the thought, he was hard again, eager to once more slide inside her and explore.

Her breath rasped in the tiniest and most delicate of snores, and he smiled at the evidence of how deeply her climax had relaxed her.

A long time had passed since she had been with a man; that was apparent. And she had never experienced her own pleasure before. Her husband must have been the clumsiest chump on the face of the earth. Lord

Reyne had planted a babe in her belly, but in all the important ways, he had left her entirely untouched.

And now she was Simon's to explore, and to enjoy. Tenderness swept over him. He wanted to wake her up and start all over again from the beginning, but he knew that she needed some time. She would be sensitive after their love play. And she would be stiff from the cool ground she lay on; despite the blanket, the earth beneath them was chilly.

"Olivia," he whispered. "Wake up, sweet."

Her eyelids fluttered, and she raised a hand to his face. The half-conscious gesture was an invitation, and his penis went rigid. Even if she wasn't entirely awake, *he* was—and she'd asked for it.

He quelled the baser side of himself and shifted away from her enough to wrap her in the blanket. She stirred as he picked her up, but her eyes were unfocused and she seemed not to know quite where she was.

He carried her to the house and managed to open the kitchen door without banging it. But the narrow, steep stairs gave him pause. She was not tall, but the ceiling was barely high enough to let her pass. He would have to duck his head as he carried her, throwing his balance into question. Even if he didn't fall over, how was he to get them both up the no-doubt creaky stairway silently enough to avoid disturbing the household? And which bedroom was hers? He could see three doors at the top of the stairs, with nothing to suggest which one was his destination. Perhaps he should try to wake her enough that she could walk up by herself.

A quavery, high-pitched voice spoke from the shadows at the top of the stairs. "Mama?"

The woman in his arms came instantly alert. "Charlotte?" Startled to find herself suspended in midair, Olivia struggled, and Simon set her down.

Now through the railing he could see a haze of white, something that must be a tiny nightgown. "Is that a bad man, Mama?"

"Not at all, darling. What are you doing wandering around?"

"I had a scary dream, but you weren't in your bed."

"I'm here now, pet." Without a glance at Simon, Olivia climbed the stairs and stooped at the top. The small figure melted into her as Charlotte buried her face in her mother's shoulder. Olivia looked over the railing at Simon and shook her head slightly as she picked up the child.

As though she thought he would follow her upstairs and insist on sharing her bed. Not that he didn't want to, of course.

He tiptoed out through the kitchen, collected his horse from the shed at the bottom of the garden, and rode back to Halstead in a sort of haze—wondering what had happened to him back there.

❧

Not only was Halstead full of unfamiliar sounds at night, but the country darkness was so intense that Penelope felt oppressed. Occupying a big bed so different from the one she was used to in London didn't help.

Neither did the fact that every time she closed her

eyes she couldn't stop herself from once more visualizing her husband's bare chest. Once, as she dozed off, she stretched out a hand as if to touch him—and the movement startled her awake again. She slept badly, woke later than she'd planned, and had to hurry if she was to ride with Kate and the bridesmaids.

The little housemaid who'd helped her dress for dinner did her best, but Penelope was too rushed to be patient over details like the firm lacing of a corset. When Maggie was summoned to poke a fire down the hall, Penelope waved her away and scrambled into her riding habit by herself, thanking fortune she'd chosen a design that buttoned up the front.

Kate was already in the hall when Penelope came downstairs. "You look tired, Penny."

A bridesmaid who was dawdling nearby snickered. "Perhaps she had a strenuous night," she said under her breath. "Newlyweds, you know."

Kate fixed the girl with a stern look, and the bridesmaid fluttered away toward the breakfast room.

Penelope tightened the ribbon that held her bonnet, hoping the locks of hair she'd stuffed up underneath wouldn't fall out. "I'm not as tired as you must be, Kate—dealing with all this."

"Oh, I'm all right. One day behind me, and only another four or five to go. I'm glad you're going along, Penny. The more eyes we have to watch over these girls…"

"They're quite a determined lot, aren't they?" Too late, Penelope heard someone behind her on the stairs and turned to see Lady Daphne, dressed in a daringly stylish scarlet habit. No wonder she'd come up with the idea of riding, Penelope thought. She must have wanted to show off another piece of her trousseau.

Lady Daphne's gaze slid slowly over Penelope. "I do hope after a few months of marriage *I* won't have ceased to care how I look."

Penelope tried to shrug off a surge of embarrassment. Were her buttons not straight? Was it obvious she had simply wound her hair up atop her head as best she could? "Why is it we have not yet met your husband-to-be, Lady Daphne? I thought you would wish him to be present for all the wedding festivities."

Daphne's eyes narrowed. "The marquess will arrive in time for the important parties."

Penelope wondered if the timing had been chosen for the groom's convenience or to keep him away from the covetous bridesmaids. What a scandal that would make, if one of Lady Daphne's dozen friends were to take aim at her marquess in the manner they seemed to be doing with every other eligible man at Halstead...

A peal of giggles cascaded from the breakfast room into the hall, and half a dozen bridesmaids fluttered out. In their midst were Andrew Carlisle and the Earl of Townsend, and the bridesmaids' attention seemed to be evenly divided.

So the young ladies were not only pursuing the eligible males, Penelope realized, but some ineligible ones as well.

Today the earl's coat was a shade of dark blue that matched his eyes to perfection. His buckskins were spotless, and his boots reflected the spot of sunlight that fell across the marble floor of the hall. He looked absolutely perfect, and Penelope couldn't take her gaze off him.

He paused in midstride and returned her look with a thoughtful head-to-foot appraisal that made Penelope felt even more unkempt than usual. Lady Daphne's stare had been a compliment in comparison, and she wished she had taken a few more minutes with her toilette. Not that it would have made much difference; sooner or later her hair would be falling down no matter what she did. At least no one could argue with the tailoring of her hunter-green habit or the gloss on her riding boots.

As the group trailed out to the stables, where the horses were already saddled and a row of grooms waited at attention to adjust girths and stirrups, the earl stayed a few steps behind Penelope. Though she couldn't see him, she knew he was there, and her heart skidded around in her chest.

Lady Daphne looked around the stable yard. "Where's my brother?"

The stable master ducked his head respectfully. "The duke went out half an hour ago, my lady. He said he'd meet up with you in the village."

"Oh, fie. I'd planned to take the river route down to the abbey ruins. But I suppose if we must go to the village first to collect Simon, then we must." Lady Daphne's gaze fell on Penelope. "No doubt we'll have to find some sort of cob you're capable of riding, even though you'll hold the rest of us up."

Penelope had reached her limit. "Perhaps, my lady, you should give me the most restive mount in the stable. After all, if the horse should throw and trample me, my husband might once more be free for your friends to pursue."

She felt the earl's quick movement behind her. She hadn't realized he was quite so close, and she hadn't intended for him to overhear the exchange. She felt herself start to color.

"We can't allow an accident." The earl came up beside her, running an eye over the row of horses. "May I choose a mount for you?"

Penelope held her breath. He'd never seen her on horseback; there had been little opportunity in London for her to ride. What if he, like Daphne, assumed she was only capable of controlling some fat and placid old nag?

He pointed out a trim little gray mare. "That one, I think."

Penelope nodded gratefully as he led the mare to the mounting block. "Thank you for not suggesting I'd be more at home on a hobbyhorse."

"Would you be?" he asked coolly. By the time she'd drawn a breath to answer, he had mounted a big gray gelding.

Penelope tentatively touched the mare with her heel and moved away from the stable, getting the feel of the horse. She stayed on the fringes of the group, expecting no problem in keeping her distance from the earl. But whenever she glanced around, there he was within a few lengths and always with his gaze on her. His unsmiling regard made her itchy, and her nervousness seemed to transmit itself to the mare, who sidled and shied at shadows.

Pay attention, Penelope warned herself, *unless you want to be thrown and trampled!*

By the time they reached the village, she had herself in hand and had convinced the mare that the horse was not the one in charge of the expedition. She tried not to notice the earl, who seemed to still hover at the corner of her eye, but studied the village instead.

On their arrival yesterday, they had swept down the main street so quickly that Penelope hadn't paid much attention. Now she realized what a neat and well-kept little town it was—with a row of shops, a cluster of cottages, and a small stone church surrounded by a graveyard full of tall, bristling stones. A perfect little English village, steeped in tradition.

Outside one of the cottages she spotted a pair of horses, saddled and bridled, standing by a garden gate. An urchin held the reins, but the animals seemed to pay him no heed; they pulled at his arm as they stretched over the wall to nibble at a flowering bush inside the garden. Coming down the walk from the cottage was the duke and beside him, with her hand on his arm, walked a woman in a well-worn dark habit.

"At least now we know why he was in such a hurry to get to the village," the earl said. "And what a reason she is, too."

Penelope shot a look at him and then turned to stare at the woman. Despite the slightly shabby habit, there was an air of elegance about her that sent shards of envy through Penelope. No matter what she herself did, she could never acquire that sort of polish—the smooth grace and the easy gliding walk that this woman displayed.

Lady Daphne's gaze was sharp enough to hone steel. "Who is *that*?"

"Lady Reyne." Kate sounded as if she had swallowed something large and hard. "But why is Olivia riding with the duke?"

"Perhaps because he asked her to," the earl said, and once more Penelope caught a tinge of humor in his voice.

"But he couldn't have, sir," Kate said. "The riding party was not mentioned until after dinner last night. I myself instructed Greeley to send word to the stables that horses would be required, but not until quite late in the evening."

"He has servants, Kate," Penelope pointed out. "Grooms, boot boys, footmen... Any of them would cheerfully run an errand for a few coppers."

The earl was smiling. "Especially to the village, where they can stop at the taproom for a moment. It's hardly any distance at all... for a man who has a mission."

Lady Daphne sniffed. "With Halstead full of eligible ladies, why would Simon want to ride with *her*?"

The earl turned to survey Lady Daphne as if he didn't believe what he was hearing. Then his gaze flicked once more over Lady Reyne as the duke helped her onto her horse.

A horn lady, Penelope thought. Lady Reyne was even graceful as she swung into the sidesaddle. And the way the duke was looking at her... He seemed entranced.

Nothing about his gaze was at all similar to the way the earl was looking at Penelope. "Ma'am, if I might have a word..."

Penelope said tartly, "You *are* having one." She noticed Kate's look of shock and thought better of her tone of voice. "Of course, sir." She nudged her mare to the far side of the road.

The earl followed. "You are a far better rider than you wanted Lady Daphne to believe."

That was what he had drawn her aside to say? "I thank you for noticing, my lord. Now that you've reassured yourself that I will not embarrass you by my performance, you no longer need to shadow me, and you may go about the business of entertaining Lady Daphne's friends." *Or staring at the duke's lady, which you'd seem to prefer.*

"Very well." His voice dripped irony. "Since I have your gracious permission, I shall take care of entertaining myself for the rest of the day." He touched his heel to the gelding's side and moved away.

Fool, Penelope told herself. Why had she spoken so sharply? She might have at least thanked him for choosing the mare, not some impossible mount. She could have expressed her appreciation for the confidence he had shown in her or for pretending he was concerned about her safety and her riding skills... No, for that would have been sarcastic. He *had* been concerned about her safety—and she ought to have acknowledged the fact.

And she would have, if not for the sudden dart of jealousy that had shot through her.

She watched as her husband paused beside the duke and his companion to exchange a few words. And she was very aware, as the group rode back through the village and took the first turning beyond the farthest cottage, that he did not rejoin the brides-maids but dawdled toward the rear instead. Was he once more watching… oh, what had Kate called her? Lady Reyne?

The riders trailed through a little wood, so crowded by low-hanging branches that they had to ride slowly and single file, and Penelope was barely out from under the trees when she realized the earl had not come out the other side with the rest of them.

She doubled back through the little grove and caught a glimpse of him wading his horse across a small stream a few hundred yards away.

Impossible for him to have missed the way, which meant he intended to go somewhere else instead.

The gelding splashed through the last of the water, climbed the shallow bank, and vanished through a small break in the underbrush.

Penelope glanced over her shoulder. The group of riders was no longer in sight, and no one seemed to have missed her.

She turned the mare toward the stream and followed her husband.

∽

For a moment when Olivia first woke, she thought she'd dreamed about the garden and the duke. Then she stretched and realized her muscles were sore. Lots of muscles, all over her. Her elbow bumped against a small, warm bundle, and she remembered the end of the evening—Charlotte's nightmare and how instead of trying to settle the child back into her own bed, Olivia had taken the little girl in with her instead.

Remorse swept over her. She'd been out in the garden consorting with a man when her baby needed her.

The only thing worse, she reminded herself, would have been if the duke had been with Olivia in her bed when Charlotte came looking for her mother. At least she'd been spared the need to explain *that*.

In fact, Olivia realized, the entire episode could be viewed as a gift—a clear message that she could not continue on this course. Though she was fortunate disaster hadn't struck last night, only a fool would take such a risk again. How could she have imagined even for an instant that she could carry off an affair in the close confines of the cottage with no one being the wiser?

"Mama." Charlotte sat up and yawned. "There was a bad man last night."

"It was only a dream, darling. You're perfectly safe. Come along. You can help me fix your breakfast."

Nurse was already in the kitchen, where she had built up the fire and set a pot of porridge boiling. She looked Olivia in the eye and said, "I don't know how Miss Charlotte got out of the nursery this morning without rousing me, but it won't happen again."

Olivia wished she herself could feel as certain. If Nurse hadn't even realized it wasn't morning when Charlotte had wandered off but the middle of the night instead… "You must have been sleeping very soundly."

"I was that scared when I found her gone." Nurse's voice shook a little. "Even after I peeked in and saw she was with you…"

Olivia scooped porridge into a bowl and set it on the table to cool.

"I want to make breakfast," Charlotte muttered, but at Nurse's look, she subsided into her chair and stirred the concoction.

Olivia tied on an apron and cut a slice of bread from yesterday's baking. "The laundry can wait until tomorrow, but the grapes won't keep. If we're to have grape juice and jelly this winter…"

So much for the idea of a ride this morning, of being out in the countryside enjoying nature and fresh air. Had she ever really let herself believe she might have such an outing? In any case, if the duke did appear this morning…

As if the thought had summoned him, a shadow fell across the kitchen door and the duke loomed up outside.

Charlotte's spoon stopped moving as her big brown eyes focused on the duke. "I remember you."

Olivia froze.

"You caught me when I fell off the wall."

The incident hadn't unfolded quite that way, of course. Memory was an odd thing, and Olivia thought perhaps that was just as well. "Charlotte, practice your curtsey to His Grace, please."

"You are not ready to ride, Lady Reyne. Is there a problem?"

The duke's rich, deep voice wrapped around Olivia as warmly as the blanket had the night before, and suddenly she felt hot and tense. This was not how she had envisioned their next encounter.

No, you imagined meeting in a quiet corner where other people couldn't intrude, where you could enjoy making love forever with no threat of interruption…

"I can't go, Your Grace. I have my daughter to

look after and far too much to do. This floor needs scrubbing, and we have grape jelly to make."

He said quietly, "Am I to understand you're going back on your word?"

"I…" She shot a look at Nurse. "Please get Miss Charlotte dressed while her breakfast cools enough to eat."

He waited until they were alone and then moved a little closer. "What happened between us last night does not fulfill the bargain we made, Lady Reyne."

"I know." She felt herself color. "That was just the—added spice."

"Perhaps you're telling me you didn't enjoy that *spice*?"

She would be wasting breath to say so. Even if Olivia could bend her tongue around the untruth, this arrogant male would never believe her. In any case, an unvarnished announcement would doubtless carry more weight than any logic or argument. "Do not fear that I shall try to cheat you, Your Grace. You don't owe me anything. The truth is I simply can't go on."

"If you do not have a distaste for my lovemaking, then it must have been your child waking that upset you so and changed your mind."

Olivia nodded. "Nurse was abjectly apologetic this morning, but the fact is… Well, she was my own nurse when I was a child, and though Charlotte loves her—"

"Perhaps she's too old to look after such an active sprite as your daughter?"

"If her only duty was to look after Charlotte, I wouldn't be so concerned, but in such a small household Nurse has many responsibilities. It's no surprise if sometimes she sleeps too soundly to hear Charlotte stirring. However, if Charlotte were to stray again and Nurse didn't hear her, and I was not at hand... I cannot take the chance."

"Certainly not."

How very odd, Olivia thought, that his stern pronouncement didn't engender even a whisper of relief. Surely she should feel reassured because he understood her dilemma.

She told herself she was only upset because the affair would have been such a sensible way to solve all her financial problems. This letdown she was feeling was nothing personal. She couldn't possibly be *disappointed*.

"Miss Charlotte needs more than one person to look after her," the duke said. "I will make arrangements."

"But... Wait. What arrangements can you possibly make? If you're thinking I need a nursery maid, please stop right now. I can't afford another servant."

He smiled, and Olivia felt her heart rock like a baby doll in a cradle. "Of course you can," he said gently. "You're to receive an annuity, remember?"

She said tartly, "All right, someday I'll be able to afford another maid. But the fact is that everyone in the district who is able to work is already employed at Halstead. Remember the maid who admitted you yesterday? She's gone to work for Mrs. Greeley."

"Have you paper and ink, Lady Reyne? I wish to send a message."

The way he said her name made Olivia's toes curl. Though he sounded perfectly respectful, the underlying note of sensuality rubbed her like velvet brushing her skin. He hadn't so much as touched her this morning, but every inch of her body was alert—especially her breasts, her hips, and the secret spots he had caressed so thoroughly last night…

"Paper?" he repeated. "Ink?"

Annoyed for letting herself be distracted by the husky note in his voice, Olivia snapped, "I'm poor, Your Grace, not destitute." Charlotte bounded back into the kitchen, with Nurse close behind. "Run into the sitting room, darling, and bring paper and ink for His Grace. Careful with the inkwell, mind."

"Go and put on your habit while I write my message, Lady Reyne. The horses are standing, and the other riders will be along at any moment." There was an unmistakable note of command underlying the duke's soft tone. "You said you wouldn't cheat me, my lady—and I shall hold you to your promise."

❧

Kate watched in astonishment as the duke gently settled Olivia into the sidesaddle, adjusting the length of her stirrup with his own hands. He had brushed aside the groom who came running up to help, to take care of Lady Reyne himself.

No wonder the stable master hadn't dared to look Lady Daphne in the face when he'd told her that her brother had already ridden to the village. No wonder he hadn't volunteered the fact that the duke had taken a lady's mount with him…

Kate stole a glance at Daphne and was not surprised to see her looking dazed. Kate felt the same way. The last time she'd seen Olivia and the duke together, they'd been sniping at each other over diamond bracelets; the time before that, they'd been quarreling over Charlotte. Now they seemed suddenly on the best of terms.

A roan gelding sidled up beside Kate's mare, so close that the white cuff atop Andrew Carlisle's boot brushed the folds of her habit. "Have you any notion what the duke is planning? Who is she, anyway?"

"Perhaps you should ask His Grace to introduce you. But I wouldn't suggest flirting with Lady Reyne. She's a widow and therefore available." Andrew looked puzzled, and Kate was ashamed of herself. "I overheard you and Lady Townsend last night as you walked her to her door," she explained without quite looking at him. "You said you were sorry you could not attend her wedding, because if you'd had the opportunity you might have stolen her away from her husband, and..."

Andrew smiled. "And she asked me whether I flirt with every woman I meet or only the ones who are safely out of reach. Yes, Penny Wise made it clear that whatever else she might be, she's not a fool. But I am flattered you hovered nearby to listen, Kate. Where were you? I ask only because I find it difficult to believe I didn't notice you. Somewhere near the top of Halstead's stairway there must be a hidden corner."

"A spot which might prove useful for a gazetted flirt like yourself to know about," Kate agreed. "However, I have no intention of telling you."

"Why not? Because it's so convenient for eavesdropping? Or because you'd rather show me?"

Kate's fingers twitched on her riding crop.

Andrew eyed her. "None of that, mind. Far too much comment would ensue if you slashed at me with your whip."

Kate smiled at him and turned to survey her charges. Things had come to a pretty pass when she looked forward to the bridesmaids' antics to take her mind off Andrew Carlisle...

"What a shame Lady Stone chose not to accompany us this morning," Andrew said. "She'd have had a grand time betting on which of the bridesmaids will fall off her horse first."

Despite Kate's best efforts, a bubble of laughter escaped her.

Andrew's gaze had slid back to the duke. "So Lady Reyne is available, is she? I must find out what sort of game Simon is playing." He touched his heel to the roan and trotted off, clearly intending to catch up with the duke and Olivia.

Suddenly Kate didn't feel like laughing any more.

Eight

When one of the grooms rushed up to help Lady Reyne into her saddle, Simon had to restrain himself from slapping the man's hand away. He settled for stepping between them, and when the groom looked puzzled, Simon held out the note he'd written at Olivia's kitchen table. "Take this message back to Mrs. Greeley at Halstead."

The groom touched his hat and rode off. Simon took his time in helping Olivia into her saddle and was rewarded with the smallest glimpse of a smooth stocking and the curve of her calf. Once he had all the straps right, he took hold of her heel and guided her boot into the stirrup.

She surveyed him quizzically. "Are you quite satisfied my foot is in the right spot, Your Grace?"

The boot was warm from her heat, tempting him to explore. Simon wanted to run his hand further up under the draped folds of her habit. He was standing between her and the rest of the group, and surely the breadth of his shoulders would keep anyone from seeing…

But a fleeting touch would not satisfy, so he gave the worn leather a last pat and stepped away.

"You have not told me what you wrote in your message," Olivia said as he swung up into his own saddle.

"Your maid will be back at the cottage by the time you return."

She frowned, and for a moment suspicion flickered in the corners of Simon's mind. Had she expected him to offer something else? Something more?

"I'm not convinced Maggie will appreciate the change of duties, sir. She was looking forward to the possibility of vails when your guests left."

"I shall make up the loss of income to her. I also requested Mrs. Greeley to provide you with enough grape jelly to satisfy your household for an entire year. I hope you have ample pantry space to store it."

She laughed, and Simon felt his distrust fade away.

Lady Daphne kneed her horse up beside him. "How very strange that you seem on such good terms with Lady Reyne, Simon, when we've heard nothing of her before."

"You shouldn't be surprised, Daphne. I'm far more discreet than you credit me for being. Lady Reyne and I danced together years ago at a London ball. And of course you've heard of her—you must have, because you invited her to your wedding."

Daphne gave a little snort and pushed her horse into a trot, startling the riders around her. "Come along, everyone. We're heading for the abbey ruins."

"I thought I taught her to ride better than that," Simon muttered.

"She looks beautiful in the saddle," Olivia said.

"Not the same thing at all. A true beauty wouldn't risk injury to the horses or to other riders. Take you, for instance…"

"Are you paying me lavish compliments, Your Grace? And here I thought you prided yourself on being discreet. So discreet, in fact, that even I did not notice this first meeting of ours. It was years ago, you said?"

"Don't be foolish, my dear. Of course you remember a country dance during your first Season."

"My *only* Season. And if you're going to invent stories about a romantic encounter at a ball, cannot you at least make it a waltz we shared?"

"If we had waltzed, I never would have let you go. Pray, my lady, do not break my heart by claiming you cannot remember our first dance. Or at least, please don't tell my mother or sister you can't recall it."

"I would not have…" She broke off, her face going slightly pink.

"Were you about to say you could not have forgotten dancing with me?" Simon was charmed. Olivia Reyne was full of surprises. He wondered how long he would take to discover them all. Perhaps he shouldn't have put a time limit on their affair.

But in fact, he realized, he hadn't. He'd said he wanted to pretend to court her until the wedding was over, that was true. But after the vows were said, while Daphne and her marquess honeymooned, the guests would scatter across the country once more and the duchess would go off to visit friends. There would be nothing to prevent him from lingering on at Halstead. He could arrange trysts and rides and outings…

As the first riders wound into a small grove outside the village where they could ride only in single file, he dropped back far enough to admire Olivia's form and the lush curves of her bottom in the worn wool habit. Desire stirred, and he tried to remember the abbey ruins. Was there a private corner somewhere to be found? And just how difficult would it be to lure Olivia there, if only for a kiss?

Not that a kiss would satisfy him. But he could wait for the rest.

❦

Wherever the earl was going, Penelope realized he knew the way. After crossing the little stream and threading through the underbrush beyond, she dawdled at the edge of an open field to watch while he crossed it and then hurried to follow. She had to push the mare to keep up with the gelding's steady trot, and every time the horse and rider vanished for a moment, her heart went to her throat. What if she lost sight of him entirely? She wasn't enough of a countrywoman to know the necessary tricks to retrace her route.

She'd been so absorbed in following his path—while trying not to be seen herself—that she'd paid little attention to the direction, other than to realize they were not headed back toward Halstead but across country. They were riding south, she thought, though it was close enough to midday that even checking the position of the sun didn't help much.

She stopped to look around for landmarks and realized she had lost sight of him again. Ahead of her, the narrow path twisted. Perhaps, just around that bend, she could catch a glimpse again and reassure herself. She leaned forward, urging the mare to greater speed…

And came around the corner to find her husband waiting for her, his horse drawn up at the side of the road.

She opened her mouth to explain and realized nothing she could say was adequate, so she closed it again.

"Very wise," the earl said. "As a hunter, you lack finesse."

Penelope bit her lip. "How long have you known I was following you?"

"A while."

"Not all that long," she argued, "or you would have stopped and sent me back."

"I'd have *taken* you back. However, I had no wish to call attention to the fact that I had left the group."

"You told the duke you were going. I saw you."

"Only so he could prevent consternation if I was found to be missing."

"That's all right, then. If anyone misses me, they won't be in the least concerned."

"I imagine they will be highly amused at the notion that we rode off together—the newlyweds wishing to be alone."

"Of course," Penelope said drearily. "So tell me where we're going."

The earl clucked to his horse and set off down the road. "No."

"Since I don't seem to be welcome, I think I'll go back."

"Suit yourself," he said over his shoulder, "though the notion of being an uninvited guest does not seem to have disturbed you when you chose to come along on this expedition."

Penelope's bravado faded as quickly as it had flared up. She had no notion where she was or how to get back to Halstead. She caught up with him before the next turn of the road. "I'm sorry, my lord," she said miserably.

He was silent for a while. "Perhaps you should see this."

They rode for another mile or so—Penelope was no judge of distance in the country—before he drew up his horse at the crest of a hill and looked out over the narrow valley beyond. At the far end, perched on the long slope, was a manor house dating from Queen Elizabeth's time, a massive, wonderful pile of brown brick. Towers on each corner wore Tudor caps—at least they should have done, Penelope thought. A closer look revealed that two of the four were missing, and in one wing, boards had been nailed where windows should have gleamed.

"Stoneyford," he said quietly. "My family's estate, going to ruin. I can't sell it, for it's entailed—and I wouldn't sell even if I could, for it is my heritage and my responsibility. Every penny that comes in from the land must be reinvested there to keep the place going, which means small hope of ever again making enough profit to repair the house."

She had known there must be an estate, for an earl always had a manor house and land somewhere. But Penelope couldn't recall giving the matter any further thought, and he had never mentioned the country. "What happened to it?"

"What usually happens to landed estates. My grandfather was a gambler. He sold off all of the unentailed property to pay for his fondness for cards and dice. My father was unwilling to admit the reality, so he continued to spend as though the estate was in fine form. By the time I inherited the title, the house was very much as you see it now. I sold the contents before they could deteriorate further and used the proceeds to board the place up."

And then you thought to mend matters by marrying a fortune, only to find you could not bear the woman who came along with the money...

"This is what you wanted from my father," she said slowly. "This is what you asked for, in the letter you wrote him."

"I hoped he would assist me to improve the land so the estate can once more stand on its own. But he refused."

My terms are clear, Ivan Weiss had said. He had meant he would not help to fund his son-in-law's estate unless there was a child to inherit.

"I can't even lease the house to bring in a little cash," he went on, "for as you see, it is falling down."

The walls were still straight, and the roof appeared solid. But even Penelope's inexperienced eye could see the task of restoring the manor would not be easy or inexpensive.

"I'd like to see it." She didn't wait for an answer, in case he tried to discourage her, but nudged her horse down the slope.

The day was beautiful, and the vista as they rode across the valley tugged at Penelope's senses. The land looked like a quilt pieced from an infinite variety of greens—crops and grasslands, trees and meadows, threaded together by the thin blue glint of a narrow river running lazily, half-concealed by tall marsh grasses. Not far from the house the river widened and shallowed, rippling over half-exposed rocks—the stony ford that must have given the house its name.

What should have been the front lawn of Stoneyford had become a hay field instead, and a half-dozen men were forking the dried grass onto a cart as Penelope and the earl rode up. One of the men stood straight and saluted; the others bowed their heads and tugged at their hats. "Welcome home, sir," the leader said. "It's past time you brought your lady to see Stoneyford."

The earl only nodded in answer. As one of the men took the horses, the earl pulled out a big key and unlocked the front door.

All through the house was the scent of stale air and dust and neglect. In a few rooms, wallpaper had peeled because of the damp air and now trailed in ribbons across the floor. Dust lay thick on the few remaining pieces of furniture, most of which must have been too old and threadbare to sell, and dimmed the windows. The floors were bare of rugs, and darker patches here and there on the walls showed where paintings must once have hung.

Only a huge fireplace and a few mismatched bits of armor remained in the great hall, but the carved paneling was intact and looked to still be in fair condition. The dining room held nothing at all, but the kitchen showed signs of occupation.

"There's a caretaker," the earl said when Penelope cast a questioning look at him. "An old fellow, one of the tenants who can't work the land anymore. He tries to keep an eye on things, but housekeeping is hardly his strong suit. Mainly he's here to discourage anyone from poking around and getting hurt."

After that, Penelope was more careful to watch where she stepped.

The staircase would have greatly benefitted from wax and elbow grease, she thought. Still, the newel post and banister were huge and heavy, and the stairs felt solid beneath her feet.

Though the house was not as large as Halstead, she lost count of bedchambers and almost lost herself in a warren of rooms at the back of the house—servants' quarters and box rooms and storerooms and twisting little staircases that led up to attics and garrets and down to stillrooms and pantries.

Finally she returned to the front of the house, where the grandest suite of rooms looked out over the hay field. At least, these had once been the grandest, with silk hangings and hand-painted wall coverings, so the house's change of fortune showed up most arrestingly here.

She stood in a doorway and looked thoughtfully at the largest bed she had ever seen. The hangings were so faded she couldn't tell what color they had been. "I'm surprised this is still here."

"It was too large to remove. My grandfather had it built right inside the room."

"Well, at least he left you something." Penelope turned her back on the devastation and went downstairs, letting her glove trail lightly along the banister as she descended. The leather would never be the same, she thought, looking at the dust she'd picked up.

And yet...

The earl stopped to talk to the men who were finishing up the haying. Penelope stood by the sagging front steps and studied the front facade of the house while she waited for him.

It was not an elegant house nor—strictly speaking—a beautiful one, especially in its present condition. It must have always been more utilitarian than graceful.

But Stoneyford spoke to her in a way the imposing new townhouse in London never had. Stoneyford must have once been the sort of home where dogs could flop down on the hearth rug and drool without anyone getting upset, and where children could play hide-and-seek or wheedle sweets from the cook or hold pretend jousting meets in the great hall on rainy days...

She caught herself in midsigh.

"You've been very patient," the earl said as he boosted her back into the saddle. "I'm used to seeing the house in ruins, of course, or at least I thought I was, until... At any rate, I'm surprised you didn't scream and run."

"Tell me about it," Penelope said. "Tell me about Stoneyford."

❧

The group of riders crossed fields and trailed along lanes so narrow that they had to ride single file. Kate had dropped to the back of the line so she could more easily keep count of her charges—and stay well away from Andrew. But as she approached the top of the last hill, she realized Andrew had been quietly sitting on his horse in the shadow of a huge old oak tree right at the crest. Her heartbeat speeded up at the thought that he had waited for her, but she told herself it was foolish to read hidden meanings into casual actions.

He nudged his gelding toward her, and they climbed to the top of the hill together. "Did you discover the duke's secret plan?" Kate kept her voice light.

"No. He just told me to go away."

He sounded quite calm, but Kate wondered if he would have preferred to hover about Olivia. Not that she cared.

She paused at the crest of the hill to look down across the ruined abbey. From this vantage point, the half-fallen walls formed an almost geometric labyrinth, a pattern of long roofless corridors flanked by multitudes of small rooms.

Kate drew a long breath. "Oh, dear. They'll be able to get lost in that tangle of hallways with no effort at all."

"It's beautiful. Look at the way the light falls across the stones, and the pattern of sunshine and shadow."

Kate looked again. Andrew was right; caught up in her responsibilities, she had seen only the risks presented by the ruin, not the beauty of sun-warmed stone heaped against rich green grass, or the sparkle of light on the river beyond. She let her gaze wander across the vista and felt her heart warm.

"There is a serenity about England," he said softly, "that feeds the soul in a way more exotic landscapes cannot."

She turned slowly to look at him. "So you *have* traveled and seen exotic places."

"As well as many that are neither exotic nor beautiful."

"But you told the bridesmaids you're an ordinary tutor."

Andrew's smile flashed. "On the contrary, Kate. I told them I didn't know enough Latin to teach it. You know quite well I'm telling the truth there."

She did indeed. Latin was only one of the subjects in which Andrew had been faltering during that long-ago summer he had spent at Halstead. But it seemed to be the one he and the vicar spent the most time reviewing. Each day, the vicar would release Simon from servitude and keep Andrew behind for a bit more practice.

And each day, Kate would manage to be nearby when his lessons were finally finished. Sometimes they shared only a word or a smile. Sometimes he lingered to talk with her about her book or her work. Sometimes he walked her to a parishioner's cottage.

Once… just once… in the garden behind the vicarage, he had kissed her.

And after that, as if that kiss had frightened him, he had made certain never to be alone with her again. For a while, she had continued to haunt the vicar's study at the end of the day—until Lady Daphne had gleefully told her how silly she looked and what a foolish girl Andrew thought she was…

Water under the bridge, Kate reminded herself. "If you

were not teaching the standard subjects, what sort of instruction did you provide Lord Winchester's sons?"

"He wanted the boys to be informed about the family business—including the pineapple plantation in Antigua, which I visited last spring because Lord Winchester did not care to leave his new bride."

"He's your employer, then?"

"Not precisely. He does not like to travel, and I do. He has considerable property he does not care to visit, and I am happy to take his place."

"How fortunate you are to have such a patron."

Andrew grinned. "Indeed. The only thing that would make my situation better is if I could convince him to invest in Brazil, so I would have an excuse to canoe up the Amazon... Shall we race to the bottom of the hill?"

~∞~

The abbey, built of native stone, had once loomed over the wide level plain adjoining the river. Now few of the walls stood more than head high, but the remains still formed a formidable maze. "I know why the stones look so familiar," Olivia said as she and the duke rounded a bend in what must once have been a long and twisting hallway. The stone floor had been overtaken by moss and grass, and she had to watch her footing. "It's because I see the same shapes and colors every day in my own cottage."

The duke nodded. "When the abbey was closed down and the abbots dispersed, scavengers hauled away enough stones to build Steadham village."

"It must have taken hundreds of cartloads." She

looked around. "I should be helping Kate to keep an eye on the bridesmaids."

"Even with their genius for troublemaking, they will take time to get into mischief."

"You're only saying that because at the moment you feel safe from their schemes."

He smiled. "It's true I can't be cornered as long as I have you to protect me." He drew her around a corner into what must have once been an abbot's cell. Now it was open to the sky, but the walls in this section remained stronger and taller than the surrounding ones.

Olivia shivered. "It's chilly in the shadows."

"Come here and kiss me," the duke said softly, "and you won't be chilly any more."

She stood her ground. "I'm quite hopeless as a mistress, aren't I? How is it, sir, that I did not anticipate your intentions?"

"I told you I was discreet. If you won't come to me, my lady..." He closed the distance between them, and before Olivia could move, he'd swept her into his arms. "And you are far from hopeless." His mouth brushed hers softly before he turned his attention to her temple, her ear, and the hollow under her cheekbone.

"If you think I'm going to make love with you here," Olivia began, "with a dozen people just outside that wall—"

The duke went still, his lips pressed against her eyelid. "I was going to say you require only practice to be the ideal mistress, but suddenly I'm inclined to think you've already learned it all. Do enlarge on this fantasy of yours, my dear, for I find it quite arousing to think of you seducing me in an abbot's cell."

"Me, seducing *you*? I just said…" Olivia gasped as he nibbled from her chin to the hollow at the base of her throat and beyond. How had he released the buttons down the front of her bodice without her noticing? Cool air flowed over her breasts, but she barely had time to register the chill before he warmed them once more with his hands and his mouth. She tried again. "Do you always make love outdoors, Your Grace?"

"Hardly ever. But since you seem to prefer it…"

Olivia's throat closed up as he traced a slow, erotic circle with his tongue around the eager tip of her breast. Shafts of heat shot through her and pooled between her legs, and suddenly it seemed quite a good idea to pull him down on the stone floor. "We can't," she moaned.

"If I reached under your dress right now, Olivia, would I find you are as ready as I am?"

I want you wet and hot and eager, he had told her before making love to her in her garden. Now she knew exactly what he meant, and if she hadn't already been aroused, his question would have been sufficient to do so.

He seemed to find her silence answer enough. He drew her closer and kissed her deeply, his tongue sampling her in gentle contrast to the hardness of his erection resting insistently against her belly. Then he said, "Regrettably, you are correct—we can't. And it was never my intention to do so. I meant only to steal a kiss."

Olivia gave a little shriek and tried to stamp on his foot.

He only held her more firmly. "As stolen kisses go, my dear, that was remarkable. For the rest of my life, whenever the abbey is mentioned, I shall remember your fantasy and picture you lying on this bed of moss as I make love to you. Unless you would care to return with me one day so I won't have rely on imagination?"

"Of course not, Your Grace." Olivia's voice felt raspy.

He laughed and let her go. In the midst of her relief, there was a thread of regret that Olivia refused to think about right now.

He leaned out of the cell to survey the twisting passageway outside. "No one is in sight. It's safe enough for you to go and meet up with a few of those dozen people now—but I shall have to wait a while before I rejoin you."

Her gaze flicked down to the front of his breeches.

"Looking at me like that won't help. It is odd, I grant, but it seems you don't even need to be touching me to make me more aroused. I wonder if the same works in reverse. If I simply look at you…"

Olivia didn't wait for him to experiment. She ducked through the door of the abbot's cell and out into the passageway. Just around the first turn, she came face to face with Andrew Carlisle and a trio of bridesmaids.

Olivia fell into step with them just as Kate spoke from the shadow of a half-fallen wall. "The footmen are setting up the picnic."

"Already?" When Olivia saw Kate's sharp look, she would have given anything to take back the comment. How much time had passed while she and the duke lingered in that quiet little cell, anyway?

The outdoor luncheon was the most elaborate

Olivia had ever seen. Several small tables complete with starched linens had been set up in what must have once been the abbey's dining hall, and the tidbits the footmen served were as dainty as anything to be found in the dining room of a fine estate.

Olivia's chair was directly across from the duke's, and though she tried not to look at him, she was quite aware he was watching her. *I wonder*, he had said, *if I simply look at you...*

She hoped he didn't realize how very effective his technique was. She felt hot and cold at the same time, and she could barely taste anything, much less swallow. Still, when the meal was finally over, she complimented Daphne on her choices.

"It was all well enough," Daphne responded indifferently as she collected a couple of friends so they could go off to further explore the ruins.

Much to Olivia's relief, Andrew Carlisle drew the duke aside, leaving her free to turn to Kate. "You must be the one who really organized the picnic, Kate."

"Perhaps I should become a housekeeper," Kate mused, "for my other options for employment don't seem to be showing much promise. Walk with me so I can follow the bridesmaids at a discreet distance."

"I'm sorry. I should have been helping you earlier." *Instead of playing delightful games in the abbot's cell...*

"I'm growing used to dealing with them on my own. Most of them are only heedless, not truly troublesome. And I'm not complaining, mind you— neither you nor Penny were foolish enough to agree to this job."

"Penny? Have I met her?"

Kate looked around. "I wonder where she disappeared to... Penny is Lady Townsend, and if you haven't been introduced, I expect you soon will—if the duke continues on this course. What is going on, Olivia? One minute you and His Grace are at dagger's point, and the next it appears he's—well—courting you."

Olivia tried to look innocent. "Strange, isn't it?"

"But he can't mean it, Olivia. Simon and you... No, that's just impossible."

For a moment Olivia was hurt that her friend was so certain—and she wondered if, despite Kate's assertion that she had no personal interest in the Duke of Somervale, she was now discovering she was jealous. It worried Olivia to think that Kate might be hurt by something that wasn't even real.

"Olivia, do take a warning to heart. Simon is extraordinarily charming, and he's far too used to having his own way. I cannot think he is serious in this."

"Of course he isn't serious. Don't trouble your head over it, Kate. I know exactly what I'm doing."

Kate looked at her for a long moment and then shook her head and led the way on through the ruins. At the moment, not a bridesmaid was within sight, but somewhere in front of them Olivia could hear a pair of girlish voices. She couldn't quite distinguish the words, but something in the tone of voice warned her there might be mischief afoot.

As they drew closer, she could make out the words. "Didn't the duke come this way?" one of the bridesmaids asked.

The other said, "Perhaps we missed the turning and ended up in the wrong corridor. I wonder..."

"I meant to ask you, Horatia, what did the earl mean this morning about accidents?"

The other laughed. "Don't be simple, Emily. Of course he can't allow anything to happen to Penny Wise. Not until she inherits from her father, at least."

"*Penny Wise*?" Olivia asked softly as they came up to a turn in the walkway. "Is that—"

Before her eyes, the wall seemed to bend, creaking and groaning. Falling stones rattled down and dust billowed as the ancient structure collapsed. Kate's eyes widened, and her fingers clenched tight on Olivia's arm.

They rounded a corner as one of the bridesmaids hurried toward them. "Emily's hurt," Horatia gasped. "Oh, do come quickly. She's on the ground—and she's lying awfully still!"

❧

The earl did not regale Penelope with memories of the days when Stoneyford had been a home, but he did at least answer when she asked a question. Sometimes the answer was very brief, and she learned as much from what he didn't say, or even simply from the tone of his voice, as from what he told her. After a while, she began to keep a sort of mental tally. Old servants, rain on the roof, a particular pony, sledding down the long hill from the house to the river's edge—those seemed to be his best memories from Stoneyford.

After a while, however, he said, "You've gone quiet. You must be quite tired of the sound of my voice after five miles of hearing nothing else."

"Not at all," she said honestly. "But I must own to being hungry, for I missed breakfast. How far are we from Halstead, my lord?"

"Another five miles at least."

"Then we can't possibly reach the abbey in time for Lady Daphne's picnic, either."

"A village lies not far off our path, with an inn where we can bespeak a meal."

The coaching inn where they stopped was small but neatly kept, with pale pink flowers spilling from wooden boxes under each window. The earl lifted Penelope down from her sidesaddle, and she would have been relieved to be on firm ground again had she not been so stiff she could barely walk. She managed just two steps before she staggered and almost fell in the middle of the yard.

The earl swept her up in his arms, and suddenly stiff muscles were the least of Penelope's concerns. She'd had no difficulty with breathing until he picked her up, but suddenly her chest was tight and every inhalation took so much effort she simply wanted to lay her head on his shoulder.

Before she could make up her mind to experiment, he'd carried her inside the inn. The landlord rushed to open the door of a private parlor, and the earl laid Penelope down on the sofa. "My apologies," he said. "You are not accustomed to days spent entirely in the saddle."

I could become *accustomed to it*, Penelope thought, *if this was the result!*

But the earl moved away to discuss their meal with the landlord, and Penelope forced herself to sit up and wiggle her feet. By the time the landlord had brought a bottle of Bordeaux, the stiffness had eased and she could walk across the room.

The earl poured a glass and held it out. "This may be stronger than you're accustomed to, but it will help to restore you."

Penelope accepted the goblet and sipped warily. The wine's bouquet was rich and fruity, and the liquid warmed her as she swallowed. The parlor was quiet except for the crackle of a small, neat fire.

"Perhaps you would like to take off your hat," he suggested.

Penelope shook her head, remembering the hasty way she had rolled her hair up that morning and shoved the loose ends under her bonnet. She swallowed another mouthful of the sweet wine and felt relaxation course through her veins.

She closed her eyes and imagined herself on the hillside, looking across the long green valley to where Stoneyford stood, looking lonely and abandoned. It was wrong, she thought, for a house like that one— once a home—to be left to sink quietly into ruin.

"You would like to see Stoneyford restored, my lord," she said finally.

"I have accepted the facts. Seeing the house again as it stands today, I know it is not to be."

"It's damaged. But I don't see why it couldn't be saved."

The earl refilled his glass. "Beware of being overcome by romantic notions. Strange though it may sound, I assure you that today we saw the house at its best. If you had been introduced to it on a December day with a gale whipping down the valley, I hardly think you would be dreaming of rescuing it."

Penelope had no difficulty drawing the picture he had evoked. Icicles dangled threateningly from every eave and overhang. A sharp-edged wet wind swirled down the cold, bleak chimneys. Snow crystals piled on the window ledges and seeped in around ill-fitting panes to drift inside the rooms.

Distressed, she blinked and the picture faded. Perhaps he was right, she thought reluctantly. Sometimes things *were* past saving.

The landlord returned with a maid and a pair of loaded trays.

The food smelled wonderful, though it was very simple—dark bread and sharp cheese, a plain roasted chicken, baked apples strong with cinnamon and wrapped in a flaky crust. But the fare reminded her of the simpler days of her childhood, before her father had made up his mind to marry her to a title. Or perhaps, she admitted honestly, she couldn't really remember a time before Ivan Weiss's dream had taken shape. She suspected he had begun to plan on the day she was born; he just hadn't spoken of the idea to her until far later.

Plain food for a plain woman… the two things were well suited. And, Penelope thought, Stoneyford fit into that pattern as well.

Suddenly the picture in her mind reformed—but it had shifted. Snow and wind still rattled outside the house, but she was inside where the rooms were warm and bright, fragrant with wood smoke and warm wax and pine boughs. She could see the glint of candlelight against the shiny green of holly wreaths and the white berries of mistletoe, and she was surrounded by people. Laughing, happy people.

Imagine the house in December, the earl had suggested, and she had done so. But she had pictured Christmas at Stoneyford.

She tore more bread from the loaf and rolled it between her fingers just to keep her hands occupied. "How much money would be required?" Her voice felt a little husky.

"Stoneyford?" He sounded wary. "Why are you lingering on the question?"

Penelope shrugged. "Because I like the house."

"Your father has made his position clear. I will not go back to him to beg for funds." He drained his wineglass and reached for the bottle. "Nor will you, for I will not allow it."

He wouldn't *allow* her to ask her father for money? Penelope bristled for an instant. But she had no intention of asking Ivan Weiss for money or permission, so there was no point in getting upset with the earl for telling her she couldn't.

"I'm not talking about my father's fortune." She held out her goblet to be refilled. "I have some money of my own."

He looked from the wine bottle to her face and filled her glass only halfway. "Your pin money, you mean? I hardly think—"

"No, though I seldom spend all my allowance. But to be accurate, I should have said I have things of value. Remember the brooch my father brought me this week, the one with the big yellow diamond?"

"I've found it difficult to forget that ornament."

"The setting is unfortunate, but the stone is good—and since it was a gift, I can do as I like with it. If I would rather have Stoneyford rebuilt than own a yellow diamond that I will never wear, then it's my business, not my father's."

She thought the silence in the parlor would go on forever, interrupted only by the snap of a log in the fireplace and the gurgle of wine as the earl refilled his goblet. He looked down into the glass as if it were a crystal ball and he was looking at the future.

When he finally spoke, his voice was quiet. "What do you want in return?"

Penelope realized she should have anticipated the question. Their entire marriage was a bargain, and she knew it had been so from the first time Ivan Weiss had approached the Earl of Townsend. Why should her husband view this discussion as anything else?

In any case, she wasn't truly upset by the idea of bartering; perhaps some of her father's business instinct had passed on to her after all. *What do you want, Penny Wise?* she asked herself.

If she demanded too much, he would walk away. If she asked for too little, he might laugh at her…

I want you to talk to me every day the way you have talked to me today.

She opened her mouth, but what came out was not what she had intended to say. "Just once, I want to know how it feels to be a wife."

The earl went as still as a frozen lake.

Penelope could have cheerfully swallowed her tongue, but whatever had made her utter that incredible sentence was still in charge, for she couldn't stop. "Only once," she whispered.

When he neither moved nor looked at her, she turned her back and tried to fight off tears. She would not cry; Penny Wise had not cried when the girls at school had ridiculed her, and she would not give in to weakness now.

The earl set down his goblet with a thump that seemed to Penelope's heightened senses to shake the table. He strode across the room and reached for the bell pull.

He'll send for the reckoning, she thought. And then they would ride back to Halstead in silence. *Why did I have to ruin things?*

She reminded herself that at least she would have the memory of today—of Stoneyford and of riding along beside him as if she belonged there and of talking together like a real couple... She reached for her gloves and riding crop.

The landlord reappeared. "What can I do for you, sir?"

The earl said softly, "Show us to your best bedchamber."

Nine

STONES STILL CLATTERED TO THE GROUND, THE RATTLE echoing in the narrow, twisting passageway as Kate sent Horatia off to fetch help and then hurried toward the spot where the wall had fallen in. Afraid of what would be waiting for her, she felt as if her feet were lead weights.

They rounded the corner and Kate's heart jolted. Hearing that one of her charges was laid out senseless was one thing; seeing the accident victim motionless on the moss-covered flagstones was quite another. Was it her imagination, or was dust still puffing up from the heap of rocks that had fallen?

But as she came closer, she realized the situation was not as dire as it had seemed. Emily's eyes were open, and though she was stretched out on the ground, she was moving. All down one side, her pale blue habit was smeared with slick green moss. Her hat had fallen off, and she was covered with dust from head to foot.

Kate knelt beside her. "Be still a moment. Where are you hurt?"

"My shoulder," Emily whimpered. "I think it's bruised."

Kate wanted to tell the girl she'd be lucky indeed if nothing was broken, but she bit back the words, unwilling to cause Emily any more fright than she was already feeling.

And, Kate admitted, since she herself didn't feel up to dealing with a hysterical maiden, she'd best not do anything that would make an outburst more likely.

Behind her, she heard the skitter of boots against stone—a tread too measured and heavy to be the bridesmaid who had run to fetch more help.

Emily squealed like a terrified rabbit.

Kate looked around to see the duke and Andrew approaching. Relief swept over her. "Mr. Carlisle, let me make way for you." She started to get to her feet.

Emily seized her skirt in a surprisingly strong fist. "Don't leave me, Miss Blakely."

"Nonsense, my dear. The gentlemen can assist you better than I."

"But it's the duke, and I look a fright," Emily breathed.

Kate unclenched Emily's fingers from the twill of her skirt and stood up. "The rocks seem to have struck her shoulder, Mr. Carlisle," she said crisply, "but I think you will find she is not seriously injured." She moved away to join Olivia at a discreet distance.

Andrew and the duke exchanged a long glance. Then Andrew bent over the patient and took hold of her wrist. "Are you able to move your arm, Miss Emily?"

Emily cried out, and a shiver ran up Kate's spine. But slowly, under Andrew's guidance, Emily was able to flex her arm with no more than a whimper.

"I think nothing is broken," Andrew said. "But she won't be able to ride, Simon."

"I'll send a groom back to Halstead to bring a carriage. If you will accompany me on my errand, Lady Reyne…"

Before Kate could object or even ask her friend to stay, the duke and Olivia were gone—and Kate and Andrew remained in the shadow of the fallen wall, with only Emily to observe.

Not that there was any call for concern. What had come over her, Kate thought, to cause even an instant's anxiety about the proprieties? She and Andrew weren't *alone*. And even if they had been, there was nothing to be concerned about. Besides, he'd seemed quite smitten with Olivia this morning, so he was hardly likely to take a second look at Kate even if not for the injured young woman lying between them.

Andrew's gaze remained on Emily's face as he gently moved her arm, checking her shoulder, her elbow, her wrist. "Miss Blakely," he said finally, "why did you ask for me just now?"

Kate was startled. "I don't know what you mean. I didn't."

"Instead of appealing to the duke, you addressed me."

Kate ran back through the memory of what she had said, realized he was correct, and shrugged. "I suppose it was because you must have seen injuries in your travels."

"The duke has traveled, too," Andrew said quietly. "I find it interesting that you put your confidence in me, rather than in him. I feel quite honored."

Kate was nonplussed. "I'm hardly putting you up for notice as a hero, Mr. Carlisle."

"Aren't you?" He grinned at her and then looked once more at the bridesmaid. "I can see nothing seriously wrong, Miss Emily, though I expect you will be bruised and stiff for a day or two. Let me help you to sit up, and we'll wait for the carriage to take you back to Halstead."

Relief made Kate's knees wobbly, and she sank down on the pile of rocks.

"I don't know if I *can* sit up," Emily said. "I feel so shaky."

"Perhaps the heroic Mr. Carlisle will let you lean against him," Kate murmured.

Andrew shot a look at her that Kate pretended not to see. She brushed at the slimy green patches the moss had left on her habit when she had knelt on the stone, but all she succeeded in doing was to stain her gloves as thoroughly as her skirt. At least the spots wouldn't show from a distance against the dark fabric of the riding habit, and there was a chance that, under the ministrations of the skilled laundry maids at Halstead, they would come out. But her kid gloves would never be clean again. She sighed.

"You seem disturbed... Miss Blakely."

There was the barest breath of hesitation in Andrew's voice before he voiced her title. If Emily hadn't been there to overhear, he would no doubt have called her Kate again. The ironic little twist in his tone, the hint of secrets shared, would have made clear to Kate—even if he hadn't said so before—that he regarded the title as a formality. Yet his words had been perfectly correct and his tone so subtle that she couldn't even call him to account for it. He would merely pretend shock if she tried, and even Emily's self-centeredness would be jolted enough for her to notice if they were to bicker over a name.

How incredibly unfair that no matter what Andrew called her, Kate was left off balance. She eyed him with displeasure. "I am concerned about Lady Reyne."

"The duke will look after her with the greatest care, I am persuaded."

"But why did he take her away at all? There was no need for her to hurry along on his errand."

Andrew helped Emily move to a more secure position with her back against a wall, though she protested that it, too, might fall on her. Once she was settled, he sat down near Kate on the fallen rock pile. "Did you wish Lady Reyne to remain as a chaperone for you?"

Kate felt herself start to flush. "Of course not. But it is hardly proper of the duke to ask her to be alone with him."

Andrew smiled.

Kate's heart turned over. She had never forgotten his smile, and the way his dark eyes sparkled and looked almost gold when he was amused. But what had been a singularly charming smile when he was a youth was now dangerously attractive.

Andrew said softly, "The key point for Simon, I believe, is that *he* is not alone."

Kate recalled the long glance that had passed between the two men. It would have puzzled her at the time, had the majority of her attention not been focused on Emily. Still, even in her preoccupation she had recognized a message in that glance…

For the first time, Kate remembered sending the

bridesmaid for help. It was odd that Horatia hadn't returned along with the gentlemen; what could have happened to her?

"I see. The duke took Olivia along to serve as *his* chaperone," she said quietly. "So Horatia—or another of the bridesmaids—could not waylay him alone in some quiet spot."

"Wouldn't you, if you were in his position?"

"But then why doesn't he mind being alone with Olivia?"

Andrew shot a quizzical glance at her. "If you really don't know the answer, Kate, perhaps we should go exploring together."

Something about the way he said the word sent a tingle of anticipation through her. "I'm not interested in exploring with you, Mr. Carlisle."

"Aren't you?" he said softly. "We could search along the passageway Lady Reyne came out of this morning—and the duke only a minute later. You remember the incident, I'm sure. We would find quite a private little spot, I suspect."

Before Kate could find enough breath to answer, a pair of young women came around the corner—Horatia had returned with Lady Daphne. Horatia shrank back as if afraid of what she might see, but Lady Daphne's gaze roved brightly over the scene until she spotted Emily. "That's what you get for climbing on walls to peek at the duke. Yes, Horatia told me what the two of you were doing. There's no damage done?" She sounded disappointed.

Emily looked pathetic. "Mr. Carlisle says I will be unable to move on my own for days."

Daphne sniffed. "Since you don't show to advantage on the ballroom floor, having such a good excuse to sit out every dance will work well for you."

Kate was aghast. "Lady Daphne, what a perfectly horrid thing to say to your friend! And Miss Emily, that is not at all what Mr. Carlisle told you."

"And you would know, my Kate, because you were listening so carefully to every word I spoke."

"I am not *your* Kate—and I hear many interesting things, Mr. Carlisle." She took a deep breath and decided it was time to change the subject. "Have you found your heiress yet?" she asked him quietly.

He smiled. "That was Simon's idea. I'm not looking for one."

"I grant that heiresses are on the whole a brainless lot. But surely that's not a huge consideration in your case."

"Why? Because you believe I'm brainless enough myself that I should not notice the lack, if I were to marry a woman who has a shortage of intelligence?"

Kate hadn't intended to insult him—at least not quite so thoroughly as he seemed to think she had set out to do. But shouldn't he have been aggravated by such an implication? Possibly even had his feelings hurt? Instead, he'd sounded amused.

"Not at all, Mr. Carlisle," she said crisply, "for you likely wouldn't be at home to be bored with her anyway. If you were to marry a woman with enough money, then you would not be limited to going where your patrons wish to send you. You could go adventuring to your heart's content."

Andrew let out a low whistle. "What a very good idea, Kate!"

"If you choose a woman who is more interested in having a home than a husband, she might not even notice you were gone. She might even be glad of your absence."

"And all I'd need to do is come home once a year to get her with child."

"I didn't say anything about…" Kate noted the twinkle in his eyes and swallowed the rest.

"I think you've hit on the perfect plan for my life. No doubt you will also volunteer to choose the perfect heiress for me?"

"Oh, no. I've done my share—though I'm surprised you haven't thought of it yourself."

"Come now, Kate. You've already spent quite a lot of time with each of these young ladies—more than you believe I should spend with just one of them in my entire lifetime." He shifted on the rocks, turning to face her. "How could you possibly be so cruel as to refuse me your guidance in choosing which of them I must wed?"

❧

Penelope couldn't believe what she was hearing. A bedchamber? Perhaps her ears weren't working correctly, for the landlord merely bowed and stepped out into the hall. Surely if the earl had really requested a bedchamber at this hour of the day, the landlord would have expressed surprise, not acted as if it was the most commonplace of requests.

"This way, my lady," the landlord said respectfully. "My good wife keeps our best bedchamber always ready."

Penelope stared at the earl. "*Now?*" Her voice was no more than a squeak. "But it's still…"

"Daylight?" the earl said. "Indeed it is. No time like the present."

Penelope let out her breath in a rush. He had no intention of carrying through this scheme; he was trying to shock her out of a truly silly notion. Now the earl had made his point, she realized how far outside the bounds she had gone.

"Don't make fun," she whispered. "I only meant…"

"I have no intention of ridiculing you. You expressed a desire, and I am waiting to fulfill your wish—right now."

"My lady?" the landlord asked, and Penelope realized his voice had gone sharp. He must be questioning why there seemed to be a difference of opinion between his guests. And no wonder, she thought. A bedchamber in the middle of the day… did he think they were indulging in an affaire? Or perhaps he was wondering if they were eloping. Possibly even suspecting she might have been carried off against her will…

In any case, the landlord was sweet to stand up for her, since interfering with the desires of a young, active, athletic member of the *ton* was hardly good business.

Right now, the earl had said—and he was looking impatient. If she backed down now, the opportunity would never come again. Which was, of course, exactly what he intended to happen.

Wasn't it?

"I am quite all right," she told the landlord. "Please show my husband and me to…" Her lips refused to form the word, but the landlord bowed again and led the way.

The stairway was narrow and twisting, and each step seemed to be a different height. At least, the toes of Penelope's boots kept awkwardly bumping the treads as she climbed. Or perhaps her clumsiness was only because she was so fiercely aware of the earl just a step behind her.

The bedchamber was small and painfully neat. It might be the best in the house, but it was no competition for the guest suite at Halstead. The bed was far smaller and less ornate, with no elaborate hangings, no counterpane. Instead, a pieced quilt, made of fragments of cloth so small Penelope couldn't imagine stitching enough of them together to cover a mattress, draped the bed. The frame was homemade and the carving crude. The mattress was uneven and looked lumpy.

This bed was not only smaller than the ones at Halstead, but it was far more intimate—more personal. And somehow, Penelope thought, that fact made this bed even more intimidating than the grand one she had slept in the night before. She brushed her fingertips across the quilt. "It's really very pretty."

She heard the door close behind the landlord and turned around slowly to face her husband. She couldn't meet his gaze so she focused on the knot of his neckcloth. "I… I don't know what to do," she admitted.

"The custom is to remove one's clothing. All of it."

Penelope's mouth went dry.

"If you are having second thoughts, ma'am, we need not proceed."

He might as well have come straight out and

called her a coward. And perhaps she was, Penelope admitted. For an instant she wavered.

Then she straightened her shoulders and said, "No second thoughts." Before she could think any further, she took hold of the top button of her habit. Her fingers shook, but she kept at it, working her way slowly down the front of her bodice until it gaped open and her white linen chemise peeked out.

For a man who had twice casually stripped off his coat and shirt in front of her, the earl seemed in no hurry to undress himself. Appearing perfectly at ease, he stood in the center of the room. His gaze didn't leave her, though he appeared no more than mildly interested.

But then that was no surprise, Penelope thought bitterly. She had realized long ago she was not to his taste. Perhaps on a moonless night they could have pretended. But it was midday, and despite the drawn curtains over the small windows, the inn's best bedchamber was perfectly light. There would be no confusion.

She couldn't bear to see whether he showed disappointment when he saw her body, so she turned away as she pushed her habit down over her hips. She caught the garment and laid it carefully aside. She felt incredibly bare with her arms and shoulders entirely exposed to his gaze. Her breasts, pushed up by the lacings of her corset, peeked out through the thin fabric of her chemise, and even though she had turned aside, she felt his gaze on her. A deep, uncomfortable flush started in her breasts and worked up her throat, washing over her face.

For a moment she had no idea how she could

continue. If he was simply going to stand there and watch while she stripped naked…

You asked for this, she reminded herself.

She sat down on the room's single chair and pulled up her petticoat a few inches to take off her boots. Footwear hardly mattered, and the boots had to come off sometime—even though she knew in her heart it was only a delaying tactic, intended to give herself another few moments to get used to the idea of being totally bare in front of him.

She raised her foot and bent to reach the fastenings of her boot. She felt as if she might spill out of her corset. She'd never had such an odd sensation before, as though her breasts had grown and her nipples were swollen and warm and eager to be free.

The earl dropped to one knee in front of her, gently pushing her hand away. He cupped her calf directly below her knee, supporting her leg with one hand as he efficiently tugged her boot loose with the other. His hand was big and warm and gentle, and a tingle ran up each of Penelope's legs in turn, meeting deep in her belly where the sensation grew into a quiver of excitement.

Perhaps, she thought, footwear mattered after all.

The earl extended a hand to help her stand again. Without her boots, he seemed much taller, and suddenly she felt tiny and helpless and vulnerable. He reached out as if to cup her chin, but instead he tugged on the ribbon holding her bonnet in place.

Penelope uttered a faint protest and saw surprise sparkle in his eyes. She supposed it didn't make much sense—after all, she was standing there in her shift and

corset but making a fuss about taking off her hat... She
swallowed a sigh and pulled the bonnet off. Released
from captivity, her hair straggled down around her
face and wild curls sprang out in all directions. She
must look as if she was just getting out of bed...

Close enough, I suppose. At least he knows what he's getting.

She didn't protest when he turned her away from
him once more. For a moment he rested his fingertips
against her neck, barely touching the hairline, and
then slowly he pushed upward so each finger drew
a channel through her hair, rubbing and relaxing the
muscles in her scalp.

Penelope swayed a little and wondered how much
wine she'd consumed. She hadn't realized she'd had
so much to drink that she would be dizzy, but perhaps
she had lost count.

A moment later she felt the warm touch of his
hands against the small of her back as he released the
ties of her petticoats and let them drop to the floor.
Then he began to work the knot loose in the lacings
of her corset. "I see you do not lace yourself so tightly
that you have difficulty breathing," he said.

Unlike the other women you've undressed? she wanted
to ask. But Penelope kept her silence. He must
already have noticed she made small pretense of being
fashionable.

As the cords slackened, Penelope knew she should
be more comfortable, but in fact her chest felt increas-
ingly tight as his gentle touch worked slowly up her
back until the corset was loose enough to remove.

Finally only her chemise remained. Not only was
a good deal of leg bare, but the sheer fabric didn't

truly conceal even the sections of her body that were still covered.

The earl took a long look. Penelope wondered if he was noting how her breasts, no longer supported by the corset, sagged. Or perhaps he was wondering why the circles around her nipples were so much darker than the rest of her skin. She'd wondered herself at boarding school, when she compared her body to the other girls. But did his long survey mean there was something wrong there?

Trying to act casual, she crossed her arms across her chest.

His gaze drifted lower to the shadow between her legs. Penelope could feel her knees trembling. She wanted to lower her hands, but she wouldn't be able to bear it if he laughed at her.

The earl reached out and slowly untied the string fastening the neck of her chemise. Trailing one finger downward, he traced a line from the base of her throat through the shadowed cleavage, pushing the soft fabric aside to bare her breasts to his gaze.

He has every right to look, she reminded herself. *And to touch.* But if he didn't like what he saw…

Under his steady gaze, she felt as if her skin was on fire. Simple embarrassment? Or something else, something that heated her from the inside out?

Was he breathing just a little faster, or was it only her imagination?

When he took his hand away, she felt as if a cool breeze had drifted across her skin—but rather than feeling refreshed, she wanted to shiver and press herself against him so she could be warm again.

He continued to look at her as he undressed. Every movement he made was efficient and refined. He was even graceful as he pulled off his boots, and he displayed not so much as a hint of self-consciousness. But she understood. Unlike her, the earl knew he was pleasant to look at. No doubt all his previous feminine audiences had made clear how much they appreciated his broad chest, strong shoulders, and well-defined muscles.

When he unfastened his breeches, Penelope couldn't keep her gaze under control. When he stepped out of his smalls, she couldn't contain her gasp.

The duenna who had chaperoned Penelope through her betrothal had told her something of what to expect in the marriage bed. But now she couldn't help but wonder if Miss Rose had ever seen a man firsthand.

Penelope had thought her husband overwhelming the day before when he'd stripped to the waist in his bedroom, but the rest of him was even more compelling. Broad shoulders narrowed to hard, well-defined hips, and the strong angles of his body drew her gaze on down to what Miss Rose had coyly called man-parts.

If that was what made a man, Penelope thought, then the earl must be more manly than most.

Her lips suddenly felt dry. Half-consciously she ran the tip of her tongue across them, and she was startled when his penis seemed to grow longer and thicker and stand out even more strongly from his body.

He gently unfolded her arms from across her chest and pushed the straps of her chemise off her shoulders. The garment dropped to the floor, pooling around her feet, and Penelope stood completely naked in front of her husband.

"Get into bed." His voice was low and harsh, and Penelope scrambled to obey.

Miss Rose's words echoed in her mind. *Do not anger your husband. Simply lie still and let him do as he wishes. It will be over quickly.*

She slid between the sheets. The cool linen was like a balm against her overheated skin, and the quilt was thick, concealing her lack of curves. At least now he would no longer be looking at her so closely—and perhaps finding her wanting—and she was glad.

But he took hold of the quilt and the sheet, stripping the covers away to drape them over the foot of the bed so she lay sprawled across the mattress entirely bare to his gaze. "That's better," he said as he stretched out beside her.

With the very tip of his forefinger, he traced a line from her forehead down past her ear, along her throat, and around the back of her neck to spread his hand over her nape as he bent to touch his lips to hers.

He had kissed her once before, and though his caress had been no more than a cool and formal end to their brief wedding ceremony, at least this gesture was familiar. Penelope relaxed a fraction, knowing what to expect.

Except… she was wrong.

This time, his mouth wasn't chilly and firm. He was all heat and motion, his lips searing hers, his hand at the back of her neck holding her, gentle but insistent. "Open your mouth for me," he said, and when she did, his tongue delved in, sweet and tangy and refreshing. He tasted foreign, different, and yet utterly right, like a perfectly executed dish from the hand of a master chef. Unable to stop herself, she darted her tongue against his, and in turn he deepened the kiss.

He cupped his palm around her breast and a shiver shot through her. How, she wondered, could his touch on her breast make the spot between her legs feel damp and warm and somehow all aglow?

As if he understood what she was feeling, he stretched his hand downward over her belly and her hip, slowly insinuating his fingers between her legs. She wriggled against him until his fingertip brushed a most sensitive spot, and she cried out.

He pulled back and said, "It's all right if you want me to stop."

But her cry had not been protest but simple surprise, and when he withdrew his hand—withdrew himself—she felt empty and cold, and as if she had ruined something wonderful.

"No," she said. "If that is what a husband and wife are supposed to do, then do it—now."

"Before you change your mind?" he said dryly. He didn't wait for her answer but bent his head to her breast. He had barely touched his tongue to her nipple before it peaked. He traced the rosy aureole and then settled down to suck and lick and tease the eager point. He divided his attention between her breasts, tracing the shadow between them with his tongue, and slipped a hand between her legs once more.

Penelope wriggled under the flood of senses—the heat of his mouth, the chill of air on her damp skin, the silky brush of his hair against her throat, the scent of his soap teasing her nose, the gentle firmness of his fingers stroking between her legs. Each individual sensation seemed to be expanding, circling outward until they collided and caused ripples to run throughout her body. She was glad she was lying down, for her knees were even shakier than before.

She was gasping, and something seemed to be wrong with her vision, for the edges of the room had grown darker and she couldn't focus. As she closed her eyes to concentrate on the heat growing between her legs, he slid one finger inside her body and nudged at a sensitive spot she'd never dreamed existed. Penelope's world tore apart. She bucked and shuddered against his hand, and he held her as she rocked against him and cried out.

He waited until the quivering stopped, and then he parted her legs and settled his weight over her. "This will hurt a little." He sounded breathless. "But it will soon be over."

Miss Rose's warnings echoed in Penelope's mind. *It will be over quickly,* the duenna had said. *Lie still...* Penelope tensed, remembering she had not exactly been still.

He nudged the head of his penis inside her and Penelope trembled. But she knew somehow that what lay ahead would be even more wonderful than what had just happened, and so she forced her muscles to unclench as she lay quietly under him and waited.

He slid slowly inside her, and she could feel herself soften and stretch to welcome him. He hesitated and then pushed past her barrier, and Penelope gulped and whimpered a little with the shock.

"It's all right now," he whispered against her

temple, and when she eased once more, he slid a little deeper, inch by slow inch. She could sense the tension in him, could see the tightness of his jaw. Instinct told her to rock her hips just a little, and she looked into his eyes as she moved, seeing surprise there even as he sheathed himself completely in her. Her moment of triumph, of enjoying the power she had exerted over him, faded in fear that she couldn't contain him. But then the heat took over, and as he began to move, the pressure started to build again inside her.

He pressed deep and then withdrew almost completely, stroking inside her as thoroughly as he had caressed her breasts. Each thrust grew more urgent, and Penelope's breath caught painfully in her chest as she reached once more for fulfillment, somehow knowing an ecstasy even stronger than before lay within her reach.

With one last powerful thrust, he took her over the edge. Then, even as she shuddered with her release, he clenched his jaw and pulled away from her.

Caught up in the waves of sensation surging through her, arching in exaltation, she didn't notice for an instant that he was no longer sheathed inside her body, and when she did, she was too self-conscious to wonder why.

Ten

THE RIDERS WHO DISMOUNTED THAT AFTERNOON IN THE
stable yard at Halstead were much quieter then they'd
been on the outbound trip in the morning, and Simon
was relieved when most of them simply turned their
horses over to the grooms and straggled off toward the
house for refreshments and a rest.

He led his own gelding into the stables and reached
for a currycomb, glad to have an excuse to stay away
from the company for a while.

In a nearby stall, Andrew Carlisle put a final polish
on the gleaming coat of his own horse and grinned at
Simon. "I never knew you to be so fond of currying
your own mount before, my friend."

"The grooms have their hands full. You got back
safely with the carriage?"

"Surely you didn't doubt it, with the very efficient
Kate Blakely managing the trip. We must have been
half an hour ahead of you. Miss Emily will be safely
deposited in her bed by now with the doctor in atten-
dance." Andrew patted his horse's neck and moved
over to help Simon. "Did Lady Daphne complain all

the way back about the pall the accident threw over her party?"

"Most of it," Simon admitted.

Except, of course, when he'd tried to glare his sister into silence—for instead of taking the hint to watch her tongue, she had accused him of being every bit as irritated with Miss Emily as she was. Since Kate Blakely and Andrew Carlisle had been sent off with the carriage, Daphne had pointed out, Simon himself was required to accompany the riders all the way back to Halstead. Which meant, Daphne finished triumphantly, he could not make some excuse to stay in the village with Olivia Reyne.

Since he'd been hoping to do exactly that, Simon was particularly annoyed that Daphne had hit the nail precisely on its proverbial head. He hadn't bothered to deny his plans because a protest would only have given her more reason for suspicion. Instead, he'd contented himself with staying on the opposite side of the group from his sister and hurrying the riders along as best he could, while he daydreamed about what he'd wanted to be doing instead.

Taking Olivia out to her garden for tea—along with more creative forms of refreshment.

But a cottage garden in Steadham village in the middle of the afternoon was hardly a private enough spot for the sort of tryst Simon had in mind. To be honest, it had barely been secluded enough at midnight, considering the enthusiastic response of his lady.

Definitely his attention would be better spent in concocting a smoother scheme for their next rendezvous. Doing his planning in private might be wise, too, since even thinking about making love to Olivia again was enough to stir his blood.

"Chadwick arrived this afternoon," Andrew said. "Warren and Ponsonby should be in the village by evening, and the rest of the group are on their way. You did say you'd hired the entire inn to house your friends until the wedding? You'll need it—but with three more single gentlemen on hand, tomorrow should go more easily no matter what Daphne has planned."

"An archery contest, I believe."

"Twelve young ladies loose on the range with bows and arrows in hand?" Andrew shook his head. "I believe I'll stay in my room with a head cold. Charles can take my place—it's his turn. Where did he disappear to today, anyway?"

"He rode over to Stoneyford."

"I suppose he found something in disarray, since he has not yet returned."

"More surprising if he *didn't* find something in disarray."

"Perhaps his lady wished to closely inspect the property."

Simon paused, and the gelding stamped and snorted in halfhearted protest. "Did he take Lady Townsend along? He didn't mention it."

"You didn't notice she disappeared at the same time he did? What's the matter with you, Simon? You must have had other things on your mind today." He added slyly, "Lady Reyne could knock the sense out of most men with no more than a look."

Simon felt a sudden urge to wipe the smirk off his friend's face. Suddenly the stable was even more uncomfortable than facing the bridesmaids. He turned the currycomb over to a groom to complete the job and walked over to the house. Andrew ignored the cold shoulder Simon was attempting to give him and strolled along.

The butler greeted them in the front hall. "Your Grace, the duchess has requested you to call upon her in her private sitting room as soon as possible."

"As soon as possible?" Andrew gave a soundless whistle. "He's up to his neck in trouble this time—eh, Greeley?"

The butler said stolidly, "I have no opinion on the matter, Mr. Carlisle."

The hell he didn't, Simon thought. Greeley was just too diplomatic to express his thoughts.

Simon considered letting his mother wait while he washed up and changed his clothes, but in the end, he went directly upstairs to the duchess's rooms—the ones she had chosen for herself after the death of her husband, when she had left the principal suite for Simon to occupy. Choosing her own view, she had often said, was one of the few privileges of being the dowager rather than the duchess.

When his mother's maid admitted him, the duchess was sitting in her favorite chair in the bay window overlooking the gardens with a glass of ratafia in her hand. Kate Blakely perched on the edge of the nearest sofa.

The duchess looked up at Simon. "The ruins of the abbey must be cleared at once."

He was absurdly relieved to discover the source of her concern. "Sir Jasper Folsom owns the property. I can discuss the matter with him, but I cannot compel him to take action."

"Don't be foolish, Simon. Of course he will do as you like, for you're the duke, and he's a mere baronet."

"The remains of the abbey have stood there for two hundred years. This is the first collapse I've heard about—and I've wandered through those ruins for the past two decades. Would it not be more sensible to simply forbid future expeditions? In any case, after this week Daphne will be in Oxfordshire, and no one else at Halstead is apt to organize such a party."

"After an accident such as this, we cannot take chances again."

Miss Blakely cleared her throat. "Ma'am, Miss Emily was climbing on the wall when it collapsed. If not for her own actions, she would have been perfectly safe."

The duchess's eyes widened. "Climbing on the wall? Who dared to accuse her of such a thing?"

"Lady Daphne did." Kate Blakely's voice was wry. "Miss Emily and Miss Horatia seem to have been attempting to peer over the barrier to check whether the duke was within range."

"Indeed. One must wonder why they bothered, when he has been so very disobliging to all the girls. Thank you, Miss Blakely."

The phrase was a dismissal, and obediently Miss Blakely stood and curtseyed.

The duchess said sharply, "What is the stain on your skirt?"

"Moss, Your Grace. From kneeling on the stone floors of the abbey. I should have changed before coming to report to you, I know, but…"

Simon moved a little closer. "But knowing how anxious you must have been to hear all the news, Miss Blakely did not delay for even an instant to change her clothes."

"Well, your habit is quite ruined," the duchess said. "You must have a new one."

Kate Blakely's jaw was set, but her voice was level and calm. "At the moment, Your Grace, I have neither time nor inclination for sewing and no funds for materials."

"Nonsense. The dressmakers I brought down from London to see to the bridesmaids' gowns have nothing to do. Send the modiste to me immediately, and I shall set her staff to work. I'm certain she can find something left over in the cupboards that will be suitable for you."

Miss Blakely bobbed another curtsey. She had turned pale, but she was still in control of her temper as she left the room. Simon thought it had been a close-run thing.

"Very generous of you," Simon said dryly when Miss Blakely was gone.

"Generous? What, giving the girl a dress or two? It's simply common sense. She can't look like a ragamuffin while she's chaperoning the young ladies."

"Perhaps you could afford new materials, at least."

"There's no time to order from London. I suppose she'll need a simple ball gown too, come to think of it, and something to wear for the wedding... But that isn't why I wanted to talk to you, Simon. Daphne has been telling me that you were paying particular attention to Lady Reyne on this outing today."

His sister hadn't taken long to make her report. Simon should have expected that Daphne would rush straight to their mother. *Once a talebearer, always a talebearer.*

The duchess studied him over the rim of her wine-glass. "I was not aware that Lady Reyne had even been invited on the excursion to the abbey."

"What a surprise, Mama. I thought you knew everything." Simon sat down in the chair matching his mother's.

"Is it true?"

"That I was paying particular attention to Lady Reyne? Quite true."

The duchess sniffed scornfully and her expression changed. "Do I detect an aroma of horse on you, Simon?"

"You did say you wanted to see me as soon as possible."

"Well, I *didn't* want to smell you straight from the stables. Is this how your new—acquaintance—has affected your manners?"

"Mama, cut line. I know what you're plotting. With marriage in the air, you'd be quite content if my eye lighted on one of Daphne's friends."

"Simon, whatever makes you think I'm trying to marry you off? Though as long as you've brought the matter up yourself—"

Simon snorted.

"You're getting close to thirty, and it's time to see to the succession. Any one of those girls would be quite an acceptable match for the Duke of Somervale."

"I'm still closer to twenty-five than I am to thirty,

and you know perfectly well my taste runs to ladies who are more mature than Daphne's friends."

"Yes, yes. But not to *marry*, Simon."

And my taste doesn't run to marriage—but there's no sense in admitting that just now. "Why not? Lady Reyne is hardly past her prime. She must be twenty-three at most." He paused, but when the duchess did not comment, Simon said deliberately, "She's also a proven breeder—you must appreciate that fact."

"A *girl*," the duchess said.

Simon tried to hide his smile. "My intentions toward Lady Reyne are of the most serious. I suggest you adjust yourself to the idea."

He settled back and waited for the explosion. Watching his mother sputter and stammer and argue was going to be fun.

But he soon realized that Iris Somervale hadn't been thirty years a duchess for nothing. "Very well. If I am to welcome Lady Reyne as a potential bride for my son, then welcome her I shall. Wait, please, while I write a note."

"A note?" Simon asked warily.

The duchess smiled, showing more teeth than amusement. "Inviting her to dinner tonight, of course. Since all the servants are quite busy, perhaps you'll take it down to Greeley to be sent to the village. Unless, of course, you'd prefer to deliver it to Lady Reyne yourself?"

❧

The duke had been as good as his word, for when Olivia entered the cottage the first thing she saw was

Maggie, feather duster in hand. The maid looked very much like a whirlwind as she shook the duster around the sitting room.

Or perhaps, Olivia thought as she took a closer look, *thundercloud* would be a better description. "Do be careful, Maggie. This cottage contains little enough of value, but I must warn that breaking things will not end in you being released to go back to Halstead. The duke himself arranged for you to be here."

"Duke indeed," Maggie muttered. "Why is he concerning himself with the likes of me instead of taking care of his own affairs? That's what I'd like to know!" She gave the duster a final flourish, leaving a dainty vase that had belonged to Olivia's mother rocking on the corner shelf.

Unwilling to encourage that line of reasoning, Olivia went upstairs to change her riding habit for a day dress. She arrived in the kitchen a few minutes later to find a dozen jars of grape jelly neatly lined up on the table; her pride prickled at accepting the gift, but at least Mrs. Greeley had shown restraint and not sent over a cartload. Nurse was placidly shelling beans at the table, while Charlotte dashed around the room holding a long stick between her knees.

"Why is my daughter wielding a branch in the kitchen?" Olivia asked.

"I should think you'd recognize a horse when you see one, Miss Olivia. A dead limb from a tree, a bit of paper to draw a head, a yard or so of yarn to make mane and tail, and a ribbon to serve as reins, and she's been content for more than an hour. You used to do the same thing yourself."

Olivia walked around the makeshift horse and took her apron down from the hook by the door. "Did Mrs. Greeley send the beans as well? They can't be from our garden."

"No, for that would require magic. Somehow the last hills of our beans have been cut off right at the ground. Sir Jasper Folsom's man dropped these off this afternoon."

Olivia's fingers tightened on the apron's ties for a moment. She doubted Sir Jasper had intended the gift as a neighborly good deed or even charity, but instead as a reminder.

The day when her rent would once more be due was drawing closer. But despite the bargain she had made with the Duke of Somervale, Olivia was in no better financial condition than before. The promise of an annuity was all very well, but collecting might be another matter. If she only knew what to expect, what she could rely on… What had she been thinking last night, not to insist on having a definite understanding with the duke?

But doing so—demanding a cold and practical discussion of financial terms—would have made it impossible to pretend their arrangement was anything but business. Trading her virtue for money carried an ugly name, and one she didn't want to think about, but as long as there was no direct payment…

Don't be foolish, she told herself. *Just because you'd prefer not to admit the facts doesn't mean there's anything romantic about this bargain!*

She checked the hidden fold of her skirt where she had fastened the duke's sapphire stickpin. She had carried it with her since he had pressed it into her hand the afternoon before. Perhaps keeping it on her person was risky, since there was a chance of losing it—but she could hardly leave it anywhere in the house. If Maggie were to see it as she dusted, or if Charlotte spotted the bauble and decided it would be the perfect decoration for her horse's mane, there would be more questions than Olivia could answer. So the sapphire rested under the edge of her apron, even though it seemed to weigh her down.

She didn't offer to help shell the beans. She couldn't bring herself to touch something that had come from Sir Jasper.

After her outing, Olivia was both tired and out of sorts, and she had difficulty settling down to work. She looked in the larder, taking inventory of the contents. If she made a pastry crust and put in all the bits and pieces of meat and vegetables, she could create a sort of shepherd's pie that, along with the beans and the rest of yesterday's bread, would fill them all.

As she was rolling out the crust, Maggie sauntered into the kitchen. "It's the duke come to call. *Again.* I put him in the sitting room."

Olivia's heart gave a little jerk. Only two hours earlier, he had said a hasty good-bye at her garden gate and then caught up with the group of riders as they left the village. What was bringing him back so quickly? Surely he wasn't foolish enough to think she could invite him upstairs at this hour of the afternoon…

On the other hand, since there was no possibility of indulging his sensual appetite, perhaps this would be a good opportunity to have the unpleasant but necessary conversation that she should have demanded the previous night.

She shifted the pastry into a shallow pottery dish and arranged the bits of meat and vegetables, pouring gravy over the mixture and adding a layer of potatoes on top.

Maggie looked at the pie and said wistfully, "Even in the servants' dining room at Halstead, the table is so loaded down that it groans."

"And if you ate all that rich food, you'd be groaning afterwards," Nurse put in.

Olivia slid the pie into the oven niche at the side of the fireplace and dusted flour off her hands. "Charlotte, dear, your horse is growing loud. Perhaps it's time to put it out to pasture."

Charlotte galloped off into the garden.

Olivia brushed off her skirt and went into the sitting room. The duke was occupying the same spot where Sir Jasper had stood on the day he had propositioned her, and for an instant, time seemed to fold in around her. They were such different men—and yet, when all was said and done, the situation she found herself in today was not much different from what Sir Jasper had suggested.

His gaze roved over her face so intimately that Olivia could feel his touch. "I came in the hope of a friendly greeting." The duke's words were perfectly amiable, but his tone—lazy, sensual, like melted butter flowing over newly baked bread—made clear what he had in mind. He took a step closer. "It has been hours since I kissed you, and I feel the lack."

Her insides began to quiver, and she felt an embarrassing rush of warmth between her legs. She shifted uncomfortably, and Simon smiled—a knowing, predatory smile.

Bad enough, she thought, that all he had to do was murmur in her ear and she grew wet and ready for lovemaking, but worse yet was the fact he knew it.

"I should like to speak with you in private," she said firmly.

"That is my dearest wish as well. Except for the part about speaking." He captured her hand and lifted it to his mouth. His lips moved with agonizing slowness down her fingers. "My dear, you smell of lovely things. Chicken, perhaps?"

"Only gravy." She could barely hear herself think. "It's shepherd's pie for dinner."

"Then I wish I could stay and share it."

"You would have trouble explaining your absence to your guests. In any case, there isn't enough for us to invite an extra."

He turned her hand over and touched the tip of his tongue to the center of her palm, sending a dart of sheer pleasure through her. "Fortunately, the pie need stretch only to serve three, for you are summoned to dine this evening at Halstead."

"Whose mad idea was this?"

"My mother's. She sent a note inviting you. I beg you not to inform her that she is mad. She takes the suggestion badly, you see."

"I can't come to Halstead."

Suddenly the lover was gone and he stood before her every inch a duke. "If my mother is to be convinced I am courting you, it will be necessary for me to appear to court you."

Olivia quailed for an instant. Then she rallied, reminding herself that this man was not her husband and she had not given him power to compel her. "You cannot flaunt your mistress directly under your mother's nose, sir."

"Exactly," he said softly. "Which is precisely why you are coming to dinner not as my mistress, but as a potential wife. If you recall, my agreement regarding an annuity was based on that performance, not on whether you occupy my bed."

"Then I shall not feel it necessary to entertain further advances in *that* direction, Your Grace."

"Yes, you will, Olivia, because you want to." His voice was low and lazy. "Making love is simply an added pleasure for both of us. Don't waste your breath trying to deny it, for your face gives you away." He brushed her eyelid with his thumb. "Even now you're looking at me like a woman who's hungry for her lover."

She tried to clench her legs together to stem the flood of wet heat, but without success.

The duke smiled. "I thought so... The carriage will call for you in ample time. Until this evening, my lady."

He did not close the sitting room door behind him, so Olivia heard the clatter of Charlotte's galloping come to an abrupt halt in the hallway.

"I thought you were afraid of horses, Miss Charlotte," the duke said.

"Only if they're big ones," Charlotte admitted shyly. "Like yours."

"So that's a pony you're riding now? What is his name?"

"*She*," Charlotte said indignantly. "She's a *girl* horse."

"Indeed. Since this is a house full of females, only a *girl horse* would fit in. How foolish of me to think otherwise!"

Olivia stepped into the hallway. "Go find Nurse, Charlotte. And as for you, sir, if you expect me to be ready when the carriage comes, you'll take your departure right now."

Charlotte frowned. "Are you going away *again*, Mama?"

"Only for a little while, my dear. I'll try to come home in time to put you to bed."

"Unlikely," the duke said.

Olivia glared at him and turned back to the child. "And if you're already asleep, I'll tuck you in again anyway. Run along, now."

Charlotte sidled past the duke, eyeing him steadily, and disappeared into the kitchen.

"How flattering that you sought once more to be alone with me." The duke lifted her hand to his lips.

An observer, Olivia realized, would notice only the cool correctness of a gentleman paying tribute to a lady—the sort of elegant gesture he might perform even in a crowded ballroom. But an observer would not have felt the deliberate caress of his breath lingering against her skin and reminding her of even more intimate fondling. Her breasts tingled, and Olivia made a mental note to keep a shawl with her all the time she was at Halstead—just in case the duke happened to feel playful.

❧

The duchess's offer to provide her with a new habit had been welcome enough, for even Kate wasn't so proud that she would refuse to accept a replacement for a garment she'd ruined while in the duchess's service. But Iris Somervale's announcement that Halstead's castoff scraps would be good enough for someone like Kate had been harder to swallow. In any case, there were things she needed much more than a new riding habit. Whatever employment Kate ended up taking, horses and rides were likely to be scarce.

When Lady Stone, coming out of a bedroom, called her name, Kate almost didn't hear her.

"Miss Blakely, I have not as yet had an opportunity to wish you well in your betrothal," Lady Stone said, her beady eyes bright. "Give me your arm along the corridor, if you please—unless you are engaged on an errand."

"I am to find the modiste and send her to the duchess," Kate admitted.

"Then you must not delay to assist me. What is the emergency, pray? Has Lady Daphne measured the pintucks on her wedding gown and found one shorter than all the others?"

Kate had to repress a smile at the picture of Lady Daphne with a ruler, checking out each line of stitching. "Her Grace has decided I require a new riding habit." She waved a careless hand at the slick spots of moss on her skirt.

"I should think so. Though, knowing Iris, she may be more concerned that the dressmakers are idle at her expense while they wait for one of the bridesmaids to tear a ruffle." Lady Stone's voice was as gravelly as always, but her eyes were alight with mischief.

For once, Kate thought before speaking. After all, Lady Stone was not simply a guest at the wedding but a good friend of the duchess, close enough to have been named Lady Daphne's godmother. "I am grateful for Her Grace's thoughtfulness, and any fabric grand enough to have been stored in Halstead's cupboards must make a far more elegant dress than anything I am able to afford."

"My dear Miss Blakely, are you truly determined to make yourself into the perfect companion for Iris? I assume in that case you aren't intending to marry the vicar after all. Of course, there is such a thing as being too close a cousin, so perhaps you're wise to think twice."

As Kate turned to offer her arm to Lady Stone, she collided with Andrew, who had just come up the stairs. He paused with his hand on the door of a nearby bedroom—the same bedroom, Kate couldn't help but notice, that had been assigned to her until his untimely arrival had shuffled her off to smaller and much less convenient quarters in the east wing.

"Our patient seems to be doing well, Miss Blakely," Andrew said. "I spoke to the doctor as he was leaving. He believes Miss Emily will be fully recovered in time to take part in the wedding festivities."

"I'm sure Lady Daphne will be relieved to hear it."

"Would anyone care to place a wager on that?" Lady Stone asked blandly.

Kate was startled when a tall chair standing in the niche at the top of the stairs seemed to chuckle. Then

Colonel Sir Tristan Huffington unfolded himself from the chair, leaning to one side to peer at them. "Whichever way you're betting, Lucinda, I'll take the other side. And if you're getting so feeble in your old age that you need an arm to support you down the stairs, I consider it my duty as an officer and a gentleman to offer my assistance."

"An officer, yes," Lady Stone sniffed. "I'm not so sure about you being a gentleman." She let go of Kate. "Thank you for your offer, my girl, but Mr. Carlisle appears to have something on his mind—though I recommend you move away from the top of the stairs before you share any more secrets." She started down the stairs, and the colonel followed.

"Is that where you were hiding to eavesdrop last night, Kate?" Andrew asked. "Behind a very convenient chair?"

"I was not hiding," Kate said. "I was merely…" *Dodging bridesmaids.* "Did you have something else to add about the accident?"

"No. But I couldn't help hearing what Lady Stone said."

"You *couldn't help hearing*? What an interesting distinction! When *I* overhear something, you seem to think it's because I have been hiding and eavesdropping. When *you* overhear something, it's the fault of the person who was talking." She started past him.

He stepped into her path. "Is she correct?"

"About the vicar, the duchess, or my financial state? And what business is it of yours?"

"Kate," he said gently. "I ask as a friend."

She surveyed him with irritation. "No, I haven't

turned down the vicar as yet, and I have no plans to do so anytime soon."

"Lady Stone has a point, you know—about you being cousins."

"*Distant* cousins. Neither am I trying to make myself the perfect companion for the duchess, because she's made clear she needs me only until the wedding."

"And your shortage of funds? If you would prefer not to be beholden to Her Grace, I might help."

Kate knew it was silly of her to be embarrassed; her straitened circumstances would hardly startle anyone who had given the matter an instant's thought. But her feelings were already raw, and the idea that Andrew felt sorry for her was humiliating.

"If you are offering a loan, you must know how inappropriate it would be for me to accept. In any case, since I have no idea when I would be able to repay any funds you advanced, I could not possibly allow you to commit money you will no doubt need on your next adventure. If you will excuse me, Mr. Carlisle, I must carry out the duchess's request." Kate brushed past him and went down the stairs, doing her best to blink back tears.

Eleven

PENELOPE WANTED TO WRAP HERSELF AROUND HER husband and cling tight, begging him to keep her safe until the last of her tremors had died down—and then perhaps show her once more what husbands and wives did together. But she suspected he intended to hold to their bargain. Just once, she had said, and that was all he had agreed to.

And her instinct was correct, for while she was still quaking inside, he disentangled himself from her and went to the washstand. He dampened a cloth in the basin and came back to where she still sprawled across the bed.

At the first cool touch of the cloth between her legs, Penelope jerked away.

"I'm sorry the water isn't warmer," he said, but he didn't stop until he had thoroughly washed away every trace of their lovemaking. Then he covered her with the quilt and began to gather up his clothing. "I'll send a chambermaid to help you dress."

Penelope bit her lip and wondered if there was a reason he wanted her to stay in bed for a while, or if he simply meant he had been bored with the whole experience and couldn't wait to get away. She watched him as he dressed, trying to be discreet and not stare—while wondering if she would ever again see him this way.

As he was tying his neckcloth, she mustered her nerve. "Is there anything I should do? Or not do? I would not like to harm the chance of…" Her throat felt dry. "Of there being a child."

He paused, the knot half-formed. "There will not be a child." His voice was gentle.

But how could he be so certain? Judging by what Miss Rose had said… Of course, even Penelope's painfully limited experience made it clear that Miss Rose was no authority.

Before Penelope could find her voice again to ask, the earl was gone. A moment later the chambermaid knocked and came in to assist her.

When Penelope reached the foot of the stairs, the front door of the inn stood open to the sunshine and the horses waited just outside. The earl helped her up into the saddle. "It's only a few miles now," he said and set the well-rested horses into a steady trot that didn't allow for conversation.

As they skirted Steadham village, their path crossed that of the duke. They rode back to Halstead together with the three horses abreast where there was room, the men talking easily across Penelope while she kept her silence as she rode between them. In the stable yard, the earl lifted Penelope down from her horse as casually as if she'd been the inanimate saddle instead of the rider.

They crossed from the stable yard to the house

with him still talking to Simon, and only when they reached the top of the staircase and the duke turned toward his suite was Penelope able to take a deep breath and an even deeper risk.

"Will you come into my room with me, sir?" She could feel his surprise, and she kept her voice even with an effort as she reminded, "You kept your end of the bargain, and I shall keep mine. I promised my jewels to you."

She opened the door, but instead of the quiet, cool, peaceful bedroom she had come to expect, her gaze fell on a row of open trunks with a cluster of maids unpacking under the suspicious gaze of her own lady's maid.

Etta wheeled around and her eyes narrowed. "Just two days on your own and look at you, my lady. You're wind-burnt, sunburned, and a right mess. What have you been doing to your hair—stirring it with an egg whisk?"

Penelope's hand went to the back of her neck. Her hair was trailing down despite her bonnet, and her skin indeed felt warm—whether from the sun or sheer embarrassment, she didn't know.

"I knew nothing good could come of you leaving me behind in London." Etta shook her head and clucked her tongue. "I'll be embarrassed to show my face in the servants' hall, I will. Come and let me work on you. Let's see if there's anything I can salvage."

Penelope opened her mouth, intending to silence Etta no matter what. But the earl said, "We'll speak later," and turned away toward his own bedroom before she could argue.

She only wished she believed him. But she suspected that if the question was left up to the earl, *later* would be a very long time coming.

∽

Simon had told Olivia he would send the Somervale carriage for her, and he fully intended to do so. But instead, as the dinner hour grew near, he ordered his curricle to be brought around and drove himself into Steadham to the cottage.

Olivia answered the door and looked him up and down. As her gaze came to rest suspiciously on the basket he carried, she asked, "Since when do you make deliveries?"

Simon hefted his burden a little higher. "All the urchins in the village appear to have been called in for their supper and bed, so I had to leave my groom holding my horses."

"Is that food in the basket? If you're planning another picnic—"

"It isn't for you." He dropped a kiss on her nose. She smelled delightful tonight, though he couldn't quite pinpoint the aroma. What fun to investigate, following his nose to the crook of her elbow and the hollow behind her ear and all the other delightful places where she might possibly have dabbed her scent. The back of her knee sounded promising, and the spot right under her shoulder blades...

"Your Grace?" she reminded.

Simon pulled himself back to the subject at hand. "It's hardly fair for the rest of your household to be left out while you're feasting. Lead me to the kitchen so I can rid myself of this weight, and then I'll greet you properly."

She didn't move, so he took advantage of the opportunity to look more closely. She was dressed tonight in pale-blue muslin, cut in a modest style that would have been highly appropriate for one of the bridesmaids—though in fact, Simon suspected, those brazen maidens would likely have seen Olivia's gown as far too sedate even to consider.

For that matter, Simon thought both the color and the style were all wrong for Olivia. His fingers itched to tear the garment off her and replace it with something that better suited her. Dark green satin, perhaps, as smooth as the undersides of her breasts and as slick as the welcoming passage between her legs...

No, he'd like to tear the garment off and not replace it with anything at all.

He wasn't accustomed to becoming aroused by the sight of a woman wearing a plain, ordinary, out-of-date dress that covered up everything a man was most likely to be enticed by. Except, no matter how alluring her body was, Olivia's face was what he came back to. He could fall into the depths of her big hazel eyes, and he longed to explore new ways to caress her lips and her ears and her temples—all at the same time, of course, that he made certain the curves under her dress were still exactly the right size and shape to fit neatly into his hands. And there was territory yet to be explored. Her toes, he suspected, were small and perfect, like a row of matched pearls...

If only he could manage to get her truly alone, with all the time in the world to explore. Which, regrettably, seemed unlikely. The cottage was so small that even now he could hear voices from the kitchen... including a high, childish one.

"Have you finished looking?" Olivia asked dryly. "I'm afraid this is the best I can do, so if I'm inadequate, you'll just have to leave me behind."

The saucy wench was not only challenging him; she sounded hopeful that he would find her wanting and simply go away.

So—just to prove to her that he could set her afire with a look—Simon let his gaze run slowly over her once more, from her smooth dark hair swept up into a knot atop her head to the tips of her slippers peeking out from under the ruffle that edged her hem.

Picturing all the loveliness that lay under the pale-blue muslin, without being able to act on his desires, was a delicious torment. But as he'd expected, the inspection was just as tantalizing for her. Under the thin muslin her nipples peaked, and he had to restrain himself from palming her breasts to see if they really were as hard and excited as they appeared.

"I forgot my shawl," Olivia said.

"Are you running away?" Simon asked softly. She didn't answer, so when she went up the stairs, he took the basket to the back of the cottage.

Though the sun had not set, the corners of the kitchen had already fallen into dusk. The table was a warm, bright island with a couple of candles throwing wavering yellow light across a pottery dish standing in the center. As Nurse dipped portions onto three plates, the aroma of shepherd's pie filled the air and made Simon's mouth water.

Maggie looked up and gave a little shriek. "What's in the basket?"

"I'm not certain." Simon set the basket in front of her. "But I suspect you'll find the best of Halstead's kitchen."

The maid dug past the towel that concealed the contents. Simon thought that if she could have climbed inside the basket, she'd have done so. "There's a whole slab of ham," she told Nurse breathlessly. "And there's a cheese and a bit of trifle…"

"What's that?" Charlotte asked.

"Trifle? It's a lovely sweet dish, Miss Charlotte."

"Which you will not taste unless you eat your shepherd's pie," Nurse pointed out.

Charlotte obediently picked up her spoon.

"I told you, Nurse. Things are different at Halstead," the maid said.

Maggie was right, Simon thought. Things *were* different at Halstead—all kinds of things. She had, all unknowingly, solved his dilemma.

"Pack Lady Reyne's things for a visit," he ordered. "And your own as well. I'll take her ladyship with me now, of course, but a carriage will call for the rest of you later this evening. You're all coming to stay at Halstead until the wedding."

By the time the news had a chance to register— Maggie shrieked even more loudly this time—Simon had already returned to the hall. Olivia was coming down the stairs with a light cloak over her arm and a plain gray shawl concealing even the little he'd been able to see earlier of those delectable shoulders and the inviting curve of her breasts.

His fingertips tingled with the urge to unwrap her like a long-awaited Christmas gift. Later tonight, he promised himself, he would. Later tonight—at Halstead.

❧

The evening was still warm, so Olivia concluded that the way the duke carefully tucked her into his curricle and wrapped a carriage blanket around her was more an excuse to touch her than true concern for her comfort. She realized that distracting him from his task would only cause delay, so she waited until he had set his horses into motion before she spoke.

"While I appreciate your thoughtfulness in proving a feast for my household as well as for me, Your Grace—"

"It was nothing," he said modestly. "I learned years ago that the very first rule in successfully managing an estate is to make a friend of the cook."

"The *first* rule? Surely... Never mind. The grape jelly was a thoughtful gift—but this is different. You must understand that I do not accept charity. In fact, if not for the waste, I would have insisted you take the basket back."

"I think the deciding factor was that your maid would have mutinied if she hadn't been allowed to keep the basket."

Olivia couldn't deny that Maggie's shriek of satisfaction, ringing through the entire cottage, was the greatest reason why she hadn't stood on her principles. "That's why I'm making clear that you cannot fob me off with a food basket whenever you've done something particularly outrageous. Or when you want a favor, either."

"Rather than offering you something of real value? An annuity, perhaps?"

Olivia bit her lip. "That is entirely different."

"Indeed, but now is not the moment to discuss the differences between gifts and payments. Very well, my lady—no more food baskets."

Concern still niggled at Olivia. Apart from the jibe about annuities, she thought his concession had come far too easily, and she didn't feel entirely peaceful about it. Probably he'd agreed only because appearing to give in would quiet her protests for the moment, while he continued to do exactly as he pleased.

However, she'd fight that battle when the occasion arose. In the meantime, she couldn't deny that whatever had been in the basket, life would be more pleasant at the cottage for a few days at least.

"As it happens, you're quite right," the duke went on. "Foodstuffs *would* only go to waste at the cottage when your entire household has moved to Halstead until the wedding."

Olivia choked. "You can't—"

"Of course I can. I've no idea why I didn't think of it earlier, for it's the perfect answer to make everyone happy. By the time the moon rises tonight, your maid will be back in Mrs. Greeley's service, your nurse will have all the help she requires, your daughter will be perfectly safe and entertained, and you…"

"I will be always available as your mistress," Olivia said under her breath.

He looked at her with a smile that threatened to singe her bones. "I was going to say that for a while you will not be tied to the duties of keeping a house, and so you can concentrate on convincing my mother you'll make a perfect duchess. But I must say I prefer your description to mine."

The curricle made a great sweeping turn through huge, heavy gates that boasted the Somervale crest. No time at all seemed to have passed—the ride had been so smooth, the horses so quick, the curricle so well sprung.

"You must have seen Halstead before, of course," the duke said, "but I have always thought the place loveliest in the evening light."

Far down the long lane bordered by lime trees, Olivia could catch only a glimpse of the house, little more than she had seen on the few occasions when on a long walk in the countryside she had passed by the gates. But as they drew steadily closer, the manor loomed up above them.

Even from the distance, Halstead was imposing—but from the crushed-stone carriageway directly in front, where the duke pulled up his horses, it was overwhelming.

The central block of the house was a full four stories tall, built of red brick trimmed in pale cream stone. A row of ionic-style pillars framed the main entrance under a stone pediment. Off to the sides, a pair of nearly symmetrical two-story wings curved out from the main section. To Olivia's surprise, they looked like a pair of welcoming arms, arching out to gather her in.

Welcoming was the last impression she would have expected to get when standing directly in front of the main facade of a house the size of Halstead. She was still pondering the oddity of the sensation as the duke turned his team over to the groom and offered his hand to help Olivia alight from the curricle.

She was surprised he didn't seize the opportunity to lift her down and hold her close, until the front door swung open and the butler appeared. Then she was startled to find herself longing to be alone with the duke, instead of about to face a crowd of new—and probably unfriendly—faces. If the rest of Halstead's guests were anything like the bridesmaids...

Much of the company was already gathered in Halstead's drawing room, and Olivia felt as if she was running a gauntlet as she entered. Had the bridesmaids really formed a line as if closing ranks against her?

She saw only a couple of friendly faces—Kate, of course, smiled at her from beside the fireplace, where she was standing with an elderly gentleman of military bearing, with the beady-eyed Lady Stone on his other side. From a long sofa at the far end of the room, a young woman with curly dark hair inspected Olivia at length. The young, slightly shabby-looking gentleman who was leaning over the back of the sofa to talk to the young woman seemed to realize he'd lost the lady's attention, and he too looked closely at Olivia.

The duke took Olivia straight to his mother, who was seated in a tall-backed chair that managed to look like a throne. "Ah yes," the duchess said coolly as Olivia made her curtsey. "I remember you and your little girl. You were harvesting grapes at the time we met, I believe."

One of the bridesmaids tittered.

"You'll have an opportunity to get to know them both far better, ma'am," the duke said easily. "I've invited Lady Reyne to stay at Halstead through the wedding. And her daughter as well, of course, since she's such a devoted mother that she refuses to leave the child behind."

The duchess's face turned to stone. "That is quite impossible, Simon. I don't mean to be rude, Lady Reyne, but we simply have no space for more guests at Halstead."

"Of course I understand, Your Grace." So much for Simon's plans, Olivia thought. He hadn't bargained on his mother—and though technically he was the master here and his word was law at Halstead, Olivia wouldn't care to go up against the duchess when she wanted her own way. "The duke did indeed invite me to join the house party, but I had not yet given him my answer. How silly it would be to inconvenience your household when, as you point out, I already have a perfectly good cottage in the village."

The duke smiled. "Nonsense. I assume you haven't yet put anyone in the nursery? I thought you must have overlooked that possibility. So the child and her nurse can be quite easily situated there. Mrs. Greeley can find a cot somewhere for Lady Reyne's maid. Which leaves only Lady Reyne herself to be accommodated."

"*Only?*" the duchess said. She sounded as if her teeth were gritted.

Lady Stone gave a little chuckle and turned to the military gentleman. "Five guineas says the duke wins out," she said, not quite under her breath.

"There is still one empty bedroom in the main wing," the duke said blandly. "Since my valet has kept it locked, I'm quite certain it is not in use."

The duchess pulled herself up even straighter and puffed out her chest like a pigeon. "If you are referring to the empty room next to yours—the bedroom that will one day be used by your duchess—"

One of the bridesmaids gasped.

"—I think not, Simon. Not unless you plan to obtain a special license before the evening is over!"

The military gentleman rubbed his jaw and leaned down toward Lady Stone's ear, but his voice resounded as though he were on a parade ground. "Make that wager ten, Lucinda, and I'm in. He won't try to get past Iris on that one."

"Sadly," the duke said, "much as I would like to put your mind at ease, a special license could not be acquired on such short notice. I believe you will bear me out in that regard, Mr. Blakely?"

Until then, Olivia hadn't noticed the vicar standing in a corner of the drawing room. In his plain black, Mr. Blakely seemed to fade into the shadows.

The vicar looked uneasily from the duke to the duchess, clearly trying to calculate if there was any way to agree with one while not offending the other. "I believe you are correct, Your Grace," he said, and for a moment Olivia wondered which of the Somervales he was addressing. "Though I have heard a rumor since my arrival that the archbishop may be visiting somewhere in the vicinity. High Wycombe has been mentioned. If Your Grace were determined—"

The duke cut smoothly across the flood. "Rumor seems an inadequate foundation for making such a long ride with the outcome so uncertain."

Olivia wondered what he would have done if

the archbishop's presence had been more than just a rumor. *He'd find a different excuse to leave the archbishop in peace, no doubt.*

"In any event," Olivia said firmly, "I couldn't possibly agree to use a room that is reserved for the future duchess."

To Olivia's surprise, the duchess eyed her with something resembling respect. "Your guest has far more common sense than you do, Simon. Lady Reyne, I am sorry to be so disobliging, and I am in your debt for understanding my predicament."

The curly-haired young woman on the sofa stood up. "An easy solution is available, Your Grace—one that would suit everyone."

"Yes?" The duke and his mother spoke at the same instant. Despite their very different voices, Olivia thought she heard an identical note of fear in each one, and she had to fight down the hysterical urge to laugh.

The duchess glared at her son before she turned to the young woman. "Do share your insight, Lady Townsend."

So that was Lady Townsend, Olivia thought, the young woman Kate had called Penny.

Lady Townsend moved away from the slightly shabby gentleman who had been leaning over her on the sofa. "We—my husband and I—are perfectly content to share a room." She laid a hand on the arm of a handsome dark-haired gentleman who had been standing by the mantel and looked at him with what appeared to be adoration in her eyes. "I would be happy to have my things moved into your room, my dear, unless…"

For the barest instant, the gentleman beside her looked as if the mantel had come loose from the wall and tumbled onto his head.

Lady Townsend went straight on. "Unless you would prefer to come to me instead and leave your bedroom free for Lady Reyne to use?"

❧

By the time Etta had finished pulling, tugging, poking, and prodding, Penelope was relieved to go down to the drawing room to face Halstead's other guests and wait for the dinner hour to arrive. Most of the company was assembled already when she came in, but she barely glanced at the other faces once she noted the earl was not yet present.

Kate gently freed herself from yet another of Colonel Sir Tristan Huffington's seemingly interminable stories about the war.

Penelope said, "I'm sorry, Kate. I had intended to help you today, and then I... well, I forgot entirely."

"It all worked out. But I'm longing to know where you disappeared to instead, you and your husband. How lucky you are to be able to just go—without chaperones or... And what has happened to you, Penny? You seem so *different*."

Penelope couldn't stop herself from giving a little squeak. If Kate could see at a glance that something enormous had taken place today...

"Indeed she does." Andrew Carlisle lifted two glasses from a footman's tray and handed one to Penelope. "I was just telling myself you're looking even more delightful than usual tonight, Lady Townsend, very sleek and modish. What have you done differently with your hair?"

Kate rolled her eyes and walked away.

Penelope knew she should have been relieved to discover that her unusually glossy curls, and not her afternoon in bed, were making people notice her. No doubt Andrew Carlisle had really meant that she'd been quite the antidote before Etta had arrived to take her in hand, but Penelope couldn't find space in her heart to care what Mr. Carlisle thought. Or perhaps her lassitude was only because Etta had laced her corset so tightly tonight that Penelope had no room for *anything*. For the other women in the room, the discomfort of being limited to shallow breathing might have been a small price to pay for a compliment—but not for Penelope.

"Tell me how you and Charles found things at Stoneyford," Andrew said.

Penelope considered. The earl had been so secretive about his intentions to visit his estate that she suspected few people had any suspicion how bad conditions really were at Stoneyford. Was Andrew Carlisle fishing for gossip? "Much as he expected, I believe." She kept her voice expressionless. "Relatively unchanged from his last visit."

"If the situation has not grown worse, it is good news. Come and sit down and tell me all about it." He guided her to a long sofa and sat down beside her. But after a few minutes of jumping up repeatedly as each new lady came into the drawing room, he gave up his seat with a smile and leaned against the back of the sofa instead.

"I think your questions would be better directed to my husband," Penelope said.

"You're plainspoken, my lady. It's a refreshing attribute, you know. Very well, if you don't wish to speak of Stoneyford, we shall not. How is it you had lost touch with Miss Blakely?"

Suddenly, as surely as gravity pulled a dropped handkerchief to the earth, Penelope's gaze slid to the doorway where her husband stood.

Always before when Penelope looked at him, she had seen the earl—aristocratic, elegant, perfect in dress and bearing. This time she saw him differently—as a young man bearing up under burdens she could not imagine. She could even detect traces of the boy who had watched helplessly while his inheritance was ruined.

His gaze flicked past her and on to the group by the mantel, and a moment later he joined Colonel Huffington and Lady Stone.

Penelope bit her lip. How easily he had dismissed her!

Andrew Carlisle leaned a little closer. "If I might offer a word of advice, my lady. A little light-hearted flirting with another gentleman often brings a husband's attention back where it belongs."

Was she so very obvious? "Your knowledge of such things must arise from your vast experience as a flirt, Mr. Carlisle, since I believe you have exactly none as a husband."

He grinned. "That's precisely the way to do it, ma'am! Now you lean a little closer and smile at me as if I've amused you greatly. And if you could manage just a tiny giggle…"

Penelope couldn't help laughing. "You *do* amuse me greatly, Mr. Carlisle." However she behaved, she told herself, the earl would probably not notice. He had turned his back toward her to concentrate on the colonel. So she might as well occupy herself in whatever way she could find to make the endless hours pass more quickly.

"Amusing people is my greatest talent," Andrew Carlisle confided.

"And I am persuaded your willingness to be of assistance to a lady has no connection with your desire to discourage the attention directed at you by the bridesmaids."

"I believe I have already been successful there." His gaze roved over the guests. "Yes, not a one of them is paying me the slightest heed. Being a mere wage-earner has advantages, my lady."

"But are you fulfilling your promise to the duke by taking yourself out of the running?" Penelope looked up archly only to realize Andrew Carlisle was not looking at her any more. She followed his gaze to where the duke and Lady Reyne had just appeared in the arched doorway.

No wonder Mr. Carlisle was staring, she thought. Even in an outdated dress, Lady Reyne had a presence Penelope herself would never be able to command.

Her flirtation with Andrew Carlisle had died aborning, before she could take it too seriously. She let her gaze drift once more to her husband—only to realize he, too, was focused on Lady Reyne.

Penelope told herself not to be silly. She wasn't *jealous*. Every eye in the room, not just those of the gentlemen, was upon Lady Reyne. The way the duke and his mother were squabbling—with level voices and perfect manners, to be sure; but the truth was they were squabbling all the same—over whether Lady Reyne should remain at Halstead or be sent home to her dour little cottage had drawn everyone's attention.

Penelope knew she couldn't have handled the strain with anything like the calm Lady Reyne did. Perhaps that was the true difference between ordinary people and the quality.

She looked back at the earl, and this time she couldn't pretend she wasn't feeling green with envy. If just once he had looked at her in the way he was studying Lady Reyne… But he was her husband, and there was no changing the fact. Perhaps she should act the part.

"Lady Reyne, I am sorry to be so disobliging," the duchess said, "and I am quite in your debt for understanding my predicament."

Penelope stood up. "An easy solution is available, Your Grace—one which would suit everyone." She felt the gaze of every person in the room turn toward her. The enormity of what she was about to do made her light-headed, and she took an instant to get her balance before she moved slowly toward her husband.

"We—my husband and I—are perfectly content to share a room." Her timing had been impeccable; before her words had a chance to register, she laid her hand on the earl's arm and turned her face up to his with what she hoped looked like adulation. "I would be happy to have my things moved into your room, my dear, unless you would prefer to come to me instead and leave your bedroom free for Lady Reyne to use?"

The earl's arm twitched under her hand. "What the devil are you thinking?" he said quietly.

Penelope didn't bother to lower her voice. "Only that you are always so thoughtful of a lady in need. Surely you would not want to see Lady Reyne be required to undertake the journey back to the village late at night."

The duke seemed to be trying not to laugh. "It's very generous of you, Charles, even though I'm sure you'll be... ah... suitably rewarded for your selflessness."

Penelope noted the morose look on the earl's face. Was he struggling to keep from pointing out that he was not the one who had made the offer, generous or otherwise?

Colonel Huffington nudged Lady Stone, who looked disgruntled. "That's ten guineas you owe me, Lucinda. I told you the duke wouldn't buck his mother."

In the doorway, the butler cleared his throat and announced dinner. The ladies gathered up their possessions, and the gentlemen began to seek out their dinner partners.

The earl stood frozen. "We will discuss this later."

Penelope's knees were quivering, but she kept her voice level. "Yes." She flipped her fan open and looked at him over the lace trim. "I just made certain of it."

Twelve

PERHAPS THE DUCHESS HAD TIRED OF HER EXPERIMENT in seating her dinner guests purely at random, Kate thought. Or maybe the addition of a few more gentlemen had encouraged her to return to the usual pattern of arranging her table by rank.

Though Kate realized where that system would place her—toward the center of the table, well away from the titled guests who clustered around the duke at one end and the dowager at the other—she hadn't given thought to the question of who her dinner companions might be. So she was startled when Andrew Carlisle bowed before her in the drawing room and offered his arm.

"You?" she said, before she could bite her tongue.

Andrew merely looked thoughtful. "Surely you're not suggesting the duchess could have erred in her calculations of our respective ranks? Let's see. The daughter of a vicar and the younger son of a baronet… Ponsonby, Chadwick, and Warren all outrank me, so…"

"I was not impugning Her Grace's manners, merely regretting the way I snapped at you earlier,

Mr. Carlisle. Under the circumstances, it cannot be comfortable to be dinner partners."

"No, Kate. I am the one who must apologize for asking uncomfortable questions."

The knot inside Kate's stomach unclenched a little. He sounded sober, thoughtful, and considerate.

"As for going in to dinner together," Andrew went on, "I think Her Grace is correct that we make a good match."

She shot a wary look up at him. Surely he didn't realize how suggestive he'd sounded. On the other hand, he had not missed the opportunity to flirt with Penny or to stare at Olivia, so he might see pretending to dangle after Kate as mere practice.

She tried once more to escape. "You're certain no bridesmaid requires your escort?"

"None of them wants me any more." Andrew sounded pitiful. "I was too successful at discouraging them before you came up with your plan for me to marry the richest one. Which of them would that be, by the way?"

"So you can set about ingratiating yourself with her? If I knew, I wouldn't tell you."

Andrew smiled. "I wonder why you have had such a change of heart. But I suppose I must not put you to the blush by asking why your scheme to marry me off to an heiress no longer appeals to you."

Kate stared at him for a moment, speechless. How had he taken a firm refusal to participate in his game and turned it round to imply that she was flirting with him? "I should think not. Let us change the subject, Mr. Carlisle."

"As you wish, my Kate. Perhaps later—in

private—you will explain." As they walked across the wide entrance hall, he nodded toward the head of the procession, already at the dining room doors. "Lady Stone looks quite put out. Do you suppose she is trying to renege on her wager?"

"I think she'll pay the Colonel and then attempt to recoup her losses from Penny."

"It does seem hard on Lady Stone. She had a sporting chance, I think, until Lady Townsend stepped in to prevent the question from playing out."

"Yes," Kate murmured. "Lucky girl."

"I beg your pardon?"

Had she truly spoken the thought aloud? "Oh, I just meant this entire household has been scrambling to accommodate the number of husbands and wives who are required to attend Lady Daphne's wedding together but who prefer not to share a roof."

Andrew's voice dropped to an intimate whisper. "Much less a bed. Yes, I see what you mean. How interesting that you, too, feel Lady Townsend is lucky in her match. As for the idea of a wife wanting—to put it in delicate terms—to share a room with her husband... Miss Blakely, have you any idea how exciting it is for me when I hear you speak of such things?"

Delicate? He didn't know the meaning of the word. "And have you any idea how improper you are to speak of it, Mr. Carlisle?"

But they had reached the dining room, and he showed her to a chair next to the vicar's.

Just when I was thinking things couldn't get worse, Kate reflected. She noted the sparkle in Andrew's eyes and braced herself.

The gentlemen sat down, and as the scrape of chairs faded, to be replaced by the soft clink of serving spoons against china, Andrew said, "Miss Blakely, I hope you were able to remove the moss left on your skirt by this afternoon's adventure."

The vicar's ear perked up and he turned toward Kate, ignoring the young woman with whom he was supposed to be conversing over the soup. "Adventure? My dear Miss Blakely…"

Andrew leaned across her to confide, "I regret to say she appeared to have rolled in the stuff, Vicar."

"Mr. Carlisle exaggerates. Miss Horatia is waiting to speak with you, Mr. Blakely."

Andrew settled back into his chair and waited while the footman served their first course. "I don't think the vicar will thank you for reminding him of his manners," he said softly. "Did you see the way his jaw went white? Did you get rid of the moss, by the way?"

Over the venison, the vicar questioned Kate about moss stains and the accident in the abbey until she was ready to scream. But eventually, he seemed to accept that she had comported herself like a lady and not a trollop, and he ended by congratulating her for her Christian sacrifice of a riding habit.

"I notice," Andrew pointed out when she turned back to him with the start of the next course, "*he* didn't offer to loan you money to replace it. Tell me, Kate—now that you know the vicar better, do you think he's truly a man of God? Or does he simply think he *is* God?"

Kate's head was starting to pound.

After dinner, as the ladies returned to the drawing room, she had the first opportunity of the evening for a word with Olivia or Penny, who had been seated at the far ends of the table.

As Kate came up behind them, however, the duchess intercepted her. "Miss Blakely, I need you to run an errand for me."

Kate forced a smile. "Of course, Your Grace."

"Please look in on Miss Emily to see that she's comfortable. Do you know if the dressmakers have set up their tables as I instructed?"

"I believe so, Your Grace. I suggested they take over the east wing hall, which is the only place with adequate space to work and the necessary privacy for fittings. With only ladies passing through that corridor…"

"You must tell Mrs. Greeley to issue instructions for the footmen to announce themselves before they walk through the hall, so any lady caught in a state of dishabille can safely remove to her room." The duchess took the arm of one of the bridesmaids' mothers and strolled off toward the drawing room, talking about gardens.

Kate delivered the order to the housekeeper and went up to the east wing to check on Emily's bruises. The hall had been transformed, with a row of tables down the center and a bevy of dressmakers wielding scissors. Kate looked at the array of fabrics in surprise. The range of colors made a rainbow look dim.

This was the sort of thing that had been stashed in Halstead's cupboards?

Nearby, the modiste looked up from where she was fitting the bodice of a silvery-gray dress on a young woman who stood patiently, arms out, while the modiste pinned. "Miss Blakely, you're in good time. Sally, take that dress off instantly so I can check the fitting on Miss Blakely."

By the time Kate returned to the drawing room, the ladies were comfortably disposed. She waited patiently for the duchess to finish a comment about the upcoming ball and said, "Miss Emily is asleep, ma'am, with her maid watching in case she calls for anything, and the dressmakers are proceeding well. I wish to thank you for the gowns you've planned for me."

The duchess's eyes gleamed. "I hope you're not offended by my choice of colors? Black was in short supply, I'm afraid, but since it has been three months since your father's death, surely navy and gray and lavender are reasonable alternatives."

"Yes, ma'am. The modiste said all the dresses would be ready for fitting by morning."

"Very well, then. Make certain every lady is entertained, if you please."

Kate worked her way around the room, starting a conversation here and asking a question there. Finally, feeling free to follow her own interests for a moment, she sought out Olivia and Penny. They had taken a sofa in a secluded corner, and as Kate approached, she heard Penny say earnestly, "What I'd really like, my lady, is your advice on…" Her voice dropped. "Seduction."

Olivia's face turned the color of Halstead's red brick walls. "What in the world do you mean?"

"Well… you were married, and you have a child. So I thought perhaps…" Now Penny was turning red too. She took a deep breath. "I thought perhaps you could give me some advice about how to… get my husband to…"

Kate felt her eyes widen. Perhaps Penny wasn't so lucky in her marriage after all.

"I can't say I ever tried to seduce Lord Reyne," Olivia said dryly. "But in general, I suppose…"

Much as Kate would have liked to listen to rest of the conversation, she was drawn away by a pair of bridesmaids with a complaint about the fire smoking in their bedroom. While she listened to the litany, she noticed that Olivia and Penny had moved closer together and seemed so absorbed in their discussion that they were oblivious to everything going on around them.

Kate suspected Penny might have been a good deal wiser to have asked someone besides Olivia for advice. Andrew Carlisle came to mind; he could probably teach a brick wall how to be seductive…

Penny seemed on the brink of tears, and Olivia reached into her reticule to offer a dainty handkerchief. Penny started to blot delicately around her eyes, but then she gave a little gasp of pain and pulled the linen away. Kate saw a tiny cut oozing blood on Penny's cheekbone.

Something glinted in the folds of the handkerchief—something gold-colored, with a flash of blue. As Penny unfolded the fabric, a piece of metal fell into her lap, gleaming for an instant against the shimmery yellow silk of her skirt before it slid off and bounced on the carpet.

Olivia's face went pale. Quickly she bent to snatch

up the bauble from the floor, and an instant later it had once again disappeared into her reticule. "Just wire from a… from a comb I broke a few days ago. I am sorry you are injured, my dear."

The tiny crack in her voice would not have been obvious to others, but Kate would have spotted the falsehood even if she hadn't known Olivia had no gold combs to break.

That bit of metal hadn't looked anything like a piece of a comb, anyway. It had resembled a gentleman's stickpin—one Kate had seen before, though she could not remember where. But how had Olivia come into possession of such a thing?

Kate's headache came back with a vengeance.

⁂

Simon was not aware of feeling impatient for the evening to end, but as the port made its way around the dining table for the third time, Andrew said, "You're damned poor company tonight, Your Grace—and you keep looking at the clock as if you think the hands aren't moving at all."

"You're imagining things, Andrew, but if you're in a hurry to get back to the bridesmaids, don't let the rest of us keep you."

"A most charming group of young women," the vicar said. "Lady Daphne is to be congratulated on the beauty and elegant manners of her friends."

Silence dropped over the room for a moment.

"Indeed," Simon said. "I think on that note, gentlemen, we should rejoin the ladies, since we seem to be missing their company."

At his right, he thought he heard the Earl of Townsend murmur, "Speak for yourself, Simon." But the earl drained his port glass and pushed back his chair along with the others.

Simon dawdled behind the others as they entered the drawing room. The vicar made straight for Kate Blakely and began what looked like a monologue. The three newcomers—Ponsonby, Warren, and Chadwick—carried out their assignments with the same military precision with which they had executed maneuvers on the Peninsula; they fanned out to create multiple diversions, and each was soon surrounded by young ladies.

With the bridesmaids distracted, Simon strolled through the drawing room, pausing to chat with each of the older ladies, his path precisely arranged to end beside the sofa where Olivia sat with Lady Townsend.

If he couldn't be in bed with Olivia, Simon thought, then the next best thing was to sit beside her. He could think of worse ways to spend an evening than flirting with Olivia. Scheming to find ways to touch her even under his mother's watchful gaze was entertainment enough for the moment—and since she was so delightfully responsive to every glance and breath and word, he looked forward to an even more enjoyable night when they were finally alone.

The sooner, the better.

❦

Only a moment after Olivia had retrieved the stickpin and tucked it safely away once more, the gentlemen returned to the drawing room. Olivia was still vibrating from her close call—in another few seconds, Lady Stone would have seen the sapphire. Or worse, the duchess herself might have turned her head and recognized it.

A pretty problem it would have been to explain to the duke's mother why his stickpin was in Olivia's possession. What on earth would she have said, anyway? *"I found it in the hall just now. One of the gentlemen must have dropped it, so I mean to ask as soon as they rejoin us. Unless one of you recognizes it?"*

But the duke was wearing bottle green tonight, with a glorious diamond in his neckcloth, so he couldn't have lost a sapphire at dinnertime. And since Olivia couldn't even make *herself* believe a valuable stone could have lain in the hallway for hours without Halstead's vigilant staff noticing, she knew better than to try that story on the duchess.

Stop it, she told herself. The stickpin was safely back in her reticule. The mark on Penny Townsend's cheek was tiny, barely a pinprick, and would quickly heal. No real damage had been done.

But Olivia had thought the stickpin was safe before, bundled into an extra handkerchief and tucked deep into her bag. She couldn't keep taking chances.

She sat quietly and tried to listen while Daphne and her friends entertained the company with music, even though in Olivia's shattered state, cats screeching on the garden wall would have sounded better. The duke sat beside her, looking like the perfect gentleman. There was not even a touch that would appear anything but proper to an observer.

And yet there was nothing at all proper about the

emotions he roused in her. Every word, every glance, every half smile made her feel naked and as though she was sprawled across a blanket somewhere with him leaning over her and looking his fill.

The music finally ended, and as Olivia lifted her hands to applaud, her reticule slid off her lap. As the bag hit the carpet she saw that the drawstring had come open, and her heart went to her throat. If the stickpin fell out now…

Simon swooped up the bag and laid it in her hands. What no one could see, Olivia was certain, was the way he slowly stroked the underside of her wrist just beyond the edge of her glove, sending a torrent of sparks along her skin.

The duchess said, "Perhaps on another evening, you might be persuaded to entertain us, Lady Reyne."

"I'm afraid the few feminine talents I have are far too rusty for that, ma'am."

"A pity. But perhaps your daughter will have a gift for music or dance."

How could she have forgotten about Charlotte? "I beg your pardon, but if I might be excused from the company, I am anxious to look in on my daughter."

The duchess nodded. "Miss Blakely, please show her ladyship to the nursery wing."

Kate made the quickest curtsey Olivia had ever seen as she excused herself from the vicar. "Thank you for the rescue," she told Olivia as they started up the stairs. "I really thought I was going to scream if I had to listen to one more admiring comment from Mr. Blakely about the girls' performances!"

Olivia managed to get her first deep breath in an

hour. "I hope when he renews his offer of marriage, you will remember his conduct from tonight."

"Even being Colonel Sir Tristan Huffington's private secretary and writing down his memoirs would be less trying," Kate said gloomily. "Though perhaps not a great deal more exciting."

"Has he asked you? The colonel, I mean."

"No. Perhaps Daphne is right—she says he's the poorest of poor relations, retired on half pay from the Army."

They were out of the public areas of the house now. The stairway here was both narrower and steeper, and they stopped to catch their breath on a landing so high above the entrance hall that the marble floor looked no bigger than a chessboard.

Kate said softly, "Are you all right, Olivia? I couldn't help but notice, back there... with Penny... You looked so upset."

"Kate, please. It's nothing, really." Olivia smiled, though every muscle in her face felt stiff. "I just need to hold my little girl for a while, and then I'll be fine."

❦

After Simon dismissed his valet, he sat by the fire in his bedroom toying with a glass of brandy while he waited for enough time to pass so he could go to Olivia.

A stolen kiss in the abbey ruins was not enough to satisfy, and the sort of light flirtation he'd been able to indulge himself with this evening had simply made his hunger grow. Last night in her garden had provided only a taste of what he wanted from Olivia Reyne. He wasn't finished exploring her...

He checked the clock. Less than half an hour had gone by since he'd dismissed Hemmings, not long enough for the house to quiet sufficiently for him to steal down the hall and around the corner to visit her. He should wait until midnight—if he could hold out so long. Olivia's bedroom was directly at the head of the stairway, so everyone in Halstead would pass as they went up and down. Until every last person was safely tucked away for the night, he couldn't make a move.

A pity he hadn't been successful at establishing her in the room directly next to his. Then there would be no sneaking up and down corridors, no watching at corners to be sure no one was observing, and no waiting until the dead of night to safely visit.

Simon refilled his brandy glass and crossed his room to the connecting doorway. He hadn't so much as peeked through that door in a year at least. Though he didn't deliberately avoid the duchess's bedroom, he also didn't have any reason to visit. Most of the time he forgot the room was even there. It was a good thing Hemmings had thought to lock it; Simon might have forgotten entirely.

He simply didn't think about the part of his future that would require him to choose a duchess. He was a long way from thirty yet, so there was plenty of time to set up his nursery.

The very idea of a nursery reminded him of Olivia's daughter, and he wondered how she was adapting to her new surroundings.

Despite the fact that Halstead's nursery wing had not been used since Daphne grew big enough to rebel at being treated like a baby, Mrs. Greeley would have kept it ready to use—just in case. And no doubt somewhere on Halstead's enormous roster of employees the housekeeper would have found a maid or two with experience in caring for younger siblings. So Miss Charlotte was without a doubt safely watched over. By now, she should be tucked securely in one of the narrow cots in the night nursery, sound asleep.

After the cramped quarters of the cottage, however, the child must be overwhelmed. Simon remembered lying awake and watching the shifting shadows of the firelight on the angled ceilings, imagining monsters creeping silently out from under the bed ready to attack. He suspected—remembering her stick horse— that Charlotte was even more imaginative than he had been. What if she saw monsters? What if she again suffered the nightmare that had awakened her and sent her wandering the night before?

He shook his head at his own wild speculations and pushed open the door of the duchess's bedroom next to his own. The furnishings were sparse, for his mother had moved much of her favorite furniture to her new suite. Simon had never bothered to replace the missing pieces, for surely a new duchess would wish to choose her own.

Furnished with only a bed, a bureau, and a couple of small tables, the room looked huge, and despite the weak light of the candlestick he carried, Simon could easily cross the carpet without fear of stubbing his toes. He touched the flame to the lamp standing atop the bureau, and the wick caught instantly. He lit candles at each side of the great bed, setting them safely away from the bed curtains. As each wick caught, another pool of warm light sprang to life and rippled outward, overlapping until the pale gold hangings and draperies seemed to glow.

The icy colors of the room had been exactly right for his mother. But Olivia would require brighter shades. Scarlet, perhaps, to match the flame of passion that lay deep inside her. Or would that be entirely too predictable—and overwhelming, as well? Royal purple would be just as dramatic with her dark hair and milky skin. Yes, he thought. A variety of shades of purple could be restful. Paired with pristine white to emphasize her grace and purity…

What in hell was he thinking? Even if he'd been able to sneak her into the adjoining bedroom, an affair of a few days' duration was hardly cause to redecorate. And even if he stayed on after the wedding, he could not keep his mistress right here at Halstead.

He was losing his mind, Simon thought. The best cure would be to find Olivia, take her straight to bed, and work out these strange ramblings of his through an energetic romp. He must take full advantage of the short time while she would still be so conveniently near at hand.

Though the house was not yet utterly quiet, and night lamps still burned here and there to see the last of the guests to their beds, no one was in sight as Simon left his bedroom. The curving wings presented considerable danger, however, because he couldn't see far enough down the passages to be certain he was alone. If someone came around a corner while he was tapping on her door…

But which door was hers? Simon had had no reason to care which room the Earl of Townsend had occupied and which one had been assigned to his countess. They were in the blue suite, he remembered. But the odds were fifty-fifty that he would knock at the wrong door. Being discovered in the act of tapping on his mistress's door would be embarrassing enough, but if he chose wrongly and interrupted his friend's amorous plans, he might as well stand in the entrance hall and shout his intentions of making love to Lady Reyne.

Simon paused at the top of the stairs, senses tingling. An instant later he had confirmation he was not alone when Charles Townsend leaned around the side of one of the tall-backed chairs on the landing. "I thought that must be you, Simon. What are you doing tiptoeing around wearing a jacket that looks awfully like a dressing gown?"

"I have a better question," Simon parried. "What are you doing out here when your countess is waiting for you? A shared bedroom, Charles… The *ton* will be shocked when they hear. So if you're going to have to hold your head up under the gossip, you might as well have the fun to compensate."

"Thanks for the advice, old friend. If you're about to tell me you're headed down to the library for a book of sermons to help you sleep, don't bother. Lady Reyne's room is that one, by the way." Charles pointed at the door nearest the top of the stairs.

Simon felt a wash of relief. "Why would you think I'm interested?"

"But she's not there just now."

"What? Where is she? And how do you know?"

Charles snickered. "You gave yourself away there, my friend. Miss Blakely came down perhaps half an hour ago. She told Lady Reyne's maid that her ladyship was going to stay upstairs with Miss—whatever-her-name-is."

"Charlotte," Simon said absently. "Lady Reyne promised Charlotte she'd tuck her in tonight—before she knew they'd be here instead of at the cottage, of course. I wonder if the child is too frightened up in the nursery to go to sleep."

"Watch out there, Simon. Talking about nurseries and remembering little girls' names... You're starting to sound like a man who's ready to settle down."

"And you're starting to look like one who's had his wings clipped. Do you always jump when the heiress demands it?"

Charles's voice was low and even. "That's my countess you're referring to, Simon."

Simon could have cheerfully eaten the words. "Sorry. I didn't mean to sound... I'm sorry, Charles. Daphne's breaking out the archery equipment tomorrow. If you'd like to take a shot at me for that insult, I'll stand still and pretend to be the target."

"No—it wouldn't be sporting, to say nothing of raising too many questions. How about I beat you senseless in a game of billiards instead?"

"Good idea. And since I appreciate your gentle-manly conduct, I'll let you win."

"We'll see about that." Charles stood up and stretched. "Shall we go down?"

"Surely you can't mean right now."

Charles laughed. "So you do have plans for tonight!"

The door of the second bedroom—the Countess of Townsend's room—opened, and a stern-looking maid came out with a neat pile of clothing in her arms. She glared at the gentlemen before she stalked off down the hall toward the back stairs.

"She must be one dragon of a female," Simon said under his breath. "No wonder you were waiting here till she cleared out. Have a good night, Charles." He waited until the earl closed the door behind him and then considered his options. He could go back to his room and try again later, roughly doubling the risk of being spotted. He could wait for Olivia in her room, but hadn't Charles said her maid was there?

He heard voices from the foot of the stairs—Lady Stone and the colonel, he thought, debating which of them owed the other ten guineas. "It was not a fair bet," Lady Stone said firmly, and Simon heard the deeper notes of the colonel's voice as he argued his case.

Simon hoped the colonel came out the winner. Lady Stone could afford her bets, but Simon suspected the old soldier couldn't.

The voices drew nearer as the pair started up the stairs. With just moments to decide between his options—rushing down the hall to his own room, or bursting into Olivia's and hoping her maid wasn't there—Simon found himself instead sprinting straight up the stairway all the way to the top, where the nursery was tucked under Halstead's sloping roof.

He'd forgotten how low the ceilings were here. Even the passage running down the center of the house, where the roof line was highest, was small enough to make Simon feel like a giant.

No one was in the day nursery, though a lamp burned near the door. Hearing the soft murmur of a lullaby from the night nursery, Simon tiptoed across to peek in. Olivia was sitting on the edge of a cot, while Nurse rocked by the fireplace as she darned a sock. He wondered if she managed the work purely by feel, since the only light in the room, apart from the glow of the coals, came from a dim lamp on the table beside her.

Olivia turned her head as he came in, looking startled. "I didn't expect to see you anywhere near a nursery, Your Grace." Her voice was low and soft, brushing over his skin like the warm tickle of gentle fingers, and he wondered how it would feel to hear her say his name. Then he noticed she was gently and rhythmically stroking her child's back, and envy ran through him. To have her touch him like that...

Though perhaps his back wouldn't be his first choice of locations.

He realized she was waiting for an answer. "I always liked this wing."

"I suspect you feel more secure here, since this is the last place the bridesmaids would be likely to look for you."

"That's true," Simon admitted. "Still, a good host makes a habit of greeting all his guests, so naturally I came to check on Miss Charlotte."

"She was overexcited and enamored of the hobby-horse. I believe she would have much preferred continuing to explore—the nursery alone is as large as our entire cottage."

"The third duke and his duchess were a prolific pair, so when he built Halstead, he designed the nursery to accommodate a crowd."

"How long ago?"

"A century, give or take. We have cousins all over England because of him."

"Charlotte will be quite above herself with all this space at her command and a full staff to wait on her. I'm sure when we go home in a few days she will find the cottage very dull in comparison."

"And what about you, Olivia? Will you find the cottage dull?"

"Of course. Halstead is nothing if not exciting."

And me? Simon wanted to ask. *Will you miss me?*

She tucked the blanket more closely around the child. "She's safely asleep now, I think. I'll tell her tomorrow she was honored by the duke himself coming to visit." Olivia eased herself from the cot and stood up.

"Then if your duties here are complete, may I escort you downstairs?" Damnation, what was wrong with him? His voice had cracked like a schoolboy's.

She gave a long sigh. Speckles of apprehension danced through him. Surely she didn't intend to refuse him, did she?

She reached for her reticule, lying on the table next to Nurse's chair, and led the way out to the corridor. She stopped there and opened her bag. "First, I have something I wish to give you."

The dim light that filtered out from the nursery lamps caught on the object in her hand, and for an instant it flared brilliant blue.

Simon looked down at his sapphire stickpin, lying against the smooth, creamy skin of her palm, and felt his mouth go dry with dread. She was returning his gift.

But why?

Thirteen

PENELOPE BORE ETTA'S BEDTIME FUSSING WITH ALL THE
grace she could muster, but finally even the maid had
to admit she could do nothing more to add to her
lady's allure. Gathering up the clothing that needed
laundering, Etta pulled the door of the blue bedroom
shut behind her, leaving Penelope alone.

She sat up in the big bed with pillows propped
behind her and candles burning on either side,
wondering whether the earl would come to her or if
he would find some other place to spend the night.

Her brazen challenge had seemed such a good idea
when she had tossed it out in the drawing room. She
had even managed to eat a few bites of her dinner,
though perhaps only because she'd been seated at the
far end of the table from her husband.

But now Penelope was alone in the shadows,
waiting to see whether he would take up the gauntlet.

Asking Olivia Reyne for advice had been one of
the most difficult things Penelope had ever done, but
at least now she knew what had happened this afternoon and what had gone wrong. Her physical needs

had been met, but her husband's had not. Instead of satisfying himself by spilling his seed, he had withdrawn from her... and that, from what Lady Reyne had implied, was so unusual where husbands were concerned as to be unheard of.

The door opened and the earl came in. Penelope sat up a little straighter.

His gaze flicked across her as though she was just another pillow. "Is there a dressing room?"

She pointed toward a door half-hidden in the paneling. "It's very small."

The earl pulled off his coat and untied his neckcloth. "I assume there is a cot I can use."

"No. The duchess must have needed it elsewhere."

He paused in midmotion. "The duchess? Or you? You've managed everything else to your own taste. I must assume you capable of arranging that, too."

He didn't sound angry or bitter, just resigned.

Suddenly the challenge she had flung down before him with such high hope and confidence seemed merely pathetic.

"Put out your candle," the earl said.

"Why? I've seen..." *Your very intriguing body—all of it—before.* Penelope stopped herself. Perhaps he meant this time he would prefer the dark.

Obediently, she wet her fingertips and pinched out the wick. Only the candle on the far side of the bed still burned, and as the earl undressed, his shadow reeled around the room, making Penelope feel dizzy.

Or perhaps it was simple anticipation.

She toyed with the edge of the linen sheet, trying not to watch as he disrobed. But she couldn't help but feast her eyes on him as the candlelight kissed his skin, making the hair on his chest gleam gold.

He didn't bother with a nightshirt, and Penelope suddenly felt very overdressed in her fussy satin and lace gown.

He pushed back the coverlet and sat on the edge of the mattress for a moment, his back to her, as if bracing himself. Then he pinched out the candle's wick.

In the sudden darkness, the rasp of linen sounded loud and harsh against his skin as he slid into the bed. Penelope scooted down from her pillows to lie flat, waiting for him to turn to her, to reach for her.

He didn't.

She lay rigid in the big bed and listened to him breathe. Gradually, as her eyes became accustomed to nothing but firelight, she could see the room nearly as well as she had when the candles were lit.

Finally, she said, "Is the fire too much?"

For a moment she thought he was going to pretend he was asleep. As though she could be convinced he had drifted off. "Too much what?"

"Is there too much light to let you pretend I am someone else? If you need the room to be darker—"

The earl swore. She'd never before heard some of the words he used—but she had no trouble understanding the gist, and she felt as if her stomach was turning miserable flips. What had she done? How had such a simple plan gone so badly awry?

"I am sorry, sir." Penelope's voice was little more than a whisper.

The earl sat up, punching at his pillow. "I should think you would be. You chose this course. *One time,* you said, and I agreed. Now this. What in hell did you think you were doing, making a public farce of this?"

She couldn't exactly argue. But she'd said she was sorry, and now Penelope was feeling so mulish she couldn't back down. "Yes, you agreed—and then you didn't do as you promised!"

"What are you talking about?"

"I asked to be shown how it feels to be a wife. This afternoon hardly addressed the question."

"I'm not surprised you were shocked by the process, ma'am."

"No, I mean a *husband* would have attempted to give his wife a child!"

He went still, as though he'd frozen in place.

"I may have been a virgin this afternoon, but I know more than you think I do. That wasn't how a man treats his wife. That was how a man acts with his mistress when he doesn't want to be saddled with a bastard child!"

As soon as the words were out, Penelope knew she had gone too far.

He moved so suddenly she didn't have even an instant to contemplate his intentions before his hands were on her. "You're wrong. A mistress is an entirely different thing." He seized her nightgown with both hands. The sound of satin and lace ripping echoed through the room. Three quick wrenches laid the gown open from neckline to hem, exposing her completely. "*This* is how a man treats his mistress."

He captured both her wrists and dragged them above her head, holding her wrists with one hand while he plundered her body with the other. His fingertips seemed to be everywhere, leaving a trail of flame wherever he touched—the line of her throat, the hollow under her collarbone, her painfully aroused nipples, her waist, her hip, her thigh. He nudged her legs apart enough to plunge one finger inside her, and Penelope felt a surge of slickness as she welcomed him. He released her wrists and slid down her body, his tongue greedily claiming every spot his fingertips had touched, sliding across her belly, dipping into the small indentation of her navel, and moving on down...

Shocked, she clamped her legs together.

"Oh, no," he said. "We'll have none of that. Not from a mistress." He moved over her, kneeling between her thighs. With one hand on each of her knees, he spread her legs wide. For a long moment he only looked. She felt the brush of cool air moving across the damp heat of her most private parts and was embarrassed to admit she found even the small touch stimulating. Or was the sudden rush of wetness between her legs purely because of the way he was looking at her?

He bent his head and flicked his tongue against her, and Penelope arched off the bed. As if in retaliation, he pushed her knees wider yet and settled down between her legs, licking and sucking and lapping at her. He found the sensitive nub of her clitoris and blew gently on it, then casually rubbed his thumb across it, setting off an earthquake deep inside her.

Penelope moaned. He was deliberately driving her mad, she knew, and there was nothing she could do but let him watch while she came apart under his relentless stroking.

She was still shaking from her orgasm when he released her knees, positioned himself over her, and plunged inside with one long deep thrust. She cried out in surprise and he paused, holding himself still.

He intended to withdraw again—she could sense it. But this time, she swore, he would not be able to pull away. Guided by a primitive instinct she did not understand, she wrapped her legs around him and locked her ankles together, holding him inside her.

"You learn very quickly, *mistress*," he muttered and began to make quick thrusts, moving only an inch or two, stroking her sensitized flesh.

But the rest of her was just as hungry for his touch. "More," she whimpered.

He stopped moving altogether. "Then you have to let go."

If he withdrew again without finishing, Penelope thought, she would die right there in his arms. But she couldn't stand this either, to have him inside her but quiescent. Reluctantly, she relaxed her legs.

Instantly, he pulled almost all the way out of her. For a long moment he stayed poised there, with only the very head of his penis teasing inside her. Penelope felt betrayed, wounded—but then he delved again, sheathing himself completely. She clenched her muscles tightly around him, stroking him in return.

He said something under his breath—she thought it might have been "Vixen"—and then she was past thinking or hearing. All she could do was feel as his thrusts, long and deep and hard, took her over the brink. But even as she lost herself in utter fulfillment, she felt a burst of heat and joy as he cried out and spilled his seed deep inside her body.

&

When Kate and Olivia reached the nursery, Charlotte was wearing her nightgown but sitting up in her cot, fighting sleep and arguing madly to be allowed to continue exploring. "There's a real horse!" she told Kate.

"It's a hobbyhorse," Nurse said. "Quite an elaborate one, too, compared to her stick creation. The mane and tail are made of real horsehair."

"I'll show you, Miss Kate," Charlotte offered. She squirmed off the cot before Olivia caught her by the back of her nightgown.

Kate decided to remove one potential distraction. "Tomorrow, my dear, I will come and admire the horse. For now, I must go back downstairs to see the duchess, and it's time for you to go to sleep so you're not too tired tomorrow to ride."

"I would like to see the duchess, too," Charlotte said hopefully.

"I think I'd better stay here till she's settled," Olivia said.

Kate met the duchess on the first landing. She hadn't realize it was so late, but if the duchess was retiring to her room, the company would soon scatter; once the highest-ranking lady had excused herself, the rest of the ladies were free to do the same. The gentlemen would likely return to their own pursuits for an hour or two before retiring, but Kate's duties would be finished for the day. "Is there anything else you would like me to do this evening, ma'am?" she asked.

A couple of minutes later, with the duchess's instructions still echoing in her ears, Kate paused on the threshold of the drawing room. At a table in the far corner, Andrew Carlisle, the colonel, and a couple of the bridesmaids' mothers were playing whist. Kate hoped the stakes were low—for the colonel's sake, of course, she told herself.

Standing by the pianoforte, one of the newly arrived gentlemen turned pages for the lone bridesmaid who displayed actual musical talent. He looked moonstruck; Kate wondered if he was really impressed or was simply an excellent actor.

On the long couch, Lady Stone had taken up Olivia's seat beside Penny and seemed to be quizzing her. The hairs at the nape of Kate's neck stood up. If Lady Stone had overheard the conversation about seduction, or if she had gotten a better look than Kate had at the gold trinket Olivia had dropped, or if she was trying to dun Penny to pay the bet Lady Stone had lost...

As she headed in their direction, the vicar intercepted her. "Miss Blakely, if I might have a word."

Kate managed a smile. "Of course, sir. The duchess requested me to discuss a few last arrangements for Lady Daphne's wedding with you. If you have no objections to displaying flowers on the altar for the ceremony, the gardeners will send over the best blooms Halstead can produce."

"Yes, yes. Whatever Her Grace wishes." He took her arm and drew her off toward a corner. "We've had scarcely a moment alone. Even at dinner, that officious Mr. Carlisle was continually making his presence felt, so I could not express my feelings."

Kate pretended not to hear. "If Her Grace's notion is satisfactory to you, sir, then I will undertake to arrange the flowers myself on the afternoon before the wedding."

"I shall look forward to the occasion. Such a feminine pursuit, flower arranging! I will accept no other engagements. What a charming idea you have had, for us to meet in the church to become better acquainted since the church has brought us together. My dear Miss Blakely, I cannot tell you how delighted I am at the prospect."

He sounded as if he hoped she was plotting to drag him into the vestry and ravish him. "The duchess felt I would be the best person to carry out her wishes, since I know where the vases are kept in the church and how the altar is decorated to best advantage."

"Of course." He smiled broadly. "When a lady arranges matters to suit herself, she should never admit it—and a gentleman must never call attention to the fact she has done so. My apologies, I am sure. I am properly set down, but how gently you did it. I am impressed with your tact, surely the best of all traits for the wife of a vicar, my dear."

Kate bit her tongue until the tip ached. "Sir, I have not given you leave to address me as such."

"And again you show your sensitivity to what is right and proper, Miss Blakely. I wish I could say the same for some of the company gathered here." He glared past her in the direction of the card players. "For instance, I must question your acquaintance with Mr. Carlisle. You seem on easy terms with him."

"He is a friend of the duke's. I could hardly give him a direct cut."

"Still, a lady may be cool, distant, and remote to such approaches. He is irreverent, impertinent, and capable of leading a young woman astray."

"Surely you are not implying I am foolish enough to be led about by such a man?"

The vicar smiled. "Indeed not. You have reassured me. I should have realized your appearance of cordiality toward him rose from your tactfulness and discretion. I shall say good-bye for now, but I look forward to meeting you again in the church when you come to decorate with your presence as well as with flowers." He gave a creaky little bow and pressed his lips against the back of her hand. "Until then, my... Miss Blakely."

The ladies soon began to trickle off to their beds and the gentlemen to their various pursuits, leaving Kate thinking longingly of her own room. At least there she could be quiet and alone—unless, of course, one of the bridesmaids or one of their mothers found something new to fuss about and came seeking Kate to complain.

Finally, the only female remaining in the drawing room was Lady Stone, absorbed in a game of piquet with the colonel. Kate couldn't imagine anyone who needed a chaperone less than the tart-tongued Lady Stone, so she didn't interrupt their game to say good night.

Two steps outside the drawing room she pulled up short, realizing the vicar was still standing by the front entrance, chatting with the duke. Kate had assumed he would simply walk across to the stables—but how silly of her not to realize Mr. Blakely was the sort to stand on ceremony and insist his horse be brought to him at the front door instead.

Kate ducked sideways into the library. If some of the gentlemen were there, she'd simply say she'd come to get a book for the duchess.

But the room was dim and quiet. The fire had burned low and a couple of lamps, barely glowing, made only a feeble attempt to keep the shadows at bay. Kate picked up a candle from the desk, lighting it from a lamp as she wandered toward a corner where she had seen some novels. She would browse to while away a few minutes, until the vicar was gone. And perhaps taking a book upstairs wasn't a bad idea after all; though she was tired, she was not in the least sleepy.

Just as she put her hand out to brush the green leather spine of a promisingly thick volume, she heard someone moving behind her. The flame of her candle wavered as she spun around.

Andrew rose from a wing-backed chair, a book in his hand. "You look as if you've seen a ghost, Kate."

"I thought no one was here." Her hands were trembling. She ran a finger across the books, trying to steady herself, and gave a little laugh. "I must have read too many silly novels. Letting myself be so startled—"

"You should read all the novels you desire now, for I doubt the vicar would allow you to spend your time with such frivolous pursuits after the wedding."

"Thank you for the warning. I shall certainly keep it in mind."

"But you believe novels would be a small thing to sacrifice, in return for the secure position he offers, don't you? What has happened to you, Kate?"

"When one lives in complete security, the idea of taking risks has a seductive appeal. But when the future is doubtful, security looks quite attractive."

Andrew shook his head. "When the future is doubtful, taking risks makes me feel more fully alive."

"Clearly we are quite different in our perspective. What are you reading, Mr. Carlisle? And if I may ask, *how* are you reading with so little light?"

"I confess I was doing more daydreaming than studying." He set his book down on the nearest table. "This is a survey of the new section of America, the Louisiana Territory."

Kate tugged the fat green volume off the shelf. "It sounds like a wonderful place for an adventurer."

"Do you really think so?" His voice was soft. "Why don't you come with me and find out for yourself?"

Her heart gave a strange little flutter.

"Your skills at organizing would come in quite handy in my travels."

Kate told herself she should have expected something like that. She kept her voice carefully level. "I doubt your patron would appreciate that plan. Good night, Mr. Carlisle."

"*Are* you going to marry the vicar, Kate? He seems confident you will."

"I haven't made up my mind."

"Now there's a reply worthy of the most flirtatious of the bridesmaids—keeping all your options open as long as possible. I am disappointed."

"And what business is it of yours?"

"You really don't know?"

He moved closer, and Kate, caught in the corner

with a heavy book in one hand and a burning candle in the other, felt trapped. Suddenly he seemed larger, though surely that was only because of the weird shadows cast by the low-burning lights.

Why had she not felt danger in the air the moment he had made himself known? She had been startled, yes, but not worried. Why hadn't she excused herself immediately?

Because the vicar's just outside and you're tired of dealing with him. But she knew better. Part of her had wanted to stay, to talk with Andrew, to banter, even to flirt just a little...

"I'm not preventing you from leaving, you know," he said softly. "All you have to do is walk past me."

Her feet seemed to be frozen to the floor.

"That's what I thought." He took the book from her hand and set it on the table atop the one he'd been reading. Then he unfolded her fingers from around the candlestick and put it aside.

"Why did you do that?" she whispered.

"Because any man can take a woman unawares when she has her hands full—and she can blast him afterward. But you're going to kiss me because you want to, Kate, not because I've left you no choice in the matter."

His big, warm palms cupped her jaw and turned her face up to his. She felt the slow surge of his heat warming her blood as his fingertips massaged the delicate skin just in front of her ears, brushed across her lobes, and settled along her neck in the hidden spots under the low swoop of her hair.

For an instant, she considered resisting, and then

she tossed the notion aside. Only one thing would burn away the silly, sentimental memory she had carried with her so long. Better to get on with it and let him kiss her again, so she would see there was nothing special about his touch. Then she would understand how foolish it was to still dream of the long-ago summer when she had been just seventeen. The summer when Andrew Carlisle had come to the vicarage each day for tutoring, but also, Kate had sometimes allowed herself to hope, to see her. The summer when, just once, he had kissed her...

His mouth brushed hers as softly as the touch of a butterfly's wing, his lips firm but gentle. Yes, just the same as all those years ago—and nothing special, really, to have hung her dreams on. A good idea, really, to have come here to revisit the single minute that a foolish girl had believed so important. In just a moment now the kiss would be over, and her foolish fantasy would be gone.

He traced the line of her mouth with the tip of his tongue. "Such a prim little miss you are," he whispered. "All puckered up and firm... Relax your lips for me this time, Kate. Kiss me back."

All part of the experiment, she thought. Now that she had gone this far, she might as well finish. Then her illusions would be truly exploded and the vague longing she had always felt for him would be healed...

She let her mouth soften under his. Slowly he nibbled at her lips and then gradually deepened the kiss. What a very interesting sensation, Kate thought. He tasted of something fiery and hot, something that felt intoxicating and robbed her of breath. Something that made her open her mouth wider and seek his tongue with her own.

Andrew's hands slid to the back of her neck, holding her mouth tightly against his, but the firmness of his touch kindled a sense of urgency within her. She tilted her head to one side. All her senses seemed to be concentrated on his mouth. Why had she never realized before how very sensitive a tongue could be?

He pulled her closer, crushing her breasts against his coat. Kate felt tiny and helpless and weak, able only to melt into him and whimper a little as he stopped kissing her. His lips moved to the point of her chin; she arched her neck and he kissed her throat with tiny nibbling caresses as he worked his way down. His hands slid over her back, sending pinpricks along each muscle, until his palms rested snugly over her derriere and fitted her tightly against him. As his erection snuggled between her legs, Kate gasped, and he kissed her mouth again, this time not gently at all but plundering, demanding, wordlessly showing her what he would like to do…

What should really terrify her, Kate thought with her last fragment of reason, was the fact she was neither shocked nor frightened, but eager. She wanted to find out what came next. Her skin was on fire, and if she could have managed to take her hands off him, she might have torn off her clothes herself.

The library door swung wide, creaking just a little. By the time the butler was fully in view, Kate and Andrew were standing several feet apart. She didn't know whether she had moved or he had. She felt a flood of relief that sanity had returned.

But her relief was mixed with another emotion—one she didn't want to study too closely.

"My apologies, sir, Miss Blakely," Greeley said. "I believed the room to be empty and came in to extinguish the lights."

Kate's voice was—miraculously—steady. "We're just leaving, Greeley. Carry on with your duties."

She was crossing the hall with her head high when Andrew caught up with her. "I was right, Kate. We are not so different after all. You *are* an adventurer—in the ways that really count."

She shrugged. "An interesting sensation, I suppose, but that is all. Hardly something I care to repeat."

He laughed softly. "Then we shall not repeat ourselves but go forward instead. You will let me know, will you not, when you're ready for the next stage of the journey?"

❧

Olivia reached for Simon's hand and tipped the sapphire stickpin into his palm. He looked down at it and then up at her. "This is yours, Olivia. You—"

Stung, she said fiercely, "Don't you dare say I earned it!"

"I would not insult you in such a way. This was a gift—a symbol of a promise."

"Well, that *symbol* nearly undid me tonight when I dropped it in the drawing room. If your mother had gotten a better look…"

He smiled slowly. "You were carrying it with you, my dear?"

"What else am I to do with a valuable piece of

jewelry? Leave it lying on my dressing table for any chance intruder to find?"

"If you're giving it back because you have nowhere safe to keep it, I shall hold it in trust until you can safely possess it once more. Or would you prefer something else instead? It is not a lady's jewel and would have to be reset before you could wear it. And though the sapphire would look lovely against your hair, it's not at all the right color for your eyes."

"I am not bargaining for a replacement."

He didn't seem to be listening. "An emerald clasp, perhaps. Or a pair of hair combs."

Olivia shivered. "Not combs! I mean what I say, Your Grace. I never should have let you leave the trinket with me, and I never want to see it again."

He turned the jewel over in his hand. "Never? Now that seems harsh, my dear. To say I can't wear a particular jewel because you are offended at the mere sight of it—"

"I didn't mean anything of the sort, only that I want no more responsibility for keeping your jewels safe."

"I own I am glad the stickpin has come back to me, for it has always been a particular favorite. Now, however, I will enjoy not only a treasured bauble but a lively memory as well."

She tipped her head back and stared up at him. "You're enjoying this, aren't you?"

"Well, yes. You said you dropped it in front of my mother?"

"Very nearly." Once more, Olivia felt the sheer terror of the moment. "And if you dare to say *that* only adds to its charm, I'll take it back and stab you."

He laughed and tucked the stickpin safely away. "Now may I take you downstairs, Lady Reyne?"

She picked up her lamp and put her hand on his arm. "Part of the way, perhaps. It would be obvious if you came to my room."

"True enough," he mused. "A risky business for you, smuggling a gentleman in and out of a bedroom right at the head of the main stairs. One would think my mother had planned the location for you, rather than arguing against it. At any rate, I have a better idea."

Olivia stopped walking. "If you have some sort of mad notion of taking me to the duchess's bedroom, I won't do it."

"My mother's? Why would I…"

Olivia wished she hadn't said anything, but his quizzical gaze demanded she give him an answer. "No. I meant your wife's room."

He took advantage of the pause to draw her close. "Since I have no wife," he said against her lips, "one room is as good as another."

"No, it isn't. I suppose you won't understand, but you must not defile the room reserved for your wife by taking a mistress there. You may not care now, but someday when you bring a wife to that room, you would regret the memories."

"Then let's go to my room." His mouth moved with aching slowness over her temple, her cheek, her throat. "I would have given it up for you."

"No," Olivia said tartly. "You would have offered to share it with me."

He smiled. "True enough. I honestly don't care where we go, Olivia my sweet, as long as we make love. In a bed, without interruption." He planted his feet wide apart and pulled her into him, clamping his thighs securely against her legs, wrapping his arms around her, and kissing her until she forgot how to breathe. "And more importantly, without delay."

Olivia couldn't deny the thrill she felt with the evidence of his desire pressing against her. Her own heartbeat had speeded up. There was something compelling about his urgency—and the risk of being discovered added an extra level of excitement.

But she realized to her own surprise that down deep she didn't believe the danger was real. The duke would not be caught, for a man of his experience would have planned everything, avoided any possibility of exposure... She was perfectly safe in his arms in whatever bed he chose.

"Your room is closer." His voice was hoarse. "Or else I'm going to take you right here. It's up to you."

For a mad instant she considered. "There's no bed here," she pointed out, and reluctantly peeled herself away from him to lead the way down the stairs.

He stopped her halfway down the last flight and blew out the lamp she carried. Then he went ahead, walking as silently as a cat, to peer around the landing. "It's safe," he called softly, and she tiptoed down to him as he stood just outside her bedroom door. "Your maid won't be waiting?"

Olivia shook her head and pushed open the door. She didn't know how they got across the room to the bed, but she thought she was the one who lost her footing and overbalanced them. The duke twisted as they fell, so she landed on top of him.

"You're not nearly as soft as a mattress," she whispered, and he rolled until she was under him, pressed into the featherbed and unable to move. She looked up at him in the firelight, and the harsh beauty of his features made her insides melt with longing. She struggled to free herself, and he let her go—but she moved only enough to tug at her skirt.

"Does taking off your clothes feel like a waste of time?" he muttered, and at her nod, he laughed. "Then we are in agreement." He raised her skirt, released the fastenings of his breeches, and answered the aching need inside her with a hard, deep thrust.

Their coupling was fast and tense, and for a moment Olivia gloried in the ferocity of her own needs, the throbbing and painful dark side of passion.

But something black hovered at the corners of her mind, swelling out to smother her desire. Something shrieked in her ears, growing louder until she couldn't bear the sound. She went rigid in his arms, tried to push him away, and uttered a single tiny sob.

Instantly, the duke's hold gentled. "I've hurt you. My sweet—"

"No." Olivia could only gasp. "Not really. It was just... memories."

"Memories? Tell me."

How foolish of her. She tried to concentrate, letting herself feel the heat of him still fully sheathed inside her. But the magic had flown.

He seemed to know that too. He withdrew, very slowly as if giving her every opportunity to protest and draw him back—but she could not. Still, Olivia felt both bereft and guilty.

The duke kissed her temple and drew her gently against his side, almost in the same way she had cradled Charlotte against her body the night before to soothe the child. "Memories of Lord Reyne, you mean," he said.

"I'm sorry."

"The sorrow is mine. In my clumsiness, I reminded you of…"

"No!" She wiped away tears with her fists, suddenly anxious to take away the heaviness in his voice. "You *weren't* clumsy. And I wanted to make love this time. I truly did. I don't know what made me stop. Perhaps just because it was so fast… so hard…"

"You're saying Lord Reyne raped you," he said flatly.

"No." Olivia's voice was quiet. "He was my husband. He had the right."

"The right of a husband to make love to his wife carries the responsibility to make the act of love pleasant for her. He was obliged to seduce you, not to take his own satisfaction without concern for yours."

Olivia's eyes filled with tears again. "You're really very special."

"Get up." He rolled off the bed and pulled her to her feet.

"What—?"

"Don't look at me as if I'm about to beat you." He turned her around to face the bed and began undoing the ties at the back of her dress. When the garment was loose, he lifted it over her head and bent to kiss the exposed skin of her shoulder where her chemise ended.

Olivia couldn't bear his gentleness. After what she had done…

Slowly he removed her petticoat, unlaced her corset, released the painfully creased folds of her chemise, slid off her slippers, and gently rolled down each stocking to her toes. "Where will I find a nightgown for you?"

"I don't know. I don't care."

"Then you'll sleep in your shift tonight." The bedclothes had been turned back partway, and he tucked her gently underneath the blankets. "Rest well, Olivia."

Olivia clutched at his neck. "Don't go. Please—stay with me. I don't want to be alone."

"You don't know what you're asking."

"I'm sorry. I have no right to demand. But…"

"Just until you go to sleep, then." He took off his brocade jacket, and she held up the blankets invitingly. He slid underneath and turned her away from him, spooning her into his body with her back pressed tightly against his chest.

She snuggled back against him and felt his erection prodding her bottom, reminding her he had not been satisfied. She nudged him a little and felt his penis stir against her.

"Stop it, Olivia. You're feeling guilty because we didn't finish, but there's no need."

"No." She turned over to face him. Her breasts, under the soft lawn of her chemise, brushed his chest. "It's not guilt. I just… I *want* to finish."

"You don't have to do this."

She closed her eyes and looked into her heart. "Yes, I do. I want to be free, Simon. Free of those memories."

He was very still for an instant. "I like the way you say my name. Say it again."

Feeling suddenly shy, she whispered, "Simon."

He kissed her. "And again, for I want you to remember who is in this bed with you."

As if she could forget! "Simon," she said, and this time she let a tart edge creep into her voice. "Stop talking now and get to work."

He kissed her long and softly, and she shifted impatiently against him. He toyed with her breasts, licking and nibbling. Curious, Olivia let her hand wander down his chest and across the flat stomach until her fingertips brushed against his erect penis. How could something be both so rigid and so velvety smooth at the same time?

He seized her wrist. "You can explore some other day. Tonight you're not going to hurry me, Olivia. I won't make that mistake again."

His caresses grew to a torment. When he held her legs apart and kissed her, she felt a gush of warmth. "Hold still," he said. "If you can."

She twisted her hands into the sheets, but she couldn't remain motionless under his gentle assault. Soon—though not soon enough for her—she shuddered in a more powerful release than she could have imagined, her body quaking through waves of sweet agony. "Simon," she gasped. "I never dreamed…"

He watched her in something like awe and then poised himself above her. "Would you like another, Olivia?"

"Yes," she breathed, and as he once more slid inside her, she gave a little murmur of sheer satisfaction and tilted her hips to pull him deeper within her until she had her fill.

This time was just as hot and intense, but slower—achingly slow sometimes, as he stroked her. When she was once more on the brink, he reached down and thumbed the sensitive button of her clitoris. She arched against him with a shriek, and as she tumbled over the edge, he thrust once more and joined her in the maelstrom.

She drifted a little, warm and secure in his arms. "Have you made love in every room in this house yet?" she asked sleepily.

He kissed the top of her head. "Come to think of it, I haven't. But what a very good idea."

"What about this room? Have you visited any previous guests here?"

"Not a one."

"That's nice." Olivia set about exploring his body as thoroughly as he had studied hers.

"We still have two nights before the wedding," Simon murmured. "Shall we see how much of Halstead we can cover in that time?"

Fourteen

IN THE DIM WARMTH OF THE BLUE BEDROOM, PENELOPE lay on her back, still feeling the aftereffects of their lovemaking. Now everything made sense; now all felt right. *This* was how things were supposed to be, with her husband sated and relaxed, still half-lying atop her, his weight cradled in her arms.

She lifted one hand—her arm seemed heavy, and moving was an effort—and brushed a lock of hair back from his forehead.

As if her touch had startled him, he rolled away. "I am sorry. I didn't intend to do that."

Penelope felt cold and forlorn. "I know you didn't. I drove you to it. But I'm not sorry." She pulled the ripped nightgown more closely around her. "Thank you, my lord."

"How amusing—and how very ladylike of you—to thank me for treating you like a…" He sat on the edge of the bed, his face in his hands.

How very ladylike of you. Must he turn the term into an insult? "…Like a wife," Penelope said softly. She slid out of bed and picked up the candlestick.

Then she took a twisted bit of paper from a jar on the mantel, held it against a glowing coal until the spill flared, and lit the candle once more. "Your part of the bargain is satisfied. Now I shall keep mine."

He didn't move. Didn't even appear to hear what she had said.

Penelope took her jewel case from the drawer. She lit the second candle, laid the jewel case out on the rumpled sheets, and opened the first compartment. The yellow diamond, the biggest stone in the case, winked like the eye of a malevolent cat.

"Put that away," he said.

"Please, my lord. The mistake has been made and we cannot undo it. We are chained together for life."

He rubbed his forehead as if it hurt.

Penelope said softly. "But at least I can give you Stoneyford."

He looked at the yellow diamond gleaming in the candlelight and shook his head. "I couldn't take it. But the simple fact is—well, it's not enough."

The words struck dread into her heart. "I cannot give you freedom," she whispered. "I know you want nothing of me. But if we can rebuild Stoneyford…" She couldn't finish the thought—not aloud. *Then perhaps someday we might find our way… not to happiness, for that is too much to ask. But perhaps we could be contented together…*

"That's not what I meant," he said harshly. "Do you believe me so ungrateful as to throw your gift back in your face because it isn't large enough?"

"Then I don't understand, sir."

"Have you any idea how much money it would

take to put the house in order? I have consulted builders and craftsmen, and I know it is more than a few diamonds can bring. It is very generous of you to offer, but your jewels would be wasted and Stoneyford would still stand in ruins."

"The jewels are mine to waste." Penelope paused, frowning. "You knew this afternoon I didn't own enough diamonds to make a difference?"

"I thought it quite unlikely you did."

"Then why did you agree to the bargain, my lord?"

Finally, he drew a deep breath and said, "Because you asked. Because that was what you wanted."

Tidbits fell together in her mind until certainty formed. "But you made certain there would not be a child because you do not want my father to get what *he* wants."

"You took care of that problem tonight, didn't you? He will be very pleased with your performance, if you are with child."

"You think that's why I goaded you tonight? To please my father?"

"You may be willing to knuckle under to Mr. Weiss's demands, but I am not."

"Then we are at a standstill."

"Indeed we are. I am glad to know you understand so much, for I have never thought anything else."

With shaking hands, Penelope folded up her jewel case and put it away, then crept back into the great bed, where she lay as close to the edge as she could and pretended to go to sleep.

⤲⤳

Though of course Simon was pleased to be of assistance in Olivia's quest to banish her bad memories, the truth was she had worn him out. When she finally dozed off, he gathered her carefully into his arms and settled down for a quick nap himself. He still had time enough to get safely back to his own room before the servants started to stir. Besides, his own bed would be freshly starched and cold—while hers contained not only her alluring warmth but the soft scent of her hair spilling across her pillow and tickling his nose. Sheer comfort drew him down into a spiral of relaxed, peaceful exhaustion.

He dreamed of emeralds. She had said she did not want jeweled combs, and Simon had to agree. He much preferred her hair loose and trailing around her shoulders.

But he could still picture her draped in emeralds. A glowing blue-green necklace, a row of bracelets, a pair of eardrops, perhaps a tiara. And nothing else.

He woke with the image filling his mind and desire burning through his body, and leaned over Olivia to kiss her awake. She stirred and opened her eyes and curled herself around him.

"What time is it?" she asked. "Is that sunlight I see?"

The sun was not yet up but dawn was breaking, and Simon realized he had slept far longer than he intended. He pushed aside the blankets and scrambled into his clothes and then came back to the bed. "One last kiss to hold me through the morning," he said, and though Olivia laughed at him, she cooperated so enthusiastically that he wanted to climb back in with her.

With his senses so fully aroused, he should have

sniffed danger long before he collided with it—but perhaps he wouldn't have heard telltale sounds from the landing anyway, for the door was thick and the servants were well trained. He opened the door just as Maggie, with a tray balanced on one hand, turned the knob. He almost pulled her off her feet.

"Good morning, Your Grace," she said pertly and stepped around him to cross the threshold. "Good morning, my làdy. The duchess would like to see you this morning."

"My mother is already up and about?" Simon said warily. "And she wants to see me?"

"I think she gave the message to her maid last night to pass along through the servants' hall." Maggie's voice took on a saucy edge. "And it's Lady Reyne she wants to see. She'd have hardly counted on me as a messenger to *you*, Your Grace—seeing as how you're the last person she'd expect me to run into while carrying up a tray of morning chocolate for her ladyship."

He was being particularly dense this morning, Simon realized. "So the Inquisition begins," he muttered and then fixed a stern look on the maid. "Maggie, I'll make it well worth your while to keep silent about this."

She sniffed. "Do you think I'm mad, Your Grace?"

"Very well, then." He tried not to wonder why Maggie hadn't seemed surprised to see him or shocked to find a man just leaving her mistress's room.

As he put his ear to the door, Maggie set the tray down and went to open the curtains. "My apologies for being so early, ma'am, but I have a dozen trays to deliver. I thought I could tiptoe in without waking you—or at least you'd not bite my head off if I made a noise, as some of the other ladies do."

Simon could detect no sounds from the corridor, but he opened the door cautiously and then sneaked around the corner into the hall and down to his own room as quickly as he could, feeling disgruntled about the whole episode. There was something wrong when the master of the house was reduced to sneaking around and hiding in shadows to avoid the servants.

He'd been right about his bed being cold, and the sheets felt stiff and scratchy. After Olivia's glowing warmth and satiny softness, it was torment to stretch out here and try to settle himself to sleep. Maybe if he counted emeralds... how many could he fit onto Olivia's slim form without weighing her down?

A foolish game, of course. She would never keep emeralds or anything so valuable. Olivia had been quite clear about her goals and her methods. He was foolish to think of elaborate gifts for a lady who had made it clear that she found cold cash a far more attractive option. She had only kept the stickpin close and protected because of its monetary worth, not its sentimental value.

And that was exactly the sort of bargain he had asked for, Simon reminded himself. Exactly what he had wanted.

With the very notion of sleep banished, he climbed out of bed and rang for Hemmings to bring his shaving water. The valet did not comment about the near-pristine state of Simon's bed or about the early hour of the summons or even—while he was carefully inspecting every piece of clothing—the sudden reappearance from a pocket of a once-lost sapphire stickpin. But his eyebrows kept climbing higher and higher until Simon expected they'd soon meet Hemmings's receding hairline.

"I presume I should lay out your riding garb this morning, sir? Shall I send word to the stables to saddle your gelding?"

Simon paused and then thoughtfully scraped the razor down his jaw. "No. This morning, I'm in the mood for a pony ride instead."

That did it, he observed. Hemmings's eyebrows might *never* come back down into line.

❧

Olivia dawdled over her chocolate and took her time in getting dressed before eventually finding her way to the sunny suite at the back of the house.

Large though the duchess's rooms were, they seemed uncomfortably full of people. Kate was there with a cluster of bridesmaids, and Lady Stone occupied the chair nearest the duchess's. Perhaps it was a good sign, Olivia told herself, for surely the duke's mother would neither interrogate nor castigate a guest in such a public setting.

However, as soon as the dowager's gaze fell on Olivia, she shooed everyone else away. "Go and get ready for the archery tournament," she urged. "You will want to finish your exercise before the day grows warm and leave yourselves time to rest before the ball begins. Come and sit here with me, Lady Reyne."

While shepherding the bridesmaids out, Kate cast a worried look over her shoulder at Olivia.

Olivia tried to smile back with a reassurance she was very far from feeling. The sudden silence felt oppressive, dangerous, and threatening.

"Would you like tea?" the duchess asked, and poured a cup without waiting for an answer. "Lady Reyne, I am charmed to have the opportunity to know you better. Tell me about yourself." She leaned back in her chair with an air of being ready to wait forever for an answer.

"I… My father was Sir Ralph…"

The duchess waved a hand. "No, my dear. I know where you come from, who your people are, when you came out, who you married. Lucinda Stone may be an old gossip, but she's also a treasure trove, for she knows everything about everyone. I am asking about *you*."

"Not much to tell, Your Grace. I was married and widowed…"

"Within the last year, I collect."

"It's been just under a year."

"Yet you are not in mourning."

"When I left my husband's home, I was able to take very little with me. Since then, a lack of funds has not permitted me to purchase a new wardrobe." Olivia added wryly, "Of course I considered dying the clothes I had—but dye takes so unpredictably that I felt it unwise to risk the few dresses I owned to make an outward show of mourning."

The duchess's eyes gave away nothing of what she might be feeling. "You felt the appropriate levels of grief, of course."

"Yes, ma'am." *Depending on how one defines appropriate, of course.*

"How did you meet my son?"

Olivia sipped her tea to give herself a chance to think. It was hard to tell if the duke's tale of dancing at some unspecified ball had made its way to his mother's ears, but Olivia suspected the story was not a safe refuge. The duchess was capable of demanding the hostess's name and the date, and with Lady Stone's seemingly endless knowledge to draw on...

Olivia forced a smile. "The duke insists we danced together once at a private ball in London—but I am afraid I can neither confirm nor deny that. I simply don't remember, you see."

The duchess sounded startled. "You don't remember dancing with a duke?"

"So very odd of me." Misleading as Olivia hoped her interpretation was, it at least had the advantage of being true—to an extent. The fact that she could never have forgotten the duke, had she met him before he came to Halstead, was entirely beside the point.

"Indeed." The duchess set her cup down with a clink. "I presume your limited wardrobe does not include a ball gown."

"No, ma'am."

"I do not like for a guest in my house to be uncomfortable, so I have taken the liberty of asking the modiste to create a gown for you to wear for Daphne's wedding ball."

"But the ball is tonight."

"Yes. I need hardly say the time constraints mean the gown must be simple."

"Your Grace, that is very generous of you. But I really cannot allow you to provide such things for me."

"Nonsense. The entire staff of dressmakers has been taking up space and, I suspect, using the time to catch up on their London commissions. I'm merely putting them to work."

"But the materials... I must at least pay for the materials they use." Olivia still had the money she'd set aside to pay Sir Jasper, tucked safely away in the bottom of her reticule. She suspected it wouldn't go far to buy the sort of fabric the Duchess of Somervale had in mind, but at least paying something would soothe Olivia's pride.

And when Sir Jasper came back to collect the rent payment... *I'll worry about that when the day comes.*

"Nonsense. They are also creating a dress or two for your daughter." The duchess offered a plate of small cakes. "My initial opinion of Charlotte will come as no surprise to you. I thought her precocious and forward, as well as entirely lacking in discipline."

"The grape juice accident was entirely my fault. I assure you that in general my daughter..."

"Is graceful for her age, possesses the rudiments of manners, and—overall—seems to show promise that one day she might have the makings of a lady."

"You sound as if you know," Olivia said faintly. "How...?"

"I made a visit this morning to the nursery so we could become better acquainted." The duchess refilled the tea cups. "You seem startled, Lady Reyne. Let me assure you, I have not forgotten where the nursery is located. Neither, I understand, has my son, if the report is accurate that he visited you and Charlotte there last night."

"It's accurate."

"Do you object to my taking an interest in a child my son seems to intend to bring into my family?"

Olivia hadn't thought about it in those terms before. "As to that…"

"Yes?" The duchess went still. "Are you referring to the duke's intentions toward you?"

She knows it's all a pretense, Olivia thought. *She's laying a trap.* "The duke has not made his intentions clear," she said carefully. "Unless he does, I am unable to—"

"Pish. You're not a debutante, Lady Reyne. I'm convinced you have a very good idea of exactly what the duke means to do."

"No, ma'am. I mean—yes, ma'am." Olivia's head was spinning. Had the duke been even more successful at convincing his mother than any of them had dreamed possible? Or had something essential changed while Olivia wasn't looking? *A child my son seems to intend to bring into my family…*

No, she thought. The duke was simply putting on a good show for his mother, pretending to contemplate such a thing.

"Very well, then." The duchess glanced out the bay window, and a little frown crossed her brow. She picked up the glass bell that stood on the tea tray and rang it sharply.

I'm to be dismissed, Olivia thought with relief. She had survived—at least, she hoped she had not destroyed everything—but now she understood why the duke had muttered something this morning about the Inquisition.

When the maid appeared, however, the duchess said, "Go and tell the modiste she'd better add a riding habit to the list I gave her this morning."

"A habit?" Olivia protested. "But why—?"

"For your daughter. I suggest you look out the window."

Olivia stood up. The view across the lawns and gardens from the bay window of the duchess's suite was lovely, but that was not what took her breath away. What caused Olivia's throat to close up was the sight of a short, fat gray pony waddling placidly across the lawn—with Charlotte perched on his back. Beside her walked the duke, his hands at the child's waist to hold her steady, smiling proudly as she clutched the reins.

⁂

By the time all the bridesmaids had found their hats and gloves, quite a little time had passed. But eventually the group trailed out of Halstead and across the gardens to where the archery range had been set up in a shady little hollow on the far side of a brook. As the bridesmaids crossed the arched footbridge over the gurgling water, Kate looked across to where a pair of footmen were adjusting the target against a tall earthen bank, under the direction of Andrew Carlisle and Viscount Chadwick.

Not far from the range and at a safe angle behind the spot where the archers would stand, another pair of servants, working under Lady Stone's critical eye, set a big upholstered chair in place. Kate felt a pang of sympathy for the footmen who had been required to haul that bit of furniture all the way from the house.

The girls were soon milling around the target and trying out bows from the rack nearby.

Lady Stone settled into the chair. "Very wise of you to hang back, Miss Blakely. We should be safe enough here and able to observe some real sport. Of course, I don't mean the one that uses arrows. It will be amusing to watch them circling the targets and adjusting their aim."

"I hope Lord Chadwick is prepared for the onslaught."

Lady Stone eyed Kate with interest. "You feel no concern for Mr. Carlisle?"

"He can manage for himself. It's the viscount they'll go after."

"Yes—despite the minor nature of his title and some wildness in the family, which would be a draw for this empty-headed lot."

Kate tried without much success to bite back a smile.

"So you do have a sense of humor," Lady Stone said slyly. "I was starting to wonder."

"Where is the duke, Lady Daphne?" one of the bridesmaids complained. "You said he'd help us with our aim."

Kate had no trouble picturing what the bridesmaid had in mind. A lithe and yielding young woman, practically in the arms of the duke as he showed her how to properly draw the bow and take aim…

"Any competitor who received the duke's assistance in shooting—or help from any of the gentlemen— would have an unfair advantage," Kate said firmly, "and thus would be ineligible to win the contest. Since none of you wishes to be out of the running…"

"That depends entirely on what the prize is to be,"

one of the bridesmaids said. "If it's only a dance at the ball tonight…"

"Still," another said. "A dance with the Duke of Somervale—that's something to remember."

"Indeed," Lady Stone murmured. "One wonders how any impressionable young woman could possibly forget such a thing, no matter when it is supposed to have happened. Which reminds me to ask what the duke is scheming over, along with your friend Lady Reyne."

Kate pretended deafness.

Lady Stone sniffed. "Oh, very well. I hope you're happy with yourself, by the way. I was about to offer a small wager as to which of them would be able to act the most helpless and win the largest share of the duke's assistance."

"I'm sorry to cheat you of your entertainment, ma'am."

Colonel Sir Tristan Huffington's deep voice broke in. "I'll wager with you, Lucinda—if you give me odds."

"Odds? I should think not."

"Then I shall stand with Miss Blakely and chat instead." He planted his stick firmly in the ground between his feet.

"Bore her with more of your prosy stories, you old fossil?" Lady Stone scoffed.

"She doesn't think they're prosy," the colonel objected. "As a result of Miss Blakely's encouragement, I am of a mind to write a book about my experiences."

"A great aid to the insomniac *that* will be. Oh, very well, Colonel—I'll be pleased to take back the ten guineas you cheated from me."

Kate moved off to the side to leave them to their squabbling. The first bridesmaid to step up to the mark took a shot, but her arrow twanged into the hillside, missing the target altogether. Her second arrow clipped the edge and spun off, narrowly missing Viscount Chadwick.

The colonel winced. "It's a good thing the riflemen in my regiment were better marksmen than these girls, or we'd have gotten our tails kicked by those chappies in the Colonies like the rest of the army did. I recall a time when I was just a captain. We were in a skirmish near Philadelphia…"

Lady Stone gave a huge and theatrical yawn, took out a small notebook and a pencil, and started making a tally. The next arrow hit the target, but the following two missed entirely. Lady Stone nodded sagely and marked her paper.

"Is she figuring odds?" Andrew asked in a low voice as he came to stand beside Kate.

Kate's skin quivered at his nearness, remembering how hungrily he had kissed her the night before and how her body had strained against his, longing to be closer. *I was merely exhausted and off guard*, she told herself. *Of course I wouldn't have given in to temptation.*

But she knew she was lying. If Greeley hadn't chosen that moment to put out the lights in the library…

She took a firm hold of her self-control. Andrew appeared just the same as ever—friendly, calm, and perfectly relaxed, as if the few minutes they had shared in the library had never happened. To him, no doubt, everything *was* normal—and so Kate would be a fool to let him guess that she even remembered. She kept her voice level. "It's possible she's simply keeping track of how many times she's heard each of the colonel's stories."

He clicked his tongue. "Shame on you, Kate. Colonel Huffington was speculating this morning about whether he could hire you away from the duchess to assist with his memoirs."

Kate blinked. "Really? I thought he had no money for such a thing." It might not be the most exciting employment, she told herself, but balanced against the pitfalls of being a governess or a companion, the opportunity was inviting. She looked over at the colonel, but he seemed absorbed in his story. She could not interrupt.

"Come off for a walk through the gardens with me, and I'll tell you what I think."

"I'm not at liberty to stroll off with you." And a good thing, too, she thought, for the very idea of wandering through the flower beds with Andrew—or of getting lost in the maze with Andrew—was enough to speed up her heartbeat and make her breath catch in her throat.

"The bridesmaids can't get into trouble with Lady Stone sitting right there."

"A dozen young women armed with bows and arrows? You're jesting. Philippa has already tried to skewer the viscount."

"Entirely his own fault. Chadwick never was any good at understanding geometry, but if he insists on standing at that angle to the target, he deserves to be hit."

"How unkind of you. Come now, tell me what the colonel said about his book."

Andrew's gaze dropped to her mouth. "I'll share if you will, Kate. Information in return for a kiss."

"The bargain you offer is not to my taste, Mr. Carlisle."

"The hell it's not. I can see the pulse fluttering in your throat as you think about it."

Kate decided to ignore him. "Here comes the duke."

"With the delectable Lady Reyne—looking as if they're having the same sort of conversation we are."

Kate shot a look at him. "About kissing? You must be joking."

Andrew grinned at her. "It looks to me as if they're quarreling. But if you'd like to chat about kisses, my dear—"

Kate felt her stomach tighten. Deliberately she turned away to watch the duke and Olivia. She wouldn't have said they were quarreling herself, though there was a definite air of tension about Olivia. And now that Kate looked more closely, the duke seemed to be ill at ease as well, raising his hand in a nervous gesture to tug at the stickpin in his neckcloth.

A gold and sapphire stickpin, glinting and flashing in the sunlight.

Kate remembered where she had seen the pin before—not only as a glimmer of gold and blue as Olivia had palmed it from the carpet in the drawing room on the previous evening, but displayed against the pristine white of the duke's neckcloth as he and Olivia had squabbled over diamond bracelets in the village. How had it come to be in Olivia's possession? It wasn't the sort of thing that was easily lost... unless he'd deliberately taken it off. Which he simply wouldn't have done anywhere except his own rooms, unless…

The duke and Olivia had been talking, Kate recalled, of diamond bracelets—and of mistresses.

The very next day, she had seen the two of them coming out of an isolated corner of the abbey ruins, and Andrew, with a wicked little smile, had said something about a very private spot they had been visiting…

No, Kate told herself. Olivia wouldn't—she *couldn't*—be the mistress of the Duke of Somervale.

"I'm glad of one thing, however," Andrew said. "If you're considering the colonel's offer, then you've definitely decided against the vicar. I'm proud of you, Kate."

❧

As dawn cracked across the horizon, the earl rolled from the bed they had shared—and *not* shared—throughout the night. Penelope thought about pretending to still be asleep. But playing possum was the coward's way out, and in any case she was fairly sure he knew she hadn't slept any more than he had. She sat up and nibbled a thumbnail.

He looked a fright, she thought. His hair was wildly mussed; there was a shadow of beard on his jaw; and he had picked up the same shirt he'd worn yesterday instead of searching the wardrobe for a clean one. This was a far cry from the cool and elegant man with whom she had shared a London townhouse for three months.

"There's no need for you to rush around to escape," she said quietly. "I'm not going to make another scene."

He didn't look at her as he pulled buckskins from the wardrobe. "I'm only going for a ride. Long and hard—and alone."

Only going for a ride? In London—and here at Halstead, before today—he would not have set foot outside his bedroom in such a state, no matter what activity he had planned. Though Penelope had not needed such a clear demonstration to understand his state of mind, there was no denying the evidence. She had sought to change her husband, and what a transformation she had wrought!

"I was just trying to make things better," she said, and he shot a twisted smile at her and opened the door.

Etta was outside, and the earl stepped back with a courtly air to admit her. A moment later he was gone, and the latch clicked with an awful finality.

Etta stood just inside the room with her mouth hanging open, staring at Penelope. The tray she carried took on an ominous slant, the china chocolate pot sliding unheeded. "My lady!"

"Oh, do stop going on about my hair, Etta," Penelope said impatiently. "I don't know why you even try to control it overnight, anyway. It's a wasted effort to braid when it starts coming down the minute you finish." She tried to brush the wiry mass—even bushier than usual—back from her face. Perhaps her hair helped explain why the earl had been eager to leave the room rather than look at her any longer.

But she understood the urge he felt to get out into the fresh air, to be active—and to avoid other humans. Horses didn't ask questions.

Penelope reached up to push the bed curtains out

of the way. As she moved, she felt the rush of cold air against her skin and realized Etta hadn't been looking at her hair after all. The maid was staring at the indecent display where Penelope's torn nightgown gaped open all the way down her chest and beyond.

"My lady, I am horrified. *Horrified!*"

"It's only a nightgown, Etta. I must own two dozen so this one will hardly be missed." Irritated, Penelope pushed the blankets back. She couldn't bear to stay in bed any longer and think about the previous night. The earl was planning to clear his mind with a furious ride; perhaps she would go for a long, long walk.

"It's not the loss of a nightgown, my lady. It's the... the wantonness."

"Wantonness? What on earth do you mean?"

Etta stuck her jaw out. "Only a common trollop would cavort around in a nightgown that's torn from top to bottom. I knew no good would come from this scheme of sharing a room."

"*Cavort?*"

"Making *you* into a lady is impossible—as I told your father when he hired me."

Penelope kept a thoughtful silence as Etta helped her dress, with the maid muttering all the while. When the last button was fastened and the final hairpin in place, and Etta began to pick up the debris, Penelope rose from the dressing table. "You were quite right about the difficulty of making me into a lady, Etta, and there's no need for you to ruin your reputation by continuing to serve a hopeless cause. Pack your things. I'm sure the coach to London stops at Steadham village. You can wait at the coaching inn."

Charlotte's riding lesson had just ended when Olivia reached the lawn at the back of the house. The pony ambled off toward the stables with a groom in charge, while Charlotte's nurse led her toward the house. When Charlotte saw her mother, she broke free from Nurse's hand and came running across the lawn. Not far behind her, the duke strolled toward them, looking indecently pleased with himself.

Olivia wanted to kick him, but instead she listened to Charlotte's triumphant recital with all the patience she could muster. When the peals of childish glee came to an end, Olivia sent her daughter off to the nursery, waiting with lips pursed until the child and Nurse were out of earshot. Only then did she turn to face Simon, and the first thing her gaze fell on was the sapphire stickpin gleaming brazenly in his neckcloth.

As though it was a trophy, she thought, and rage rose in her.

"What do you think you're doing?" she demanded. "Giving my daughter pony rides as if this is some sort of village fair—"

The duke pulled back as if she'd slapped him. "It wasn't just a pony ride—it was a lesson in managing a horse. What's wrong with that?"

"You didn't have to take charge yourself. *That's* what's wrong!"

He frowned. "You would prefer me assigning the task to the head groom?"

"And you didn't have to carry out this performance on the lawn!"

"The lawn is softer. If Charlotte was to take a fall—which I made certain she wouldn't, of course—this would be far safer for her than the stable yard, and here the pony couldn't possibly be distracted or spooked by another horse."

The fact that all his arguments were sensible ones only made Olivia more furious. "But you would never have thought of giving her a riding lesson if you hadn't been showing off for the duchess, would you?"

"Of course I would. As soon as I saw that ridiculous stick horse of hers, I thought, *There's a child who needs a pony.*"

"So you used my daughter as a tool. A device to convince your mother that you're—" *Seriously thinking of marrying me.* The words were so ridiculous Olivia couldn't even bring herself to say them. "You were showing your mother how much you enjoy being a family man."

"Speaking of my mother," the duke said, "perhaps we should take this discussion somewhere else so she cannot observe us from her window."

"Then you admit you chose this location because she would be likely to see!"

"Nothing of the sort." He offered his arm, and Olivia reluctantly let him guide her into the garden. "I must remind you that you agreed to take part in this performance."

"For myself, yes. But I never agreed to let my daughter play a part in your hoax. She's only a baby. She doesn't understand that what you do and say means nothing."

"Olivia, it's not as if I've hurt her in any way.

Charlotte's already told you how much fun she had. She even asked if she could ride again tomorrow."

"But she can't," Olivia said, "because tomorrow is the wedding, and you—along with everyone else on the estate—will be far too busy for riding lessons. By the day after, we will be at home in the cottage once more, with no ponies and no indulgent dukes to walk alongside."

She saw the very instant he understood why she was objecting, for his jaw tightened. *Of course*, she thought. *His Arrogance doesn't like to have anyone point out the error of his ways!*

She went on a little more gently, "When the excitement is over, Charlotte will not understand why her great friend the duke doesn't come around any more. Please don't pay such attentions to her. Don't make things harder for her."

"Do you want me to ignore her altogether or just stop being polite to her?"

"I want you to stop petting and spoiling her and treating her like a princess! And stop encouraging your mother to do so. She's already ordered the dressmakers to create an entire wardrobe for Charlotte."

"That was none of my doing," the duke protested.

"Not directly, perhaps, but the duchess would never have done such a thing if she hadn't believed your intention is to make Charlotte a part of the family."

"That's good news. The fact she's convinced, I mean."

Olivia gave a furious little shriek.

"All right," the duke said. "No more riding lessons."

"An easy enough promise, since there will be no time for them." She considered. "No more visits to the nursery, either. And no seeking Charlotte out if she happens to be playing within sight of the duchess. In fact, don't seek her out at all."

"Are you finished?"

She didn't trust his mild tone of voice. "If I think of anything else, I'll let you know."

They walked on in silence, approaching the arched footbridge over the brook just as an arrow zinged from a bridesmaid's bow, ricocheted off the edge of the target, and sent Viscount Chadwick scurrying for cover.

The duke let out a low whistle. "I thought Chadwick had more sense."

"One more thing," Olivia said suddenly. "No gifts sent upstairs in your name—in fact, no gifts at all."

"No *more* gifts," the duke agreed.

Olivia stopped walking. "What have you done?"

"Nothing big, just a riding crop that isn't even new. I found it in the tack room, a small one that probably belonged to Daphne. I sent it up to the nursery so Charlotte can use it on the hobbyhorse for practice."

Olivia shook her head. "How will I ever explain to my daughter, as she's living in a cottage, why she has such strong memories of an enormous house and a nursery with servants and a duke teaching her to ride a pony?"

His voice grew suddenly stern. "You'll tell her she was a guest at a house party, Lady Reyne. No more, no less. As are you, in case you need the reminder."

Fifteen

Olivia stared at him as if he'd stolen the last rays of sunshine from the world, and suddenly Simon realized how very much she and her daughter looked alike. The perfect oval of the face, the soft curve of eyebrow, the slender neck and well-shaped head—all were identical.

And as for the look of reproach in the huge hazel eyes speckled with gold, Charlotte had looked at him in precisely the same way when he had told her it was time for her lesson to end.

Olivia's voice was low and sweet. "How kind of Your Grace to make my position clear, in case I had forgotten myself."

"Olivia. I didn't mean—"

"A moment ago you called me by my title. I suggest you remember it in future. Thank you for your escort, sir." As they reached the end of the arched footbridge, she released his arm and, without a backward glance, went to join Kate Blakely and Andrew Carlisle as they stood watching the archery match.

Simon paused at the end of the footbridge, feeling

foolish and very much at loose ends. Suddenly becoming aware that Lady Stone was watching him from her absurdly fancy chair on the little knoll, he tried not to catch her eye, but to no avail. She raised a hand to summon him, and he smothered a curse and joined her and the tedious colonel.

"Nice stickpin, Somervale," Lady Stone said. "I have always had a weakness for gentlemen who can wear jewels without looking like fops."

"Thank you, ma'am."

Her gaze drifted off to rest on Olivia. "Of course, you should take better care of your playthings. You seem to be growing careless."

What in the world was the harridan talking about? The stickpin, perhaps; had she seen it drop in the drawing room? Or was she—somehow—referring to Olivia?

Guilt lent a sharp edge to Simon's voice. "I have no idea what you're referring to."

"Oh, no—of course you don't." Lady Stone gave a little cackle. "You told your mama you met Lady Reyne in London and danced at a ball with her."

"What of it, ma'am?"

"Lady Reyne's only Season was four years ago… the same winter you spent in Greece, as I recall."

There was no way out except through, Simon told himself. "Make of it what you wish."

"Oh, I shall. I wonder whether it will be more amusing to tell the duchess or not to tell her. Perhaps you will advise me on that question, Somervale." She shifted in her chair. "Colonel, a guinea says the next three shots all miss the center circle."

"Only a guinea? What a miser you are, Lucinda."

"I'll take your bet, Lady Stone," Simon said suddenly. "I say at least one will hit the mark. Only let's make it more interesting. Ten guineas?"

Lady Stone looked down her nose at him. "Twenty, and I'm in."

"Done." After all, Simon thought, what was a little genteel blackmail between friends?

The colonel shook his head sadly, but he didn't comment.

Neither of the next two shots hit the center of the target—exactly as Simon had expected. One of them stuck feebly off to the side; the other struck at an angle and slid down the surface into the grass.

However, the next archer to pick up a bow was his sister, and as Daphne pulled her bowstring taut, Simon began to have second thoughts. Deliberately losing a bet was one thing—a far more tactful way to buy silence than simply handing over a bribe. But if Daphne loosed an arrow straight into the target and Lady Stone ended up owing him twenty guineas instead of pocketing a payment as he'd intended...

Slowly and carefully, Daphne sighted along her arrow. Just as she released her grip, one of the bridesmaids let out a squeal and pointed at something behind Simon.

Daphne's arrow missed the target altogether.

Simon released a relieved breath and turned to see what all the excitement was about. Daphne's betrothed was walking across the bridge, and a moment later Daphne brushed past Simon and flung herself against the man who tomorrow would become her husband.

"Good to see you, Harcourt," Simon said. "Excellent timing."

Lady Stone's face went all wrinkly. Simon thought she must be smiling. "I'll come to collect before luncheon. It's been nice doing business with you, Somervale."

❧

The head groom helped Kate up into her saddle, frowning as the fresh and frisky mare danced across the stable yard. Kate ignored his concern, for she was fully occupied.

Just as she thought she had the mare settled, Andrew Carlisle rode in. He paused to close the gate and then drew his gelding to one side and sat easily in the saddle, watching. "Perhaps a calmer horse," he said to the head groom.

The groom nodded. "As you wish, sir."

"Nonsense," Kate said. "She's just excited about going out. Once we're away from the yard, she'll be fine."

"If she doesn't run off with you," the groom muttered. "She's a well-named one, Fancy is. Wait here a minute, miss, till I get you a different mount."

Kate would have argued, but the groom was already gone. She turned on Andrew instead. "Since when do you give orders in the duke's stables?"

"When you don't use common sense. Where are you going, anyway?"

"Just to the village." Kate nudged the mare toward the gate. "And I'm late, so I'm not waiting for another mount."

"Then if you insist on riding a streak of lightning, I shall accompany you."

"No need. I'm perfectly safe."

He smiled. "I recall an errand I forgot to carry out, so I must go back anyway."

Kate gave up. It was only a mile to the village—not far enough to truly relax and enjoy being outside even if she was alone.

"What takes you to the village on such a warm afternoon?" he asked as they reached the long avenue lined with lime trees.

"I'm to arrange the flowers for the wedding tomorrow. What about you? What errand is it that you forgot to complete?"

He stumbled a little and looked a bit ashamed.

"Next time," Kate recommended, "think of a story ahead of time. Perhaps one of the bridesmaids asked you to bring her ribbons for the ball."

"That's it exactly!"

She shook her head. "Then you would not have forgotten the commission—for by now you must have discovered which of them is the greatest heiress."

"I'm still relying on you to tell me which one I should court."

The idea pinched a little somehow. Had she asked because she hoped he would laugh and tell her that he had given up the notion? "Then you'd best make other plans."

"And exactly why will you not advise me which of those girls I should choose as a wife?"

It's far better to ignore him, Kate. "If you don't marry an heiress, what will you do? Go back to Lord Winchester? Or look for another patron to fund your travels?"

"Not immediately. I have some money put aside, and one can live quite cheaply in Italy, I understand."

Italy. Sunshine and villas and canals and vineyards and brilliant blue seas and dusty ruins... All places she would never see. "Not America?"

"Does that sound more inviting to you? What is your grand plan for after the wedding, Kate? Will you help the colonel with his memoirs? Take a position with one of the bridesmaid's families? Or was I wrong and you're still thinking of marrying the vicar?"

The matter-of-fact summary of her prospects shot gloom through Kate's veins, but she wasn't about to admit it to Andrew, who didn't seem in the least concerned which option she chose. "I might become a housekeeper," she said lightly. "Though not for a family with eligible daughters. Have you noticed that Mrs. Greeley's hair is much whiter now than earlier in the week?"

When the village came into sight, Kate was startled by how quickly the ride had passed.

Olivia's cottage looked almost like a painting, still and quiet in the afternoon heat. As they passed, Kate noticed a gentleman standing on the front step, hand raised as if to knock. She drew up her horse in the road by the garden gate and called, "Sir Jasper, Lady Reyne is not at home. May I assist you?"

Sir Jasper Folsom turned. "Not unless she has entrusted you with the rent payment that is due in two days." His eyes narrowed. "But perhaps you were unaware Lady Reyne could not pay the entire sum due last month? She asked me to wait to collect the rest."

"Oh, no," Kate breathed. Suddenly it all made a

dreadful kind of sense. Olivia's assurances that the duke was indeed not courting her and that she knew what she was doing. The high color in her face this morning, and the fact she had been on the edge of tears. Even the wandering stickpin fit in somehow, Kate was certain. "I shall tell Lady Reyne you inquired after her."

"Remind her that I'm waiting to see whether her fancy friends pay her debts."

Andrew said softly, "Want me to knock out a few of his teeth? It would be a pleasure, just on general principles."

"Not today," Kate managed to say.

The church was silent and, to Kate's relief, empty. The windows stood open to the perfect summer afternoon, and the front doors were propped wide. Near a table set up under the balcony stood big buckets of roses and lilies, ready to trim and arrange.

"There are enough blooms here to decorate three churches," Andrew said. "At least, if you're going to leave any room at all for people." He tugged a rose from the bucket and snapped the stem between his fingers.

His hands were not those of a gentleman, Kate thought. They had been once, and they were still well-shaped, with long, strong fingers. But now there were small scars and the mark of physical work done without gloves. His skin was not rough, but it had been used, not pampered as many gentlemen did. She didn't recall the slightest discomfort when he had touched her the previous night, only a sort of heightened tension when his fingers had brushed the soft skin at the nape of her neck…

Enough, she told herself.

He dried the stem on his coat sleeve and tucked the rose into the smooth braid above Kate's left ear. He was so close that she could smell his shaving soap…

"I'll have plenty of blooms to choose from." She didn't even sound like herself. "Will you help me to get the vases before you go about your errand?"

"My errand is to take the horses to the coaching inn while I drink a tankard of ale in the taproom and wait for you to finish. Unless you would like me to buy ribbons for you, for the ball?"

Kate's senses thrummed at the idea. "No, for the shop here has little to choose from."

"Then a tankard of ale it must be. Shall I come back in an hour?" He carried the silver vases she chose to the worktable and lounged beside it, watching as she selected tall-stemmed lilies to form the basic lines of the arrangement. "It must be very difficult for you to see Mr. Blakely here instead of your father."

"I will grow used to the change. You need not stay, Mr. Carlisle."

"Are you anxious to be rid of me so you can be alone with the vicar?"

"He's here?" Kate jerked around, slopping water across the table.

Andrew laughed. "That's what I thought." He strolled off. She watched as he untied the reins from the gate and led the horses down the street toward the coaching inn.

Kate stopped mooning about, mopped up the mess she'd made, and went back to her work. With an effort, she put Andrew out of her mind to think instead about Olivia, Sir Jasper, and the overdue rent.

Kate couldn't help but feel at least partly to blame for the situation Olivia was facing. The budget in the little cottage had been very tight, and Kate had done everything she could to help—but it hadn't been enough.

She gave a final tug to a pink rose that insisted on facing the wrong way and carried the first vase up the main aisle to set it in place, pausing on her way back to straighten the needlepoint kneelers and hymn books.

Olivia had been there for Kate in her time of need, providing her with a home. Now Olivia needed help, but there was only one way Kate could think of to return the favor.

If she were to marry the vicar…

The sound of a masculine throat being cleared drew her attention to the back of the church, where Mr. Blakely stood just inside the door, square and stocky and entirely dressed in black. She curtseyed and walked back to her table to arrange the second vase.

"Miss Blakely," he said. "What a joy to see you here."

If marrying him is the only way to save Olivia, Kate thought, *then perhaps that is what I should do.*

Her face felt frozen, but she forced herself to smile. "It is indeed good to see you, Vicar."

He seemed to be startled, even nervous, as he slowly came closer. "Do I see you wearing *blue*? With your father not yet gone four months?"

Kate looked down at the skirt of her new habit. "It's such a dark shade…" She caught herself up short. He was being ridiculous. Her father would never have made such an objection to a member of his parish who could not afford to buy the trappings of mourning.

"Wearing a dark blue riding habit is hardly the same as gadding about in scarlet, sir." She wondered what he would have said about the new lavender day dress she'd tried on this morning and planned to wear for the wedding. Or the deep purple gown the duchess had provided for the ball.

The vicar shook his head sadly. "I am growing to fear the influence the duchess has had on you, but I suppose I have no choice but to bide my silence." He stood with his hands behind his back, studying the chiseled inscriptions and memorials on the wall.

Kate worked quietly until the second vase matched the first. She put it into place on the altar and, returning to clear the table, took a deep breath. "When you first arrived in Steadham, sir, you were good enough to make me an offer."

"Yes, Miss Blakely?" His eyes brightened. "Have you an answer for me?"

"Not as yet—but I do have a question. *If* I were to accept, would you be agreeable to giving a home to my friend Lady Reyne and her daughter?"

He looked appalled. "Are you mad? You cannot expect me to take in a woman who possesses such a reputation and house her in the vicarage."

Kate's heart sank. If rumor was circulating about Olivia... "What reputation are you referring to, sir? What evidence do you have?"

He shook his head sadly. "I cannot share what was told me in confidence, and in any case I would not sully your ears with the details."

"She is my very good friend. I feel a responsibility toward her."

"That fact causes me to question my assessment of your own character, Miss Blakely, and to wonder if I may have acted too quickly in offering for you. However, I am under an obligation to your father, good Christian gentleman that he was, to see you cared for. I will stand by my decision to marry you, for withdrawing my offer would reflect on my own honor. But I must warn you that when you are my wife, the loose ways you have learned while sharing a house with Lady Reyne, and at Halstead, will no longer be tolerated."

In silence, Kate cleared up the last of the stems, wiped down the table, and carried the empty buckets to a side door where Halstead's gardeners could retrieve them later. When she was finished and believed she once more had control of her temper, she returned to the back of the church.

The vicar was rocking on his heels as he studied the memorial plaque the duchess had placed in honor of her husband shortly after the sixth duke had died. "How fortunate this church is," he said, "to be the burial place of so many notables, and how fortunate they are to have such beautiful surroundings for eternity. But that is nothing to the point. I hope you will keep in mind what I have said as you reflect on your future, Miss Blakely."

"Oh, I shall," Kate said crisply. "And now let me make myself clear. You may be a vicar, sir, but you are anything but a Christian gentleman. You are not worthy to fill my father's shoes. As for your offer of marriage—before a day comes when I would exchange vows with you, there would be a snowstorm in hell. Good day, sir."

She walked out, her head held high, and made her

way toward the coaching inn. And while she thought about what to do next, she might even give in to some of those loose ways she had learned and join Andrew in a tankard of ale.

❧

Every lady at Halstead was excited about the ball—with the possible exception of Penelope. And every lady at Halstead was closeted with her maid as the hour grew nearer for the guests to gather—again, with the exception of Penelope, who was even beginning to regret that she had sent Etta back to London.

When the door of her room opened, she didn't spare a glance for the little maid who was supposed to be coming to help her dress. "At last—I've been waiting for you forever." She stood up, dropping her blue velvet robe onto the stool by the dressing table.

"Have you indeed?" the earl said coolly.

"I…" Penelope felt every inch of exposed skin flush with shame—and there was plenty of skin on display, for she found herself standing in the center of the bedroom wearing nothing but her chemise and stockings. She hadn't even been able to don her corset by herself, much less the petticoats and ball gown that lay ready across the bed.

"The effect has been worth your patience. You must know you make quite a picture there, with the fire behind you. The light shines through your chemise and makes your hair look like gold—but perhaps you planned that effect."

"I wasn't waiting for *you*." She knew she sounded sulky.

He tipped his head to one side. "Then who is the lucky guest for whom you arranged this tableau?" He came across the room toward her, his step light but firm.

"I didn't arrange…" Penelope's heart started to thud as he advanced. Did he think she had invited some other man into her room? And if that was the case, what would he do about it? She couldn't quite stop herself from shivering at the thought, though the frisson running through her might be either fear or anticipation. "I was expecting Maggie. The maid."

He stopped a foot from her. "Where's Etta?"

"I paid her off this morning and sent her back to London."

"Why?" He wrapped her robe closely around her.

The warm brush of velvet against her skin confirmed for Penelope that the little shiver she'd felt had been anticipation—with perhaps a sprinkling of hope—for she didn't feel relieved that he had covered her.

How perfectly stupid she was being, Penelope told herself, to hope that simply seeing her in such a way might rouse him to desire. After all, he'd seen much more of her on other occasions, but he had only made love to her when she had pushed him.

She sat down at the dressing table again and picked up her hairbrush just to keep her hands busy. "Because I am bone-weary of being told I will never be a lady."

He paused, hands raised to the knot in his neck-cloth. "She told you that?"

"Frequently. She was not *my* choice, you know. My father hired her and assigned her a futile task. But I do regret she is not here to fix the mess I've made of my hair." She tried again to smooth the mass into a knot at her crown. A lock fell out and tumbled down her back. Penelope let her curls fall around her shoulders.

The earl hadn't moved.

"Tomorrow is the wedding, my lord," she said quietly. "And then we are free to go back to London." *And start the game all over again...*

He started to unbutton his shirt. "I'm not going to London. At least, I shall not stay. I'll take you back if you wish me to, though I imagine you would prefer to join some of the other ladies on the journey. The duchess will be going in that direction, I believe, and she would be pleased to give you a seat in her carriage."

Penelope's heart twisted. She felt for a moment as though he had reached into her chest and squeezed. "And you, sir?" Her voice was low, husky.

He didn't answer.

Tears stung Penelope's eyelids. "I believe I have a right to know where my husband is, my lord."

"Why would you want to know? Tell your father what I did. If there is any way to free you, Ivan Weiss can find it."

"You sound so noble, as though my wishes were supreme. At least be honest with me. If you find me so repulsive you cannot bear to keep the bargain you made—"

"No," he said under his breath. He reached out gently to touch the springy curls that had fallen down her back. "Your hair fits you. It's just like you, in fact—unexpected, unpredictable, always going its own way."

Penelope could scarcely believe her ears. He sounded approving and not at all repulsed. Very well, she thought. If he liked *unexpected* and *unpredictable*, then she would be those things. "My lord, you said last night that you wished me to have what I wanted. What if I told you I don't want to be free? I want to have your child."

"Only because your father desires it so strongly that you believe you wish it, too."

"No. My father wants an *heir*." She looked straight at him. "I want a *child*."

"I admire you for wanting to make the best of things. You were given no choice. He bartered with your life—"

"I agreed to the bargain."

"But you had no real understanding of what the bargain meant. Not until you were, as you yourself said, chained to me for life. On our wedding night, you were terrified and yet rigidly determined to do what your father required."

Penelope shivered under the memory that cascaded over her. Her wedding night had been warm, a beautiful spring evening in London, but Penelope had been as frozen as if she was naked in the snow...

"I could not force you," he said softly. "And I couldn't bear to look at what I had become. I had not allowed myself to think until then, you see. But when I realized what I had agreed to... Your father sold you—just as surely as he transfers a cask of spirits from one owner to the next—not for money, but to breed a noble heir for him."

She had thought on their wedding night that he had turned away from her in disgust. But if that was not true...

"You were a stranger then," she said. "Now you're my husband." *And my love.* But he would never believe her if she told him. "And now that I know what I was missing, I am not willing to return to the pattern of the past. I am, admittedly, inexperienced— but I find I like being a wife."

His hand stilled. She relished the weight and warmth of his palm against her hair.

"You say I do not repulse you," Penelope went on steadily. "But if it is only your refusal to allow my father to win that prevents you from taking me to your bed, then you are hurting us both in the effort to injure him."

"I hadn't thought of it in that way before."

"Of course, you hadn't. Because you believed me to be unwilling, you didn't see yourself as stubborn but as honorable." She took a deep breath. "I believe there are ways to satisfy ourselves while still allowing you to enjoy taking revenge on my father."

"What are you suggesting?"

"We could, for instance, give him a string of granddaughters."

The earl seemed to freeze, and Penelope thought she had gone too far, risked too much, pressed too hard. A wave of pain flooded over her, but she felt a glimmer of satisfaction, too—for at least she had reached out for what she wanted. Not getting it made her sad, and she would cry over the loss as soon as it was safe to do so. But she had given her all.

The earl snickered.

"Sir?"

"I was picturing your father with three or four little girls, all with your curly hair, as he ties up ribbons one after another." He was laughing outright now, a deep, rich belly laugh Penelope had never heard before, not even when he was with his friends. "And every time one of them bobs a curtsey, another hair ribbon comes loose. He'll never be done with hair ribbons!"

Penelope felt as though she'd unexpectedly stepped off a ledge, for everything inside her seemed to shift and twist and settle into a new spot as she fell more deeply in love.

He lifted her hair and kissed the nape of her neck, then gently tugged her dressing gown loose until it pooled on the bench around her hips. He traced the edge of her chemise with his tongue, pushing the strap aside and unfastening the strings to give him access to more bare skin…

Conscience made her say, "We'll be late for the ball, my lord."

"Do you mind?" His fingers skimmed over her shoulder blades to push the chemise down and then brushed over her ribs until he could cup her breasts. "Shall I stop—my lady?"

He had never before called her *my lady*. Confidence surged over Penelope. If not for her father's bargain, the earl would not have married her, and that she could accept. But if he was proud enough of his wife to give her the title…

"No," she whispered. "No, don't stop."

He made love to her with agonizing slowness, tasting and savoring every inch of her, until Penelope thought she would scream with frustration and desire. To distract herself from the torment he was causing, she mimicked his actions, exploring his body with her hands and her tongue. She learned her own power when she ran her fingers lightly up and down the velvet surface of his penis and felt it grow even harder under her touch. As she started to investigate the fascinating sac that lay below, she found herself flat on her back, her wrists pinioned as he loomed over her. "What do you want, Penny?" he asked hoarsely.

"You," she gasped, and then she stopped thinking and let herself be swept away on the tide of exultation as he plunged inside her and took her to the heights of satisfaction.

∽

His valet hovered anxiously as Simon finished arranging his neckcloth. A timid scratch on the door made Hemmings jump and drop the diamond stickpin he was holding out. He scrabbled around on the carpet and handed it to Simon. "I thought we were finished with the young ladies' stunts," he muttered as he went to answer the door.

Simon had thought so, too. His scheme to court Olivia while providing an alternate supply of young men to distract the bridesmaids had turned out to be as shrewd and effective as any sleight of hand supplied by a stage magician.

But then he and Olivia had quarreled. Though it really wasn't correct to call it a quarrel, Simon told himself. Nothing more than a disagreement, really— and over such a thing as a pony ride! Despite her obvious efforts to maintain a bright facade, Olivia had been distracted all day, and the pack hadn't taken long to pick up the scent and embark on the hunt again.

Things would still work out well in the long run, he told himself. He only had to survive the ball and the wedding itself. By the time the wedding breakfast was over, Olivia would create a scene as planned, making it clear he was no longer welcome to pay court to her. Then everyone would remember how moody she had been, and the break would come as no real surprise.

Hemmings came back. "Not a bridesmaid after all," he said. "Just the tweeny pressed into service to carry a message from the duchess. She would like you to come to her rooms before dinner."

The duchess was already dressed for the ball, resplendent in mauve satin and diamonds, when her maid showed Simon in. Her gloves and fan lay on a chair, however, and she was sorting through a pile of correspondence roughly the size of a haystack.

Simon wouldn't have been surprised if the spindly little French table she used as a writing desk had collapsed under the weight of all her letters. "You wished to see me? Are you ready to go downstairs?"

"Not just yet." The duchess didn't look up. "I wish to discuss arrangements for the wedding."

Simon suppressed the urge to swear. "The wedding is tomorrow, Mother. Daphne hasn't time to add any grand plans. Or is it Harcourt who's coming up with ideas? Would you like me to take him aside and remind him the time for suggestions is long past?"

"Not Daphne's." The duchess pulled a letter from the stack. "Your wedding."

Your wedding. The words seemed to skewer him to the carpet. "Oh, there's plenty of time to think about that."

The duchess looked up, finally. "Is there, really?"

"No need to get into a fuss while Daphne's big event is still hanging over us. Nothing can be formalized until Lady Reyne's period of mourning is over, anyway. She's something of a stickler about waiting a full two years."

The duchess snorted. "I'd find it easier to believe that Banbury tale if she were wearing black now. In any case, if you wait another year, Simon, the child who should be the next Duke of Somervale could be three months old at his parents' wedding."

"Damn it, I *knew* I shouldn't have trusted that girl to keep her mouth closed." He recalled, too late, that Maggie hadn't actually promised to be silent…

"Which girl are you referring to?" the duchess asked politely.

Simon realized his mother hadn't known after all. She'd been fishing for information, and she'd landed herself a whale.

"Thank you for confirming my suspicions. And pray, do not at this stage try to convince me that you and Lady Reyne have been simply playing piquet in her bedroom instead of… other games." From under a pile of letters, she drew out a small velvet box. "I had this sent up from the bank vaults in London, since you will soon need it."

"The Somervale betrothal and wedding rings," Simon said. Reluctantly, he took the box.

It's all right, he told himself. What did it matter if, when Olivia publicly jilted him, he happened to be in possession of the Somervale rings? An increased level of public embarrassment might even win him sympathy from his mother, and if he was lucky, a reprieve from further matchmaking efforts.

He didn't feel lucky.

The duchess stirred through her correspondence again and drew out a letter. "You should also know, Simon, that Mr. Blakely—though always annoying—is occasionally quite correct. The archbishop *is* visiting in the neighborhood. I have invited him to dinner before the ball, and he has accepted. So you can take care of arranging a special license tonight."

Simon swallowed hard and told himself having a license was one thing; standing up in front of a priest and taking vows was another.

"The wedding will have to be a quiet one, of course." The duchess raised her voice. "Miss Blakely? Come in, please." She flicked her hand at Simon, shooing him away. "That's all, dear. Go and take care of the arrangements now. And if you haven't yet offered for the lady, perhaps you should think about doing so—and *quickly*."

Sixteen

KATE COULDN'T OVERHEAR THE LOW-VOICED CONVERsation going on in the duchess's sitting room, though she had to admit she'd tried to listen. Which, she supposed, only confirmed what the vicar had said about the effects of her time at Halstead—for Kate couldn't recall feeling the urge to eavesdrop before.

Still, only a saint could have sat there and not wondered what the duchess could possibly be saying to her son that left the duke so nearly speechless.

"Miss Blakely?" the duchess called. "Come in, please."

Kate shot a look at the duke as he left. He looked pale. And perhaps—determined?

The duchess surveyed Kate critically. "I must commend the modiste for her selection of fabric, but I think the simple style must have been your choice."

"Yes, ma'am."

"A very good result—and with the dull surface of the fabric and the deep color, no one could think it in poor taste."

The vicar could, Kate thought. But what the vicar thought was no longer any worry of hers.

"You will be wondering why I asked you to take a moment from your busy day to see me, Miss Blakely. I am extremely grateful for the assistance you have given in the past few days. In fact, I cannot express how much I appreciate you, so I hope you will not be offended by a token gift."

Kate's heart beat a little faster. What the duchess called a token would no doubt look like a fortune to someone in her circumstances.

The duchess picked up her fan and gloves. Underneath them lay a small leather-bound book with an elaborate design picked out on the front cover in gold. "This prayer book was a gift to me long ago. I hope you will find the study of its contents to be as rewarding as I did."

A prayer book, Kate thought helplessly. What more useless gift could the daughter of a vicar receive? She owned half a dozen already; what was she to do with yet another? The duchess must still think she was going to marry Mr. Blakely—for a prayer book, even though redundant, was a gift the vicar would approve.

I should tell her I've refused him, Kate thought. But something inside her shuddered at the thought of talking about it. She was too embarrassed even to confess she had given Mr. Blakely's offer serious thought...

The calfskin warmed in her hands as she held the little book. The worn satin ribbons that held the book closed slid across her wrist, tickling her.

The duchess had given her a ball gown that she would have no opportunity to wear again and a prayer book...

And it wasn't even a new prayer book.

"I don't know how to thank you, ma'am," Kate managed to say.

The duchess smiled. "It's nothing, my dear. Run along—and enjoy the ball this evening."

❧

Though the duchess had warned that a ball gown made in such a hurry must of necessity be a simple one, in fact Olivia thought her dress the loveliest thing she had ever owned. Each time she moved, the silver tissue skirt drifted lazily around her, as light and airy as clouds in the summer sky. She felt quite elegant even before she went up to the nursery and watched her daughter's eyes widen.

"You look like Cinderella," Charlotte whispered.

Complete with borrowed finery, Olivia thought. Her lacy shawl and fan and shoes were on loan from Lady Townsend, who had flung open her trunks this afternoon for Kate and Olivia to choose from. And though the silver nosegay holder full of baby roses had arrived with the duke's card attached, Olivia knew that was nothing special, for Kate had told her every lady at Halstead was meant to receive a similar one tonight.

Charlotte settled back into her cot. "The duchess will bring me a sweet from the ball."

Olivia's heart sank. Obviously Simon had not passed along her strictures on visiting to his mother. "Did she say she would?"

Charlotte nodded firmly.

"Then I'm sure she meant it. But she will be busy with all her guests until long after you're asleep."

"But she promised!"

Olivia thought, *And when she realizes you're not going to be a part of the family after all...* "You must not count on her. She will be fully occupied tomorrow with the wedding, Charlotte."

"I want to see the bride!"

"I think there can be no objection to you and Nurse watching Lady Daphne get into the carriage that will take her to the church." Olivia looked down at her daughter. "Everyone at Halstead is making you feel very special right now, Charlotte. But in a day or two we'll be going home to the cottage, and then things will be as they always have been before."

Charlotte considered. "My pony?" she asked hopefully.

"The pony is not yours, dear. He belongs to the duke, who only loaned him to you for a ride today. In any case, we have no place to keep a pony."

The child stuck out her lower lip. "But the duke said—"

"The duke said a good many things." Olivia knew her voice was sharp, and she almost wished Simon was here right now so he could see firsthand the results of his spoiling. "Your pout is most unattractive, Charlotte. It's time for your prayers."

Charlotte's list of people to bless had grown immensely in just one day. She rattled off names from the duke and duchess to the nursery maids and the tweeny who had brought her supper upstairs. But perhaps, Olivia thought hopefully, Charlotte was merely groping for people to bless, to keep her mother beside her for another minute and delay sleep. Perhaps her enthusiastic prayer didn't mean she would miss those people or even remember them when they vanished from her life.

Finally, however, the amens were said. Olivia scooped up Charlotte for a good-night hug and then went down to dinner.

Most of the ladies hadn't yet appeared—Olivia thought they were doubtless still primping for the ball, which would begin shortly after dinner was over—but the duke was already in the drawing room, and the instant she came in, she could feel his gaze on her.

She hadn't seen him all afternoon, not since the archery contest had ended and the winner had laughingly claimed his arm to walk back to the house.

She had to admit she had missed him, and her heart lifted when she caught sight of him. When his gaze ran slowly over her, from the cluster of roses she had woven into her glossy curls all the way to the toes of her borrowed slippers, heat followed, pooling in her belly and making her feet clumsy. He knew it too, for he smiled and let the very tip of his tongue graze his lip, reminding her of the delight he had given her and would no doubt give her again tonight, if this ball was ever behind them...

Not only Charlotte needed to be reminded that none of this was real, that nothing would last. The transformation would not happen precisely at midnight, and Olivia's dress would not change into rags—but when her time was up, all the special treats would wilt just as quickly as the roses in her nosegay, and she would be back in the cottage among the cinders...

But that would come later. For now, she would enjoy the remaining time. She smiled at the duke and was pleased to see she could have something of the same effect on him that he so effortlessly created in her.

His eyes widened just a little, and he came across the room to her. "Lady Reyne." Even the soft syllables of her name were a caress that whispered along her skin and made her ache for his touch.

His gaze slid past her to the door. Olivia glanced over her shoulder to see a tall, thin gentleman all in black.

"Archbishop," the duke said. "I am so pleased you could join us this evening."

Olivia's stomach lurched.

"As it turns out," the duke said softly, "my mother discovered he was in the vicinity after all. And since she is daydreaming of special licenses and hurried ceremonies—"

"The sooner the duchess is disabused of her notion, the better." Olivia's voice sounded calmer than it was. "We have not discussed, as yet, how to end this. I suppose I could slap you and walk off the ballroom floor."

"You needn't sound gleeful about the possibility. And tomorrow is soon enough."

Olivia considered. "Because you're afraid all the bridesmaids might line up to console you overnight?"

"You saw what happened today when you quarreled with me. They were like a pack of flies again."

"That was not a quarrel. That was a—" She stopped herself short; in a day or two, nothing she had said to him would matter anyway. She would never see him again unless perhaps she chanced to be in the garden some day when he rode through the village. But she would not think about it now. "When *do* you wish me to jilt you? In the church?"

"I have put the archbishop off until tomorrow so he may enjoy his evening. He and I have an appointment just before Daphne's wedding."

"I could throw coffee over you at breakfast."

"Must you take pleasure in this? I am to meet with the archbishop at ten in the library. If you are there already when he arrives, perhaps even shedding a tear as you tell me that after long reflection you cannot bear to violate your period of mourning, and so you must for the moment decline my offer and postpone our marital happiness…"

"*Postpone?*" Olivia said. "You said you wanted me to jilt you. That's an entirely different thing."

"Yes, but I've reconsidered. Leaving my mother with a flutter of hope seems more practical."

"Practical for you, perhaps, because as long as she thinks you besotted with me, she might not force other young women to your attention. But for me, it's hardly a pleasant alternative."

He smiled. "I wish we were alone, Olivia, so I could show you how wrong you are." He raised his voice. "Archbishop, may I introduce a very special person? I'd like you to meet my… Lady Reyne."

❦

With a dozen bridesmaids keeping score of who he danced with, to say nothing of the other ladies of rank who were present and expecting notice from their host, fully half the ball had passed before Simon had a break from the dance floor.

Finally, however, he bowed before Olivia for the first waltz. "I should turn you down," she said.

"Then I would be left standing alone, for I could never honor one of the bridesmaids with a waltz when the others have received only country dances. How dreadful for the host to be unable to find a partner."

"They're all staring. What if I stumble?"

"I shall hold you closely so you can't."

She flicked a look up at him through her lashes. "And *that's* supposed to comfort me?"

Simon noticed that his mother was watching them, her lips pursed thoughtfully. He swept Olivia onto the floor, which fortunately was so crowded that the dance was more intimate than usual. Her steps matched his perfectly; her height was exactly right for him to look into her eyes as they danced; and the brush of her skirt as they spun around the room reminded him of other touches during last night's long and luxurious love-making. He was impatient for the ball to be ended, so he could have her once more under him in an entirely different sort of rhythm.

"You waltz as deliciously as you make love," he whispered as the music ended, and delighted in the wash of color over her face.

She refused a cold drink, so he walked her over to a corner of the ballroom to join Kate Blakely and the bridesmaid who had fallen down in the abbey ruins. Though the bridesmaid had managed to hobble downstairs for the ball, she was looking interestingly pale, and Simon passed a few minutes in polite conversation lest she feel slighted in favor of the other bridesmaids.

Finally, with his obligations complete, he turned back to Olivia to ask for the next dance. "I have promised it to the colonel," she said, and though Simon laughed at the idea, she went off with the elderly gentleman who, to Simon's surprise, was quite good at the country dance.

At loose ends, Simon retreated to the refreshment room and sent one of the footmen after something more substantial than the ratafia and punch his mother had ordered for the ladies.

As he was waiting, Sir Jasper Folsom came in, and Simon—so recently reminded of the bridesmaid's accident—recalled telling the duchess he would take up the matter of the abbey ruins at the next opportunity. He just hadn't expected the baronet to be on the guest list for Daphne's ball. "Sir Jasper, I would like to consult you in a matter that concerns us both."

"I've been expecting you would, Your Grace. A matter of a lady, is it?"

Simon frowned. "My mother has expressed concern about the condition of the abbey ruins, after one of our guests had an accident there."

"I hope no one's trying to blame *me* for it. Anyone foolish enough to walk around on those slimy stones deserves a fall."

"You know how females can be," Simon said, and hoped his mother would never get wind of what he'd said. "She'd like to see the whole lot pulled down. Now you and I are men of the world…"

"Indeed we are," Sir Jasper said. "And this is about far more than a set of ruins, isn't it, Your Grace? I'd consider pulling the rest of the abbey down, if…"

Simon's fingers itched with the desire to push Sir Jasper's oily voice down his throat. "If…?"

"I should say, *when* we come to an arrangement. That's a lovely lady you were just waltzing with. Of course, things aren't always as they seem. What's it worth to you, Your Grace, to find out why Lady Reyne is really here in Steadham, and what happened to her husband?"

❧

The dancing was already well under way when Kate reached the ballroom, for Emily had insisted on walking in by herself rather than letting a footman carry her. Kate supposed the injured bridesmaid thought she made a more sympathetic picture than if she'd merely been carried through the crowd to the small sofa that had been reserved for her. But it took forever for Emily to hop the full length of one of Halstead's main-floor wings with a walking stick, wincing as she tried to protect both her sprained ankle and her bruised shoulder.

By the time Kate had pulled the sofa around to give Emily the best view, propped her injured foot up on pillows, and arranged her ruffled skirt to the bridesmaid's satisfaction, the first group of country dances was coming to an end.

"Here comes Mr. Carlisle," Emily said in a voice loud enough to carry over the music. "I hope he's not planning to prose on to me about Latin, for none of the other gentlemen will come around if he does."

Kate set a chair next to the sofa in a position that would not require Emily to turn her head to an uncomfortable angle to chat. But Andrew only made a sketchy bow to the bridesmaid. "I have no Latin prepared for you, Miss Emily. Miss Blakely, may I sign your dance card for the set that is just coming up?"

"I am not planning to dance tonight, Mr. Carlisle."

Andrew looked around. "Why not? The vicar seems not to be present."

"I do not base my decisions on the vicar's opinions," Kate said, more sharply than she had intended, and she watched Andrew's eyes narrow. "In any case, Miss Emily needs me."

Lady Stone craned her neck around a nearby pillar. "Nonsense. The foolish girl is perfectly safe here, and I'll keep an eye on her. Go and have fun."

Emily looked horrified. She seemed to think that even listening to Latin would be better than being supervised by Lady Stone.

Andrew offered his arm. "The set is forming, Miss Blakely. I see the archbishop already in position with the duchess. Unless you'd prefer to stroll about the room so we can chat?"

Outnumbered, Kate surrendered.

"If the vicar's opinion is no longer of interest to you," Andrew said, "then you must have refused him after all."

Valid though his conclusion was, the casual statement annoyed Kate in more ways than she could count.

"I thought you said you would not answer him until after the wedding. What did he do, Kate, to make you reject him now? And what do you plan to do instead, with the security of the vicarage no longer in your future?"

I wish I knew, Kate thought.

Andrew looked down at her. "My offer is still open."

Kate's breath froze for an instant before she remembered what he was talking about. "Coming with you to the wilds to organize your travel? Do be serious, Mr. Carlisle." Kate took her place among the dancers, ending up a couple of positions down the set from Olivia and Viscount Chadwick. Kate hoped the young man would prove more adept in the ballroom than he had on the archery range.

At least it was a country dance, not a waltz—and, she realized, as long as she stayed on the ballroom floor Andrew could not quiz her further. So Kate danced one set after another, barely noticing her steps.

The satisfaction of having said her piece to the vicar had died away as the hours slipped by, and though Kate knew she could never regret the decision she had made or the fact she had stood up for herself, reality had begun to settle in. Losing one more option from the pitifully few at her disposal stung. Her time at Halstead was coming to a close. Her hopes, so high when the duchess had first offered the opportunity, had sagged to nothing. There seemed no one except the colonel who wanted a secretary, and no one—at least no one she could hear—who might hire a companion.

Penny was settled; at least Kate was reasonably certain that since neither the Earl nor the Countess of Townsend had appeared for the ball, they were having their own private party upstairs. And as for Olivia… Perhaps she had a point in choosing to be the duke's mistress, Kate thought as the first waltz started and Olivia whirled about the room in Simon's arms. Tonight, at least, Olivia seemed contented. Kate alone was at loose ends.

Reluctantly, she returned to the corner where Emily sat. "You've been having a good time," the bridesmaid said between clenched teeth. "You were supposed to stay beside me."

Lady Stone intervened. "The secret to a satisfying relationship with a companion, Miss Emily, is to make the expectations clear. For instance, I expect my companions to be saucy, pert, and opinionated—so not just anyone will satisfy."

The duke and Olivia came up to them, and Emily dimpled prettily as she chatted to the duke. He stayed a moment and then excused himself and moved off. Kate saw Olivia watching him wistfully.

Lady Stone's beady gaze rested expectantly on Kate. "I've been watching you this week. You would do for the post, if you're interested. I'd hate to see you wasted on the colonel."

Saucy. Pert. Opinionated. Yes, Kate thought, *I can do that.* "I'm very interested."

"Good. We shall consider it settled and discuss the details tomorrow."

Emily shifted fretfully on her couch. "I want a cold drink."

Kate didn't realize Andrew had returned until he said, "Miss Blakely and I will fetch it."

Still overcome by the sudden shift in her circumstances, and feeling dazed at the idea of working for Lady Stone, Kate obediently took Andrew's arm to go down the hall to where refreshments were laid out.

They were barely outside the ballroom when Andrew said, "You're to be Lady Stone's companion?" His voice dripped disbelief.

"I gather you've been eavesdropping again."

"It seems to be the only way to discover anything where you're concerned!"

"Kindly do not lecture me, Mr. Carlisle. I had my fill of that this afternoon."

"So you did turn the vicar down. Or was he ungallant enough to withdraw his offer?"

"The question is insulting." *Even though it cuts uncomfortably close to the truth.*

Caught up in her own feelings, Kate almost missed the low-voiced conversation going on in the corner of the refreshment room until she heard Olivia's name. Only then did she realize that the man who was face to face with the duke—the man who was talking about Olivia's late husband—was Sir Jasper Folsom.

Now Kate knew where the vicar had heard the gossip about Olivia. And she had a fairly good idea of what Sir Jasper had told him, and what he was now telling the duke.

She turned to Andrew, eyes wide. "Do something to stop him! I'm going to warn Olivia."

⁂

Penelope's ball gown and petticoats had slid off the bed and lay rumpled on the carpet. Candles glowed around the bed, and she felt a delicious lassitude as she lay curled against her husband. Her left hand lay against his chest, the gold of her wedding ring gleaming in the candlelight as she savored the strong beat of his heart against her palm. "Where were you planning to go," she asked lazily, "when you said you weren't coming back to London?"

"Stoneyford, of course. I've camped out in worse conditions." He smoothed her hair back from her face and twisted the full length of a curl around his finger.

"But you must come to London. We need to sell my jewelry at once so we know what moneys you will have to work with."

"At that moment, my plan did not include your jewels."

"Then you need a new plan," Penelope said firmly, "for I want to be a partner in this effort."

"At least wait till I've told you what I want to do before you agree. If we spend your money on the house as you suggested, we could restore a wing. We'd have a place to live, but the land would still be unprofitable. If instead you are willing to invest in the land, then I can make the estate pay—and with luck, sooner or later we may rebuild the entire house and make it our home. That is what I asked of your father, in my letter—to invest in the land."

Penelope was startled. "Not the house?"

He shook his head. "I cannot justify spending on the house because it will not turn a profit. But if this plan is not to your liking…"

"The jewels are yours now, sir. I have confidence you will use them to best advantage. But if I choose to spend my pin money on the house, you will not object?"

"The decision is up to you. But enough about business tonight. If we are going to be partners in this, Penny, I should like to hear you use my name."

She whispered, "Charles," and felt her world shift again as he smiled at her.

He pulled away and came back a moment later with her jewel case. Slowly he sorted out the contents, putting each piece on her. "How did I miss the amethyst and garnet necklace before?" he muttered, clasping it around her throat. He pinned the yellow diamond brooch into her curls as though it was a hair clip and fastened a particularly gaudy bracelet around her slender ankle.

"What are you doing?" Penelope asked finally, as he laid the empty case aside.

"I'm arranging all your gifts to me so they will adorn the best gift of all." And before she could think it through, he was kissing her again. "I want to hear you say my name while I am inside you," he said against her lips.

Before the night was out, she had said his name, shrieked it, whispered it, murmured it... and each time, she fell more deeply in love.

❧

As soon as Sir Jasper had gone, Simon tossed back his brandy, hoping it would burn out the ugly aftertaste of the man's words. He put the brandy glass down with a thump and went back to the ballroom to seek out Olivia.

She was going down the set with his friend Warren, and Simon leaned against a pillar and watched her with appreciation. The slim, dainty figure—had he once thought her too slender, her bosom not generous enough? How wrong he had been, when her breasts were exactly the right size to fill his hands. She was incredibly graceful, spinning through the figures of the dance in a way which made every other woman in the set look as clumsy as an elephant.

What was happening to him, anyway? When she'd first come into the drawing room tonight, he'd been afraid she was still angry. Then she had smiled... and he had felt as if the floor was sliding out from under his feet.

He remembered thinking how stunningly beautiful she was. But surely it was odd that he had been startled, for her beauty was the first thing to attract him.

No, on the contrary. He had thought her unusual and striking, but far from his usual idea of beauty. Then he had made love to her and found her both lovely and beautiful. But in the last day or so, he must have stopped noticing she was beautiful. She had become simply Olivia...

He wished he'd had another brandy, even though the fire of the alcohol hadn't washed out the taste of Sir Jasper's words.

Nothing would, he realized, except perhaps clearing the air with Olivia.

✑

Kate wanted to run back into the ballroom, but she knew hurrying was the worst thing she could do. Drawing attention to herself and to Olivia right now would only make matters worse.

When she rejoined Lady Stone and Olivia beside the invalid's couch, Emily said fretfully, "Where's the cold drink you promised, Miss Blakely?"

Olivia smiled. "Where did you lose Mr. Carlisle, Kate? That can't have been easy."

"I need a moment with you," Kate said under her breath. Drawing Olivia away, she added, "Sir Jasper is in the refreshment room, and he's telling the duke about you—and Lord Reyne."

Olivia closed her eyes for an instant. When she opened them, she was pale but resolute.

"I'm so sorry," Kate said.

"I'm not. I'm glad I seized the opportunity."

Olivia's partner for the next set presented himself, and with a smile that would have fooled most people—though not Kate—she went off to dance.

Seizing opportunities, Kate thought. She'd done some of that herself of late, though taking a job with Lady Stone—or even telling off the vicar—really didn't compare with having an affair with the Duke of Somervale. At least working for Lady Stone would be more interesting than chaperoning girls like Emily, and the old lady did seem sincere in preferring honesty over mealy-mouthed agreement.

Seizing opportunities…

Penny was upstairs with her husband; she'd made the most of her stay at Halstead. And even though Olivia was facing disaster, she had no regrets about the choices she had made.

While Kate would be the companion of a sharp-tongued old lady, starting tomorrow—which left only tonight for seizing opportunities. If she dared.

❧

From the moment the invitation to Lady Daphne's

wedding had arrived, Olivia had been half-expecting that at least one of the many guests gathered at Halstead for the festivities would have heard the stories.

She hadn't expected it to be Sir Jasper Folsom.

She had not yet regained her poise after Kate's breathless warning when her partner claimed her for the next dance. But the duke couldn't interrupt the set, so she'd have a few more minutes to gather herself.

Simon was waiting for her at the edge of the floor when the set ended, and Olivia knew as soon as she saw his face that Kate had been right. Sir Jasper had indeed passed along whatever poison he had been able to collect. And it must have been quite a deadly poison, for there was pain in Simon's eyes and a set to his jaw that sent a tremor through her.

By tomorrow, when she was supposed to jilt him, the word would have spread throughout the assembled guests and it would be too late to protect him from the gossip. She had to act now, so the duke would not be hurt.

"Come with me, Olivia," he said quietly.

She smiled and fluttered her fan. "Sir, your attentions have been amusing and a pleasant way to pass the time for a few days. But you must not think I meant any more than a flirtation."

"And my offer of marriage?"

The music seemed to fade; at least, Olivia could hear only a strange buzz in her ears. If only it had been true, she thought. If only he *had* wanted to marry her...

Only now, when it was too late, could she finally see the truth. Being his wife would be the culmination of her dreams. She hadn't merely been enjoying having a lover; she had fallen in love with Simon—with the man, not with the duke.

But grieving must wait for later. Just now she must play her role.

"You were mistaken, sir. I did not regard your talk of permanence as an offer, only as coquetry."

"So you're a heartless jilt, leading me on and pretending I misunderstood?"

How much it hurt to laugh and agree, when with all her heart she wanted to do the opposite—to fling herself against him and beg him to mean what he was saying. "I suppose I am," she said lightly. "What a terrible thing to have to admit about oneself!"

"Indeed it would be, if it were true. But I have it on the best authority that only a fool would jilt a duke. You, my dear, are not a fool, and you will find I am very patient."

And that was just another line from the drama, Olivia thought, for he had shown no signs of patience up until now—certainly not as a lover. Why had he not simply seized on the escape she had offered?

"Let us go somewhere private to finish this discussion."

Olivia made a last stab at escape. "I am engaged to Mr. Carlisle for the next dance."

"Andrew will understand." Simon drew her hand firmly through his arm, strolling through the ballroom to the terrace doors and out into the perfect summer night.

Olivia tried to pull away, but he had clamped his hand over hers and would not let go.

"What is wrong with you?" she said furiously.

"You wrote this script. Can't you recognize a cue when you hear it?"

"Tell me about your husband, Olivia."

"What could I possibly add to what Sir Jasper has already said?"

"He told me he'd heard that up in Lincolnshire they call you the Dark Widow."

She shuddered. "I didn't know that. But I am not surprised."

The silence drew out. "You will not even attempt to defend yourself?"

"He told you one side of the story—that of my late husband's brother and heir. I presume it goes something like this: I did not realize my husband's miserly habits were from need, not from inclination, so I hastened his death to free myself. Then when I realized I would not benefit, I stole what I could and ran away."

"That was the gist," Simon agreed. "And now tell me what really happened, Olivia."

He sounded as if he cared—as if he would truly listen.

She sighed. "Despite his ill health, Lord Reyne was trying furiously for a son, for he wanted desperately to keep the estate from his brother. Little though there was to inherit, they had always been rivals. He died… in the effort… and there was talk."

"I imagine there might have been," Simon said dryly.

"But I did not understand the true nature of my position until the new Lord Reyne arrived to claim the estate."

"Nasty sort, was he?"

"He took one look at me and announced that I was

comely enough to earn back what his brother had cost the estate through his foolish marriage—so he would make arrangements with a friend who would pay well to have me in his bed."

"So, of course, you ran."

"That was not the entire reason. Though he was not named Charlotte's guardian, I feared he would find a way to change the situation, and he would be able to sell her in a few years. So I packed what little I could hide away—some bits of my mother's china, a few sentimental things I had brought with me. I stole away, I came as far as I could afford to do, and I have lived quietly on the minuscule funds left me by my father—and hoped it would be too much trouble and expense for the new Lord Reyne to hunt me down."

"And you waited for him to move on to other schemes."

She nodded. "I should have changed my name, I suppose, but that did not occur to me until after I had made myself known in Steadham village, and then it was too late."

The music stopped, and the dancers' applause drifted out across the terrace. Then the orchestra began a waltz. The slow, dreamy beat of the dance made Olivia want to cry, and she knew she would never again hear a waltz without remembering Simon.

"Yes," he said slowly. "A very good idea, to change your name—next time you move."

Seventeen

KATE WAS STILL THINKING OF OLIVIA SAYING SHE WAS glad for everything she had done when Andrew Carlisle came up beside her. Had he come to take up their quarrel? She had broken away from him in the midst of it, but if he started in again to quiz her about the vicar and Lady Stone…

"Did you talk to Lady Reyne?" he asked.

Kate relaxed a bit. "Only for a moment. She's out on the floor." She turned to watch the dancers. "Did you stop Sir Jasper?"

"It proved impossible. He was already winding down by the time I reached the duke."

"What does the duke intend to do?"

"Simon did not take me into his confidence." Andrew drew her hand into the crook of his arm. "The less made of it by people staring, the better. Starting with you."

Kate knew he was right, but she couldn't entirely keep herself from looking back. She saw the duke and Olivia face off at the edge of the dance floor. "I must do something to help."

The colonel caught her eye and came briskly across the room toward them. "Not a bad idea," Andrew said. He sketched a bow to the colonel and led Kate out into the hall. "This way, I think—quickly. Now that the colonel has caught a glimpse of us leaving…"

"What are you doing?"

"Creating a distraction. Something else for the crowd to chatter about."

"The fact we've disappeared together?"

"You did say you felt you must do something to assist your friend," Andrew reminded. His voice was low and almost rough. Before Kate could object, he whisked her around a corner into a small, empty anteroom and closed the door. "With luck, no one will find us here."

So now he would kiss her. *Seizing opportunities*, Kate thought.

But Andrew didn't move.

Why not? Because—despite what he'd said about distracting the crowd—if someone were to follow and find them here locked in an embrace, it would ruin her? Or because it would ruin *him*? Had she missed her chance altogether?

If Greeley hadn't interrupted them that night in the library, would she have reached out with both hands to experience the passion, excitement, and adventure he offered? Or would she have let the invitation slide away? And was it now too late?

She looked up at him. The brilliant green blaze of his eyes heated her blood. She could see and feel his desire calling out to hers. But still he didn't reach for her.

It was up to her, Kate knew. She could seize the opportunity now or let it pass—but this would be the last chance. From tomorrow, she would have to answer to Lady Stone.

She flicked the tip of her tongue across dry lips and whispered, "I don't want to quarrel with you, Andrew." She took a step closer. The soft purple ruffle that edged the neckline of her ball gown rose and fell with her uneven breaths, brushing his coat, and her breasts tingled with anticipation. "I'm ready for the next stage of the journey."

Slowly, he put his arms around her, drawing her into the shelter of his strength. Andrew's mouth was warm, soft, and mobile. His kiss questioned, rather than demanded, and Kate felt her entire body soften in response. His hands slid slowly over her. Her breasts pressed against the hardness of his chest, aching a little until he turned his attention to them. He freed her from the restricting bodice and licked gently until her nipples peaked eagerly.

He pulled her closer against himself, his erection gently nudging between her legs and heating her through the thin fabric of her skirt. She felt damp and hot and confused, not knowing quite what she wanted, but eager nevertheless. She whimpered a little and tugged his head down to kiss him, darting her tongue against his in a silent appeal.

"Come upstairs with me," he said, "where we won't be interrupted."

Kate's head spun at the idea. Down the length of the ballroom wing, across the wide entrance hall, up the wide-open staircase… how did he plan to accomplish that without being discovered? She didn't think she could walk the distance alone; her knees had gone too weak to hold her up. "How do we…?" she managed to say.

Andrew's grin flashed. "I used to play hide-and-seek in this house." His breathing had grown ragged. Or was that hers?

Kate lost count of the anterooms they ducked through, with Andrew peering around each door. They waited in the last one for a chattering group of bridesmaids to pass. Kate felt one short quiver of conscience that she was not supervising them tonight, but then Andrew kissed her again, and she forgot. As soon as the girls had passed, he pulled her across the passage and opened a door to reveal a narrow, twisting staircase. At the top, he urged her down the hall, stopping where the curving wing joined the main house to be certain no one was in sight.

Finally they reached his bedroom—the bedroom Kate had occupied when she first arrived. She felt as though she was coming home, stepping once more into that quiet, welcoming room. Or perhaps she simply felt safe because he turned the key to shut out the world.

But that was the last instant when Kate felt entirely secure. As soon as Andrew touched her again, desire flared more strongly than she had ever imagined it could—a flood tide of longing, impatience, and hunger. She pressed herself against him, her rock in an unsteady world.

His lips trailed slowly down her throat to the low neckline of her gown, and her nipples peaked again

in anticipation. "You are so lovely, so responsive…"
Her gown slid slowly off her shoulders. How had he
managed to unfasten the back without even looking
at it?

With her petticoats and corset gone, Kate began
to feel shy. As if he understood, Andrew turned her
away from him and kissed her nape, following her
spine downward and feeding the heat within her while
allowing her to gather herself once more.

"So utterly beautiful, Kate." Andrew's voice was
like a caress, low and soft, curling around her and
pulling at her heart. She let her head fall back against
his shoulder, and he kissed her lips again and ran his
hands down to cup her breasts through the thin fabric
of her chemise.

She was sorry when he let her go, until she realized
he didn't take his gaze off her even while he undressed.
Perhaps that was the advantage of a gentleman not
being a dandy, she thought; he didn't seem to care
what happened to his clothes. She wondered idly why
she felt so warm despite her state of undress, and then
she forgot everything else as he came back to her,
naked and powerful—for it felt so very right to be in
his arms.

He released the ties of her chemise and peeled it
slowly away from her body, and then gathered her
close against himself and lifted her onto his bed.
The hair on his chest rubbed her tender skin as he
leaned over her and drew her into the hardness of
his body. Her head was spinning. What a different
sensation it was, she thought muzzily, to be kissed
while lying down. She could really concentrate on

his lips when she didn't have to give thought to keeping her balance...

Andrew shook his head as if he, too, wasn't quite able to focus. "Did I do something wrong?" she whispered, and he smiled and kissed her again.

He explored her slowly but as thoroughly as he had once talked of exploring continents—and he claimed her as completely as any adventurer had ever claimed a mountain peak or an island. He brought her to ecstasy with his hands and his mouth, and held her while she trembled through her first orgasm. Only then did he slide inside her, slowly and gently stroking her—until Kate whimpered in frustration and his control broke. He surged deep inside her, thrusting hard, until to her infinite satisfaction they reached the pinnacle together.

❧

Simon's calm agreement—his matter-of-fact assessment that Olivia should change her name when she moved on from Halstead—chilled her heart and made her wonder if this conversation was only an intellectual exercise to him.

What was wrong with her, anyway? She had never expected faithfulness, for she had never considered it possible for Simon. But had she truly been foolish enough to hope she might be different from his other mistresses, that her moment in the sun might actually last?

Simon went on in a matter-of-fact tone. "You require a protector who will assure that the scum up in Lincolnshire is no longer in a position to harm you."

"A protector," Olivia said slowly. Was he suggesting

that she simply move on to another man, another affair? "No. I have no intention of… of becoming a lightskirt."

"Olivia—"

"Please, Simon, just let me finish. I beg you, help me to go away. Help me to find a place where we can live quietly."

He frowned. "Is that what you want?"

"I don't expect anything further from you—just a little help to get myself away, to reestablish myself somewhere else. You must see that even if it wasn't for the gossip, I can't let Charlotte grow up just outside the gates of Halstead, wondering why she's never invited to the manor anymore when she remembers being an honored guest."

"No, you *can't* let her grow up outside the gates of Halstead."

It was all the confirmation she needed; this was the end, then. Sadness washed over her.

"Stay *inside* Halstead, Olivia," he said softly. "Stay right here with me."

If she was starving and staring at a loaded table she was not allowed to touch, it would not have hurt her so much as to be offered something she wanted so badly but could not have. "I can't," she whispered. "I don't ever want to have to explain to Charlotte what I did to secure her future."

"Marry me," Simon said, "and you need never tell her anything at all. I will protect you both."

The words seem to echo around her.

Marry me… But she must not salve her pain by hurting him. Olivia shook her head. "You're only offering because you feel responsible for the gossip, for what Sir Jasper is saying."

"Why should I feel responsible for the insanity of your late husband's brother?"

"Because I've lived here for months without incident, until I met you. Then Sir Jasper realized it might be worth looking into my past, and here we are. But it would have happened anyway, sooner or later. You're not to blame."

"I am not offering for you out of guilt, Olivia. Or to protect you, either, though I have every intention of doing so. Sir Jasper will not say another word about you to anyone, ever."

"You seem very certain of that." She studied him more closely. "You don't *look* as though you've been in a brawl."

"Drawing his cork would have been satisfactory but crude—and within minutes everyone in the house would have known, which would hardly have put a stop to the gossip. However, I know a few things about Sir Jasper that he would prefer not to become common knowledge."

"Blackmail?"

"He seemed to grasp the concept readily enough when it was turned back on him."

"You are very kind."

"Dammit, I'm *not* kind. I'm a selfish brute and I want you." He leaned his chin against her hair. "I *need* you, Olivia. There must be a hundred and fifty rooms at Halstead, and so far I've made love in just one of them."

She blinked. "That can't be correct."

"You told me quite emphatically that I should never

bring a mistress to the duchess's room, and I haven't. But as it happens, I've never brought a woman to Halstead at all—not until now. Not until you."

"Never?" Her voice was little more than a squeak.

"Never. There were always more convenient options to carry out my affaires. I didn't know I was saving Halstead for you, but that's the fact."

Her throat had closed up so completely that she couldn't speak.

"Somewhere between the grape juice and the abbey, I fell in love with you. Marry me, and make this our home. Be my duchess, and the mother of our children—Charlotte, and the others we'll have."

"I—Your Grace…"

"*Simon*," he reminded. "I'd marry you tonight if I could, darling, but it's almost midnight and I think the archbishop would balk at giving up dancing to write out a special license."

Olivia didn't know whether to laugh or cry, to agree or to protest. Was it possible he was telling the truth? He reached into his pocket and pulled out a ring set with a huge emerald and slid it onto her finger. "It's the Somervale emerald, but you can't keep it unless you agree to keep me as well."

Even then, she hesitated. It was only when he kissed her—the soft, gentle kiss of a lover—that she relaxed and melted into him, feeling as if she had indeed come home. With her surrender, he grew more demanding, until the air around them sizzled with the strength of their passion.

Finally it was Simon who broke the kiss. "Though I would dearly love to take you to your new bedroom right now, a wise woman told me to reserve that room for my duchess on our wedding night. So we have time on our hands. Perhaps we should go peek into the nursery and check on our daughter?"

&

Less than two hours before Lady Daphne's wedding, Penelope ventured out of her bedroom and ran into Kate in the entrance hall. When Penelope saw the appraising look on her friend's face, she felt her cheeks flush.

"I was starting to think you might miss the wedding as well as the ball," Kate said.

Penelope's embarrassment flared into scorching mortification. Even if the guests hadn't noticed for themselves that the Earl and Countess of Townsend had not appeared for dinner or for the ball on the previous evening, she suspected it was too good a bit of gossip for the ones who *had* paid attention not to pass on to everyone who was present. "Do you happen to know where my husband is?"

"He was in the breakfast room a few minutes ago. Some of the guests overindulged last night, and the earl was doctoring them with a sobering potion he said was your father's recipe."

The butler approached and presented a tray with a calling card lying in the center. "Lady Townsend, you have a caller."

Penelope picked up the pasteboard and tapped the edge against her wrist. Then she sighed and crossed the hall to the room Greeley had indicated.

Her caller had not bothered to sit down, but when

Penelope noticed the straight-backed wooden chairs, she wasn't surprised. "Hello, Papa. What brings you to Halstead?"

"I'm not delivering barrels of ale for the wedding," Ivan Weiss shot back. "I hear tales."

"Do you? Etta reached London safely, then. Would you like to walk with me in the garden." *Where we're less likely to be overheard.*

"If you're trying to distract me with flowers..." Ivan Weiss followed her through the great entrance hall and out the nearest side door. He didn't even stop to examine the justly famous hanging staircase, and his lack of interest set Penelope's senses quivering.

"What's this about a torn nightgown, Penny? Etta sounded like you were carrying on like a hoyden down here."

"*Cavorting* was the word she used. She also said I was both common and wanton."

"Yes, she told me—though I didn't believe it. My Penny acting like anything but a lady?" He shook his head. "Still, she does have an eye for details, so I came down to find out what's really going on. If that highfalutin earl has been mistreating my girl, I'll horsewhip him."

Penelope's heart warmed at the idea that her father had not taken Etta's report at face value—even if he had things entirely wrong. "What nonsense, Papa. But I am glad you are here, for I need to speak with you. You should invest in the earl's estate."

A low voice behind her said, "Mr. Weiss need do nothing of the sort. Tell me, ma'am, did you send for your father in order to make this plea?"

Penelope spun around to face the earl. "My lord!" The chilly note in her husband's voice froze her heart, and she knew she must look the picture of guilt. "No, I did not. But as long as he is here…"

Ivan Weiss cleared his throat. "As matters stand, Penny, any improvements I financed would benefit only a distant cousin of the earl's, the current heir. My investment would be lost to me entirely, should the earl die without a son."

"Blackmail will get you nowhere, Papa."

The earl stepped between them. "Sir, you may go directly to the devil. Your daughter is no longer your responsibility."

Ivan Weiss asked shrewdly, "Where are you going to get the money to support her?"

"I'm more concerned about her happiness."

"At any rate, you can't cut off my allowance, Papa, for Charles told me it's written into the marriage settlements."

"Yes, he made certain of that," Ivan Weiss said.

"That's enough, sir. Penny is no longer to be badgered about giving you a grandson or menaced by your feeble threats to leave her without funds. In short, stop making your daughter miserable or you will not see her again."

Ivan Weiss lifted an eyebrow. "What do you say about that, Penny?"

"I should not like to stop seeing you, but if my husband feels it is best…"

Ivan Weiss rubbed the back of his neck as if it hurt.

"It's time for you to back down, Papa. You must realize by now that you made a foolish move when you chose a man like the Earl of Townsend and then expected to be able to crush him under your foot."

"Foolish? That's a strong word, Penny."

"Yes, *foolish*. You can't break him. But perhaps we can all work together." She slipped a hand through her husband's arm. "We're going to rebuild Stoneyford, Papa, no matter what it takes. The only question is whether you're going to be a partner or a hindrance."

Ivan Weiss began to wheeze. Penelope, concerned he was choking, tried to slap him on the back, but her father shrugged her off, and she realized he was laughing.

Finally he wiped his eyes and grinned at her. "Formed a conspiracy against me, have you? Well, it's about time. I'll be off now, and when you get back to London we'll talk about that place of yours, Townsend. Stoneybrook, is it?"

"Stoneyford," Penelope said firmly. "And we're not going back to London, at least not to stay. We're going to Stoneyford, and we will make it our home. So if you'd like to discuss the estate or see me, you can come there and take your potluck."

The earl said, "Penny, you can't live in that house."

She raised her chin. "*You* were going to."

"But it's different for you. It's no place for a lady just now. There's nothing in the house but a…"

"Bed?" Ivan Weiss said blandly. "And such a bed it is, too… Oh, yes, Penny, I looked the place over, long since—before the wedding, in fact. I wanted to see what I was letting you in for. But I must say I didn't expect you to take this turn on me. So all the two of you need to set up housekeeping is a bed, eh?"

"There's a kitchen table, too," Penelope said placidly. "It will do for a start."

"Well, well—we'll talk next week at Stoneyford," Ivan Weiss said. "Perhaps I'll send down a chair or two for your drawing room, for comfort's sake."

The earl drew Penelope into his arms.

Ivan Weiss said, so calmly that Penelope almost didn't hear him, "Though I might better send sheets and pillows instead. No point in dropping my brass on things that won't be used!"

❧

After a while, Andrew kissed Kate's temple and said, "If I'm crushing you—"

She shook her head and wrapped her arms tighter. "No. Please don't move." She wanted to stay this way all night, to keep him close to her, to hold him inside her as long as she could. To make a memory that would have to last forever.

There would be all the time in the world to be sad over what could never be, she told herself. Tonight, she would simply be grateful. So she kissed his chin and smiled. "That was wonderful, Andrew."

"*You* were wonderful. I have wanted this since you were seventeen, when I kissed you in the garden that day. You were so perfect then, so untouched, so innocent—until I nearly destroyed everything. I could so easily have ruined you."

"And yourself as well, for my father would have come after you with a whip."

"He was amazingly understanding."

Kate gasped. "*You told my father?*"

"It was the only way I could assure it didn't happen again. He did not fault you in the least, Kate, but he made certain I never had another opportunity to give in to temptation."

"I thought you avoided me because I didn't know how to kiss."

"You didn't. But I liked teaching you—far too much to trust myself."

"Daphne said…" She broke off, but when Andrew raised his head a fraction and looked at her, she couldn't avoid his gaze. "When you stopped talking to me, she said it was because I had embarrassed you with my schoolgirl fantasies."

"Daphne has always been a little witch. She spent that summer trying to flirt with me—so no wonder she took aim at you, if she realized where my dreams had led me."

"But after that summer, you never came back to Halstead again, until now."

"I didn't dare hope you would still be here, Kate— and free. Are you as fond of me now as you were then?"

"Let me think," she said. The rumble of his laughter caressed her body, and she felt him stirring inside her once more.

He dozed off as dawn approached, and Kate slipped away to return to her own room. But she didn't sleep; she sat at her window and brushed her hair and watched the sun rise.

∽✢

Two hours before Daphne's wedding was to begin, Kate left the bridesmaids squabbling as they helped each other into their gowns and went in search of a box of rainbow-colored favors that Daphne insisted had been sent down from London.

She detoured to the breakfast room for coffee and watched in bemusement as the Earl of Townsend handed out his father-in-law's headache remedy. She ran into Penny in the entrance hall, yawning as if she'd had no more sleep than Kate had. When Penny went off to greet her caller, Kate turned toward the morning room—perhaps the blasted box of favors would be there—only to hear Lady Stone's raspy voice from the stairs.

"There you are, Miss Blakely." Lady Stone ran an eye over Kate's new lavender walking dress. "That will do well enough for a start, but you'll need a complete wardrobe for London. It gives me an ague to see a young woman wearing the same three dresses over and over. I see Iris gave you her trick prayer book."

Kate had picked up the book, along with her best kid gloves, simply because a prayer book seemed the right thing to carry to a wedding. She frowned. "Her *trick* prayer book?"

"I couldn't mistake it. I'm the one who gave it to her years ago—when she was just about to make her come out. I wasn't always the pillar of rectitude I am now."

Lady Stone as an example of moral uprightness—now there was a picture, Kate thought. "A prayer book?"

"Don't be dense, Miss Blakely." Lady Stone reached for the satin bow at the side of the prayer book and tugged. "Look inside."

At first glance the prayer book was perfectly

ordinary. Kate flicked through a dozen pages and then turned one more and gasped. Only the margins were left, just enough to hold the shape of the book. The center of each page all the way to the back cover had been hollowed out to form a little box. In the opening lay a curled slip of paper. Kate unrolled it, and out tumbled a wad of bank notes.

"I don't know what Iris used it for, but I found it very handy to pass illicit notes to a suitor." Lady Stone's tone was nostalgic. "My mother thought one young man quite spiritual because every time I dropped my prayer book, he would soon press it back into my hand."

Kate read the letter. *"My dear Miss Blakely, I know you can use funds, but it feels too cold to offer to pay you for your work, so I make you a gift as a friend. You must count on my friendship wherever you go, and call on me when you have a need. Iris Somervale."*

Once more, Kate thought, she had misjudged the duchess. She must find an opportunity to thank her. Though not, of course, for everything—such as her night with Andrew, which had come about entirely because of the duchess's invitation…

"Woolgathering?" Lady Stone asked crisply.

"I beg your pardon. When do you leave Halstead, ma'am? I ask so I can be ready to travel at your convenience."

Lady Stone looked thoughtful. "I'd planned to leave for Dorset tomorrow."

Perhaps I can have one more night with Andrew, Kate thought. "I have only a few things to pack at the cottage. My one regret is that I shall be leaving Lady Reyne in confusion." At least with the gift from the duchess, Olivia would be able to pay her rent on time after all.

"Oh, you needn't worry about her," Lady Stone said briskly. "It's a good thing for you that Iris is happy this morning, by the way, for she was not pleased last night when you went missing before the ball was finished."

Kate remembered how easily she had drowned the flicker of conscience as she'd watched the group of bridesmaids go by. "What Her Grace must think of me—she gave me a lovely gift, and then I didn't carry out my responsibilities." Even so, Kate could not find it in herself to regret her night with Andrew.

"Oh, it's nothing. It was past time for the bridesmaids' mothers to take a hand in looking after them—and so I told Iris."

"Still, I… You need not fear that I will take advantage, ma'am. I will strive to give satisfaction always as your companion."

"Must you be mealy-mouthed about it?" Lady Stone looked past Kate, her dark eyes beadier than usual. "Good morning, Carlisle. What brings you over to chat?"

Kate spun around. Andrew was only feet away, but she not felt him approaching.

"Miss Blakely." His voice was low and hoarse. "What is the meaning of this?"

"The meaning of *what*? You know I accepted a position with Lady Stone."

"That was before…" He shot a look at Lady Stone. "That was last night. If you don't mind, ma'am, I would like a private word with Miss Blakely."

"Private? You could have fooled me," Lady Stone

said. "But I must go and see if Iris needs my advice about the wedding, so carry on." She strolled off toward the morning room.

Kate's face was burning. "Andrew, what are you doing? Embarrassing me like that in front of my new employer—"

"You're acting as if nothing has changed!"

"But nothing has. Last night was..." She looked around and lowered her voice. "It was wonderful. But I had no plans or expectations beyond that, and neither should you."

"Then you should have made your rules clear last night, Kate. Because you did not, I refuse to abide by them." He caught her close, tipped her face up, and kissed her.

One of the bridesmaids, coming around the last bend of the staircase, gave a little shriek.

Kate tried to break free, but it was futile to push against Andrew's strong arms. She took one look up into his determined face and said, "All right. We'll go somewhere quiet to talk."

He marched her across to the chilly little reception room and closed the door. "It is obvious now that I should not have let you bamboozle me into making love to you without a clear understanding of your intentions. But it's too late to go back, so I'm asking now what I should have asked before I took you upstairs." He laid his hands on her shoulders. "What *did* last night mean to you, Kate?"

She was afraid to look at him, much less to tell him that making love with him had been the supreme joy of her life, a high point she would never reach again. "An adventure. You said there were all kinds of adventures, and—"

"Is that all?" He shook her just a little. "Is security so important to you that you'd rather rely on Lady Stone than take a chance with me?"

"I wasn't offered the choice of taking a chance with you!"

"I asked you to come with me."

Kate was aghast. "You were *serious*? You wanted me to go trailing across the ocean with you, helping to arrange your travel?"

"It sounded like fun. You and me, together… but when you said no, I began to think hard about my life, Kate, and about what I want. I want you, and I will do whatever it takes to have you."

She felt suddenly tired. "And what will that be, Andrew? I suppose you could still marry the richest heiress, as long as she didn't mind you having a mistress as well as a wife, but—"

"Don't be ridiculous. If security is so important to you, I will give up adventuring and buy some snug little corner of England to settle down in."

Kate blinked. "Buy?" Her voice wobbled. "With what?"

Andrew took a deep breath. "Lord Winchester isn't my employer or my patron. He's my partner. When I travel to check his property—well, it's my property too. And there's a lot of it."

"You lied about being a tutor?"

"I… let's say I edited the truth. Simon warned me the bridesmaids were a rapacious lot, so it seemed sensible to keep the details under wraps."

"You could have told me."

"Then I wouldn't have known if it was me you cared for, or the security that a whole lot of money represents."

Kate sighed. "And I suppose you never can know now."

He smiled. "But I do, Kate. You came to me last night thinking I was a penniless adventurer, relying on the good will of a patron for my next meal. You gave yourself to me thinking there was no future for us."

She nodded.

"Marry me, Kate. Not to escape Lady Stone or the colonel or even the vicar, but because it will be an adventure, no matter where we live or what we do. Be my companion and my love and my wife?"

She had worked so hard to be cheerful, to be grateful, to appreciate the memories she could treasure and not dwell on the things she could not have. But suddenly it was all too much, and Kate gave a little sob and flung herself against him. He held her while she cried and kissed her tears away and whispered nonsense until the storm had passed and she could laugh again.

"I still don't understand," she said finally. "Money doesn't come from nowhere, Andrew. You're a younger son, so where did you get a stake to invest in things like pineapple plantations and—"

"Sugar mills and a factory that builds equipment to card wool." He rubbed his jaw. "There's a substance that's used in the cloth industry to fix dyes and keep the cloth from fading. But it's terribly expensive to import from South America, so when I found a substitute on my first trip into the new Louisiana Territory, every cloth manufacturer in England happily paid for a steady supply. In turn, I invested in other things, and…" He shrugged. "It just grew."

"And you will really give all that up?"

"For you, Kate? Yes. Where would you like to settle down?"

"I have no idea. Perhaps we should look around for a while first. But before that…"

"Yes, my love?"

"Andrew, will you take me to Italy?"

He drew her closer and said against her lips, "Only if it's for a honeymoon, my Kate."

❦

After Ivan Weiss was safely out of sight, Penelope and the earl walked farther into the garden, finding a little corner of a rose garden where they were disturbed only by the splashing of water drops in a stone basin. The earl sat on the edge of the fountain and drew Penelope down onto his knee. "Your father really doesn't know you very well, does he?"

Penelope admitted, "I've never said anything like that to him before."

"Even so, he doesn't have the excuse I did for not understanding you. You were so meek and scared anytime I was within shouting distance that you barely spoke at all." He kissed her slowly.

Penelope's head was spinning by the time he let her go.

"Penny, after you made your incredible offer to sacrifice your jewels—"

"Not such a sacrifice. Amethysts and garnets all mixed in together—what was my father thinking when he bought that necklace?"

"Perhaps…" A frown flitted across the earl's brow. "No, surely not. He can't have predicted you would sell them. At any rate, your generosity made me realize I've been acting like a child where Stoneyford is concerned. I resented my father and grandfather for their mistakes, and I hated the position I've been put in. But I didn't realize I was making no real sacrifice myself in an effort to fix things, any more than they had. I don't need a stylish curricle or a stable full of high-steppers—"

"Yes, you do, Charles. You have a position to maintain so someday I can take all your daughters to London and marry them off well. It will be difficult enough for them to be known as the offspring of the very common Penny Wise, without having whispers circulating about their father, the very odd Earl of Townsend."

He laughed. "You are anything but common, Penny. Sometimes… I must admit that sometimes you frightened me. You told me what you wanted in no uncertain terms, but at the same time you shivered whenever I approached you—as if you couldn't bear to be near me. Then at the inn… you said *just once* you wanted to know what it meant to be a wife. I didn't realize you were like a drug. I couldn't stay away, but every time I broke my promise…"

"Please don't stay away," Penelope said shyly. "I like making love with you."

"You did well to rid yourself of Etta. However, I must in all honesty tell you she was right about one thing, Penny. You *are* a wanton."

Her cheeks burned.

He laughed. "But only the most fortunate of husbands has a wanton for a wife, so I promise never to speak of it to anyone but you. Did you throw away that nightgown? Because if not, I wish for you to—what was Etta's word?—*cavort* around in it for me sometimes." He buried his face in her hair. "I think I love you, Penny."

Her throat closed up. She had made up her mind to be happy with whatever he was willing to give her. Being his wife, carrying his title, bearing his children—she had told herself that would be enough, and even in the wildest of her imaginings, she had never dared to dream of more. She had been determined to be a good wife, all the while loving him silently.

"I admire you," he said quietly. "You're sweet and honorable and funny and lively and incredibly attractive…"

"You *must* love me, to be so blind." Suddenly shy, she whispered, "I didn't mean to tell you—ever—that I love you, Charles. I thought you wouldn't want to hear it, to be bothered with my feelings."

"Bother me anytime you wish. The morning the invitation came to Daphne's wedding, and you came downstairs in your dressing gown to ask if we were going, you were so naturally beautiful with your hair down and your eyes still sleepy…"

"The wedding," Penelope said. "I *knew* we were forgetting something."

"No hurry. Daphne will be late for her own ceremony. Nevertheless, I suppose we should make some effort to get to the church." He set her off his knee. "You told me once that you felt like a loaf of dark bread masquerading as cake."

She remembered saying it. He had asked, on their first evening at Halstead, why she was not wearing jewels, and she had said to do so felt like adding icing to a rough loaf, pretending to be something she was not. She nodded slowly.

"Penny, you *are* cake for me. You are every treat I can think of wanting, and though I have dealt with you badly, in the future you will have no reason to regret our arrangement."

"Charles..." she whispered against his lips.

"Hmm?"

"Will you still love me if I have a boy after all? I can't *guarantee* only girls, you know."

He kissed her for a while longer, and just as Penelope forgot the question, he said carelessly, "Whenever you like, my dear. I'm sure I'll find some other way to annoy your father."

❧

Moonlight drenched the nursery. Charlotte was curled around a doll Olivia had never seen before, and a new pale pink dress hung on the wardrobe door. Nurse had retired to her room, and the nursery maid was asleep on a pallet in the corner. Simon and Olivia tiptoed across the room and stood holding hands, looking down at the sleeping child.

"She'll be just as beautiful as you are." The low warm rumble of Simon's voice sent quivers through Olivia. He drew her down onto the narrow bed next to Charlotte's cot and sat beside her. Olivia basked in the warmth of his arms, the comfort of his presence. When she yawned, he tucked a blanket around her.

When Olivia opened her eyes, she already knew she was being watched. Her daughter stood beside her, still clutching the doll and staring. Olivia stretched and bumped into something large, warm, and solid. Simon's arm tightened, keeping her from sliding out of the too-small bed. "Running away, my duchess?" he murmured against her ear.

"Mama, did you bring me a sweet from the ball?"

"I forgot, darling. But I brought something better." *A new papa… if I can figure out how to explain it.*

"That's all right. The duchess will bring me a sweet."

"My mother?" Simon sat up and cast a quick look at the window. "She might be along at any moment, so we'd best make this quick." He shifted to sit on the edge of the bed, planted his elbows on his knees, and leaned forward until his eyes were level with the child's. "Charlotte, how would you like to live here at Halstead with Nurse and Mama and me, and your very own pony and a puppy and—"

"That's plenty of promises to go on with," Olivia said.

Charlotte considered. "Forever and ever? Just like the fairy tale?"

Olivia's heart gave a funny little bump.

"Just like the fairy tale," Simon said gently. "*And they all lived happily ever after.*"

❧

Lady Daphne's wedding in the village church was exactly the spectacle everyone had anticipated—elaborate, long, and tedious. For nearly an hour the vicar expounded on the parallels between marriage and the church, and he only wrapped up the sermon and got on with the ceremony after one of the bridesmaids fainted and had to be revived with a sprinkle of water from one of Kate's altar bouquets.

But the second wedding of the day—held immediately after the new marchioness left the church on her husband's arm—was brief, quiet, and moving, with only a dozen people present. Olivia and Simon had eyes only for each other; the archbishop presided with a smile; Charlotte, wearing her pink dress, clutched the hand of her new grandmama; and the few witnesses who meant the most to the bride and groom looked on. The Earl of Townsend held his Penny's hand quite openly, while Andrew stroked Kate's wrist using her prayer book as cover.

The moment Simon kissed his bride, Lady Stone muttered to the gentleman beside her, "That's *another* ten guineas you owe me, Colonel. But I'll give you a chance to win it back, if you'd care to lay a wager on whether Daphne has a tantrum because Simon has stolen her wedding day."

After the new Duchess of Somervale was officially introduced to all the guests, the first toast was history, and Daphne had indeed thrown a tantrum, Iris Somervale lifted a sleepy Charlotte into her lap and said, "Now I'm officially in the shade—the *dowager* Duchess of Somervale. I suppose I may as well get used to it."

"I understand one does become accustomed—and after all, Iris, it's little enough to give up." Lady Stone lifted her wineglass in an informal toast. "You're merely sacrificing one title in exchange for a slightly different one. Look at what you've gained in return— a daughter and a granddaughter, and I'll wager quite soon there will be an heir to the dukedom."

"Not *too* soon, I hope." The duchess sipped her wine and looked down at the child in her lap.

Charlotte blinked. "Is that grape juice, Grandmama? I *like* grape juice." The duchess looked bemused, but before she could answer, the child's eyes drifted closed.

Lady Stone sighed. "Yes, you have all the benefits. I, on the other hand, have had to sacrifice a perfectly good employee in the cause of love. Last time I hired a companion, she stayed with me for six entire weeks before she left my employ to get married. This one lasted barely twelve hours."

"Perhaps," Colonel Sir Tristan Huffington said, "that's because you're looking for the wrong sort of companion, Lucinda."

Lady Stone eyed him coolly. "You must give me the benefit of your wisdom, Colonel. What sort of person should I be seeking to bear me company in my declining years?"

"Me," the colonel said simply.

The dowager duchess's mouth dropped open.

Lady Stone gave a raspy laugh. "Tristan, I thought you'd never ask. Or is it just that you don't want to have to honor all those bets you've lost to me?" She laid her hand on his arm. "Come and walk with me in the garden, and we'll talk it over."

THE
MISTRESS' HOUSE

LEIGH MICHAELS

**"A work of art…Deliciously decadent from start
to finish."** — *Seriously Reviewed*

**"Deft storytelling, abundant humor…and tenderness in all the
right places"** — *Linda Banche Romance Author*

The rules are made to be broken…

When the handsome, rakish Earl of Hawthorne buys the
charming house across the back garden from his town home,
he never expects the lovely lady he installs there to ensnare him
completely…

Again…

After Lady Keighley marries the earl, it seems a shame to
leave the house empty, so she offers it to her childhood friend
Felicity Mercer, who discovers the earl's gorgeous cousin…

and again…

Finally, feisty Georgiana Baxter moves into the house to
escape an arranged marriage and encounters the earl's friend
Major Julian Hampton late one night in the back garden. The
handsome soldier is more than willing to give her the lessons
she asks for…

Plenty of gossip, scandal, and torrid speculations surround the
"mistress' house," but behind closed doors, passions blaze…

978-1-4022-4135-2 • $7.99 U.S.

Just One Season in London

LEIGH MICHAELS

"With its triple romance and delightful characters, this comedy
of errors is both a bit of love and laughter and a poignant
romance." —*RT Book Reviews, 4 Stars*

"With a generous dash of dry wit, an abundance of clever
characterization, and a good dose of sexy passion, Michaels deftly
delivers three different—yet equally—entertaining romances in
one volume."—*Booklist*

A family that courts together...

Viscount Ryecroft has a beautiful sister he needs to marry off...
if only he had the money for her Season in London. His family
is in financial ruins, and his mother is willing to do anything
to help her children, including sell herself to the highest
bidder...

Finds passion on their own...

Sophie Ryecroft will sacrifice love to marry for the good of her
family... but instead finds passion and solace in an attractive
alternative. With so much riding on their one and only Season
in London, Rye, Sophie, and Miranda can't help but get
hopelessly entangled with all the wrong people...

Celebrate _____ 3190105077764 _____ e tales of
unexpect _____ n forget.

978-1-4022-4420-9 • $7.99 U.S.